The Hound of Rowan

ROWAN ACADEMY

THE TAPESTRY
Book 1

WRITTEN AND ILLUSTRATED
BY HENRY H. NEFF

The Hound of Rowan

ROWAN ACADEMY

RANDOM HOUSE AUSTRALIA

Random House Australia Pty Ltd
Level 3, 100 Pacific Highway, North Sydney, NSW 2060
www.randomhouse.com.au

Sydney   New York   Toronto
London   Auckland   Johannesburg

Published by arrangement with Random House Children's Books,
a division of Random House Inc., New York, New York, USA.
All rights reserved.
First published in the USA by Random House Children's Books in 2007
First published by Random House Australia in 2007

National Library of Australia
Cataloguing-in-Publication Entry

Neff, Henry H.
The hound of Rowan.

For primary school children.
ISBN 978 1 74166 266 5 (pbk.).

I. Title. (Series: The tapestry; bk. 1).

813.6

Cover design by Joanne Yates Russell
Additional cover design by Anna Warren
Printed and bound by Griffin Press, South Australia

10 9 8 7 6 5 4 3 2 1

For my family, friends, and students

CONTENTS

~ 1 ~

THE BOY, THE TRAIN,
AND THE TAPESTRY

Max McDaniels pressed his forehead against the train window and watched storm clouds race across the yellow sky. With a soft patter, rain began to streak the glass, and the sky darkened to a bruise. Fogging the window, Max blinked at his own watery reflection in the glass. It blinked back at him: a dark-eyed boy with wavy black hair and his mother's sharp cheekbones.

His father's voice rumbled beside him, and Max turned in his seat.

"Which do you like better?" his father asked with an enthusiastic grin. He held a pair of glossy advertisements between his thick fingers. Max looked at the ads, his gaze settling on the image of an elegant woman at a kitchen sink, her head thrown back in amusement.

"*Not* that one," he said. "It's way too cheesy."

Mr. McDaniels's broad, smiling face drooped. Big as a bear, Max's father had pale blue eyes and a deep, dimpled chin.

"It's not cheesy," he protested, squinting at the ad and smoothing his tuft of thinning brown hair. "What's *cheesy* about it?"

"Nobody's *that* happy doing dishes," said Max, pointing at the beaming woman up to her elbows in suds. "And nobody does the dishes in a fancy dress—"

"But that's the whole point!" interrupted his father, waving the flimsy ad about. "Ambrosia is the first 'ultra-premium' dish soap! A heavenly lather that's soft enough for the tub, but still has muscle for the toughest—"

Max flushed. "Dad . . ."

Mr. McDaniels paused long enough to see the other passengers glancing curiously at them. With a snort, he slipped the ads back inside his raincoat as the train came to a temporary stop on the outskirts of the city.

"It's not so bad," Max reassured him. "Maybe you could just make her smile a little less toothy."

Mr. McDaniels chuckled and promptly slid his ample bottom across the seat to squish his son. Max elbowed back as more people crowded onto the train, collapsing umbrellas and shaking the wet hair from their eyes.

Thunder shook the car and the train started to move again.

The passengers shrieked and laughed as the cabin went dark. Max squeezed his father's arm, and the train's yellow lights flickered slowly back to life. The rain fell harder now as they neared Chicago, a looming backdrop of steel and brick set in stark relief against the summer storm.

Max was still grinning when he saw the man.

He was sitting across the aisle in the row behind them, pale and unkempt, with short black hair still damp from the rain. He appeared exhausted; his eyelids fluttered as he slouched low in his dirty coat and mouthed silent words against the window.

Max turned away for a moment, swiveling for a better look. He caught his breath.

The man was staring at him.

He sat perfectly still as he focused on Max with a startling pair of mismatched eyes. While one eye was green, the other gleamed as wet and white as a peeled egg. Max stared back at it, transfixed. It looked to be a blind, dead thing—a thing of nightmares.

But Max knew somehow that this eye was not blind or dead. He knew he was being studied by it—appraised in the way his mother used to examine a glass of wine or an old photograph. Holding Max's gaze, the man eased his head up off the glass and shifted his weight toward the aisle.

The train entered a tunnel, and the car went dark. A spasm of fear overcame Max. He buried his face in his father's warm coat. Mr. McDaniels grunted and dropped several product brochures onto the floor. The train eased to a stop, and Max heard his father's voice.

"You falling asleep on me, Max? Get your things together—we're here, kiddo."

Max looked up to find the car was light and passengers were shuffling toward the exits. His eyes darted from face to face. The strange man was nowhere to be seen. Flushed, Max gathered his umbrella and sketchbook and hurried out after his father.

The station was crowded with people milling to and from platforms. Voices droned over loudspeakers; weekend shoppers scurried about with bags and children in tow. Mr. McDaniels steered Max down the escalator toward the exits. The rain had stopped, but the sky was still threatening and newspapers eddied about the street in sudden fits of flight. Arriving at a line of yellow taxis, Mr. McDaniels opened the door to one and stood aside to let Max scoot across the long vinyl seat.

"The Art Institute, please," said his father.

Max craned his neck, straining to glimpse the tops of the skyscrapers as the cab headed east toward the lake.

"Dad," said Max. "Did you see that man on the train?"

"Which man?"

"He was sitting across the aisle in the row behind us," Max said, shuddering.

"No, I don't think so," said his father, flicking some lint off his raincoat. "What was so special about him?"

"I don't know. He was scary-looking and he was staring at me. He looked like he was going to say something or come over right before we went into the tunnel."

"Well, if he was staring at you, it's probably because you were staring at him," said Mr. McDaniels. "You'll see more kinds of people in the city, Max."

"I know, Dad, but—"

"You can't judge a book by its cover, you know."

"I *know*, Dad, but—"

"Now, there's this guy at my office. Young kid, still wet behind the ears. Well, my first day I see this kid at the coffee machine with makeup on his eyes, a harpoon through his nose, and music blaring out of his headphones . . ."

Max looked out the taxi's window while his father retold a familiar tale. Finally, Max caught a glimpse of what he had been looking for: two bronze lions standing tall and proud as they flanked the museum entrance.

"Dad, there's the Art Institute."

"Right you are, right you are. Oh, before I forget," Mr. McDaniels said, turning to Max with a sad little smile on his broad face. "Thanks for coming with me today, Max. I appreciate it. Your mom appreciates it, too."

Max offered a solemn nod and gave his dad's hand a fierce squeeze. The McDanielses had always celebrated Bryn McDaniels's birthday with a visit to her favorite museum. Despite his mother's disappearance over two years ago, Max and his father continued the tradition.

Once inside, they asked a young woman with a nametag where they could find some of Bryn McDaniels's favorite artists. Max listened as his father rattled off the names from a slip of paper: Picasso, Matisse, and van Gogh came handily enough, but he paused when he came to the last.

"*Gaw-gin?*" he asked, twisting up his face and frowning at the paper.

"Gauguin. He's a wonderful artist. I think you'll enjoy his work." The woman smiled and directed them to a large marble staircase leading to the second floor.

"Your mom sure knows all the names. I've got no head

for this stuff no matter how many times I come here." Mr. Mc-
Daniels chuckled and smacked Max on the shoulder with the
map.

The galleries upstairs were filled with color—great swirls of
paint layered thickly on canvas and board. Mr. McDaniels
pointed to a large painting of pedestrians on a rainy Paris street.

"That looks a bit like today, eh?"

"The rain does, but to look like him you'd have to add a mustache and top hat," Max mused, squinting at a figure in the fore-
ground.

"Ugh! I used to have a mustache. Your mother made me
shave it when we started dating."

Some images dominated whole walls, while others nestled in
small gilded frames. They spent an hour or so moving from
painting to painting, careful to spend extra time at Mrs. Mc-
Daniels's favorites. Max particularly liked a Picasso in which a
weathered old man cradled a guitar. He was studying the painting when he heard his father exclaim behind him.

"Bob? Bob Lukens! How are you?"

Max turned to see his father pumping the arm of a thin,
middle-aged man in a black sweater. A woman accompanied
him, and the two were offering hesitant smiles as Mr. McDaniels
cornered them.

"Hello, Scott. Nice to see you," the man said politely.
"Honey, this is Scott McDaniels. He works on the Bedford Bros.
account. . . ."

"Oh, what a nice surprise. Pleased to meet you, Scott."

"They'll change the way you think about soup!" Mr. McDaniels
boomed, shooting a finger toward the ceiling.

Mrs. Lukens gave a start and dropped her purse.

"Imagine a wintry day," Mr. McDaniels continued, bending over to retrieve her things while she retreated a step behind her husband. "Your nose is running, the wind is blowing, and all you've got to warm your tummy is a can of boring old soup in the pantry. Well, *no* soup is boring with Bedford Bros. Crispy Soup Wafers! Their snappy shapes and crisp crunch will jazz that soup right up and make your taste buds salute!"

Mr. McDaniels raised a hand to his forehead and stood at dutiful attention. Max wanted to go home.

Mr. Lukens chuckled. "Did I mention that Scott's a fanatic, honey?"

Mrs. Lukens ventured a smile as Mr. McDaniels shook her hand, then turned to Max.

"Max, I'd like you to meet Mr. and Mrs. Lukens. Mr. Lukens runs my agency—the big boss. Max and I are here to get a shot of culture, eh?"

Max smiled nervously and extended his hand to Mr. Lukens, who gave it a warm shake.

"Pleased to meet you, Max. Good to see a young man pulling himself away from video games and MTV! See anything you like?"

"I like this Picasso," said Max.

"I've always liked that one myself. You've got a good eye. . . ." Mr. Lukens patted him on the shoulder and turned back to Mr. McDaniels. "I'd ask you to compare it with a favorite of mine, but unfortunately it's gone."

"What do you mean?" asked Mr. McDaniels.

"It was one of the three paintings stolen from here last week," said Mr. Lukens, frowning. "The papers say there were two more stolen from the Prado just last night."

"Oh," said Mr. McDaniels. "That's terrible."

"It *is* terrible," said Mr. Lukens conclusively, glancing again at Max. "Say, bring Max by the office sometime, Scott. I've got a print of my missing favorite and we'll see if Rembrandt can trump Picasso!"

"Will do, will do," said Mr. McDaniels, chuckling and kneeling down to Max's height.

"Hey, sport," he said with a wink. "Dad's got to talk a bit of shop, and I don't want to bore you to tears. How 'bout you go sketch some of those tin suits you and your mom used to draw? I'll meet you down at the bookstore in half an hour. Okay?"

Max nodded and said good-bye to the Lukenses, who promptly shrank before the wildly gesticulating form of Scott McDaniels. Max clutched his sketchbook and pencil and stalked down the hall, silently seething that his dad never passed up an opportunity to talk business, even on his mother's special day.

The armor gallery was darker than the others, its artifacts glinting softly from behind clean glass. There were fewer people here, and Max was happy for the opportunity to sketch in relative peace and quiet. He strolled along a velvet rope, stopping to examine a crossbow here, a chalice there. The walls were arrayed with all manner of weapons: black iron maces, broad-bladed axes, and towering swords. He paused before a stand of ceremonial halberds before spying just the right subject to sketch.

The suit of armor was enormous. It dwarfed its neighbors on either side, gleaming bright silver inside its broad glass case. Max

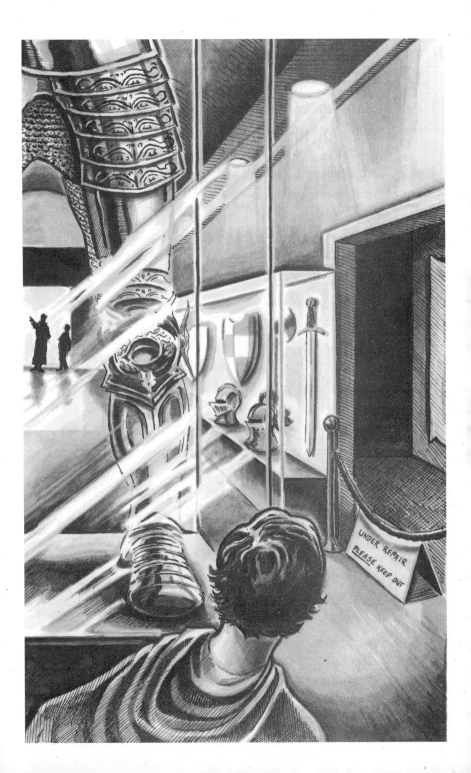

moved around to the other side, tilting his head up for a better view of the helmet. Several minutes later, he had roughed the basic figure onto the page.

As Max struggled to draw the elaborate breastplate, a commotion at the far end of the hall grabbed his attention. Max peered through the glass case and immediately caught his breath.

The man from the train was here.

Max lowered himself to a crouch and watched as the man towered over the guard at the gallery entrance. He made quick, chopping gestures with his hand. The motions became faster as the volume of his voice rose.

"This tall," he spat in an Eastern European accent. He held his hand flat to approximate Max's height. "A black-haired boy about twelve, carrying a sketchbook."

The guard was backed against the doorway, looking the man up and down. He began to reach for his radio. But then the strange man leaned in close and hissed something Max could not hear. Inexplicably, the guard nodded and hooked a fat thumb over his shoulder toward the suits of armor where Max was hiding.

Frantic, Max scanned his surroundings and noticed a dark doorway directly to his right. A velvet rope hung across it along with a sign that read UNDER REPAIR: PLEASE KEEP OUT.

Ignoring the sign, Max ducked beneath the rope and melted around the corner. He stood rigid against the wall and waited for his hiding place to be discovered. Nothing happened. It was several long seconds before Max realized that he had left his sketchbook in the other gallery. A wave of panic crashed over him; surely the man would see it and guess where Max had hidden.

A minute passed, followed by another, and another. Max

heard the footsteps and casual conversation of people strolling past the doorway. He peered around the corner. The man was gone—along with Max's sketchbook. Sinking slowly to the floor, Max pictured his name and address penciled neatly on the inside cover. He lifted his head and cast a hopeless glance at the room that had hidden him.

It was surprisingly small for a gallery. The air was musty, and the room had a soft amber glow. The sole object within it was a ragged tapestry that hung on the opposite wall. Max blinked. As strange as it seemed, the dim light was radiating from the tapestry itself. He moved closer.

The tapestry was an ancient thing. Sun and centuries had sapped its color until all that remained were splotched and faded bands of ochre. As he got closer, however, Max noticed faint hints and undercurrents of color submerged beneath its dull, rough surface.

His stomach began to tingle as though he'd swallowed a handful of bees. The little hairs on his arm rose one by one, and Max stood still, breathing hard.

Twang!

A single thread burst into bright gold. Max yelped and jumped backward. The thread flashed like fire, as fine and delicate as spider silk. It vibrated like a harp string, issuing a single musical note that reverberated throughout the gallery before fading to silence. Max glanced back at the doorway. Patrons continued to stroll by, but they seemed far away and oblivious to the small gallery, its lone occupant, and the strange tapestry.

More threads came to life, plucked from their slumber in a rising chorus of light and music. Some arrived individually, in a sudden snap of light and sound; others emerged together in woven harmonies of silver, green, and gold. To Max, it seemed he had dusted off an alien instrument that now resumed a strange and forgotten song. The song became richer. When the last thread sang into being, Max gave a sudden gasp of pain. The pain was sharper than a stitch and was caused by something deep within him.

That something had been with Max ever since he could remember. It was a lurking presence, huge and wild, and Max was afraid of it. Throughout his life he had fought with great difficulty to keep it walled within him The struggles caused headaches, including unbearable stretches that lasted for days. Max knew those days were over as he felt the presence burst free. Unfettered at last, it glided slowly through his consciousness before sounding deep within his being to stir the silt.

The pain subsided. Max took a deep breath while tears ran free in warm little rivers down his face. He brushed the tapestry's woven surface with his fingers.

The light and colors shifted to form golden, interlacing patterns that framed three strange, glowing words near the top.

TÁIN BÓ CUAILNGE

Centered below these words was the beautifully woven image of a bull in a pasture surrounded by dozens of sleeping warriors. A host of armed men were approaching from the right; a trio of black birds wheeled in the sky above. Overlooking the scene from a nearby hill was the silhouette of a tall man clutching a spear.

Max's eyes swept over the picture, but they always returned to the dark figure on the hill. Slowly, the tapestry's light grew brighter; its images trembled and danced behind shimmering waves of heat. With a rising cacophony of sound, the tapestry erupted with radiance so hot and bright Max feared it would consume him.

"Max! Max McDaniels!"

The room was dark once again. The tapestry hung against the wall, dull and ugly and still. Max backed away, confused and frightened, and crossed the velvet rope into the medieval gallery.

He saw his father's hulking figure alongside two security guards at the far end of the gallery. Max called out. At the sound of Max's voice, Mr. McDaniels raced toward his son.

"Oh, thank God! Thank God!" Mr. McDaniels wiped away tears as he stooped to smother Max in the folds of his coat. "Max, where on *earth* have you been? I've been looking for you for the last two hours!"

"Dad, I'm sorry," Max said, baffled. "I'm okay. I was just in that other room, but I haven't been gone more than twenty minutes."

"What are you talking about? What other room?" Mr. McDaniels's voice quavered as he peered over Max's shoulder.

"The one that's under repair," replied Max, turning to point out the sign. He stopped, began to speak, and stopped again. There was no doorway, no sign, and no velvet rope.

Mr. McDaniels turned to the two guards, offering each a firm handshake. As the guards moved beyond earshot, Mr. Mc-Daniels kneeled to Max's height. His eyes were puffed and searching.

"Max, be honest with me. Where have you been for the last two hours?"

Max took a deep breath. "I was in a room off this gallery. Dad, I swear to you I didn't think I was in there very long."

"Where was this room?" asked Mr. McDaniels as he unfolded the museum map.

Max felt sick.

The room with the tapestry was simply not on the map.

"Max . . . I'm going to ask you this one time and one time only. Are you lying to me?"

Max stared hard at his shoes. Raising his eyes to his father's, he heard his own voice, soft and trembling.

"No, Dad. I'm not lying to you."

Before Max had finished the sentence, his father was pulling him briskly toward the exit. Several girls his age giggled and whispered as Max was dragged, feet shuffling and head bowed, out the museum entrance and down the steps.

The only sounds during the cab ride to the train station came from Mr. McDaniels thumbing rapidly through his pamphlets. Max noticed some were upside down or backward. The rain and wind were picking up again as the cab slowed to a halt near the train station.

"Make sure you've got your things," sighed Mr. McDaniels, exiting the other side. He sounded tired and sad. Max drooped and thought better of sharing the fact that he had also lost his sketchbook.

Once on the train, the pair slid heavily into a padded booth. Mr. McDaniels handed his return ticket to the conductor, then leaned back and closed his eyes. The conductor turned to Max.

"Ticket, please."

"Oh, I've got it right here," Max muttered absentmindedly. He reached into his pocket, but procured a small envelope instead. The sight of his name scripted clearly on the envelope made him pause.

Confused, Max retrieved the ticket from his other pocket and gave it to the conductor. Glancing to confirm that his father was still resting, Max then looked over the envelope. In the warm yellow light it appeared buttery, its heavy paper folds converging to pleasing corners. He turned the envelope over and examined the silky navy script.

Mr. Max McDaniels

His father now breathing heavily, Max ran his finger along the envelope's flap. Inside was a folded letter.

Dear Mr. McDaniels,

Our records indicate that you registered as a Potential this afternoon at 3:37 p.m. CST, U.S. Congratulations, Mr. McDaniels—you must be a very remarkable young man, and we look forward to making your acquaintance. One of our regional representatives will be contacting you shortly. Until that time, we would appreciate your absolute silence and utmost discretion in this matter.

Best regards,
Gabrielle Richter
Executive Director

Max read the note several times before stowing it back in his pocket. He felt utterly drained. He could not guess how the letter had come to be in his possession, much less what a "Potential" was and what it all had to do with him. He *could* guess it had something to do with the hidden tapestry and the mysterious presence now roaming free within him. Max stared out the window. Brilliant ohafto of ounlight chaood wicpy trailc of ctorm clouds across the western sky. Exhausted, he leaned against his father and drifted off to sleep, his fingers closed tight around the mysterious envelope.

~ 2 ~

THREE SOFT KNOCKS

The next morning, Max yawned as he watched his father toss a pair of black socks into an overnight bag. Zipping it closed, his father suddenly grunted and lumbered down the hallway. He returned a minute later with a handful of television cables and video-game controllers.

"Not that I don't trust you . . ."

The tangled mess was stuffed into the bag and zipped up tight.

"What am I supposed to do all day?" Max moaned.

"Being grounded is a punishment," his father growled. "You're the one yawning—feel free to sleep the day away."

Max had to admit that didn't sound half bad. He had spent much of the night peering out of his window. The idea that the dead-eyed man might have Max's name and address and could be coming at any moment had kept him occupied until dawn. By daylight, however, his fears seemed silly.

All the same, as a taxi honked outside, Max had a sudden urge to tell his father about the man at the museum. He swallowed his words. At this point, it would seem little better than a last gasp to avoid punishment.

"I'll only be gone a day," his father sighed. Mr. Lukens had granted Mr. McDaniels the opportunity to pitch a new client, and he was off for an overnight trip to Kansas City. "The number for the Raleighs is on the fridge. They'll expect you for dinner by six, and you can sleep over there. Be good. I'll see you tomorrow afternoon."

With a peck on the head, Scott McDaniels was gone. Max locked the door, and curiosity led him back upstairs to examine his letter. Several readings later, it was still a mystery. He stood and looked out the window, listening to the wind as it shook the tall trees near the backyard fort he had built with his father. When his stomach began to growl, Max finally put the letter aside and went downstairs to make a sandwich.

He was descending the stairs when he saw a shadow moving beneath the front door. Max stopped as he heard three soft knocks. He remained still, poised between steps, when the knocks sounded again.

"Hello?" a lady called. "Anybody home?"

Max exhaled—it was not the man from the museum. Tiptoeing down to a side window, he glimpsed a plump, elderly woman holding a suitcase and glancing at her watch. Her cane was propped against the door. Catching sight of Max, she smiled brightly and waved.

"Hello. Are you Max McDaniels? I'm Mrs. Millen. I believe you received a letter that said I would be visiting you?"

Max smiled and waved back.

"Might I come in?" she asked sweetly, nodding toward the locked door.

He slid back the brass bolt and opened the door. Mrs. Millen stood on the doorstep, beaming and extending her hand.

"It's very nice to meet you, Max. I was hoping I could have a few words with you about the letter you received."

"Sure. Nice to meet you, too."

"Yes, well, can we sit down and have a chat?"

Max led Mrs. Millen to the dining room. She politely declined when he offered to carry her suitcase, leaning heavily on her cane as she swung it along. With a grateful sigh, she settled into a chair, sending up a waft of perfume. She smiled and removed her glasses to massage red, puffy eyes as Max took a seat across from her.

"Well, before we begin . . . might I have the pleasure of meeting your parents? Are they at home?"

"My dad's out on business."

"I see," she said. "And your mother?"

Max glanced at an old photo of the McDaniels family propped on the buffet.

"She's not home, either."

"Well, that certainly makes my job a bit easier," she said. Her shoulders relaxed, and she gave Max a little wink.

"How do you mean?" Max frowned, leaning back in his chair. He glanced at her suitcase, puzzled by the long, shallow scratches that scored its side.

"Oh, well, parents are often very set in their ways. For example, most parents can't really understand strange events at the Art Institute, now, can they?"

Max smiled.

"You did have quite a day yesterday, didn't you, Max?"

"Yeah—I mean yes. Yes, I did."

"And tell me, what was so special about it?"

"Well, I saw lots of weird things," Max said with a shrug. "I found a room—a room I couldn't find again after I'd left it. While I was in the room, I saw a tapestry."

Mrs. Millen nodded, tapping her finger against the table's smooth, shiny surface.

"Was it pretty?" she asked. "Was it a pretty tapestry?"

"Not at first."

Her finger froze in mid-tap.

"What do you mean?" she asked.

"It was ugly," Max whispered. But then he paused. His experience now seemed very personal. He was hesitant to share it with her.

"Yes?" Mrs. Millen said. "It was ugly? An old, ratty tapestry? Go on, dear. . . . I know it seems secret and silly, but it's all right to share it with me. Believe me, Max, you'll feel better if you do."

She smiled and leaned forward expectantly. Max suddenly felt sleepy.

"It started to glow," Max said slowly, tracing the table's grain with his finger. "There were words and pictures and music."

"And what were those words, Max? Tell me, what *pictures* did you see?"

She spoke in hushed, urgent tones. Max felt his neck begin to itch; he paused to look at her closely.

Her face was round and strangely taut. Although her smile stayed fixed, her pupils began to dilate. Max was fascinated by them as they grew. They reminded him of a polar bear he had once seen at the zoo. He had never forgotten the way its flat, black eyes had followed him hungrily from across the protective barrier.

Max blinked in alarm.

There was no barrier here.

"I have to go to the bathroom," he muttered.

"Yes, yes, certainly. But first, tell me what you saw in the tapestry!"

"Maybe we should talk when my dad gets home."

Mrs. Millen's eyes widened with surprise. The chair creaked under her shifting weight, and she sniffed suddenly as though she had a cold. Several long seconds passed as they studied each other. Then a sly smile crept across her face as though they had just shared a secret.

"Hoo-hoo-hoo!" she chuckled. "You *are* a cautious one, Max! You are one cautious, bright little boy! You just might be the one we want."

Sweat broke out on Max's forehead; his throat itched. He glanced at her cane, realizing he could run. No one had ever been able to catch him when he ran, and Mrs. Millen was old.

"I think you should go now," he said. "I'm not feeling well."

"Of course, my dear . . ."

The woman pushed back from the table.

". . . but you're coming with me!"

The smile never left her lips as her hand shot across the table to seize Max's wrist. Max yelped and shot backward, squirming painfully out of her astonishingly strong grasp and falling off his chair. At the same time, Max heard something crash upstairs in his room. Heavy footsteps were coming down the stairs.

Someone else was in the house.

Max scrambled to his feet and bolted for the back door. With a dreadful shock, he realized that the old woman needed no cane as she rounded the table and raced after him.

Fleeing into the backyard, Max made for the big pine fort. He fumbled at the rusted latch, pushing the door open and hurrying inside. He tried to slam the door shut just as Mrs. Millen crouched to barrel in after him—but she managed to wedge her arm inside, twisting it wildly about.

Max gave the door a great push with his shoulder, and Mrs. Millen shrieked and withdrew her arm. He slammed the door shut and slid its crossbeam into place.

Leaning his back against the door, he waited.

"Hoo-hoo-hoo!" she cackled. "Not so wise and cautious after all! Our little one was quick, but he has made a poor choice, indeed. . . ."

Max heard her nails dragging along the fort's walls as she slowly circled its perimeter. She paused to tap at its narrow windows. Max gulped down his fear and tried to think. He could yell for help, but his house was at the end of a quiet street, and his neighbors worked during the day. As he heard her near the fort's back wall, Max decided to make a run for it.

Just as he reached for the crossbeam, however, it dissolved into a pile of gray ash.

"Hoo-hoo-hoo!"

The door flew open, and Mrs. Millen snatched the front of Max's shirt. He gave a yell and jammed the heel of his hand into her nose. She cursed and recoiled, losing her grip on him. Backpedaling furiously, Max slammed into the opposite wall and started scrambling up the small ladder that led to the fort's roof. Max heard her muttering a few feet below him as he climbed. When he glanced down, he saw that she was standing on the lowest rung. Her ringed fingers clawed for his ankle.

"Stop right there, Max! *Astaroth!*"

At that moment, Max felt an icy numbness in his right leg. Straining, he climbed up and through the hatch and waited a moment, slamming the door down hard on the woman's head as she scrabbled up after him. His leg almost completely numb, Max dragged himself toward the roof's edge. Glancing back, he saw Mrs. Millen emerge through the hatch. Squeezing her bulk through, she crawled after him on all fours like an animal.

Max shut his eyes and rolled over the edge.

He fell with a hard, wheezing thud onto the lawn. Stunned, he opened his eyes to see her peering down at him from the fort's roof ten feet above.

"Don't you touch him," she panted, glaring in the direction of the house. "This little scrapper's mine!"

Max wildly scanned the house and yard but saw no one else. Then he realized Mrs. Millen's head had vanished. He heard the trapdoor clatter shut as she began her descent.

Moaning, Max struggled to his feet. His leg threatened to collapse beneath him as he rounded the side of the house, but he managed to limp up the driveway toward the street. Turning, he saw Mrs. Millen galloping after him.

Rounding the corner to the front yard, Max collided with a man, who let out a groan and dropped his briefcase. Max screamed, shut his eyes, and began fiercely pummeling him.

"Hey there! Ouch! Stop hitting me!" the man exclaimed, taking firm hold of Max's arms. Max whipped around, expecting Mrs. Millen to come barreling around the house. She did not.

"Are you all right, my boy?" the man asked in a subdued British accent.

Max felt the grip on his arms relax. He turned and looked up at the person before him. It was not the white-eyed stranger from the museum. Tall and impeccably dressed in a navy suit, this man had sandy hair, a high forehead, and wire glasses. He gave a nervous smile and eyed Max's hard, trembling fists.

"Was she talking to you?" Max demanded.

"Excuse me—*who?*"

Max collapsed before he could find the words.

Max awoke with a start. He was on the couch in the den, his leg no longer numb but tingling as though it had been asleep. Looking down, he saw his shoes had been removed and paired neatly on the floor. He could hear a pleasant whistling approaching from down the hallway. Max had barely managed to sit up when the man with the wire glasses entered the room carrying a plate of cookies and a mug of steaming cocoa.

"Hello, Max! I hope you're feeling a bit better," the man said cheerfully, placing the plate and mug on the coffee table. "My name is Nigel Bristow, and I'm terribly sorry to have given you such a shock! I hope you don't mind that I rummaged around your kitchen a bit. You should have a biscuit. They always work wonders for me."

Max felt too drained to be afraid or to protest. He reached for a cookie, keeping his eyes on Nigel as the man settled into his father's leather chair. Max nibbled the cookie.

"It wasn't you that scared me," he mumbled. "I was being chased."

Nigel's smile straightened into a tight line; his eyes glittered seriously.

"What exactly do you mean, Max? Who was chasing you?"

"I got a letter . . . a letter that said I was going to receive a visitor. She came to the house today and . . ." Max broke off as tears welled into his eyes. He flung his arm over his face, mortified to be in such a state in front of anyone, much less a stranger.

"I see." Nigel's voice was calm and sympathetic. "Max, I want to help you. Do you think you can share what happened with me?"

Max nodded and took a deep breath before telling Nigel the story of Mrs. Millen's visit.

When Max was finished, Nigel scooted his chair forward and patted him on the shoulder.

"It's all right, my boy. I want you to stay right here. Based on what you've told me, I need to attend to a few things. I won't be far away."

Nigel unfolded a nearby quilt and draped it over Max before handing him the mug of chocolate. Murmuring words in an unfamiliar language, Nigel left the room, tapping doorways and windows as he went.

To Max's relief, the numbness in his leg faded with every sip of cocoa. He wriggled his feet for good measure. Then, hearing Nigel's footsteps creaking upstairs, Max realized that he was expected at the Raleighs' house for dinner. Nigel returned just as Max was reaching for the phone.

"I'm not here to hurt you, Max. There's no need to call the police."

"I'm not—I know you're not here to hurt me. I'm calling my dad's friends. He's out of town and I'm supposed to stay with them tonight."

"I see. Max, I think it would be unwise for you to leave my company this evening. If you like, I can handle the arrangements."

"Who are you?" asked Max, sitting forward.

"I am a Recruiter," Nigel said, standing to inspect a photograph on a bookshelf. "I am the visitor that you were *intended* to receive. I am only sorry I did not arrive earlier."

"Then who was that woman, Mrs. Millen? I thought she was going to kill me."

Nigel frowned. "I do not yet know who *she* was or how she came to know who *you* are. This is no small matter, and I have already informed my colleagues. I'm no great terrifying Mystic, but my presence should deter any trespassers until our specialists arrive."

Max was not sure he wanted any more visitors.

"Now," said Nigel. "Let's fix another cup and I'll see if I can explain everything."

The two of them wandered into the kitchen. Max heated the kettle while Nigel hummed pleasantly and rummaged about for more cookies. Reaching into the cupboard, he pulled out a box of Bedford Bros. Crispy Soup Wafers.

"Are these any good?"

"According to my dad, they'll save civilization," muttered Max, looking down to rub the remaining numbness from his leg. A moment later, he heard a loud crunch.

"Well, I don't know about saving civilization," Nigel crowed, "but they're rather tasty!"

The Recruiter scooped up a handful of snacks and headed for the living room. It was getting dark outside; thunder rumbled in the distance. Max brought two mugs of cocoa from the kitchen and found Nigel standing before the fireplace.

"Seems we've got a storm heading our way. Let's cheer things up a bit!"

Nigel's fingers danced as though manipulating a marionette. The cold logs in the hearth suddenly hissed and popped. Yellow flames flicked along the edges. Within seconds, a bright fire was crackling merrily.

"There we go!" Nigel clapped. "A storm on the way, fuel on the fire, and a sip of chocolate to soothe the soul! Come on over here, Max."

Max gaped at the fire.

"But how did you . . . ?"

"All in due time," said Nigel, spreading the quilt on the hardwood floor so the two could sit down. "Now, Max, before we begin I need you to promise you won't tell Mum and Bob that I ate so many of these whatchacallums."

"Um . . . okay," said Max, confused.

"Excellent!" Nigel stuffed a pair of Bedford wafers into his mouth. "These recruiting trips are the only chance I get to sneak a bit of decent comfort food!" He smacked the crumbs from his hands before continuing.

"Max, as frustrating as it might be to hold off on your questions, I'd like you to begin by sharing a bit of yesterday's experience with me."

As the fire crackled and the storm approached, Max recounted the previous day to Nigel. Unlike Mrs. Millen, however, Nigel simply listened and did not press for details as Max spoke.

"I don't know what it all means," said Max when he brought his tale to a close.

"Ah, it seems someone needs an introduction to Celtic mythology! That's a most unusual vision, Max, involving the Cattle Raid of Cooley. It speaks very highly of your capabilities as a Potential."

"What *is* a Potential? That word was used that way in the letter I received."

"Why, Max, *you* are a Potential, and that is why I'm here! You are one of a handful of people on our wondrous little planet with the *potential* to become one of us. When you found that room and discovered that tapestry, we were made aware of you. I'm here to see if you have enough of that special something to merit making you an offer."

"Who is 'we'? An offer for what?"

"All in due time, all in due time. First, I need to administer a few tests."

Rain pattered on the windowpanes. Max thought he saw a shadow dart across one of the windows.

"Somebody's out there!"

Nigel smiled.

"It's quite natural to be a bit jumpy. But we are quite safe. This house is being watched by friendly eyes."

Max shivered, uncertain if he wanted to be watched by anything, friendly or not.

"What happens if I fail?"

"Then I clean up the kitchen and go on my merry way, happy to have made your remarkable acquaintance. Within a few days, you'll have forgotten all about me and this afternoon's unpleasantness. You won't remember a thing."

"But—"

"I know what you're thinking, but don't worry. I've placed this house under priority watch. Given what's happened, it will continue to be under surveillance for some time—even if the tests elude you. There may well be more than one Agent standing guard outside this house, Max."

It was clear that Nigel thought that this explanation was weighty and sufficient. It was not. Max went to look out the window.

"You won't see an Agent," Nigel said as Max peered out the curtains. "Even I might not see them. That's part of an Agent's job—to be as slippery as smoke."

Max frowned and closed the curtains; the storm was now directly overhead.

Nigel stood and motioned for Max to follow him back into the kitchen.

The Recruiter set his briefcase on the kitchen table. Opening the clasps, Nigel reached in the case and removed a digital voice recorder and what appeared to be a large silver tennis racket without any strings. Max could not see how the racket had ever fit within the slender case.

"Come over here, Max—we may as well get started. If you don't mind, hop up on the counter there and forgive me for the formalities." Nigel activated the recorder and leaned against a cupboard.

"Senior Recruiter Nigel Bristow initiating Standard Series of Potential Tests on Mr. Max McDaniels, age twelve, of Chicago, Illinois, United States of America."

Holding the recorder toward Max, Nigel continued to speak in a clipped monotone.

"Mr. McDaniels, please indicate that you have been fully briefed and agree to participate in the following trials with full knowledge that they are highly experimental and likely to result in severe disfigurement. . . ."

"Hey! Wait a minute!" shrieked Max, jumping off the counter.

Nigel chortled. "Just a bit of humor. Couldn't help myself." He waved Max back up onto the counter. "All right, then. First test to be administered: physical aptitude. Max, you've been to the doctor before, haven't you? Well, this is similar to when he taps your knee with a rubber mallet. Only instead of a mallet, I'm going to hold this little contraption. It can't hurt you, I promise."

Max watched Nigel adjust a number of tiny dials on the handle. A small screen flickered on, and a ring of white light appeared within the empty oval head. The contraption began to whine.

Max squirmed.

"Nigel, are you sure that thing is safe? It doesn't *sound* safe!"

"Perfectly safe, perfectly safe," muttered Nigel, carefully guiding the contraption around Max's dangling foot and up toward his knee. "Now, in a moment you're going to feel a bit of a shock—nothing painful, but it will make you want to kick your leg out. I want you to resist that temptation and keep your knee within the boundaries. *Do not touch the device!* Ready . . . and begin."

The machine's whine rose to a fevered pitch, and Max felt a sudden jolt to his knee. He shut his eyes and focused all of his will on controlling the powerful impulse to kick. Sweat beaded on his face and trickled down his back. Glancing down, he saw his knee moving in a blur of tiny circles that approached but never touched the instrument. Finally, the machine's pitch descended to a steady hum before slowing to a halt. Nigel studied the device's screen and reached for his recorder.

"Lactic production rate: eighty-two. Lactic dispersion rate: eighty-four. Twitch speed: ninety-five. Muscular density, current: sixty-four. Muscular density, projected: eighty-seven. Synaptic bypass: eighty-four. Mental stress fatigue: fifty-two."

Nigel frowned as he read the last number.

"Hmmm. Stress fatigue's surprisingly low. Score is likely result of subject exhaustion following preemptive Enemy intercept. Recruiter recommends retesting at later date if applicable."

Brightening, he looked up at Max, who was mopping his brow. Nigel switched off the recorder.

"Good show, my boy! Acceptable ratings across the board *and* you managed to keep from hitting the device. You're a talented devil. I've only been recruiting for seven years, but I've never tested anyone who registered a ninety-five for twitch speed. Never even heard of it, actually."

"What do those numbers mean?" Max asked.

"Oh, a lot of hogwash, really," replied Nigel, seemingly distracted as he switched off the contraption. "They're supposed to give us an understanding of your physical capabilities and, more importantly, your ability to control your actions in a stressful environment. I'm sure someone will explain all the numbers to you later if you're really interested."

Max glanced at the strange, silvery instrument.

"Is that thing *magical*?"

"Magical? Heavens, no! In fact, don't let any of the Device people hear you say that! They take a lot of pride—too much, if you ask me—in making all kinds of useful *non-mystic* things. I'm just happy this new model works. The last one was—"

He coughed and glanced at Max, who raised his eyebrows.

"Well, needless to say, it wasn't as *reliable* as this model. This one, however, is a peach!"

Nigel patted the device affectionately before letting it slip from his fingers into his case. It fell in without making an appreciable sound or dent within the smooth calfskin sides. Plucking up the recorder, he beckoned Max back into the living room.

"Right. One test down, and possibly two to go. Now, I'd like you to stand across the room and face the fireplace."

With a sweep of his arm, Nigel extinguished the lamps. The fire was now the room's only source of light.

"Wow," said Max.

Nigel smiled and placed several more logs in the hearth. Firelight danced on the walls. Max waited nervously, his eyes adjusting to the darkened room. The fire burned much brighter when Nigel finally stood and turned to him.

"Max, the first test was not so unusual—bit of an elaborate physical. This next test will be a tad strange for you. I'm going to ask you to try something that you don't currently believe you can do. I want you to extinguish this fire from where you stand."

"Are you kidding?" said Max, shaking his head and laughing with disbelief.

"You have what it takes to do this, Max. Relax your mind. Imagine this fire ebbing to a low flame, then to a trickle of smoke, and finally to a cold hearth."

Max's eyes followed the brilliant oranges and yellows that writhed about the logs. He heard the wood crackling, watched the heat rise in steady waves. A log collapsed in a shower of sparks. Max flexed his fingers. He pictured the flames slowing to a halt, losing their intensity, and leaving the space cold and dark.

To Max's utter amazement, the fire began to die. It was unmistakable, as if the wood was slowly but steadily absorbing the flames.

"Very good," said Nigel. "Now finish the job and put it out. . . ."

Max shut his eyes and focused his entire being on the glowing logs and embers. He clenched his fists, imagining the heat being drawn into the surrounding brick and diffusing throughout the house. His body shuddered; he felt utterly drained. Opening his eyes, he saw Nigel smiling at him.

"Bravo, Max. Well done, indeed." Nigel swept his arm up and restored the lights. Max winced as Nigel grasped a log that had been burning only moments before. He tossed it to Max, who instinctively backed away and let it fall to the floor in a small puff of ash and soot. Crouching down, Max flicked at it with a finger. It was cool to the touch. Beaming at Nigel, he placed it back in the hearth.

Nigel tipped an imaginary cap as he activated the recorder.

"Test two completed. Subject extinguished a confined stage-two fire from a distance of seven paces. Subject successfully eliminated flames and further sapped residual heat from logs. Test completed in one minute and forty-seven seconds."

Max's chest expanded as Nigel shut off the recorder.

"One minute and forty seven seconds is pretty good, isn't it?"

"Well, Max, not to burst your bubble, but the modern record is under five seconds by our very own Miss Hazel Boon. Your score was, well, *average* among Potentials. Not to worry! It took this poor Recruiter over three minutes to squelch his first flame, and even then you could roast marshmallows over the logs!"

Max smiled at the thought of a miniature Nigel frowning in his blue suit while a Recruiter roasted marshmallows and reported the disappointing result.

"So, what's next?"

"Oh, the last test isn't so bad—you've already had the biggies! It's just a bit of a puzzle. I've got it in my case in the kit—"

Before Nigel could finish his sentence, there was a deafening boom of thunder and the house went black. Squinting in the dark, Max saw Nigel sprawled on the floor. The back door had been smashed to pieces. To Max's horror, Mrs. Millen eyed them from the kitchen.

Her hair was matted from the rain; her makeup was smeared into dark streaks on her fleshy face. She shambled toward them, bent and furious. Her cane smacked the floor at rapid and regular beats.

"Hoo-hoo-hoo! Thought I'd just gone away? Thought your friend's little charms could keep me out?"

Max started to scream but no sound emerged. At his feet, Nigel moaned and struggled to stand, but his arms buckled beneath him and he collapsed back to the ground.

"Better run, Max!" Mrs. Millen warned. "Better run while you can! Leave that scrawny thing to me and I'll let you go!"

She was just ten feet away when Max finally bolted.

He wrenched the front door open to the summer rain. Whipping around, he saw Mrs. Millen chuckling and crouching low over Nigel, whose foot thumped dully against the floorboards.

A blind rage came over Max. "Get away from him! *Get away from him!*" He dashed back into the living room only to see Nigel sitting, comfortable and composed, by the rekindled fire. Max stalked down the hall, adrenaline now racing through his body. There was no sign of Mrs. Millen. The kitchen door was whole, solid and secure on its hinges.

Nigel smiled and spoke softly into his recorder. "Test three complete. After a brief moment of initial hesitation and retreat, Mr. McDaniels responded to phantasm with a frontal assault, exhibiting extraordinary determination and—oh dear, how should I put this—ferocity! Given that phantasm was generated from a mind cache recently exposed to the Enemy, this is particularly remarkable. It is with great pride and personal satisfaction that this Recruiter may report that Mr. Max McDaniels has passed the Standard Series of Potential Tests."

Max stared in disbelief at Nigel. "So that was all just a . . . *test?*"

"Yes, I am sorry about that," said Nigel with a sigh. "It's the only way we know of to test a Potential's courage and loyalty. Unfortunately, it's the test most Potentials ultimately fail, but we've refused to compromise our standards. You were willing to help me at great danger to your person, my boy, and I am indeed touched."

Nigel smiled and rose to place a hand on Max's shoulder.

Max glanced at the hand. He let it slip off his shoulder as he walked wearily toward the kitchen. Nigel followed.

"Don't be too angry with me!" he pleaded. "It's not so easy being on my side of it, either — what with all the screaming, the crying, the irretrievably soiled pants. . . ."

"I'm not mad anymore," sighed Max. "Just promise that you won't conjure up Mrs. Millen again. I don't think I could handle her three times in one day."

"It's a deal," chuckled Nigel. "Now, let's see if we can't find some more of those Crispy Sons Snack—*whatever* you call them."

~ 3 ~

THE TIME TO CHOOSE

Max awoke earlier than usual as Nigel's whistling and the smell of coffee wafted upstairs. It was light outside; sprinklers were hard at work. He yawned and rolled out of bed, throwing on a T-shirt and shuffling down the stairs.

Nigel was seated at the dining-room table, already dressed in a suit and tie. He perused the *Tribune* and sipped at a mug of coffee. Steam rose from a covered basket arranged on the table along with a crock of butter, several types of jam, and a glass of juice.

"And the sleepyhead emerges from his burrow! Can't say I blame you, though—you had quite a day yesterday."

"Nigel, it's six fifteen in the morning. . . ."

"Exactly. Time to rise and shine! I've got to be on my way shortly, so I thought we'd first enjoy a proper breakfast. Max, have you ever had popovers?"

Nigel peeled back the basket's cover to reveal a dozen of what looked like steaming hot biscuits.

"Are they anything like Pop-Tarts?" asked Max.

"I should say *not*," said Nigel with a shudder. "My wife's would shame these sorry creations, but I still think you're in for a treat! Here's to new discoveries!"

Max raised his glass, then spent the next several minutes attacking the hot, flaky popovers.

"Mneez uhn illy guuh!" he said at last.

Nigel looked up from his paper.

"Come again?"

"These are really good!" Max repeated, reaching for another.

"Are you admitting they compare favorably to the almighty Pop-Tart? I believe that's four you've managed already. . . ."

Max narrowed his eyes.

"Yes, well, now that we've fed the monster, perhaps we should give him a present."

Max wiped his mouth as Nigel presented him with an envelope of the same heavy cream-colored paper as the mysterious letter that had appeared in his pocket. This envelope was larger, but it, too, had Max's name scripted on the front. Max slid his hand under the sealing wax and opened the flap to remove a sheaf of papers and a glossy brochure.

"Save the brochure for later," said Nigel. "Have a peek at the rest."

Max turned the papers over and scanned the cover page.

Dear Mr. McDaniels,

It is our understanding that you passed the Standard Series of Tests for Potentials. As Mr. Bristow no doubt informed you, this is a tremendous achievement. On behalf of Rowan Academy, please allow me to extend our most sincere congratulations.

Based on your results, Rowan Academy hereby extends you an offer to join our organization as an Apprentice, First Year.

We are hopeful that you will begin the full term at the new student orientation one week from today. Details are enclosed, and we trust you will find the attached scholarship offer attractive.

A representative will visit you and your father this evening to discuss this unique opportunity and, we hope, celebrate your decision to accept. Given the unusual circumstances of your initial contact, we have taken additional precautions. You can rest assured that Miss Awolowo is indeed a legitimate representative. She will arrive at precisely eight o' clock.

Warmest regards,
Gabrielle Richter
Executive Director

"Who is she?" asked Max. "She signed my first letter."

"Ms. Richter? Oh, well, she's the boss, for lack of a better term. Quite a lady, I might add."

"Oh. And the academy—what's that?"

"Hmmm. Well, I might not be the best person to explain it to you. That falls under Miss Awolowo's responsibilities. I can say, however, that it is an extraordinary place for extraordinary people just like you, Max."

"I don't understand. Would I have to go away?"

"Well, yes. The academy is located in New England."

Max put the letter down and shook his head.

"Forget it—I can't just leave. Not after everything that's happened."

"I understand your feelings, Max—" Nigel began.

"No you don't. My dad would be all alone without me."

Nigel closed his eyes and nodded.

"My mom's been gone two years," Max blurted suddenly, his face growing hot. "My dad talks about her like she's alive, but she isn't. They never even found her."

"Do you want to talk about it?" asked Nigel quietly, wiping up some crumbs and refilling Max's juice.

"There isn't much to talk about," Max said. He felt tired again. "They found her car on the side of the road. It was still running. She was gone."

Max glowered and flicked a crumb off the table.

"Anyway," he mumbled, "I don't think moving away is a good idea."

"I see." Nigel pushed the popovers back in his direction. "I won't try to convince you, Max. All I'll ask is that you keep an open mind and listen to what Miss Awolowo has to say. In the meantime, I would encourage you to study the materials in your packet."

Nigel straightened the papers and brochure, handing them to Max before rising with his briefcase.

"I realize the timing is dreadful, but I must be going. Yesterday's events have raised questions that need answers, and I've been ordered away. Don't worry about your father and the Raleighs—I've taken care of everything."

Max was incredulous.

"Nigel! You can't leave me here by myself. My dad doesn't get back until this afternoon! What if Mrs. Millen comes back?"

"Max, this house is under priority watch. You should be just fine."

Max stood up from the table and began pacing the room.

"No, no, no! You said Mrs. Millen *shouldn't* have known I was a Potential and shown up here to begin with! Can't I come with you?"

"I'm afraid that's impossible, Max. However, I do think I can procure some company so that you're not alone."

Max paused.

"An Agent?"

Nigel shook his head. "No, not an Agent. They're under strict orders to stand guard outside. You wouldn't like their company anyway—too serious!"

Nigel placed his briefcase on the table.

"This may take a minute, depending on whether she's within call."

The Recruiter unfastened the case's clasps and buried his entire head within it. Max heard his muffled voice cooing.

"There's my girl. Oh, you're getting so big and gorgeous! No, no, I don't think you look fat. Don't tell Mrs. Bristow, but I think you're holding your shape quite nicely! Oh, well, thank you very much, indeed. Don't mean to sound immodest, but I *have* been trying to train up a bit."

Nigel pinched his rather flimsy biceps while his head remained in the case.

"Yes, well, I've got a little favor to ask. Would you mind looking after a friend for a few hours? You wouldn't? Bless you, my dear—he will be most relieved."

Max took a step back as Nigel thrust his arms into the case and strained forward to hoist something out of the bag. He withdrew and turned, cradling a pink piglet as if she were a newborn.

Max rubbed his temples and shook his head. "You've got to be kidding me."

The piglet sniffed the air and focused her drowsy eyes on Max. She blinked several times and promptly burrowed her snout into Nigel's armpit.

"Max, I'd like you to meet Lucy!" said Nigel cheerfully.

Max's voice was steady and measured.

"Nigel, you are not leaving me in the care of a *pig*."

Nigel smiled. "I'm *not* leaving you in her care; I'm leaving you in her company. You should consider yourself lucky—Lucy's the best company there is!"

Lucy wriggled to gaze lovingly up at Nigel, releasing a wheezing burst of gas in the process.

"But . . . !"

Nigel ignored Max and gently lowered Lucy to the floor. She trotted toward the kitchen, snorting happily.

"She's a snap, really—just let her have a bite, or three, of whatever you're eating. When your dad gets home, slip her out the back door and she'll find me."

Defeated, Max looked at the floor and nodded. Something fell in the kitchen. He turned to see Lucy perched precariously on a chair, nosing through the leftover batter.

"Well," said Nigel with a glance at his watch. "I am now running quite late and really must be on my way. I know it's all been a whirl, but don't let it get the best of you. Things will sort themselves out sooner than you think! It's been my pleasure."

Nigel smiled and extended his hand.

"Will I see you again?" Max asked.

"I'd like to think so—I certainly hope to see you at your orientation!" He smiled and patted Max firmly on the shoulder. "I hope you'll join the new class, Max. I think Rowan's just the place for you."

A moment later, Nigel had gone. Max watched him walk briskly down the sidewalk, briefcase in hand, before he turned off Max's street. Feeling very alone, Max locked the door and gathered up the plates and glasses. On his way to the kitchen, he passed Lucy, who trotted past him into the den. Stepping over the rather large mess she'd made, Max sighed and piled the dishes in the sink. He left Lucy in the den, where she seemed content to snort and roll.

Max was vaguely aware that the Chicago Cubs were losing to the San Francisco Giants when he heard the front door open. Bolting upright in his father's chair, he switched off the radio and skidded to the back door clutching Lucy, who had been curled up on his lap. The piglet shook herself awake with a series of startled grunts.

Setting her down outside, Max scratched her ears and whispered, "Thanks for staying with me, Lucy. Sorry I doubted you. Can you find Nigel?"

Lucy nuzzled his leg and, with a jaunty turn, trotted out into the yard, disappearing behind the fort. Locking the door, Max padded barefoot to the front hall, where his father had just let his bag thump to the floor.

"Hey, Max. How were the Raleighs?"

"Er, fine," Max said, avoiding his father's eyes. "I'm glad you're home, though."

"Yeah, well, so am I. Had a chance to cool off a bit in KC, and I think we'll ground you for one week rather than two. Cooped up for two weeks is too much during the summer. Sound fair?"

"Sure," Max said. "Um, Dad, we're going to have someone coming by the house tonight to talk with us."

"Who's that? You're not in trouble, are you?"

"No, nothing like that. I won some kind of scholarship."

Scott McDaniels glanced from the mail to Max. "Really? A scholarship? What kind of scholarship?"

"I don't know exactly, but they're offering me full tuition at some school."

"What school?" asked his father, giving an inquisitive smile.

"Rowan Academy—in New England."

Mr. McDaniels's smile vanished. "New England? That's hundreds of miles away, Max. How did you win this scholarship?"

Max began fidgeting.

"Um, I guess I did well on some tests and, uh, they found me."

"And who is this person coming tonight?"

"Someone named Miss Awolowo."

"Humph," his father snorted. "That's a mouthful. We'll see what Miss Aloha has to say."

The two made turkey sandwiches and took turns dipping

into a colossal tin of potato chips. Mr. McDaniels regaled Max with stories about a new paper towel that offered astonishing absorbency.

Miss Awolowo arrived precisely at eight o'clock. Towering to nearly Mr. McDaniels's height, she was an elegant woman whose age Max found impossible to estimate. She wore multicolored robes, a necklace of heavy beads, and carried a woven bag decorated with flying birds. She placed the bag on the step and extended her hand. Her skin was as smooth and dark as a coffee bean, her voice rich and tinged with an accent.

"You must be Mr. McDaniels. I am Ndidi Awolowo from Rowan Academy. It is my very great privilege to meet you."

Scott McDaniels paused somewhat awkwardly before concluding the handshake.

"Yes, of course. Very nice to meet you, too. Please come in."

"Thank you," said Miss Awolowo, sweeping past him into the foyer, where Max lingered nervously.

"Hello there—you must be Max! I'm Miss Awolowo."

Max took her hand and felt his apprehension wash away. As with Nigel, there was a reassuring strength and warmth to this woman. She placed a hand on his shoulder, and he led her into the living room, where Mr. McDaniels fumbled with coffee and a tray of sugar cookies. Settling at one end of the couch, she directed her bright eyes alternately between Max and his father.

"You have a beautiful home, Mr. McDaniels, and an extraordinary son. I must apologize for visiting on such short notice; we only recently received Max's results. Have you had an opportunity to review the scholarship we would like to offer him?"

"Yes, and we sure do appreciate that, Miss Ahoolaloo." Max

squirmed as his father adopted the tone of voice he used with clients. "That letter got us tickled pink, but I think we're going to have to take a pass. Max's been through a lot these past few years, and I think it's best if he stays close to home."

Miss Awolowo nodded soberly and paused before replying.

"Yes, please forgive me for being direct, but I am aware of the situation with Mrs. McDaniels. I am sorry."

"Er, yes. Yes, it's been difficult for us, but we're managing."

"Of course you are. You're doing a wonderful job, Mr. Mc-Daniels. You've raised a fine boy under very trying circumstances. I do hope, however, that you will not permit a tragedy in your son's past to obstruct a wonderful opportunity in his future."

"I only want the best for Max," said his father defensively.

"I know you do," she said soothingly. "That is precisely what we offer. Our program is better suited to serve your son than a mainstream curriculum. You see, Mr. McDaniels, a boy with Max's aptitude and creativity cannot flourish in a program that does not recognize and develop his unique skills."

"How does your academy manage to do better?"

"By placing Max among other gifted, creative students from all around the world. By providing him with teachers who understand his gifts and are capable of developing them to their potential."

"Did you attend Rowan?"

"Yes, I did, Mr. McDaniels. I was visited by a Recruiter in my village in Africa." She clapped her hands together and gave a girlish laugh. "Ah, it seems like ages ago. My parents did not want to let their baby go; they were afraid of all that might go wrong! But, after a quiet time, my father came to me and said, 'If a man does not stand for something, he will fall for anything. I want to stand *for you*.'"

Her eyes glistened, and she smiled at the memory. Mr. Mc-Daniels stared at his knobby fingers. His voice was tight when he next spoke.

"I don't know what to do here. It sounds like a good opportunity, but I just don't know if Max is ready for something like this. Max, how do you feel?"

To this point, Max had been happy to be a bystander. Now, with their attention focused on him, he became very nervous.

"I don't know. I don't want to leave you alone."

"Don't worry about me, Max. I'm a big boy."

After an awkward silence, Miss Awolowo spoke.

"Mr. McDaniels? Would it be all right if I spoke to Max one on one?"

"Max? Would you like that?"

Max glanced at Miss Awolowo, who waited patiently.

"It's a beautiful summer evening, Max. Why don't we walk around the block and get a breath of fresh air?"

Max looked at his father, who nodded his approval.

Miss Awolowo took Max's arm as they walked down the front steps. The night sky was very clear. They walked without speaking, passing quietly under the streetlamp. Giving his arm a soft pat, Miss Awolowo broke the silence.

"Nigel sends his best. You made quite an impression on him—he speaks very highly of you. You have our deepest apologies for that woman's unfortunate visit."

Max shuddered and focused his eyes on the dark hedges and lawns all around them. Miss Awolowo drew him nearer and hummed a low, pretty tune.

"You have no need to fear, Max. The Enemy is aware of me

and knows that I am no trifle. Old Awolowo can be fierce!" She flashed her eyes wide, chuckled, and gave his arm a playful squeeze. Max smiled and tried to relax.

"Miss Awolowo? Who is the Enemy? Nigel wouldn't answer my questions."

"Yes, well, that's not his job to answer questions of that sort. Will you come with me? I want to show you something."

Max nodded. Miss Awolowo straightened to her full height and looked down upon him. Her eyes shone silver, and to Max she appeared as wise and beautiful as all the queens in all his old storybooks put together. She smiled and took his hand.

Max's insides squirmed like they had when he saw the tapestry. Only this time it didn't feel like he'd swallowed bees; helium balloons now filled his stomach. His feet tingled as though he'd stepped into a bath that was too hot. When Max looked down to investigate, he gasped.

The sidewalk was shrinking.

Miss Awolowo held his hand tightly as they rose slowly above the streetlamps and dark clumps of trees. They drifted together on the night breeze, leaving houses and parks in their wake as they glided over the treetops and chimneys. They skimmed out over the lake and rose up in gentle spirals.

They soared so high, Max thought they might catch the moon. He laughed and reached out to touch it. He couldn't reach it, though. It continued to hover above them, bright and distant and cold.

"We live in a beautiful world, don't we?"

Miss Awolowo's words shook Max out of his reverie. It had all seemed utterly like a dream until he realized with sudden terror that he was indeed high above the lake with the wind whipping fiercely about him.

Miss Awolowo was serene. "Let's find a more comfortable perch, shall we?"

Max nodded enthusiastically.

With a wide, lazy turn, she guided them toward the Baha'i temple that jutted against the night sky like a massive block of carved ivory. She set them down on its dome, many stories above the trees. They sat side by side, and Miss Awolowo smoothed her robes and clasped her hands together.

"There! That's better." Running her hand over the intricate stonework about them, she declared, "I *do* love this building. Anyway, are you a bit warmer, my dear?"

"Yes, ma'am."

"Now take a look up at the sky. What do you see?"

"I don't know," Max said. "Stars. The moon."

"You also see a great deal of darkness, don't you? Max, this is our struggle. There is a force in this world that does not love the moon, stars, or sun. It doesn't care for the lights of cities, the joys of laughter, or even the sounds of grief. It doesn't care for *anything* that causes a ripple in the perfect black stillness whence it came. It would devour that moon if it could."

Max shivered and watched an elderly couple strolling in the gardens far below. Miss Awolowo continued.

"It can't devour the moon, so it seeks to devour man instead. For thousands of years, people have fought against this Enemy in all its many forms. People like you and me."

Max looked hard at her. Miss Awolowo nodded and touched two fingers to his forehead.

"Yes, Max—people like *you*. You were born a prince, a prince of humankind. For centuries, gifted people have developed their abilities to ensure man can continue to grow and create beautiful things like this very building. Without us, mankind would have perished long ago. Ours is an ancient struggle for survival."

"And you want me to join this . . . struggle?"

Miss Awolowo smiled and placed her head on Max's head.

"Nigel said you are a brave boy. But you're far too young to make such a choice. Only Rowan's graduates are asked to make that decision, and some elect to do other things. All I want you to do is to give us a try and see if you like it."

Max frowned. "What if I decide not to go? Would you be angry?"

Miss Awolowo sat quietly for several moments. Her response was measured.

"I would be disappointed, but certainly not angry. I won't lie to you, however. My desire for you to come to Rowan is very strong. Nigel's report suggests the Old Magic might be in you, that you might be a prince even among our kind. In person, I can see it might be so. The little light within you burns so bright it warms even old Awolowo!"

Her beaded necklace shook with her laughter.

"Yes, Max, that light is very bright indeed. I am only sorry that others have seen it, too. Given what's happened, I think Rowan would be a safer place for you. But I am here only to offer opportunities—you will get no judgments or false choices from me. The decision is yours alone, and it is an important one."

Max hugged his knees, listening carefully.

Max swiveled from Miss Awolowo and followed the path of a plane far away over the moonlit lake. Its signal light blinked at steady intervals against the deep blue sky. When he turned to her, his face was set and fierce.

"I want to go."

~ 4 ~

THE FLIGHT TO ROWAN

The night before he left for Rowan, Max had an extraordinary dream.

He was walking across an open field at dusk, tossing a ball high ahead of him and running forward to catch it. The wind was brisk and the moon was rising as he came to a path that led to a distant house with lighted windows.

Suddenly, something large darted from a nearby hedge and loped onto the path in front of him. It was an enormous wolf-hound. It paused and glowered at him.

Max froze. The animal's heavy face began to flicker and

shift—momentarily adopting the unmistakable features of Mrs. Millen, Nigel, Miss Awolowo, and the strange man from the train. The hound padded toward Max, a murderous rumble emanating from its throat as its face became his father's.

Max could not move. The hound reared up on its hind legs and placed paws the size of baseball mitts on Max's shoulders. It looked down at him, its breath a series of hot blasts. Growling, it pressed its forehead hard against his and spoke to him:

"What are you about? Answer quick or I'll gobble you up!"

When Max opened his eyes, he saw his father sitting at the foot of his bed. He was smiling, but he looked older and tired. Deep circles lined his eyes.

"You sleep just like you did as a little boy."

Max blinked and propped himself up on his elbows.

"I had a bad dream."

"Oh no!" exclaimed Mr. McDaniels in mock horror. "What about?"

"A big dog," Max murmured sleepily, pushing his dark hair off his forehead.

"A big dog! Well, did he bite you or did you bite him?"

"Neither," Max whispered.

His father patted his foot and stood up.

"Well, just remember—it's not the size of the dog in the fight, but the size of the fight in the dog."

Max sank back under the covers and wriggled toward the foot of the bed.

"I know, Dad. You've told me a hundred times."

"So I have." Mr. McDaniels chuckled. "Hop in the shower

and get ready. Someone from the school is on your flight, and we're supposed to meet him at the airport by eight."

Max groaned as his father whisked the covers off the bed and drew the curtains to reveal a morning sky of peach and pale gold.

Nigel was waiting near the check-in, holding up a paper sign that read MCDANIELS and looking rather bored. The Recruiter was dressed neatly in a sport coat but had seen too much sun since his visit with Max. He stopped adjusting his glasses and extended his hand as the McDanielses approached.

"Hello there. You must be Mr. McDaniels—I'm Nigel Bristow from Rowan."

"Call me Scott, Nigel," said Mr. McDaniels, taking Nigel's hand. "This is Max, your copilot for the day."

"Hello, Max," said Nigel brightly, giving a quick wink. "Thanks for coming along. Flying is such a bore without good company. We're a bit pressed for time, eh? Let's get you checked in."

Once Nigel had taken Max's duffel and stood in line, Mr. McDaniels gave Max a nudge. "Seems like a nice enough guy," he said.

"Yeah," said Max, puzzling over why Nigel would be holding up a sign with his name. Given all that had happened, Max thought his name and travel plans would be more of a secret.

Nigel called over to Max when it was their turn to check in. Max answered the lady's questions and watched his bag disappear down the conveyor.

"Well, we're all set," said Nigel, clutching their tickets. "I'll leave you a minute to say good-bye to your father," Nigel said under his breath as the two made their way back to where Mr. McDaniels stood with his hands in his pockets. "I know this sounds cruel, but try to be quick. No tears. It's important."

Nigel said his farewells and promised to look after Max before joining the long line snaking toward security. Remembering what Nigel told him, Max avoided his father's eyes. He flicked his fingers against his thumbs and looked straight ahead at Mr. McDaniels's big yellow shirt.

"All right, Max. Here's where I say good-bye."

Max nodded.

"You're just the best, you know. The best boy a father could ask for."

Max felt his father's arms wrap tightly around him. Max shut his eyes and promised to call and write and say prayers for his mother. When his father finally let him go, Max walked stiffly to where Nigel was waiting. He did not look back.

Nigel left Max to his own thoughts until they were through security.

"Well done," he said at last. "I know that wasn't easy."

"Was that *another* test?" asked Max thickly.

"No," said Nigel. "A precaution. This airport's a very busy place today. We need to avoid anything too *real*."

"What do you—"

Max cut his own question short as he saw a boy who looked very much like himself walking in the opposite direction. Max blinked. The boy did not just look like him—it looked *exactly* like him.

"Try not to stare," said Nigel casually, increasing their pace a step. "They're on our side."

Max passed himself several more times. He noticed that the boys were always accompanied by one or two serious-looking adults.

"You must be tired," said Nigel quietly as they finally took their seats on the crowded plane. "I bet you had no idea you've been taking over a dozen flights a day for the past three days. . . ."

"But—"

Nigel held up a finger to quiet him.

"Agents. Decoys. We can talk more when we get to Rowan," said Nigel, procuring a bar of chocolate and a deck of cards from his briefcase. "We're not quite out of the woods."

Max nibbled the chocolate and listened to the plane's engines as Nigel dealt the cards.

Several hours later, the plane set down. Nigel led Max out of the plane, along the moving walkways, and down toward baggage claim.

Nigel had just swung his duffel off the carousel when Max saw someone step out suddenly from behind a nearby pillar.

It was the man from the train—the man with the dead white eye.

His coat was just as dirty and his eye just as unsettling as Max remembered. He stood as still as a stone between them and the exit while people filed past.

"He's here," Max whispered.

Nigel appeared not to hear as he fumbled with Max's duffel.

"He's here!" shouted Max, clutching Nigel's arm.

Nigel shot him a puzzled glance before squinting past him.

His face went white.

The Recruiter immediately gripped Max by the collar and spun him around. Nigel marched him back up the stairs they had just descended. As they swam against a tide of startled faces, Max tried to look behind them, but there were too many people.

Nigel was speaking rapidly into a slim phone at his ear, but Max could not hear what was said. They crossed over to the next terminal, where Nigel hurried Max out the sliding doors and into a limousine that had screeched to a sudden halt at the curb.

The car sped onto the highway and made its way north while Nigel typed text messages into his phone, looking uncharacteristically grim. Over an hour passed in tense silence before they suddenly veered off the interstate and merged onto a smaller road. They were very near the coast; tall grasses swayed by the roadside as they wound their way past small farms and towns. Weathered signs advertised public beaches, fresh lobster, and clamming excursions. It all seemed very alien.

Nigel glanced out the back window. The road behind them had been empty for miles. Apparently satisfied, he pressed a button and rolled down the window. The warm summer air rushed in, fragrant and heavy with salt.

"How are you feeling?" he asked, his serious expression softening to a smile.

"I'm fine now. It was him, you know—that man at the airport. He's the one who was following me at the museum."

"Yes, I know. He matched your description perfectly. It was a nasty shock, no question about it. But mission accomplished: here you are, safe and sound!"

Max took a deep breath; it seemed the first real breath he'd taken since the airport.

"Nigel, my dad's okay, isn't he? They won't bother him now that I'm here . . . ?"

"He'll be fine, Max," Nigel said sympathetically. "You're the one they want."

Nigel looked past Max and pointed at something out the window. Max turned in time to glimpse an old wooden sign:

WELCOME TO ROWAN TOWNSHIP, EST. 1649

They passed a few tidy cottages on the outskirts. The Atlantic Ocean shimmered ahead as Max took in the clipped lawns, fresh paint, and clean awnings. The town's buildings were old but beautifully maintained. An old-fashioned movie theater rolled past, followed by a town green and a coffeehouse. Beyond these were a jumble of shops and small restaurants. Passing the row of businesses, they arrived at a small white church whose signboard indicated Rowan Academy was just ahead. Max swallowed and felt his pulse quicken.

They turned off the road onto a smooth lane, passing beneath a towering green canopy formed by the overlapping branches of tall, twisty trees lining the road. They accelerated toward a high gate of black iron flanked by a sturdy stone gatehouse. The gate swung inward as they approached. Max tried to get a better look at a striking silver crest when the limousine crossed the threshold, but the gate swung shut behind them.

The road had become a gravel lane, and the car now followed it to the right, plunging into a thick wood of ash and oak and beech.

Max turned to Nigel.

"Why wouldn't you let me say good-bye to my dad? Why did you make me hurry?"

"Oh, that—I *am* sorry. We needed to stay as consistent as

possible with the others—those decoys—that preceded you. You did very well."

"Who *were* those other kids? Are they in danger?"

Nigel smiled.

"Those *weren't* kids, and they are well equipped to deal with any dangers that might arise. You've seen your first Agents, Max."

Nigel wriggled out of his sport coat and held it up against the window. Max saw large dark stains under the arms. Nigel sighed.

"But I'm *not* an Agent, just a poor old Recruiter caught in the middle and not quite cut out for all this cloak-and-dagger stuff." He sniffed once at the jacket before folding it neatly on his lap.

"Why were you the one traveling with me, then?" asked Max.

"The Agents insisted I'd be the best decoy out there," Nigel admitted sheepishly. "They really can be brutal, you know."

"They were wrong," Max said. "That man wasn't fooled. And anyway, I'm glad I got to travel with you and not some boring Agent."

Nigel brightened as the limousine slowed for an upcoming turn.

"Thank you, Max. . . . Welcome to Rowan."

The limousine emerged from the thick wood and into an enormous sunny clearing of smooth lawns, athletic fields, colorful gardens, and old stone buildings set near the sea. Max stuck his head out the window and listened to the seagulls. The car followed the lane along a grassy bluff high above the water's edge before curving away to conclude at a large circular drive and a sprawling mansion of light gray stone. Many cars were parked in front.

Max opened his door and gaped at a marble fountain of fish-tailed horses spraying water high into the air. Through the mist, he squinted up at the mansion. He couldn't begin to count its windows and chimneys.

"One hundred and eleven," muttered Nigel, shuffling around the car with Max's duffel.

"What?" said Max, uncertain if his ears had fully popped from the flight.

"The Manse has one hundred and eleven chimneys. You were trying to count them."

"How did you know?" asked Max, troubled that his thoughts were so transparent.

"Because I tried to do the very same thing when I arrived here—oh dear Lord—some thirty years ago."

The Recruiter chuckled and stooped to pluck a white flower from among several clustered on the flagstones at Max's feet.

"Rowan blossom," he said, gesturing at the dozen slender trees ringing the drive. Nigel closed Max's door and led Max up a number of stone steps, pausing a moment before the mansion's great double doors.

"Ah—one thing, Max. I recognize the temptations, but I would greatly appreciate it if you wouldn't mention any of our *excitement* to anyone. That man, Mrs. Millen—any of it, frankly. The less gossip, the better our chances at fixing all this. Will you promise to discuss this only with the Director, and then only if asked?"

Max nodded solemnly and shook Nigel's hand.

"Good," said Nigel, visibly relieved. "Let's join the others. Orientation's already started."

Max followed Nigel through the double doors and into a tall

foyer flanked by sweeping staircases on each side. They passed through a door beneath the landing and down a long hallway, past several rooms, before stopping at a closed door of polished walnut. Max heard Miss Awolowo's rich, warm voice speaking on the other side.

"Ack! Just as I feared," said Nigel. "This door always creaks. Sorry about this. . . ."

The door gave a long, slow squeal as Nigel pushed it open. Hundreds of people turned and looked at the two of them as they stood in the doorway of a little theater. Miss Awolowo paused mid-sentence from where she stood at a podium.

"Ah! There you are! I was beginning to wonder. Ladies and gentlemen, please say hello to Max McDaniels, who joins us from the city of Chicago, right here in the United States."

Max scanned the sea of faces in mute embarrassment. He gave a little wave as Nigel led him to a seat in the back row. Miss Awolowo continued on; Max heard something about internships.

"Going to clean up a bit and make some calls," Nigel whispered, patting Max on the shoulder. "I'll check in with you later—before configuration."

Max nodded until he realized that something was missing.

"Nigel," he whispered urgently, *"what's configuration?"*

There was no answer. He turned, but the Recruiter had already slipped out. A skinny girl with braces and her mother motioned for Max to be quiet. Max scowled back at them and turned to hear Miss Awolowo.

It was mostly talk of contact information and faculty advisors and school holidays and schedules. Max tuned most of it out and studied his new classmates instead. They did not look like the students at his old school; there was much more diversity sprinkled throughout these seats. While many wore foreign clothes, Max was more interested in subtler differences, such as their posture and facial expressions. He thought many looked older and very serious. He was trying to guess their ages when the whole audience stood and began to file up the aisles.

The scene outside in the driveway was awkward, and Max did his best to keep to the edges while those who had arrived with their parents said good-bye. Tears were shed and luggage was stacked in a cacophony of sound as Miss Awolowo answered last-minute questions and ushered parents to their cars. He watched the skinny girl with braces cling to her mother, weeping uncontrollably until Miss Awolowo gently pried her away and led her mother to a taxi. Max felt guilty for making a face at them.

When the parents had all gone, Miss Awolowo led them into the great foyer. She climbed one of the staircases to address them from the landing.

"All right, children. We now must get you situated in your rooms. Before room assignments, however, I would like to make an important announcement concerning Rowan, a place very dear to me and your new home."

The air became very still; the chattering stopped immediately. Something in the older woman's voice had changed.

"Thank you. Until you are given a full tour of the grounds and premises, I ask that you stick only to those rooms and areas that I designate. As you will see, the Manse and the rest of Rowan's campus are . . . strange. This campus and its buildings possess a certain unpredictability that can baffle our most senior faculty. There are also a variety of contraptions throughout this house and grounds whose proper workings require careful instruction. As it is only our first day, I have no desire to rescue or mourn any foolhardy students. Is this understood?"

Miss Awolowo's frank and penetrating look swept from face to face just as Nigel appeared on the landing behind her.

"Wonderful." She beamed. "Now, before the configuration begins, let me say the following. If history has taught us anything, it is that some students are inevitably disappointed with their rooms or roommates or both. If such is the case, I am sorry but urge you to make the best of it. Room configurations and roommate assignments cannot be changed. So, no crying, no whining. Agreed?"

The children nodded slowly and shot puzzled glances at one another.

"Excellent. This is Nigel Bristow. I believe some of you have already made his acquaintance. He'll be showing the boys their rooms. The young ladies will come with me."

"All right, then," Nigel called down to them. "Up here and follow after me."

Max swarmed up the stairs with the other boys. Miss Awolowo's voice called after them.

"Good luck, Nigel! Good luck, boys! Meet back in the foyer at five for a quick tour before dinner. Listen for the chimes!"

Max hurried after Nigel, alongside dozens of other students.

"Okay, boys—keep up, keep up," the Recruiter said. "North Wing's for the gents here at Rowan; the ladies stay in the South Wing, so if you find yourself without a urinal in sight, you know you're in the wrong place."

The boys giggled as they climbed a spiral staircase whose

creaky wooden banister had been worn to a smooth polish. Nigel's voice echoed from above.

"As it happens, your class is on the third floor. Unlucky you. Third and Fourth Years will torment you from the second floor. Fifth and Sixth Years enjoy first-floor convenience and feel very much entitled to it."

Max emerged from the stairwell into a long, broad hallway arched with heavy beams. It was lined on either side with dozens of gleaming green doors. Nigel led them toward the far end of the hallway. Straggling behind, Max noticed that each door had a large, ornate keyhole and a shiny silver numeral in its center. Next to each door was a towering plaque of polished black wood and brass, the first two dozen of which were engraved with names.

Reaching the end of the hall—where, Max noted, the plaques were blank—Nigel turned to the boys, who began to fidget.

"Let's see . . . sixty-nine, seventy, and Omar there makes seventy-one. Excellent—didn't lose anyone along the way! Hooray for me. Now, when I say the word, go hunt for your name on the plaques next to the doors. When you see your name, hold right there and do nothing else. Everyone understand?"

A stocky, handsome boy with chestnut hair and bright blue eyes raised his hand. His Irish accent was so thick that Max could hardly understand him.

"Our names are already on them?"

"What's your name, O curious creature?"

"Connor Lynch."

"No," said Nigel, rubbing his hands together. "But they *will* be. That's part of the fun. You don't pick your roommates and neither do we; that's the Manse's job. . . . Everyone ready? Go find your room!"

To Max it seemed like a frantic Easter egg hunt as the other boys sprinted or bumped into one another to scour the name-plates up and down the hall.

"I've found mine!" called a short boy who looked like a mouse.

"Me too!" cried another, losing his retainer.

Max walked slowly down the hall as the other boys shouted in excitement and jumped about. Max wanted to be excited, too, but he felt queasy—the lurking presence within him was stirring once again. He stopped before Room 318 and stared at the plaque next to the door. As though scripted by an invisible hand, two names appeared where before there had been none. Max ran his fingers over his name, feeling the letters etched deep into the brass. A cough sounded behind him.

"My name's there, too, isn't it?"

Max turned at the voice, which sounded American. He looked down at a small boy with skin as pale as milk. The boy's features were small and faint, except for purplish circles beneath his eyes. He looked unhealthy, like an underexposed photograph.

"Are you David Menlo?" asked Max.

The boy nodded and coughed again.

"I'm Max."

Just then, Max heard Nigel's voice rise above the din.

"*Aha!* Stop right there, Jesse Chu! Didn't you hear me before? Do *not* do anything else until I instruct you to!"

A chunky Asian boy across the hall scowled and yanked his hand away from his doorknob as though it was hot. Nigel walked briskly toward him, wagging a finger. He stopped, however, as he saw Max and David standing by their door.

"Hey there—who are you two missing?"

Max glanced again at the plaque, realizing the other groups had four or even five boys in them.

"No one," said Max. "Our names are the only ones."

"Really?" said Nigel, giving a curious smile and leaning in for a closer look. "How very strange."

He shook his head before cupping his hands to be heard throughout the long hallway.

"Now, *when I instruct you to,* I want you to open the doors and step inside your respective rooms. Once inside, you will lock the door behind you and shut your eyes. You will soon feel dizzy—it is to be expected. Keep your eyes shut until the feeling subsides entirely. To be safe, I recommend that you count to three once the dizziness stops before you have a look around. Everyone clear?"

Max nodded with the others, terrified.

"All right, gents. Please enter your rooms and let the configurations begin."

Max looked at David, who inclined his head, suggesting Max should open the door. The two tentatively stepped into a small dark room with a plain stone floor and knotty wood walls.

"Are you ready?" Max whispered. "When I lock the door, shut your eyes. When the dizziness stops, let me know and we'll both count to three. Okay?"

Taking quick, shallow breaths and trying to ignore the furious patter of his heart, Max locked the door and squeezed his eyes shut.

For a moment, nothing happened.

Slowly, however, his body felt as though it was accelerating to a tremendous speed while spinning like a top. The sensation intensified for what seemed to be a full minute, culminating in a gagging wave of nausea.

He was on the verge of being sick when the spinning stopped. His body felt almost weightless, as though drifting slowly back to the earth. Moments later, the feeling had subsided. He hissed at David.

"David? Has it stopped?"

"I think so, yeah."

"Okay. Count with me. One. Two. *Three!*"

Max opened his eyes and drew a sharp breath.

Instead of the small square room, they now stood on the top stair of a very large circular chamber with a glass-domed roof. Through the glass, Max gazed up at the moon and stars, but they appeared much larger than he had ever seen with his naked eye. They rotated slowly beyond the glass. Max gasped as faint gold threads materialized to outline a celestial centaur before silently fading. A moment later, a giant scorpion was highlighted from among the many stars twinkling above.

At the level of the door and top step was a broad, brass-railed balcony. It led in either direction to enormous, curtained sleigh beds of polished wood, positioned at opposite ends of the room.

Without a word, Max and David descended the steps to a sunken floor. At its center was a large octagonal table inlaid with designs of moons and stars, resting on a thick ivory-colored rug. Beneath each balcony were identical curved niches. Each niche had a cozy couch, tall bookcases, and a wardrobe, all lit from above by lights recessed into the surrounding golden wood. At the far end, a stone fireplace crackled with a small fire. With a shock of recognition, Max saw his duffel bag folded neatly by the wardrobe along with his drawing pads and pencils. The rest of his things were similarly arranged.

"What do you think?" David breathed beside him.

Max whirled and shook David by the shoulders.

"I think it's amazing!"

With a series of triumphant whoops, the two raced up to the balcony and then ran in opposite directions to leap onto the sleigh beds. Max sprawled on a soft comforter stitched with golden suns before brushing aside the curtains. David was grinning from the opposite bed, kicking his feet against its navy curtain embroidered with silver moons.

There was a knock on the door.

"Hey there!" Nigel's voice sounded a bit worried. "Max? David? Open up, boys, and let's have a look. Boys?"

They galloped back along the balconies and swung open the door. Nigel stood outside with the Irish boy, Connor.

"Oh, thank goodness! Had me worried there that you'd gone and lost yourselves! Mind if I have a peek? I'm always curious how these configurations turn out—never seen two the same."

As Nigel entered the room, he froze and scanned the threshold.

"No vomit. Well done, gentlemen! These are new loafers, after all!"

He stepped past them and gasped.

"Oh, this is *wonderful*! Much more inspiring than my old room! I begged to switch the god-awful thing. You would, too, if you'd gotten a Mongolian yurt!"

Max and David savored their triumph as Nigel poked

around, muttering the occasional "Would you look at that!" and "Those lucky devils!"

Connor Lynch stepped in after Nigel and stood gaping at the ceiling. His bright blue eyes blinked in wonder, and he delivered an impressed thumbs-up to Max and David before stepping back into the hallway. A minute later, Nigel sauntered up the steps, shaking his head and scowling at the two of them.

"I don't want to hear even a *peep* of complaint from you two for the next six years! Oh, my wife would kill for those bookcases, you scoundrels! I'll never understand how this old Manse works." He threw his hands up with feigned disgust, brushing past them into the hallway, where the others were now darting in packs to explore the various rooms in a chorus of shouts and slamming doors. Max and David peered in at a medieval bedchamber high atop a tower and a Japanese temple before stumbling into a very plain room across the hall.

They looked around in awkward silence. Connor was lingering in the room alone; his roommates had apparently left to explore. The only sounds came from a small fire sputtering in a modest brick hearth. The room was not any bigger than the bare room Max had entered before the configuration. Narrow wooden bunk beds were stacked beneath a low, flat ceiling of dark beams. The room was otherwise furnished with only one small desk and a red rocker positioned near the fireplace. Two small windows were cut through the plaster walls. They looked onto a lazy, sun-lit meadow dotted with wildflowers.

Nigel poked his head in and broke the silence.

"A cozy little nook to hang your hat in, eh, Mr. Lynch?"

"Yeah, Nigel, home sweet home. Not a traffic-stopper, but it'll do."

Connor hopped up onto one of the top bunks and dangled his legs over the side, grinning at them defiantly. Max liked him immediately.

"C'mon, boys," said Nigel. "Help me round up the others, and let's get back to the foyer."

Nigel hurried down the hall as Max, David, and Connor looked down into a sunken room that appeared to be the captain's quarters of a luxurious galleon. Three large portholes showed a distant sunset and dark blue waves lapped at the glass. The room's four occupants were laughing as they sat on the cozy beds that were sunk into deep alcoves. Sea chests and old maps and bright yellow lanterns were scattered about. Connor spoke up just as a brightly colored fish leapt past one of the portholes.

"Hey—Nigel wants us out there. Come on."

The boys nodded and took turns climbing up the brass ladder.

"Honestly," said Connor as they filed past, "if any of you boys get the wobblies down there, just let me know and we can swap out. You there!" He shot a finger at the last boy to climb out. "You're lookin' awfully pasty. We should probably switch rooms, mate."

"Never!" shouted the boy, running after Nigel.

Connor sighed and fell in step with Max and David. By this time, Nigel had managed to gather most of the class back near the staircase.

"Right, then, congratulations on completing your configurations. You're a lucky lot, you know. Some of the chaps in my class got stuck with a dungeon, a moldy wine cellar, and a chicken roost!"

"But, Nigel," said a boy, "*how* did the rooms change? Did you change them?"

Nigel shook his head.

"Dear me, no. This is Old Magic—far older and far stronger than anything Nigel Bristow can conjure up. But more of the Manse and Old Magic after dinner."

The chimes began just as Nigel herded them down the stairs.

~ 5 ~

EVILS OLD AND NEW

The boys and girls met outside by the fountain, where room configurations were discussed in a buzz of competing voices. Max found it hard to keep track as he overheard breathless girls talking about a pharaoh's throne room carved with hieroglyphics and snug lodges in the mountains. Nigel stood near him looking bemused while Miss Awolowo shielded a tall, plump red-haired girl from the onrush of a petite black-haired girl who stabbed an accusatory finger while muttering in her native language. The red-haired girl looked miserable.

"What happened with them?" Max asked Nigel.

"Oh—happens every year. Roommates blaming one another for how their rooms turned out during the configuration. My Italian's atrocious, but I believe Lucia is upset over the leaky hovel they'll be sharing. Thinks it's all Cynthia's fault—something about an English preference for miserable weather . . ."

Nigel frowned and glanced at Max.

"That last part's not true, by the way. We merely *cope* with miserable weather—we cope out of sheer necessity!"

Miss Awolowo restored order with a calm snippet in Italian that left Lucia in smoldering silence. Nigel took his leave as Miss Awolowo addressed the group.

"All right. Now that the configurations are complete—Lucia, stop that!—we'll take a brief tour of Rowan's grounds before we have supper. If you'd please follow me to the orchard . . ."

They walked around to the back of the Manse, passing between low hedges thick with flowers, and arriving at a large stone patio. Just beyond the patio, separated by a strip of lawn, were long rows of apple trees. Max walked along with Connor and David as Miss Awolowo gathered the group by the closest tree.

"The apples!" a girl exclaimed. "They're made of gold!"

Max looked up to see a number of small apples that appeared to be cast of gold. Jesse Chu slipped past Max and stood on his tiptoes to reach one of them.

"Do *not* touch that apple!"

Jesse recoiled as if he had been stung. Miss Awolowo slipped past several students, lifting the hem of her dress above the grass.

"Forgive me for startling you, Jesse, but these trees are sacred. Let me explain a bit about the Rowan orchard. Omar, will you please read that plaque for me?"

A dark-skinned, studious-looking boy with glasses bent down and read the stone tablet embedded at the base of the tree.

"*Fiat Lux*—Class of 1653."

"Thank you. Does anyone know the expression or why we are looking at this tree?"

A tall blond boy, whose nametag said he was Rolf from Düsseldorf, raised his hand. Max thought he must be at least fourteen.

"*Fiat Lux* is Latin," Rolf said in a heavy German accent. "It's translated 'Let there be light.' According to the brochure, 1653 is when Rowan graduated its first class."

Miss Awolowo smiled; the boy looked very pleased with himself.

"Very good, Rolf—correct on both counts. This is a sacred tree—a Class Tree representing Rowan's very first graduating class. They chose *Fiat Lux* for their class motto, as they arrived here in a time of great darkness. There is a sacred tree in this orchard for every class at Rowan.

"Every year, a Class Tree will bear one apple for each living member of that class. When a member of that class has passed on, his or her apple turns to gold. Thus we remember them, and these apples we do not touch. Take a few moments and walk among them."

Fanning out with the others, Max threaded his way through the rows of trees whose golden apples gleamed brightly in the summer sun. He tried to imagine the people they represented and what they had made of their lives. After a few moments, he noticed that gold glinted from most of the trees, including some of the younger ones.

Miss Awolowo called, and they continued through the orchard

and into a dense wood of ash, oak, maple, and beech. Sunlight twinkled through the leaves as they followed a meandering path through the trees before stopping at a long, low building set in a small clearing. Its windows were dark, but small puffs of white smoke issued from a chimney.

"This is the Smithy," said Miss Awolowo, pointing at a formidable-looking door of black iron. "As Apprentices, you will not yet take Devices, but during the school year you may have occasion to visit."

Connor mouthed the word "Devices?" at Max with a quizzical look. Max shrugged with a smile as Rolf shot his hand in the air.

"Speaking of classes—when do we get our class schedules? My parents insisted that I'm to be enrolled in advanced math."

Max saw Lucia roll her eyes.

"Class assignments will be distributed tomorrow, Rolf," Miss Awolowo answered.

She continued their tour through the forest, pointing out notable trees and deflecting questions regarding the small side paths that veered off the main way to disappear into the thick undergrowth. There were several of these, and Max was curious about them. David paused so long at one that Max had to trot back to pull him along.

"Wait a minute," said David, fishing in his pockets.

"C'mon," said Max, watching the tour disappear beyond a bend in the path.

David retrieved a coin from his pocket. He scratched at the soil and buried the coin beneath the twisty root of a sagging elm. Apparently satisfied, he brushed the dirt from his hands and hurried with Max after the others.

"Why'd you do that?" asked Max.

David did not seem to hear him.

As they rounded the bend, Max heard the neighing of horses. Miss Awolowo and their classmates were circling around several long buildings and a fenced ring where a dozen unsaddled horses capered about. Beyond the buildings was a high, mossy wall with a heavy door. The wall continued out of sight; the hedge and trees behind it were very tall. Max wanted to go through the door, but Miss Awolowo kept them moving, calling out over her shoulder as she went.

"These are Rowan's stables. Beyond that wall is the Sanctuary—you'll be visiting it tomorrow. No time to stop now. Please keep up!"

The children hurried after her. She waited for them on a path that curved out of the forest and led back to the main campus. Emerging into the sunlight, Max gazed at the Manse and orchard far away to his right across the clipped lawns. The group continued along the forest's edge and gathered at a rocky outcropping above the sea.

"Wow," said Connor, reaching the edge before Max and looking down.

Max looked over his shoulder to see a large ship with three masts, creaking as it bobbed slightly in the waves. Well over a hundred feet long and looking very old, it was anchored to a long dock with a heavy chain. A rough stone staircase led down from where they stood to the narrow, rocky beach below. Max strained to hear Miss Awolowo's voice over the wind.

"That, children, is the *Kestrel*. You'll be hearing more about her tonight."

She waved to a tall man stacking driftwood down on the

beach and herded the class away from the water, back toward two imposing buildings. They were made of gray stone and faced south on the lawns between the Manse and the beach. The class approached along their long shadows cast by the sun sinking over the woods to the west.

Max found the buildings foreboding as he approached; they loomed high above him, and their many windows were still and dark. The farther one had a tall clock tower topped by a turret and a fluttering copper weathervane. The children jumped as the clock boomed six. Miss Awolowo waited for the chimes to cease.

"These are Maggie and Old Tom, our main academic buildings. You will have most of your classes here. Old Tom's our timekeeper, too; his chimes will often tell you where you need to be. Right now, he's telling us we're expected at the kitchens. It's been a busy afternoon and you all must be hungry. Please follow me."

Max walked and chatted with David and Connor as the three trailed the group back to the Manse.

"It's my first time out of Dublin, much less here in the States," Connor said, taking long strides with his hands stuffed deep in his pockets. "I suppose the two of you live in mansions back home, eh?"

David Menlo laughed. "Yeah. My mansion's got four wheels. My mom and I live in a trailer."

Connor shrugged and turned to Max.

"How 'bout you, then? You live in a mansion?"

"No. My dad and I live in a regular house. . . . We're not rich," he added defensively.

"You got a computer?" asked Connor.

"Yeah."

"You got a car?"

"My dad does."

"You got a job?"

Max looked at him, confused. "No."

"Congratulations, Max, you're rich!"

Connor ran ahead to catch up with some girls. A moment later, they were all giggling. Max flushed and turned to David.

"What do you think he meant by all that 'you're rich' stuff?"

David shrugged. "I don't know—probably nothing. Connor's weird. He tried to bet me that he'd get Lucia to kiss him before school starts."

"Not a chance," Max muttered as he watched Connor walking next to Lucia and gesturing wildly. Lucia looked bored.

As Max and David strolled past the fountain, Miss Awolowo was waiting in the Manse's doorway. She tapped her watch.

"*Please* try to keep up, you two. Mum and Bob have been working very hard to prepare dinner for us, and your classmates are hungry. We might lose an orchard apple to Jesse if we're not quick!"

She laughed and led them to join the others in a great hall off the foyer filled with glistening portraits. From there they descended some stone steps that curved down and down until they arrived at a large dining hall. The hall's vaulted ceiling was hung with massive chandeliers, and the long room was furnished with many wooden tables and benches. Light, steam, and noise issued from a pair of swinging doors, at the far end.

"Now, children," said Miss Awolowo, leading them to the swinging doors, "I want to warn you that Mum and Bob are not your typical chefs. . . ."

Max and David glanced at each other.

"They can be a bit startling at first glance, but I promise you'll grow to love them."

As they got closer, Max heard another woman's urgent whisper from beyond the doors.

"Quiet, Bob! Put that pot down! Shhh! I think they're here! Ooh! I can practically *taste* them!"

"Shush yourself, Mum!" rumbled a deep voice with a strange accent. "I hear them, too. You remember to behave!"

The students froze as they heard a bloodcurdling giggle from just behind the door. A pear-shaped boy, who was closest, whimpered and edged away. Miss Awolowo stepped past him.

"Mum? Bob? It's Ndidi. Could you come out, please, and meet the new class?"

The pear-shaped boy scurried to the back as the woman's voice cackled and shrieked. "Oh, they're here, they're here! The darlings are here!"

The door flew open, flattening Miss Awolowo. The children screamed as a panting, gray-skinned woman as short and stout as a pot-bellied stove burst from the kitchen to envelop Jesse in a fierce embrace. Jesse's legs buckled; he fainted into her arms. Her shiny face looked the children over, grinning hideously to reveal a mouthful of smooth crocodile teeth.

"Oh, Ndidi! You've outdone yourself. They're wonderful! Oh, they're so wonderful and *plump*!"

The panting woman crushed Jesse against her side and reached out with her free hand to squeeze Cynthia's ample arm as if she were examining a tomato. The red-headed English girl buried her face in Lucia's shoulder, and Lucia swatted furiously at the woman's hand while Max looked on in horror.

Suddenly, a strong voice filled the hall.

"Mum! Release that poor boy and stop pinching that young lady!"

Immediately, the woman whipped her hands behind her back, shifting her weight from foot to foot. Jesse slid to the ground.

"I was only welcoming the children, Ms. Richter," the woman mumbled.

Max turned to glimpse the unseen speaker, but several taller classmates blocked his view. Ms. Richter sounded important; she was a person accustomed to giving orders. A second later, the name came back to him—it was her name at the bottom of his letters.

His classmates parted as she came closer.

"That was not a welcome, Mum. That was an ambush. Totally unacceptable for a *reformed* hag. It simply won't be tolerated. Please apologize to the children and Ndidi."

The hag stared sheepishly at the floor. "I just got excited, Ms. Richter. I wouldn't really have eaten them."

"Well, I should hope not, Mum," said Ms. Richter. "You promised there wouldn't be any more incidents, and I took you at your word. I won't ask again for your apology. . . ."

"Oh, I'm *sorry*! I'm sorry, I'm sorry, I'm sorry, I'm sorry!" Mum bawled, bolting back into the kitchen past Miss Awolowo, who had slowly regained her feet. The door swung wildly back and forth. The same deep voice Max had heard before boomed out from the kitchen.

"I told her to behave herself, Director!"

Ms. Richter advanced slowly, and Max could now see her clearly. She was tall and had pretty, if severe, features that reminded

Max of a photo he'd once seen of a frontier family. It was a hard face, a face accustomed to work. Her hair was gray, as was the suit jacket draped over her arm. She sighed and smiled at the students around her. When she spoke again, it was in a gentler voice.

"Hello, children. I'm Ms. Richter. Welcome to Rowan."

She turned to Miss Awolowo, who was now standing by the door.

"Ndidi, thank you for covering for me while I was away."

Miss Awolowo nodded gracefully. Ms. Richter replied in kind before saying brightly, "Let's go meet Rowan's chefs, shall we?" She strode through the swinging door. Miss Awolowo steadied a woozy Jesse and motioned for the rest to follow.

Inside was an enormous kitchen where great clouds of steam rose and hissed from copper pots. Max smelled a delicious aroma. Moving forward to make room for more classmates, he smacked into Lucia, who had stopped short in front of him.

Max saw the reason.

A lanky old man, ten feet tall with yellowing skin, sank an enormous butcher's knife into a thick cutting board and smoothed his spattered apron.

The First Years screamed and stampeded for the exit. Ms. Richter's and Miss Awolowo's voices rang out above the commotion.

"Children! It's all right. It's all right! This is Bob. He's our head chef!"

Max tried to avoid getting trampled in the doorway, bracing himself in the jamb and pushing back against Jesse, who attempted to tunnel through him into the dining hall. Lucia scurried under an industrial sink, covering her eyes and muttering in Italian. David screamed and bolted past Bob, disappearing into the side pantry. He slammed the door shut behind him, triggering what sounded to be an avalanche of fallen items. Miss Awolowo and Ms. Richter herded the children back with a quiet word here, a firm tug there. When Ms. Richter finally pried Omar off her leg, she called to the huge man, who was now sitting on a reinforced stool and cleaning his monocle.

"I'm so sorry, Bob. I suppose it's to be expected after Mum frightened them so."

"Perfectly understandable, Director. Take your time."

From his seat, Bob reached a long arm over toward a gas range and stirred a bubbling cream sauce until the children had crowded behind Ms. Richter and Miss Awolowo. Connor whispered something to Lucia, who sniffled and crawled from beneath the sink to join them.

"What is it?" Rolf hissed. "Is it dangerous?"

"First things first, young man," said Ms. Richter. " 'It' has a name, and *his* name is Bob. Second, Bob is not dangerous. He is a consummate gentleman and the finest chef we've ever had at Rowan!"

Bob adjusted the flame beneath a saucepan and smiled gently at Ms. Richter.

"You flatter me, Director," Bob said, his basso voice vibrating the glass panes in the cabinets. He turned his gaze to the children, speaking deliberately.

"Hello, students. My name is Bob. I am pleased to make your acquaintance. Welcome to Rowan."

He stood and bowed, lowering a massive head covered in lumps and knots. His jaw was sunken with age, and he gummed his lips nervously.

Max found the ensuing silence unbearable.

"Hi, Bob," he said.

Bob nodded his head at Max appreciatively. Ms. Richter seized the moment to continue.

"Bob is an ogre, children. Yes, I know what some of you have read about ogres, but our Bob is a *reformed* ogre and has been with us for almost sixty years. He sought us out himself, traveling all the way from his native home in Siberia. He's been taking care of us ever since."

She gave Bob a light kiss on the cheek. He smiled and looked expectantly at the children. Lucia raised a trembling hand, asking her question in halting English.

"What does . . . what does *Bob* eat?"

Bob opened his mouth wide like a hippopotamus, revealing a cavernous space with no visible teeth. Closing his mouth, he chuckled.

"They are wary, Director. That is good, no?" Bob then turned to the group. "After I swore off . . . meat . . . I remove my teeth with pliers. Today, Bob prefers tomato soup and grilled cheese."

As Bob finished, Ms. Richter walked over to a large cupboard and knocked sharply on the door.

"Mum, are you going to join us or are you going to sulk?"

Max heard a bloodcurdling shriek from the cupboard, followed by several angry thumps.

"*Go away!* I'm not *ever* coming out. You *hate* me! I know you hate me!"

Mum's voice trailed away into pitiful, quavering sobs. Ms. Richter tapped her foot and smiled apologetically at the students. Kneeling by the cupboard, she spoke in a soothing voice.

"Now, Mum, please don't be difficult. The children want very much to meet you properly, don't you, children?"

The Director ignored their horrified faces.

"Come now, Mum. We're all very hungry, but we won't sit down to eat until you join us. Dinner smells wonderful, and we can get the sniffing ceremony done and out of the way."

Max grimaced as he wondered what Ms. Richter meant by "sniffing ceremony." Bob continued to stir the sauce attentively, ignoring the scene. There was a muffled thump followed by Mum's teary voice.

"Well, I wouldn't want anybody to go hungry. You don't hate me, do you, Director?"

"Of course not, Mum," Ms. Richter said reassuringly.

"And the darlings . . . they find me . . . *colorful*?" Her voice struck a hopeful note as she stretched out the word. Ms. Richter sighed impatiently.

"Yes, Mum, they find you colorful. Now please do us the courtesy of leaving your cupboard."

Mum peeked from the cupboard. She looked apprehensively around the kitchen. Her round face was tear-streaked; her stringy black hair lay across it like clumps of seaweed. Wriggling to dislodge her sizable bottom, she spilled onto the tiled floor. She scrambled quickly to her feet, rearranging her hair in a series of frantic motions. She abruptly stopped to gaze upon the students with a startled, sweet expression.

"Oh, hello. Is this the new class, Director? They're such dears!"

"Mum, please don't pretend you haven't seen them before."

Mum scowled and shot Ms. Richter an angry glance. The Director shook her head and turned to the class.

"Children," said Ms. Richter, "please return to the dining hall and form two lines. Mum, please come out here with us. Bob, can you see to it that dinner is served immediately after the ceremony?"

Bob nodded as they filed back out the swinging doors. Max found himself sandwiched between Cynthia and Rolf near the doors. Connor took a spot across from him as Ms. Richter escorted Mum into the dining hall.

"All right," the Director called out, walking down the lines while Mum remained near the doors. "Take a deep breath and try to be very still. When it's your turn, please hold out your arm so Mum may sniff it."

A tall black girl nearby raised her hand. Max blinked; she looked like she could be Miss Awolowo's granddaughter.

"Ms. Richter, is Mum planning to remove *her* teeth with pliers anytime soon?"

"No, dear—Sarah, is it? The sniffing ceremony ensures such measures won't be necessary. Mum, please begin."

Mum was pacing back and forth near the doors, clapping her hands excitedly. Suddenly, she lurched forward and seized the arm of the girl next to Connor. The girl shut her eyes and stood ramrod straight. Holding her arm gingerly, Mum stood on her tiptoes and sniffed greedily along its entire length before flinging it aside.

"Done!" she shrieked, shuffling over to Connor.

"Hello, Mum," he said. "Dinner smells lovely."

Mum cooed appreciatively and took his hand, looking him up and down.

"Oh, you're a handsome one!" she said. "You remind me of a young lad I ate on the outskirts of Dover. He was such a *nice* boy."

Connor moaned and turned his head as she dragged her nose along his arm like a pig rooting for truffles.

"Done!" she shrieked, moving over. Connor was green.

Max leaned forward and looked helplessly down the line; he'd be one of the last she'd sniff and the anticipation was unbearable.

"Ms. Richter!" cried Jesse with mounting desperation. "Do we absolutely have to do this?"

Mum sidestepped closer to him with hideous efficiency. Ms. Richter raised her voice above Mum's periodic shrieks and mumbling commentary.

"Once Mum's sniffed you, she knows not to *bother* you. She's really as gentle as a lamb."

When she was two students away, the escalating dread overcame Max and he shut his eyes. A minute later, he felt a soft, strong grip on his hand. He opened one eye a smidgeon and looked down.

Mum was pinching his arm thoughtfully. She lifted it up with surprising delicacy and dragged her quivering nostrils along its length. Max groaned and shut his eyes again; every instinct screamed for him to get away from those sharp, slavering teeth. When the snuffling stopped, he glanced down to see a wet trail that meandered from his wrist to elbow. Mum leaned close for a conspiratorial whisper.

"You'd be lovely with potatoes, dear. Done!"

Max wiped his arm against his shorts. He heard Cynthia whimper several "Hail Marys" as Mum seized her.

"Ah! You're the plump lass from the doorway! Like a great trussed roast you smell! No, no, not for Mum, not for Mum. Done!"

The sniffing ceremony complete, Mum stood before the doors and faced the students. Rising up on her toes, she spread her arms like an orchestra conductor and bowed with slow majesty.

"It was lovely to meet you all, my darlings. Welcome to Rowan! Your dinner is served."

The children sat at several of the long tables while the tables were piled high with roasted chickens, steaming bowls of vegetables, and rich, savory breads. Ms. Richter and Miss Awolowo sat at the table nearest the kitchen, their faces illuminated by candlelight.

Max could not remember such an exquisite meal. Normally a picky eater, he found himself wolfing down mounds of chicken served with a creamy sauce, crisp string beans, and golden potatoes. He further helped himself to two slices of homemade pie and a fat dollop of ice cream.

A shadow fell over Max and he looked up to see Bob leaning over him to fill a pitcher of lemonade. He gave Max a craggy smile.

"I did not get your name before, young man," the ogre said.

"Oh, my name is Max. Max McDaniels," he replied.

"My pleasure, Max. I hope you will visit us in the kitchens."

Bob extended a gnarled hand the size of a serving tray. Max shook it carefully. It smelled of soap. Bob chuckled to Miss Awolowo, who sat at the next table.

"He's a good one, eh, Miss Awolowo?"

Miss Awolowo nodded thoughtfully, her dark eyes glittering.

"We think so, Bob. Yes, indeed, we do."

Bob plucked several empty platters off the table and ducked nimbly through the swinging doors.

* * *

After dinner, the students carried lanterns, following Ms. Richter in a single-file procession across the grounds. Max looked west to where fading bands of scarlet blended into starry blues.

They descended the steps to the beach where the dark ship bobbed on the water. A bonfire was burning brightly with many logs and tree stumps arranged around it like little stools. Ms. Richter motioned for them to take seats as she sat with her back to the sea. Her solemn voice rose above the waves and the crackling flames.

"Tonight is a night when we remember, a night when we share with the new class a bit of Rowan's history and their own. It has been centuries since our kind fled the Old Country and arrived on these shores. We landed on this very stretch of beach, borne here by the *Kestrel*."

Ms. Richter turned to look at the barnacled, hulking vessel behind her. She began to walk among them, her feet crunching softly on the sand. Max followed her gaze as she stopped and looked up at the stars.

"It may surprise you to know that our world is still a very young world and that mankind is a very new thing upon this earth. Indeed, others were here long before us." Ms. Richter bent down and scooped sand into both her hands. "The greatest among them came to help shape this world, to watch its beauty and possibilities unfold. . . ."

The sand within her hands began to bubble and melt. Max gaped as it formed itself into a small, beautiful ornament of glass. He stared at it hovering above the fire like a brilliant jewel while she resumed her walk and glided behind him.

"They delighted in the waters and the woods and the

creatures that came to inhabit them. Eventually, they departed, leaving the care of our planet to others. These caretakers were lesser beings and we call them the Stewards. To mankind, however, they were as gods and goddesses—great spirits of the elements that watched over the world while we were still but infants. Alas, their vigilance failed."

Max and his classmates jumped as the hovering glass fell and shattered in the fire.

"Their vigilance failed, and others came, too—other things from dying worlds with nothing left to feed them. Quietly, they seeped and crept into the deep places of this world to gnaw at its roots. Their very presence corrupted some of the Stewards. . . ."

Ms. Richter's eyes hardened as a log collapsed into the bonfire, shooting plumes of sparks like fireflies.

"The corrupted Stewards lost interest in mothering the world and sought mastery instead. Humans were given a simple choice: to serve or to perish. Fortunately, a few men and women refused this choice and chose instead to resist.

"The remaining Stewards let some of their power pass to those who would fight. The first to receive this spark were very great—almost Stewards themselves, as they were granted a measure of wisdom and Old Magic to stem the darkness. And you have inherited this spark, my dears. Each and every one of you sitting here with me!"

Ms. Richter stopped walking and looked from face to face around the fire, finally locking her gaze on Max as she continued.

"We do not know how this spark comes to be within you; we cannot anticipate who will be blessed with it. The only thing we do know is that it has faded over time. Our numbers and potency today are mere echoes of the past. But they have not faded entirely! At Rowan, we gather these sparks and nurture them and so continue the Great Struggle. Rowan is the last school for our kind, founded when the others were destroyed."

She blinked as though lost in thoughts of her own. She placed her suit jacket over the shoulders of a shivering girl and sat down once again near the fire.

"Solas was the last and greatest of these schools to fall. We chose to build it in Ireland—a good choice, as the land was riddled with Old Magic and enclosed by water and mist. In Ireland, our kind made peace with the Tuatha de Danaan, the fading Stewards of that realm. They were inconstant allies but capable of powerful aid when they could be roused from their slumbers beneath the hills. It was they who laid the foundation for Solas."

Ms. Richter raised her hands and the fire writhed and grew. Within it Max saw a great castle with many towers and gabled roofs on a mountain of rock high above the sea. He squinted to see it more clearly, but the flickering flames and smoke obscured it.

"By all accounts, Solas was a wonder! The greatest minds and Mystics of the age were tutored within its walls, veiled in secrecy from the Enemy until they were strong enough to take their proper place outside. From Solas came those who would bring the Dark Ages to an end.

"After their triumphs, mankind was left in peace. For centuries, no great evil emerged, and we began to hope that we had finally succeeded! We believed that the corrupted Stewards and their many minions and offspring had abandoned this world for another. We were wrong."

Ms. Richter stood again and backed away from the fire. The image of Solas was lost in flames that swept higher and higher until the beach was filled with strange light and shadows.

"Astaroth came."

Max froze at hearing the name again—Mrs. Millen had said it. She had *shrieked* it when she chased after him and his leg had gone numb.

"Astaroth was much more patient and clever than those before him. He did not declare himself, but instead remained hidden, manipulating men and countries like chess pieces across the continents. By the 1640s, our world was in great turmoil. The Ming Dynasty collapsed; the countries of Europe fought with one another; England was consumed by civil war. Brilliant minds were imprisoned and tortured for heresy. . . ."

Ms. Richter frowned and gazed at the fountain of flames before her.

"The wisest among us, Elias Bram, perceived that these events were not random follies of man. He sensed that the world's troubles were stirred in secret by a greater mind and malevolence. Astaroth's true name and form were revealed, and our people unraveled many evil works near completion. Enraged, Astaroth bent his cunning mind on finding the source of those who opposed him.

"In the end, we were betrayed. Astaroth learned of us and our school. The great gates were thrown down, and many brave souls were lost. The Enemy paid a heavy price, however. Solas was broken, but Astaroth was broken with it. Bram came and fought with him, and the towers and halls toppled down around them. Bram fell, but not in vain—a great evil was removed from this world."

The roaring pillar of flame began to die and wither to quiet licks of flame among the spent logs.

"The students and teachers who survived fled Astaroth's armies and sought aid from the Tuatha de Danaan. These precious few were spirited here aboard the *Kestrel*, and Rowan was raised from the countryside. It is Old Magic, children, that hides this place and makes it strange."

Ms. Richter sat down once again and took the hands of the two nearest children, giving them a gentle smile.

"And, now, you are here. *We* are here so many years after our allies secured this haven and enabled our kind to continue. I am so pleased to have you among us. You have been called to Rowan not to fight, but to learn—to develop that noble spark within you. As the Director and a fellow human being, I hope that you will do your best to kindle that spark within you. Much depends upon it."

Max could not tell how long they sat in silence, huddled around the flames as they finally died to embers. He struggled to imagine what his role could possibly be in such a vast history. He turned to David, but his roommate was watching the stars, his small face thoughtful and serious. After a time, Ms. Richter broke the silence.

"It is late and there is much to do tomorrow. I will lead you back to the Manse."

The children picked up their lanterns and followed behind, making the long trek across the lawns to their new home.

~ 6 ~

THE LAST LYMRILL

The clanging chorus of Old Tom's chimes brought Max from his slumber with a shout. He had been dreaming of the hound again, and it was several moments until he remembered where he was. Lying back on his bed, Max watched the constellations rotating slowly, their golden contours fainter from the tints of pink and gold peeking from the dome's bottom rim. The chimes counted seven.

Max yawned and swung his feet over the side of the bed. Stumbling downstairs, he found his fuzzy yellow towel hanging from a hook by his dresser. David was already downstairs, coughing hard.

"Hi," said David, turning his back to slip on a T-shirt.

"Hey—I guess this is as close to morning as it gets in this room!"

David laughed and pulled on a pair of shorts.

"Are you gonna shower?" asked Max.

David turned around quickly with a nervous expression. "Oh, no. I'm okay," he said.

Max left the room and walked barefoot down the hall carrying his towel and toiletries. Hearing his name, he turned to see Connor trotting after him.

"Morning, Max! Reckon they could have told us Old Tom would turn up the volume for the bell."

Connor grinned and pushed through the door to Room 301. Max followed and saw him standing speechless.

The bathroom was a huge space filled with cedar lockers, slatted benches, and tropical plants. Max could hear classical music over the light babble of a marble fountain. One long wall was lined with gleaming sinks and silver faucets shaped like leaping dolphins. Across the room were three archways with brass signs indicating toilets, showers, and spa.

The door opened behind them, and Max turned to see Rolf, Jesse, Omar, and several other boys.

"Wow!" exclaimed Omar, his eyes widening behind his glasses. "Did you guys *configure* this?"

"Someone had to," said Connor humbly, examining his nails. He slung his towel over his shoulder and headed for the spa.

Max remembered the time and hurried to the showers. Stepping inside a stall, he was puzzled at what he found. Instead of normal faucets, there were six small silver levers protruding from the marble wall. Max pulled the one on the far left, then hopped up and down as cold water sprayed from a showerhead above him. He turned it off and tried the next only to have hot water—*much* too hot—pin him into the corner until he could kick the lever upright with his toe. Wincing a bit, he pulled the third lever and let out a sigh of relief as a heavy jet of warm water burst from the showerhead.

A frantic shriek sounded from several stalls over.

"Third from the left!" Max shouted.

"Thank you!" piped a grateful voice in reply.

After tugging at the fourth lever, Max jumped back as soap bubbles ran out of a little hidden spigot and quickly filled the stall, cascading over the door before Max could slow the stream. Lever five produced an emerald dollop of shampoo that he caught in his hand. Lever six sputtered once before releasing a steady stream of warm shaving cream. Max laughed and dabbed a bit on his chin, then sculpted a white beard of foam. He peered out the shower door to look at himself just as Omar did the same. The two burst into laughter and disappeared into their respective stalls.

Standing in puddles of water, dozens of boys were brushing their teeth and chatting when they heard a loud "Ahem!" Turning, Max was startled to see a bald three-foot-tall man who looked like a leprechaun wearing an old blue suit and massaging his jowls as he surveyed them. He smelled very strongly of musky cologne, and he looked angry.

"Enjoying yourselves, are you? Fun business making a mess of Jimmy's bath, is it?"

The little man stepped toward them.

"Well, what's the matter, lads? Mum got your tongues? Old enough to shave, but too young to answer for yourselves?" He flashed a dark look at Omar and Max, who shrank against the wall. Several faucets continued running behind them.

Connor stepped forward.

"Sir, we didn't mean—"

"*Silence!*"

Max shot a glance at Connor, who looked just as frightened and confused as Max felt. The man took another step toward the group, his face turning crimson.

Just then, the door swung open and Nigel's head popped in.

"Hurry up, boys. Ms. Richter's already in the orientation—Jimmy! How are you? Long time."

The little man rolled his eyes.

"Oh, you had to come just now and spoil my fun! I was going to get these tadpoles to mop this place for a month!"

Nigel chuckled and walked into the bathroom. Taking a silver dollar from his pocket, he went to the last sink, lifted the lid off a fat porcelain Buddha, and dropped the coin inside.

"Sorry, Jimmy. Next time, I'll leave them to you."

"Oh, it's all right. Need to get hopping anyway if we're gonna spiff 'em up for the morning session. You want a little zing of the good stuff, Nigel?"

Nigel smiled politely.

"No, Jimmy. No, thank you. I'll, eh, tell the Director the boys are . . . just making your acquaintance." Nigel paused before adding, "Boys, be sure to bring Jimmy a present later. Remember—it's the *thought* that counts!"

"Okay, then! See you later!" Jimmy called out. He was already bustling about, gathering armfuls of spray bottles and jars that he laid out on a folding table. Turning to the boys, he clapped his hands.

"Right, then, who are gonna be the lucky lads to get spruced up, Jimmy fashion?" the little man inquired. "I can't get to you all, so who's it gonna be?"

"Er . . . I don't understand," said Rolf, sniffing at his armpit. "We just showered."

Jimmy looked at Rolf as though he must be daft.

"It's your first full day, isn't it?"

The boys nodded.

"And there're some lookers among the ladies, aren't there?"

The boys looked at one another and shrugged.

"Well, then, a shower's just a start! You need the old Jimmy treatment to make 'em sit up and take notice! Quick! You six into a chair."

Jimmy snapped his fingers, and six wicker chairs zoomed across the room and arranged themselves in a row.

"Ugh, I knew we'd be the lucky ones," moaned Connor as Jimmy showed Max to his seat. Those without a chair before them made a hasty retreat out the door.

Max squirmed while Jimmy went to work, running up and down the line and slathering their hair, cheeks, and necks with a variety of gels and sprays. Frowning with concentration, he produced a comb and parted each boy's hair carefully down the middle. The boys watched themselves in the mirror, sitting in silent horror as Jimmy clapped in sudden satisfaction.

"Well, boys! Now you're looking dandy. Good material to work with, of course, but now you've got the special Jimmy touch!"

He whistled merrily and rearranged his bottles as the six boys filed out, looking glum.

Max ran to his room and dressed quickly, rejoining the others in the hallway as Old Tom's chimes started ringing. They sprinted down the stairs and skidded to a halt in the little theater. All of their other classmates were already seated. Several girls giggled as they saw the boys' old-fashioned hairdos. Even Ms. Richter, leaning against a piano, had an amused expression on her face as she casually reached for a handkerchief.

"Be seated, gentlemen. As I was telling your classmates, today is a very important day. You will be visiting the Sanctuary for the first time. There you will be paired with a good friend for the next six years. Perhaps even longer."

Ms. Richter frowned and waved the handkerchief before her face. A group of girls giggled as they whispered to one another. Pinching their noses, Cynthia and Lucia moved several seats farther away while David coughed into his hand and blinked at the boys. Avoiding his classmates' stares, Max reached up and patted the shellacked mass on his head. He was amazed that hair could be so smooth and brittle.

After a momentary silence, Ms. Richter breathed deeply into her handkerchief and continued. "Yes, well, after this morning's visit to the Sanctuary, you'll receive your semester schedules and meet with your class advisors, who will—oh dear Lord, it's simply *overpowering!*"

The girls shrieked with laughter. Max blushed and turned to Connor, whose neck was now bright red from scratching.

Ms. Richter rose from the piano. "Boys, I assume that Jimmy is responsible for your . . . grooming?"

They nodded. Cynthia's shoulders pumped like pistons as she laughed. Lucia's face was scarlet. Ms. Richter motioned for quiet.

"Jimmy has been with us for some time and he means very well, but the sad truth is that his sense of smell seems to be waning. Strike that—it is gone. In the future, I'd recommend that you politely decline his grooming services. He will undoubtedly pressure you, but you must be strong—for all our sakes. Now, let's continue this conversation outside."

Handkerchief pressed to her nose, Ms. Richter led them through some French doors and out onto the orchard patio. Their classmates ran ahead giggling; Jimmy's victims shuffled sheepishly in tow.

Exhaling, Ms. Richter folded her handkerchief and waited for the students to gather round. Clouds were building in the sky; the wind had picked up.

"That's better! Now, as I was saying, the Sanctuary is a very special place at Rowan. There is nothing more important on this entire campus. You see, children, we champion not only our fellow man, but many other creatures and spirits that inhabit this world. Not all mystical creatures are aligned with the Enemy. Those that wish may find refuge here at Rowan—in fact, you've already met some of them. Unfortunately, many of these creatures are very young or vulnerable and require your care. Today, you will be paired with one of them."

Ms. Richter fixed a stern eye on the students.

"This is a great honor being conferred upon you. Many of these creatures are exceedingly rare. Some may be the last of their kind. It is important that you take this responsibility very seriously; it is a critical aspect of your education. There is no greater shame than having to relinquish one's charge."

The idea that Max would have to care for something mystical made him very nervous. He had never even owned a pet. Most of his classmates, however, looked enchanted and gossiped in excitement as Ms. Richter led them through the woods. When they reached the high, mossy wall near the stables, Ms. Richter stood by its stout wooden door set with a heavy brass ring.

"I know you are nervous, children. After all, there are so many new things! Take a deep breath and enjoy this next experience. For many students, the Sanctuary is their favorite place. Many forge lifelong bonds with their charges. Just be yourselves and trust your charge's instincts."

The door creaked open. Beyond it, Max saw a narrow way hemmed so closely by low trees and hedges that it was more of a dark tunnel than a path. Following after the others, Max stumbled along for twenty or thirty yards when he suddenly felt a drop of rain on his nose. They had emerged into an enormous clearing whose tall grasses rippled in the wind.

Max looked back through the tunnel; it hadn't been raining on the other side of the door. Several of his classmates were already commenting on it.

Turning back to the clearing, Max squinted at a distant backdrop of forest and the surprising sight of snowcapped hills. Clumps of trees and great rock formations dotted the clearing at irregular intervals. A herd of cows grazed and lowed in the distance. Directly ahead was a long, low building set near a lagoon that was bordered by a strip of beach and royal palms.

Suddenly, something enormous plummeted from the sky to seize one of the distant cows in its talons. With a screech, a bird the size of a small airplane soared off with its struggling prey, making for the far hills.

"Good to see Hector's eating again," exclaimed Ms. Richter with satisfaction. "He hasn't touched a thing in weeks!"

A number of children retreated into the leafy tunnel until the Director beckoned them back out.

"Don't worry about any Sanctuary inhabitants mistaking you for food," she assured them. "Nothing here normally preys upon humans, and they're all very well fed."

Rolf scoffed loudly, drawing a warning glance.

"Hey," said Connor, trotting a few steps and peering east. "Where's the ocean?"

Max was startled to see Connor was right; instead of the ocean there was a series of sand dunes that rose in gentle swells for miles until they stopped at a wall of dark rock that extended to the horizon. Ms. Richter smiled.

"As Connor has noticed," she said, "our Sanctuary is a very different place from the world back through that tunnel. Like many things here at Rowan, the Sanctuary has its own space: space that is 'borrowed' from other places in the world. This provides our guests with a safe haven and a variety of habitats reminiscent of their homes. The only way in or out of this Sanctuary is through this tunnel. Remember, Old Magic can be raw and unpredictable, and thus it is important not to wander too far."

Max elbowed Connor.

"Is there anything here that can't hurt, kill, or eat us?" he whispered.

Connor grinned. "Keeps you on your toes, don't it?"

"Do you think we could ask *not to* have one of these?"

"I highly doubt it," Connor replied quickly as Ms. Richter glided past them.

"Ah," said the Director, glancing at her watch. "I think Nolan's ready for us."

A lanky, tanned man was walking toward them from the building near the lagoon. He had something that seemed to be wriggling in his arms. At fifty yards, he laughed and placed it on the ground. Max grinned with recognition. Lucy's head bobbed up above the tall grass as she quickly closed the distance, barreling into Max with a snort. Max hoisted her in his arms.

"Hey there, Lucy!" he exclaimed. "Good to see you!"

Lucy squirmed in his arms, scrambling up his chest to sniff at his cheek. Max laughed and turned toward the others.

"Ah," said Ms. Richter. "I'd almost forgotten that Max has met Lucy before! Class, come and meet Lucy. She's been Nigel Bristow's charge since he was an Apprentice, some thirty years ago."

"This is more like it," Cynthia breathed as she scratched Lucy behind the ears.

"Hello, Lucy," cooed Omar, patting her belly.

"There's a good girl," chirped Connor, shaking her foot.

Lucy tossed frantically, trying to look at each student as they introduced themselves. It was too much. With a grunt of shock, she released a burst of gas, looking hurt as the children fled with shrieks of laughter. She buried her head in Max's armpit.

"Now, now, you've hurt her feelings!" the man said with a laugh. He had dark hair, a mellow drawl, and bright blue eyes with crow's-feet at the corners. He wore jeans, a thick leather apron, and gloves that bore a variety of deep gashes and punctures. Max recognized him as the man they had seen the previous day on the beach when they had taken their tour with Miss Awolowo.

"Hey, students," he said, waving at them. "You ready to make a friend for life?" he inquired with a loud clap of his gloves. Taking Lucy from Max, he whispered something in her ear and placed her on the ground. She trotted back toward the lagoon.

"Children," said Ms. Richter, "this is Mr. Nolan, Head Groundskeeper at Rowan."

"Just 'Nolan' is fine with me," he said with a wink. He glanced over at Cynthia, who had looked petrified ever since the predatory bird had appeared. "Will you be my assistant, young lady?"

She nodded slowly.

"Thank you." He smiled at her, offering his arm and starting toward the building. "Let's all head over to the Warming Lodge. We've got some beautiful creatures that are dying to meet you!"

The Warming Lodge was made of dark, unpainted wood and covered with weathered shingles. Several bales of hay were stacked on a covered porch that faced the lagoon. Gathering the children around the porch, Nolan motioned for quiet. He produced a small silver bell, ringing it three times. The porch's planks began to creak as something large moved inside.

"Kids, I'd like you to meet YaYa. She looks after all the animals in the Sanctuary. She is the Great Matriarch of Rowan and has been here since it was established."

The children stepped back as the head of a massive jet-black lioness emerged from the doorway. Bigger than a rhino and crowned with a single broken horn of speckled ivory, she stepped heavily out onto the porch. Her black fur gave off a faint white shimmer. The great creature lowered herself slowly onto the porch, folding her black glossy legs beneath her. Her eyes were clouded with milky cataracts, and her sides rose and fell with her labored breathing. Trotting out the door, Lucy snuggled beneath the whiskers on YaYa's great chin.

Max thought the piglet looked like an appetizer.

"She's beautiful, Mr. Nolan," said a girl in front. "What is she?"

"I'm sure she'd prefer to answer that herself."

Max stood riveted as the creature raised her head. Her voice sounded like several women speaking simultaneously.

"Thank you for your kindness. I am a ki-rin. Greetings and welcome to Rowan." Breathing deeply, she lowered her head once more, covering Lucy.

"YaYa is very old," Mr. Nolan said. "Seven hundred years is a long life, even for one of her kind. Today we ensure that YaYa can spend her days resting and tending to the injured. As the Great Matriarch of Rowan, however, she's the one you'll have to answer to if she hears you're shirking your tasks."

YaYa spoke, her voices soft as the subsiding drizzle.

"Do not frighten them, Nolan. I'm sure the charges will be in very good hands. Lucy already speaks highly of them."

The cloudy eyes turned toward Max.

"YaYa," said Nolan, "with your permission, we'd like to introduce your charges to the class."

"Of course," she replied. "With the exception of Tweedy, they're very excited."

Nolan led the students behind the building, spacing them well apart in rows. Ms. Richter, YaYa, and Lucy settled onto a large woolly blanket the Director had spread on the grass. The sky was threatening and Max was very nervous.

Several minutes later, Nolan reappeared along with a dozen other adults. A motley assortment of creatures followed in a strange procession behind them. They came in all shapes and sizes, peering anxiously at the students. Some towered above the adults leading them, but most were smaller and huddled around them, murmuring or purring or chattering in their own tongues. A nametag hung from each neck.

"All right," said Nolan. "There's really nothing to this. All you have to do is stand in your places and let our lovelies take a look at you. Most are quite young, so don't be insulted if some are less polite than they should be. Part of your job will be to teach them proper manners. Okay, then—let's get started."

Max tried to calm his breathing as the creatures stepped, crawled, and hopped among them. An enormous winged bull with the head and face of a young man stopped to loom over him. It gazed at him impassively as Max read ORION, SYRIAN SHEDU on its nametag. The shedu did not move. It merely stared at Max, a small frown on its face. Max was at a loss.

"Hello, Orion. My name's Max."

Nodding stonily, the shedu lifted its head and walked down the line toward Lucia. Max heard a jingle and looked down to see a small striped dog sniffing at his ankles. It sat on its haunches and looked up at him, its nametag indicating that its name was Moby, a Somerset bray.

"Hi, Moby."

The dog wagged its tail and gave an earnest little yelp that sounded like brass horns. Max clapped his hands to his ears and the dog trotted away. Poked from behind, Max turned to see two Normandy fauns eyeing him suspiciously. They each had the hind legs of a slender goat, but the torsos and faces of a young boy and girl. They appeared to be twins: Kellen and Kyra. They spoke in French.

"Il n'est pas pour moi," sniffed Kellen.

"Moi non plus, mon frère. Je préfère Connor," replied Kyra, peering back down the line.

Max felt insulted without knowing why, when a shiny red bullfrog bigger than a toaster landed on his shoe. Clammy, padded fingers gripped Max's leg as its throat inflated like a balloon. Max sought out its nametag.

"Hey, Kettlemouth. I'm Max."

The frog blinked several times before leaping away onto Jesse Chu's head. Jesse shrieked and nearly toppled over as he tried to pry off the sleepy-looking frog that now clung to his collar. Max saw David sitting nearby, cradling the head of a silver gazelle on his lap. David whispered to it and raised its head to look at Max.

"Max, this is Maya. She's an ulu and she's chosen me!"

Max grinned and waved, privately annoyed he had yet to be chosen. A small hare hopped before him. Standing on its hind legs, it fixed Max with a brilliant orange eye. Max spoke to it slowly.

"Hello, Tweedy," Max intoned. "My name is Max."

"Why are you talking to me like I'm an imbecile?" the hare asked, its whiskers trembling with indignation. "Are *you* reading Dante in the original Italian?"

Max clapped a hand to his mouth.

"Uh, no."

"This whole business is ridiculous! I should be taking care of *you*, not the other way around. Oh, you're totally unsuitable!"

The Highlands hare turned up its tail and hopped away, frightening a tiny brown being who ducked quickly out of the way.

Max's eyes met Orion's once more as the shedu clopped past again. It stepped nimbly over a stunning three-legged peacock trilling musical harmonies as it passed.

Many children were now sitting on the grass, their charges

settled beside them or, in some cases, clinging to an arm or leg. With a flash of jealousy, Max saw Orion had chosen Rolf. Cynthia was apologizing profusely to a bawling imp no taller than a footstool. The imp was inconsolable. Cynthia was imploring YaYa for help when Max yelled and jumped.

Something sharp had punctured his foot.

Frightened, Max looked down and stared at a strange creature. It resembled a small otter, but its fur was a shimmering red-gold. Lethal-looking metallic quills ran along its neck and back toward a thick, foxlike tail. It had curling black claws like a grizzly bear, and it was one of these that had pierced Max's shoe. Max yelped as the creature gathered itself and leapt at him with astonishing force, knocking him back onto the grass. Opening his eyes, he saw the heavy animal lying on his chest. Its face was inches from his. The creature nipped his nose and began to vibrate its tail like a rattlesnake. Max held his breath as the animal's murderous claws stretched and squeezed for a better grip.

"I see you've met Nick, but I haven't met you."

Nolan's grinning face was upside down.

"Hi, Mr. Nolan. I'm Max McDaniels. Er, Mr. Nolan?"

"Just Nolan is fine," the man said. "What's up, Max?"

"Okay," said Max, trying to gently pry a large claw away from his throat. "Nolan, what exactly *is* Nick? I didn't get a chance to read his nametag."

"Nick's a Black Forest lymrill, and we're darn lucky to have him. We thought his kind was extinct until one of our Agents stumbled on him in Germany."

"Uh, Nolan? I think his claws are cutting me."

"Oh, he's just *excited,* son!" laughed Nolan, smacking his knee. "You can tell by his tail flutter. Fascinating creatures, lymrills—never thought I'd get a chance to see one. I think Nick's chosen you, Max. Congratulations!"

Max looked at Nick, who had flattened his quills and retracted his claws. His surprising weight eased off Max's chest, and he settled onto the grass. Max rubbed his chest. There were holes in his T-shirt and several small drops of blood. He glared at Nick, who was now dozing.

Far in the distance, they heard Old Tom's chimes sound ten o'clock. With a low-throated growl, YaYa stood and addressed them.

"When I call your name, please come forward with your charge. . . . Sarah Amankwe."

Max watched as the pretty black girl he'd noticed in the kitchen glided forward with the strange three-legged peacock beside her. They stood for several minutes before YaYa and Ms. Richter, and then it looked as though Sarah took a pen and signed her name before the two went back to their place.

Students were called forward, in turn, and stood before YaYa to sign their names. Max felt like dozing along with Nick by the time he heard his name called.

"Max McDaniels."

Max tried to shake Nick awake, but the animal did not budge. When his name was called again, Max slid his hands under the lymrill, hoisting it up like a toddler. As he hurried forward, he noticed out of the corner of his eye that Nick was perfectly awake and utterly content.

A choice phrase for Nick was forming in Max's mind when

he arrived before YaYa. The ki-rin towered above Ms. Richter; Max did not even stand to her shoulder. Her eyes gazed down at him, like great saucers swimming with milk. Max clutched Nick closer.

"Max McDaniels, Nick has chosen you to be his Guardian Keeper. Do you contest this choice?"

His voice sounded very small in answer.

"No."

"By signing your name in the Sanctuary Tome," continued YaYa, "you hereby pledge to care for Nick and to look after him to the best of your ability. Understand that faithful service will be recognized in kind; inconstancy will result in abandonment and shame. Do you accept this charge?"

Max looked down at Nick; he felt the lymrill's strong heartbeat beneath his hand as the animal's small, eager eyes studied his face.

"Do you accept this charge?" asked YaYa patiently.

"Yes," said Max. "I'll look after Nick."

Ms. Richter presented him with a very old book to sign. Looking down at the frayed parchment, he saw that the pledge had already been inscribed in black script. At the bottom was a blank line, next to the Rowan seal. He signed his name, startled to see the date appear underneath. Ms. Richter smiled and motioned for him to rejoin the others.

The rest of the oaths went smoothly except for Omar's. He had the misfortune to be chosen by Tweedy, the Highlands hare, who noisily protested any sort of contract with a minor. The hare wasn't satisfied until he was permitted to ink his paw and sign the book as well. Omar looked mortified throughout and meticulously cleaned his glasses.

When all of the students had taken their oaths, Nolan and his assistants gave each of them a navy booklet. Max read the words stamped in silver on his booklet's cover: THE LYMRILL: KNOWN HISTORY, HABITS, AND CARE. He was about to flip it open, when Nolan dismissed the students to explore the Sanctuary for the rest of the morning. The students scattered in different directions with their charges. Max saw Connor chasing after Kyra, the female faun, who now sprinted for a pine forest. David and Maya had not moved; she merely lay on his lap, her eyes thin slits of gold. Lucia took Kettlemouth toward the lagoon, where the red bullfrog promptly splashed into the water. Orion had permitted Rolf to climb up on his back, and the two plodded out toward the dunes.

Nick's tail fluttered and he bolted in the direction of the trees near the Sanctuary gate. His claws churned clumps of dirt as he went.

By the time Max arrived at the hedge, the lymrill had disappeared. Max rubbed his arms as raindrops began falling and thunder rumbled from the hills. He stepped under a large, bent tree near the canopied tunnel. For ten minutes he paced back and forth, peering deep within the surrounding hedge for any hint of red or gold, listening for the telltale sound of Nick's tail. The rain fell harder and Max kicked a nearby tree.

"I can't *believe* I lost my charge on the first day!"

A voice nearby startled him.

"If you're looking for the lymrill, he's right above you."

Max jumped back and looked straight up to see Nick

crouching on a knotty bough. When Max spied him, his tail began to flutter, its rattle faint in the breeze.

Max whirled to find the source of the voice.

"Who said that?"

"I did."

A plump goose waddled out from the tunnel, followed by a dozen goslings that began to honk inquisitively. As they ambled by, the goose turned and dipped her bill.

"I'm Hannah. Would love to chat, but it's feeding time and they're terrors when they're hungry. Mind you teach the lymrill to watch his claws!"

"Uh, okay. Thanks!"

The goose raised a white-feathered wing in farewell as she herded her goslings toward the lagoon.

Scraps of bark began to fall on Max. He looked up to see Nick sharpening his claws and peering down at him. Yawning dramatically, the lymrill suddenly leapt up to a higher branch and began to send more bark at Max.

"Oh, all right, I'm coming!" Max sighed, grabbing a limb and hoisting himself up. A few minutes later, Max was at eye level with Nick, who fluttered his tail with pleasure.

"Hey there," panted Max, finding a perch at the base of a thick branch. Nick circled Max's lap and curled into a ball, nibbling on the end of his tail. His quills smoothed to a metallic taper. Within seconds, he was fast asleep, his broad black nose whistling as he breathed slow and steady. Max eased a stray claw off his leg and looked out over the Sanctuary. Being in the tree reminded him of his fort back in Chicago. He watched raindrops patter on the outer leaves, thinking how his mother would laugh if she could see him.

Since Nick showed no sign of stirring, Max leaned back and flipped open his booklet:

Lymrill (also known as: Kingmaker and Roland's Folly)

Mystic tree-dwelling mammal found in Central and Western Europe. Identified by its compact size, sharp claws, thick fur, and metallic quills, which possess valuable properties.

Prized for its pelt, the lymrill was hunted to near extinction by knights and kings who believed its skin could be used to forge armor and weapons of unsurpassed hardness. Legends suggest that the lymrill must surrender its quills willingly, lest the animal die and its pelt lose its reputed properties. Last known specimen was captured on the Iberian Peninsula by the famed warrior Roland who coveted its magic but inadvertently slew the animal in his impatience for its quills.

Lymrills are considered intelligent, displaying an ability to communicate with—

Max stopped reading as he heard voices below. He looked down and saw Ms. Richter arrive from the clearing to meet Miss Awolowo, Nigel, and two other adults at the tunnel entrance. Ms. Richter sounded agitated.

"What's the latest news on Lees?"

"We know he made it to the airport," muttered Nigel, sweeping wet hair off his brow. "It appears he simply never landed. Isabella insists he never got off the plane at Logan."

"What of the others?"

"All signs say that they're gone, Director." Max squinted to make out a young woman in a gray raincoat and glasses. "Disappeared shortly after they triggered their letters. They've all been reported missing within their communities."

Ms. Richter's tone was sharp and brisk.

"Exactly how many children are missing, Ndidi?"

"Mickey Lees, who passed the tests two weeks ago, and seventeen Potentials who haven't yet taken them," said Miss Awolowo. "The last Potential disappeared three days ago in Lima."

"And how many paintings have been stolen, Hazel?"

"Fifty-two," said the woman in the raincoat. "But the thefts seem to be somewhat random. We can't conclusively say that the Enemy is involved."

"Joseph, do we have any reason to suspect internal treachery? How was Isabella's last performance review?"

"Hmmm, always possible, always possible," answered an elderly man in a burgundy sweater. "But I don't think so, Gabrielle. Isabella's never been our best, but you know as well as I do that she's trustworthy."

"Nigel," said Ms. Richter, turning suddenly.

"Yes, Director?"

"You believe McDaniels has shared everything with you? Everything about that woman at the house? And everything about Varga?"

"Yes, I do believe he did."

"Hmmm. I'll still need to interview him. I do believe that you and Ndidi may be right about him, however. David Menlo, too. What this means is anybody's guess. These missing children, however, require more than guesswork. Assume *nothing*—about the children or the paintings! I'll expect more information by to-morrow morning."

Ms. Richter turned and started back for the Warming Lodge while the others disappeared into the hedge tunnel. Frowning, Max watched Ms. Richter stride across the clearing.

"Nick, something is very, very wrong."

~ 7 ~

A FULL HOUSE

Upon returning to the Manse, the First Years were divided into five sections. Max's section was directed upstairs to the Bacon Library, where the wet children crowded round the fireplace. The library was located on the third floor and faced south, where Max could see a large athletic field. Turning away from the window, he scanned the stacks, seeing sections dedicated to philosophy, the arts, and literature. Thousands of books lined the shelves.

While some of his classmates were soaked, Max was merely damp; he and Nick had stayed up in the tree until they heard Old

Tom's chimes. The class had left their new charges with Nolan before dashing through the gate to escape the rain that had begun falling in heavy sheets.

The door to the library opened, and in walked the young woman and old man Max had seen speaking to Ms. Richter. The man had a patient face, thick glasses, and a trim white beard. The woman was much younger with short brown hair. She was pretty but looked very serious and scholarly behind small, rectangular glasses as she leafed through a stack of papers.

"All right, children, gather round," said the man, looking up.

With some reluctance, the students pulled away from the warm fire and took closer seats. David coughed in fits, rubbing his nose.

"Are you David?" asked the man.

David nodded.

"Perhaps you'd better stay near the fire," said the man with a kindly smile, before turning to address the group.

"Hello. I'm Joseph Vincenti and this is Hazel Boon. Among the faculty, I'm the Department Chair of Devices and Miss Boon is a Junior Instructor of Mystics."

Max glanced at Miss Boon; her name was familiar. Suddenly, he remembered Nigel had mentioned that she held the modern record for extinguishing flames when she had been tested as a Potential. She sat patiently, her arms folded.

"As your class advisors we're here to look after you, to make sure you're progressing as you should be. We'll be your advisors until you begin to specialize at the end of your third year—at that point you'll have an advisor within your specialty. Miss Boon?"

Miss Boon looked up, and Max was startled to see that her

pupils were different colors; one was brown, the other a brilliant blue. She looked at the students with a solemn expression. Max squirmed as her gaze lingered on him.

"Hello there. I feel very privileged to have been assigned your class advisor—you're my first class. The Recruiters have raved about you, and consequently I expect great things. Great things require real work, however, so without further ado, allow me to distribute your course schedules."

Circling the table, Miss Boon handed out the laminated sheets. Max shook his head in disbelief. The room was nearly silent for fifteen minutes while the students examined their schedules with gasps and quiet mutters. Cynthia was the first to raise her hand.

"Am I reading this right? It says my day starts at six thirty in the morning and that I'm taking almost ten classes in addition to taking care of my charge."

"That is correct," replied Miss Boon, walking over to stoke the fire. "Rowan has a challenging curriculum, and certain disciplines, like Physical Training, Languages, and Mystics, must be done each day."

Max stared at the table while Miss Boon and Mr. Vincenti answered or deflected questions about grades, room locations, class awards, and school supplies. For Max, the only bright spot was when they mentioned that Rowan had no curfew, but his excitement diminished when he realized any free time would be spent studying. They were dismissed and told they would be free to explore the Manse and grounds until dinner.

Max stalked back to his room and flung his schedule on the bed. Walking downstairs, he wet a towel at his vanity and scrubbed the gels and sprays out of his hair. The sky dome was darker and the constellations had brightened since the morning.

Dinner was soup and sandwiches, as Mum and Bob were busy preparing for the next evening's feast. The dining hall was dark, the candles of one chandelier providing the only light as thunder rumbled outside. Max saw Nigel stride briskly down the stairs accompanied by several other adults before they disappeared out another door. The girls sat at a separate table, shooting angry stares at Jesse, who had loudly predicted that the boys would sweep the class awards. Feeling a tap, Max jumped at the sight of Mum standing behind him.

"Phone call for you, love. In the kitchen."

"Oh! Thanks, Mum," said Max, pushing up from the table and following her through the swinging door.

Bob was hunched over an enormous tray of pastries, applying delicate waves of icing to chocolate ladyfingers. He looked up and smiled at Max, his crooked grin softening his craggy features.

"I think you have a phone call," he said.

"He already knows, you dolt! Why do you think he's back here?" hissed Mum, running to the phone on the far wall. The hag spoke into the receiver in clipped, snobbish tones.

"Yes, sir, we have notified Mr. McDaniels for you, sir. He shall be arriving presently."

"Mum . . . ," Bob warned, turning from his ladyfingers.

Mum clamped her hand over the phone and jumped up and down, making hideous faces. Bob sighed and turned away to mix another batch of icing. Max reached for the phone, but Mum ducked below his reach.

"Back again, sir. I think I hear him arriving as we speak, sir. He's been enjoying a cocktail on the *ve-ran-da*—"

Max snatched the phone away. His dad's voiced boomed from the other end.

"—oh, well thank you very much."

"Dad!"

"Hey, Max! I thought the receptionist was still on the phone. She's, er, very professional."

"Yeah, she's great," muttered Max as Mum clapped her hands and giggled. She rushed past him to shoulder an entire side of beef and disappear into another room.

"Well, I just got back from another trip to KC," said his father. "Home again, home again, as your mother would say. How are you? How're things?"

"Things are . . . okay." Max faced the wall and traced a crack with his finger.

"What's the matter, kiddo?"

"Nothing. It's just . . . it seems like it's going to be really hard. And I miss you."

Max squeezed his eyes hard. There was a long pause on the other end of the line.

"Well, I miss you, too."

Max was struck by a sudden longing to be back at home, his feet planted on the fort ceiling as he lay on his back, sketching throughout the afternoon.

"Dad, do you think it's too late to come home?"

"No," said Mr. McDaniels. "It's not too late, but that's not the issue. The issue is seeing through a commitment you've made. You made a decision—a tough decision—and I'm very proud of you for making it like a man. The first couple weeks will be tough, but I expect you to stick it out. If you hate it, next year you can go to school here."

Max nodded, before realizing his father could not see him. Hearing an urgent whisper behind him, he turned to see Lucia beckoning from the doorway.

"Max, they're asking for you," she said. "We're getting our books and uniforms."

She disappeared behind the swinging door.

"Dad, I have to go. They're handing out our books and stuff."

"Okay, then. Be a good boy and do your best—for me and your mom."

"Okay," said Max quickly. "Love you."

"Love you, too, kiddo. I'll call in a couple days."

Max hung up the phone and walked around the long island toward the door. Just as he reached the exit, he felt Bob's enormous hand reach out and tap him on the shoulder. The ogre extended a specially decorated pastry. Icing spelled WELCOME, MAX in a beautiful, delicate script. With a wink, Bob placed the treat in his hand and ushered him out the door.

The next morning, Max paused outside Room 301 as he heard laughter inside the bathroom.

"Aw, man, you gotta be kiddin' me, Jimmy!" said a deep voice with a heavy Southern accent.

Jimmy's voice cackled something unintelligible in reply. Max opened the door slowly. Jimmy was sitting on the counter, his legs dangling over the side while he spoke with an older boy wearing a towel and flip flops. They turned as Max entered.

"*There's one of 'em!*" Jimmy roared, leaping off the counter and hobbling at Max, who backed against the door. "*There's one of the thieving ingrates!*"

Jimmy's face was purple as he came at Max, but the fit-looking blond boy intercepted the little man, stooping to place his hands on Jimmy's shoulders. Max sighed with relief.

"Whoa, Jimmy!" the blond boy drawled. "Relax. Relax, man."

Jimmy glared at Max, his chest heaving as he stabbed an accusatory finger.

"That tadpole let me slave over 'im! *Insisted* on the ol' Jimmy treatment to get 'im spiffed up for the ladies! I told him I was busy, but he begged for a little zing of the good stuff! And does he have the decency to thank me properly? Not on your life! Not *one* of 'em gave me a present!"

The blond boy turned; his grip was still firm on Jimmy's shoulders.

"Is that right?" he asked Max.

Max turned red. "I didn't know! I-I'm sorry!"

The older boy winked at Max.

"Well, Jimmy," said the boy, "you leave this kid to me. I'll take care of him for you."

Jimmy suddenly looked concerned, alternating worried looks between Max and the older boy.

"Promise not to be too hard on 'im, Jason!" pleaded the little man. "He's just a tadpole, after all!"

Jason frowned and shook his head. "You know my ways, Jimmy."

"*Don't you lay a hand on 'im!*" roared Jimmy. "*If you do, you'll have me to answer to!*"

Jason released Jimmy and put up his hands in a defensive gesture.

"Okay, okay. I'll let 'im go!"

With a snort, Jimmy brushed past him and beckoned Max to lean in close.

"Sixth Years," he whispered. "Think they run the place. He bothers you, you let me know, eh?"

Max raised his eyebrows and nodded, glancing over Jimmy at the grinning boy. Jimmy patted him on the shoulder, then went to retrieve a mop from across the room. Jason put out a hand to Max.

"Hey, bud, I'm Jason Barrett. You must be a new Apprentice."

"Yeah," replied Max, shaking his hand. "I'm Max McDaniels."

"Good to meet ya, Max. Welcome to Rowan."

Glancing over his shoulder, Jason lowered his voice.

"Listen, Max," he said. "Jimmy might be a lot of bark, but you've still got to bring him a present if he does something for you. Doesn't have to be fancy. Anything will work, really—a piece of gum, half a bagel, a stamp, whatever. He just likes to be in your thoughts, you know what I mean?"

Max shot Jimmy a wary look as Jason continued in a lighter tone.

"Fortunately, you won't have to worry about Jimmy too much. You see, this here is the 'Big Daddy' of the boys' bathrooms at Rowan. We kind of reserve it for the Fifth and Sixth Years. Apprentices use the one down in Room 101." Jason patted Max on the shoulder and steered him gently out the door. "Start small, Max—it'll give you something to look forward to!"

Max found several of his classmates huddled outside the door, looking tense.

"We heard Jimmy shouting," Omar whispered. "Are you okay?"

"Yeah, I'm fine. But I guess we're supposed to use a different bathroom. Room 101. This one's for the Fifth and Sixth Years."

"That's ridiculous," muttered Jesse, making for the door. "This bathroom's on *our* floor."

Jesse bulldozed through the door. The others stayed put, jumping as they heard Jimmy's voice bellow from within.

"Another one! Out of my way, Jason—leave him to me!"

Jesse came screaming out of the bathroom, slamming the door and leaning heavily against it. Glancing at the others, he started for the stairs.

"Max, you said Room 101?"

Room 101 was a small, dingy space with a dozen gray stalls, toilets, and sinks. A dead spider lay in a dusty bathtub, spotlighted by a lone bare bulb hanging from a mildewed ceiling. The walls were lined with rusty lockers. Peeling back a shower curtain, Rolf poked his head inside a stall and quickly turned to the others.

"I'll go second," he volunteered.

"I loved that other bathroom," sniffed Connor, stepping past Rolf and turning the faucet.

By the time the boys left the bathroom, the Manse had become a much busier place. Shouts of greeting rang through the halls. There was a constant racket of luggage and doors slamming. Arriving back at their floor, Max found the hallway filled with suitcases and duffel bags as Second Years lingered about, getting reacquainted and comparing class schedules. But when Max and the others stepped out into the hall, the conversations abruptly stopped.

"Oh no," breathed Connor as the first yells started.

"Tadpoles! Tadpoles!"

The First Years ran a screaming gauntlet toward their rooms, past the older students who yelled and threw wadded packing tape in a stinging whirlwind of flying objects.

Max practically dived into his room as bits of cardboard and wadded tape came hurtling after him. David was on the upper level, sitting on the floor with his back against his bed.

"Terrifying, isn't it?" he said. "I went to pee and they chased me back here." He added thoughtfully, "I forgot I still need to pee."

"That's not so bad," Max panted. "I almost got killed by Jimmy this morning before a Sixth Year told me that we have to use the bathroom in Room 101."

"Why do we have to do that?"

"You'll know when you see Room 101," sighed Max, flopping onto his bed.

After making their way across the bustling campus, Max and David emerged from the Sanctuary tunnel just in time to see a herd of glossy black horses thunder across the clearing. The horses were ridden bareback by a mix of older boys and girls who laughed and shouted to one another as they cantered past the lagoon and up toward the dunes. Several students sat under the palms, tossing live fish to a pair of gargantuan seals that had dragged themselves from the lagoon onto the sandy beach.

"Do you want to help me feed Maya?" asked David. "It shouldn't be too bad—she only eats melon, nuts, and grasses."

"No," said Max, "I have to feed Nick tonight and I don't even know what he eats. I'd better read my book. If I mess it up, YaYa will probably eat *me*."

Taking the lymrill booklet from his pocket, Max waved good-bye and started toward the lagoon. The seals were gone, but he saw Kettlemouth and Lucia sunning near a palm. He waved and circled around to the other end, settling on a low, grassy patch dotted with small white flowers. For a moment, he just lay back and watched the towering clouds scoot by overhead. He peeled off his shirt and slid out of his shoes to lie barefoot. Closing his eyes, he let the sun warm his face. Soon, he was fast asleep, entertaining a strange dream in which his father had his mother declared deceased so he could marry Mum, who promptly turned him into a casserole.

Max awoke suddenly as something bumped him. Opening his eyes, he saw that he was sandwiched between two shiny, rippling mounds. He yelped and jumped high into the air before racing away from two twenty-foot seals that had slid up on either side of him. He heard a giggle and whirled to see a girl snapping photos. She lowered the camera, revealing the prettiest face he had ever seen, with long brown hair, bright blue eyes, and faint freckles dotting each sunburned cheek.

Max was horrified.

"Gotcha!" she crowed. "Was wondering when you'd wake up! That'll make the newspaper for sure. Yearbook, too, probably."

"Awful, Julie. Shame on you," chastised one of the seals, rolling over on its side. "We three very peaceful, just now."

"Oh, I couldn't resist," the girl said with a shrug. Max blinked at her dumbly. "How often do you get a First Year surrounded by two selkies during his midmorning nap?"

"Apologize, you should," sniffed the other seal with an agitated ripple.

"Oh, okay. I'm sorry . . . eh, what's your name?" She paused, raising her eyebrows expectantly.

"Max. Max McDaniels. It's okay. It just startled me." He turned and raised a hand to the two seals, which were now blinking at him. "Sorry."

"Understandable," rumbled the selkie. "You were sleeping. We give you shock. I'm Helga and this is my sister, Frigga. Scandinavian selkies. You look so comfortable, we thought we join you and sun our blubber." She smacked her flippers on her belly with a loud slap.

"Well, I'm Julie Teller," offered the girl, putting away her camera. "I'm a Stage One Mystic and head photographer for the paper—a Third Year," she added, seeing the look of confusion on Max's face. He had no idea what to say. All he knew was that he wanted her to keep talking.

"Is it okay with you if I use this in the paper?" she asked.

"Uh, sure. I guess so," said Max, reaching for his shirt and suddenly feeling very young and scrawny.

"Thanks," she said brightly. "Where are you from?"

"Chicago."

"Ooh! Cool city. My family and I visited there once a couple years ago. I'm from Melbourne."

Max gaped at her.

"That's in Australia," she added.

Max nodded, feeling stupid. They looked at each other for several moments.

"Well," Julie chirped. "Got my shot for the morning. Good to meet you, Max. I'll see you later."

Before he could speak, Julie was gone, walking quickly toward the hedge tunnel and pausing to greet Hannah the goose, who was waddling with her goslings toward Max. Max's attention was interrupted by a solid thump on the ground nearby.

"I go get a bite. Nice to meet you, Max," rumbled Frigga, turning to shimmy down to the water.

"Frigga!" Helga exclaimed, rippling after her sister. "We fed one hour ago. This must stop; you getting *huge!*"

The two erupted in a series of angry seal barks before disappearing smoothly below the surface. Max felt a peck on his calf and turned to see Hannah and her goslings crowded around him.

"Hello again," said Hannah, sounding very flustered. "Word around the Sanctuary is that you're free for a little babysitting. Is this true?"

"Oh. Well, I guess so," said Max. "Lymrills are nocturnal and—"

"Wonderful! I've got to get my down fluffed properly and one of the dryads offered to do it for a song. You can watch them for a couple of hours, can't you?"

Hannah turned and swept a wing over the goslings, who honked and bopped into one another.

"This is Susie, Bobbie, Willie, Millie, Hank, Honk, Nina, Tina, Macy, Lillian, Mac, and Little Baby Ray. Goslings, you behave yourselves for Max. Be back in a few, dear."

Buffeting Max's leg appreciatively with her wing, Hannah waddled back toward the forest. Max's eyes followed her helplessly as the goslings hopped onto his feet and began pecking his shins with their sharp little bills.

He spent two hours with the goslings, letting them jump up and down and run on his body as he lay in the grass and tried unsuccessfully to read his booklet. Every half hour, he would take them down to the lagoon, wading in and playing with them as they swam about the reeds in happy little circles. The water was warm, but every several seconds Max could feel a strong, cool current hint at greater depths. Older students waved and laughed when they saw Max had been drafted into babysitting service. The goslings demanded constant attention, and Max was relieved to see Hannah return.

"I feel like a new goose!" she exclaimed as the goslings clamored around their mother. "Hmmm. Seems like *someone* here made himself a dozen new fans. Thank you, Max, you're a dear. The children would love it if you could visit sometime. We live in a little nest by the orchard, just behind the Class of 1840 Tree. Come by anytime."

"Sure thing," said Max, grabbing his booklet. He said farewell and headed for the hedge tunnel. One of the goslings (Max thought it might be Lillian) tottered after him until Hannah herded her back with the rest.

That evening, hundreds of students streamed into the great dining hall, which was now golden with the light of many tapered candles lit among the chandeliers. Max fiddled with his tie as he and his classmates were directed to tables strewn with wildflowers and set with crystal glasses and horn-handled cutlery. Full-grown fauns with curling hair plucked at lyres, the music strange and soothing as more students filed in.

Seated between Cynthia and Lucia, Max studied the faces around him. The candlelight and formal uniforms made the students look much older. Across the hall, Max saw Jason Barrett seated with the Sixth Years, chatting with the girl on his right.

Ms. Richter and the faculty sat in blue robes at the head table. They engaged in quiet conversation, giving an occasional nod to an older student or an inquisitive glance at the new arrivals. The music came to a gentle close, and Ms. Richter stood to address them, her voice clear and strong.

"Please stand."

Max looked at the others and stood, uncertain of what was next. Ms. Richter's voice filled the hall.

"This is a House of Learning and today is the Day of Return, when teacher and pupil reforge their bonds and resume their progress on the path."

The faculty and students raised their glasses in a silent toast. Ms. Richter continued.

"This is a House of Learning and today is a Day of Remembrance, when we gather to honor our past, embracing both its joys and sorrows."

Again, the glasses were lifted in salute.

"This is a House of Learning and today is a Day of Renewal, when Rowan welcomes a new class bringing with them life and promise to grace these halls and grounds."

Max jumped as the dining hall erupted in a chorus.

"We welcome them with open arms. We will help them on the way."

The students and faculty raised their glasses toward the First Years' tables and promptly drained them. Lucia did the same, but Max wrinkled his nose and took only hesitant sips of his wine.

Ms. Richter took her seat. The dining hall burst into a chorus of cheery conversations as dozens of students streamed in from the kitchens bearing heavy silver serving trays.

The feast was extraordinary and soon the table was engrossed in Cynthia's story of how she had come to receive her letter from

Rowan. With a blaring voice and dramatic sweeps of her arms, Cynthia reenacted how she had been visiting the aquarium when a school of tropical fish began to swim in hypnotizing patterns. After concluding that it was all "very freaky," Cynthia yielded the floor to other classmates, who began to share their stories. Max did not share his, choosing instead to feast on roast pheasant stuffed with wild rice, miniature lamb chops, mountains of fresh vegetables, and little dishes of assorted sweets and chocolates. Periodically, older students and faculty wandered over to say a quick hello between courses. At the meal's conclusion, a great clamor swept the dining hall.

Max grinned as Mum and Bob were dragged from the kitchens by a gaggle of students insisting they take a bow for their efforts. Bob, wearing a starched blue shirt and clean white apron, hastily wiped away a tear and waved before ducking back through the swinging door. Mum capered to and fro, clapping her hands and issuing curtsy after dramatic curtsy until the very same students politely, but firmly, escorted her away. This drew a final round of hearty applause until Ms. Richter rang her spoon against her glass and stood once again. The candlelight cast an enormous shadow on the wall behind her. A smile spread across her face.

"Welcome home, students. As Director, I declare the school year officially in session!"

A raucous cheer erupted from the students, accompanied by enthusiastic banging on the tables and the stamping of many feet. Max was stamping away with the others when several Second Years strolled over and sat down at the table.

"Hey there," said an olive-skinned boy with jet-black hair. "I'm Alex Muñoz."

"Yeah, I'm Anna Lundgren," said a pretty girl with short blond hair.

"Welcome, guys. I'm Sasha Ivanovich," said a boy with shaggy brown hair.

Several of the First Years enthusiastically introduced themselves while finishing off the last of the sweets. Jesse looked miserable, groaning as he held his stomach and leaned against Omar.

"Are you guys excited for the big campout?" whispered Alex, twisting his finger around a wildflower stem.

"What campout?" Cynthia inquired, pushing away her plate.

"The one tonight," said Anna, "out on the *Kestrel*. Didn't anyone tell you?"

"No," said Connor, leaning closer. "What's it all about?"

"It's kind of a First Year tradition, for class bonding," answered Sasha. "The First Years sneak out and spend the night on the *Kestrel*. Out by midnight, back by sunrise."

"Isn't that against the rules?" asked Omar, wide-eyed.

"Yes and no," answered Alex. "According to 'the rules,' the *Kestrel*'s off-limits, but the tradition's been around a long time. As long as you're careful and quiet, the faculty looks the other way."

"I don't know," murmured Cynthia, looking nervous.

"It's your decision," Anna said, shrugging. "We had a great time last year. If you want to be the first class not to do it, though . . ."

"We didn't say that," said Connor, his eyes flashing. "C'mon, guys, let's do it. It'll be fun."

Connor's smile was contagious, and soon the others were grinning, too. They looked from one to another and nodded.

"Okay," muttered Rolf. "I'll bring some snacks."

"I've got a radio," volunteered Lucia.

"Everybody bring a sleeping bag or some blankets, a pillow, and a flashlight if you have one," whispered Connor. "Pass it on to the other tables. We'll meet near the stairs down to the beach at midnight. Go in ones or twos and don't get caught!"

Turning to Alex and Anna, Connor continued.

"Can we just get aboard the *Kestrel*? Isn't it locked or something?"

"Nope," said Alex. "Just tiptoe down the dock and climb the rope ladder on the side. It's a really cool ship and it's pretty warm tonight. You guys are lucky; it rained on us last year."

"But it was still fun!" chirped Anna, smiling and standing up. "Nice to meet you all. Can't wait to hear about it tomorrow." She and the others rejoined the table of Second Years.

Max was excited at the prospect of a secret sneak-out. He spent several minutes planning with the group before he saw Mr. Vincenti making a beeline for him from the faculty table.

"Sorry to interrupt," said the elderly man with a smile. "Max, could I speak with you?"

"Sure," said Max, fearful that their planning had been over-heard. Mr. Vincenti ushered him away from the table to a nearby pillar.

"Max, the Director would like to have a word with you," said Mr. Vincenti, "concerning certain events . . . events that happened before you arrived at Rowan."

"Oh," said Max. "But I have to go to the Sanctuary—my charge is nocturnal."

"This is more important," said Mr. Vincenti. "I'll see that your charge is cared for. You'd best get going—she's expecting you."

* * *

Ms. Richter's office was located off the foyer, at the end of a hall way decorated by glistening portraits of past Directors. The door was slightly ajar, letting a sliver of warm yellow light into the hall. Max's heart beat quickly as he knocked.

"Come in."

Max entered and saw Ms. Richter hanging up her blue robes. She still wore a business suit, although she had removed her shoes and stood in stocking feet. She offered Max a tired smile and gestured toward a polished armchair across from an enormous desk. Max was surprised by the relative modesty of the room. Other than the desk, it had a small couch and a coffee table with several small chairs. French doors led out to some gardens near the orchard. A small hearth stood cold and quiet in the corner.

Max seated himself as Ms. Richter arranged some wildflowers from the feast in a crystal vase. She eased into a leather chair and leaned forward to extend her hand, her bright silver eyes snapping Max to attention. Her hand was warm and dry and strong.

"Hello, Max. It's nice to meet you and chat one on one."

"Nice to meet you, too," he said.

Ms. Richter rested her elbows on the desk, her eyes assuming a deadly seriousness.

"Max, it is unacceptable that the Enemy knew who you were and how to find you. You represent a new generation at Rowan, and I shudder to think of the consequences should the Enemy find the means to identify and target our Potentials."

Max nodded, trying not to betray that he knew seventeen Potentials and a student were *already* missing.

"I want you to tell me everything that has happened starting with the day you had your vision. Anything you can remember. Spare no detail, no matter how trivial you think it may be."

Max told Ms. Richter everything he knew. Her questions came quickly, forcing him to search his memory and recall details he had forgotten. When he had concluded, Ms. Richter picked up a folder and opened it. She glanced quickly at its contents before selecting a photograph and holding it up for Max to see.

"Is this the man that has been following you?" she asked.

Max squinted at the picture and recoiled in shock. The figure was indeed the strange man from the train and the museum, although he looked younger and less haggard in the photograph. He was sitting at a sidewalk café holding a newspaper, but his gaze was directed at the camera. The man's good eye displayed a mixture of alarm and rage as he had evidently just spied the photographer, who, from the look of the photo, was in a moving car. Max shut his eyes and nodded. Ms. Richter put the photograph away.

"I'm sorry to frighten you, Max," she said, her features softening, "but I needed to confirm Nigel's account. That's all I need at present. I'd ask you not to speak of this matter with anyone until we have more information. Okay?"

"Okay. Can I go now?"

"You can go, but, Max, I need you to remember something."

"Yes, Ms. Richter?"

The Director's expression became deadly serious again. She spoke in tight, urgent tones.

"If you ever see that man again, I want you to run and call for help as loudly as you can. Do not answer or speak to him; it could be very dangerous. Do you understand?"

Max nodded mutely, his insides frozen. Ms. Richter got up from her chair and ushered him out the door, suggesting that he swing by the kitchen for some cocoa. But as soon as she closed the door, Max ran down the hall and up to his room.

David was dead asleep when Max and Connor began to shake him. He blinked several times before flipping over and burying his head under a pillow. Max hissed between his teeth.

"David! C'mon, David. Wake up! We're camping out on the *Kestrel*. Remember?"

"No need to whisper, Max," laughed Connor. "You're still in your room!"

Connor jumped up and landed on David, who gave a muffled groan.

"C'mon, Davie! It'll be fun. Ladies and adventure on the high seas, eh!"

"Okay, okay. Get off of me," pleaded David's voice from beneath the pillow.

Max clutched several blankets and a flashlight as the three stole down the hallway. Reaching the foyer, they nearly bumped into Cynthia and Lucia, who were tiptoeing toward the door. Connor motioned for them to go first, and the pair slipped quietly outside. Several moments later, Connor turned to Max and David, his grin visible in the dark.

"You boys ready?" he whispered. "Stick close to the Manse and stay low until we're beyond the lights. When you have to leave the house, crawl—you'll cast a smaller shadow. When we reach the grass, we'll run the rest of the way."

Max nodded and moved past Connor to the door. Sticking his head outside, he turned and motioned for them to follow. The three hugged the perimeter of the Manse, crouching below the windows, and crawled to the grass. Max found it hard going while carrying their blankets and the flashlight. One by one, they rose and ran into the darkness.

The night air felt cool as Max raced along. Old Tom and Maggie were given a wide berth; several of their upper windows were lit with a pale green light.

As they reached the steps, they saw many silhouettes moving against the moonlit ocean. A few dozen students were already there, whispering excitedly and tallying the goodies that had been brought. Omar and Jesse came panting up a few minutes later. Connor scanned the group and furrowed his brow.

"Where's everyone else?"

"A bunch of people aren't coming," said a girl. "They don't want to get in trouble."

Connor rolled his eyes and made a noise in his throat before starting down the stone steps. Max swatted a mosquito and hefted his pack, laughing with Cynthia as they followed along.

It was a peaceful night, gentle waves lapping at the *Kestrel*, which rose black and tall on the water. Connor turned on his flashlight and jogged down the dock, the light bobbing wildly as the others trotted after. He stopped abruptly and Max heard him swear. As they caught up to him, Max saw why: the *Kestrel* *did* have a rope ladder hanging from its side, but the ship itself was moored fifteen feet away. They would have to swim to it. The water looked inky and cold. Connor kicked a wooden post.

"They might have told us about this!" he fumed.

"Let's just forget it," muttered Rolf, looking back toward the stone steps set in the cliff.

"I am *not* going in the ocean at night," a girl said, and shuddered, peering over the dock at the water.

"Yeah," said another boy. "I vote we head back."

Max stood quietly, watching the ship, as the others debated what to do. He noticed that its rocking motion brought it closer at regular intervals.

Max backed away down the dock. For several seconds, he studied the ship's movement in the water. When he saw its mooring chain begin to slacken, he sprinted toward the edge and leapt high into the air.

For a moment he thought he had misjudged badly.

He plummeted toward the water, grabbing wildly for the rope ladder as he fell. With a sudden snag, his fingers caught it and he crashed against the side of the ship. There were surprised gasps and cheers from the dock as his feet scrambled for a hold and he began climbing. Swinging over the ship's side, he spilled onto the deck, rolling over something hard and uncomfortable. He looked to see what it was and smiled, standing to cup his hands around his mouth.

"Hey!" he called back to the dock. "There's a gangplank on the deck—no one has to swim!"

The others began chattering; the atmosphere was electric once again. Grunting from the weight, Max swung the gangplank over the ship's side and fed it slowly toward the dock, where Sarah and Rolf reached out to grab it. Securing the end of the plank into its groove, Max signaled it was ready. They proceeded in single file; Connor was first up, carrying Max's gear with his own.

"You've got some serious springs, don't ya, Max?" Connor grinned, dropping the gear on deck and looking around.

"Yeah, I call Max for my basketball team!" piped David, who began rummaging through Rolf's pack for snacks, to the visible annoyance of its owner.

The students fanned out and began exploring up and down the deck. Several took turns playing with the wheel. Lucia and Cynthia crawled up to a crow's nest, raining hard candies down on the rest as they spread out blankets and sleeping bags. Connor strolled toward the cabin, returning shortly with a disappointed expression on his face.

"There are locks on all the doors and hatches; looks like we're staying above."

"That's fine by me," squeaked a girl from Denmark. "It's probably scary down there!"

"I'll bet it's cool down there," said Connor wistfully. He took a seat on a nearby blanket and turned on someone's radio, quickly lowering the volume as an opera singer blared an impressive tremolo. He began scrolling through the stations.

Soon all of them had settled down in their impromptu campsite. Huddling in a small group as the boat rocked, Max laughed and played cards and devoured Rolf's snacks while he learned about his classmates' hometowns and families. Omar was telling Max about his baby brother back in Cairo when the boat pitched wildly.

Playing cards slid across the deck. The masts creaked noisily and the children stopped talking.

For a moment all was silent again. Then the boat shuddered as a massive wave rose beneath it, crashing the children into one another as they scrambled for a hold.

Thump.

Thump, thump.

Something was thudding loudly against the side of the ship, below the waterline.

The children felt the boat strain against its moorings. Lucia shrieked as the gangplank slipped from its hold and splashed into the water. Max looked frantically over the railing to see something, *anything* that would indicate what was churning the sea. All he saw was swirling, fathomless black.

Keening wails suddenly filled the air, causing Max to fall back onto the deck as the others covered their ears. The *Kestrel* now bobbed like a toy boat as seawater frothed and spilled in foamy waves over the sides.

"Run!" screamed Connor over the noise, pulling Lucia to her feet. "All of you, run!"

The children staggered toward the bow of the ship, falling now and again as it pitched back and forth. The keening increased; the timbers of the boat began to vibrate and hum. Many of the children leapt over the side, plunging some fifteen feet into the water and flailing through the chop for the beach. Max saw David bob up in the foamy water when he suddenly felt a hand seize his arm. Sarah was shouting at him in terror.

"I can't swim!"

The wailing became deafening; the boat lurched away from the dock as one of the mooring chains strained near snapping.

Max grabbed Sarah and hurled the two of them over the side. They plunged into the sea. Swallowing a mouthful of salty water, Max clutched Sarah's shirt and stroked wildly with his free arm for the beach. The water was cold and swirling in wild currents; beds of kelp dragged against his legs like clammy fingers. At any moment, Max expected something horribly strong to clamp on to his foot and heave him out toward deeper waters.

Brine splashed in his face, and a great black wave rolled over his head, pushing them under. Sarah was screaming and thrashing crazily in his grip, her sharp elbows hitting him on the side of the face as he labored.

As Max's grip threatened to give, their feet met the rough sand. Sarah flung herself away from him and scrambled through the surf. The keening began to die as the children fled up the stone steps and across the lawns.

The Manse's lights were on. A crowd of students and faculty had gathered onto the drive by the fountain. Ms. Richter was among them, her bright lantern casting her anger into sharp relief.

~ 8 ~

THE NEW AND WEIRD

Stifling a yawn, Max stumbled down the hallway with his classmates shortly before six o'clock Monday morning. Many were exhausted, having spent Sunday cleaning out the stables as punishment for their foray aboard the *Kestrel*. The task had taken most of the day, leaving them drained and filthy. Ms. Richter had been sparing with her words, muttering only that she had never seen a class so determined to exterminate themselves.

When Mr. Vincenti asked why they had elected to do such a foolish thing, Connor insisted that it was his idea, staring all the while at Alex Muñoz, who gawked from the dwindling crowd.

Despite their questions, no one told them what had churned the seas and wailed so horribly. No students seemed to know, and no faculty would say.

Max was particularly tired. After the day's labor, feeding and playing with Nick had proven to be no trivial task. Following the instructions in his booklet, Max murmured, "Food for Nick: Black Forest lymrill," into a stained and spattered wooden bin in the Warming Lodge. The bin rumbled and shook, its lid clattering and spilling beams of light onto the stalls. While his reading had braced him for Nick's diet, Max still retched upon opening the lid. The bin was piled high with crates of writhing rodents and worms along with small stacks of thin metal bars.

Nick's tail fluttered wildly, and he zoomed up and down the corridor as Max loaded the crates into a wheelbarrow and staggered outside. He looked away as Nick methodically devoured each crate's contents: first bloodying his snout in the wriggling piles of vermin before extending his tongue to deftly separate, lift, and swallow whole each of the small metal bars. After cleaning himself vigorously in the lagoon, Nick then chased Max about the clearing, racing ahead in tremendous bursts of speed to ambush him from outcroppings of rock or swatting playfully at his ankles to spill the boy into the grass as he fled. When Nick finally stopped and curled himself into a dozing ball, Max almost wept with gratitude. Scooping the lymrill into his arms, he walked down the Warming Lodge's rows of stalls until he found the door for Nick's. After laying the sleeping lymrill in the boughs of the stall's small tree, Max dragged himself to bed.

"How are you feeling?" inquired Omar, stumbling along next to Max as they descended the stairs for their first class. Omar was in

Max's section, one of five groupings of First Years who would be taking all of their classes together.

"I can't even see straight," moaned Max. "Nick kept me out until eleven."

"Can Nick talk?" asked Omar, rubbing sleep from his eyes.

"No."

"Well, you should be thankful. Try caring for Tweedy. He's making me memorize the life works of his favorite composers. . . ."

Max grunted in sympathy as they entered the basement classroom, a large space whose floor was covered in firm, spongy mats. A tall, wiry man with close-cropped black hair and heavy-lidded eyes stood in the middle of the room. He wore a loose-fitting shirt and pants; his feet were bare. He sipped from a bottle of water as he perused a clipboard, not bothering to look up as they entered.

"Remove your shoes," he murmured with a slight accent. "Start jogging around the room. Clockwise. Quick, quick!"

Max jogged along with the others, shooting curious glances at the instructor as they lapped doggedly around the room. "Faster," the man's voice snapped like a whip. After a few minutes, Max was huffing; he noticed Jesse and Cynthia were several laps behind. The man took another distracted sip, sat on the ground, and murmured, "All right. Over here. Spread out along the floor, facing me. Stretch your hamstrings, like so." He spread his legs and smoothly lowered his forehead to a knee, holding it there. As Max and the others seated themselves and struggled to emulate him, he abruptly stood and started walking around the room. "Do not bounce!" he hissed, passing Connor, who promptly groaned and forced himself back down.

"I am Monsieur Renard. I will be your instructor for Training and Games. You will either love or hate me. This does not concern me."

Max's eyes widened. He shot a look at Connor, who had unwisely taken a break just as M. Renard passed behind him.

"Many of you are fat and lazy," the instructor hissed, digging his toe into Connor's midsection. "Little sausages that have burst their casings. That ends today. Cynthia Gilley?"

"Over here," wheezed Cynthia, red-faced in the corner.

"Cynthia Gilley," he read off the clipboard. "Lactic production rate: forty-nine. Lactic dispersion rate: thirty-four. Twitch speed: fifty-one. Muscular density, current: thirty-six. . . . Hmmm. You might have to be a special project. And I do not like special projects."

Cynthia looked helpless.

"Rolf Luger," he continued, scanning down the list. "Not bad . . . not bad at all. We'll see what we can do."

Rolf suddenly looked very serious and grunted through his stretches.

"Max McDaniels?" M. Renard inquired, raising his eyebrows and scanning the room for Max, who raised his hand. M. Renard walked over, looking him up and down with a stoic expression. "Your ratings are unusual—*most* unusual. Are you aware that a ninety-five has *never* been recorded?"

"Nigel said something about it," said Max, ignoring the glances from his classmates.

"Are you lazy?" asked the instructor, looking down his nose.

"I don't think so."

"We shall see," mused M. Renard, turning on his heel. It was a punishing hour of exercises and stretches. Cynthia had been reduced to tears; M. Renard simply stepped over Omar's inert body when he assumed the fetal position during sit-ups. When M. Renard finally announced that class was finished, the students rushed off to shower and breakfast before their first academic classes.

Clutching a slice of buttered toast, Max ran up Maggie's steep stone steps as fast as his tired legs would allow. His school uniform felt hot and stifling. Other students disappeared quickly down hallways; doors began closing.

This classroom was smaller and cozier than the Manse's basement gymnasium, its desks and chairs raised in a small amphitheater to look down on the instructor's desk and blackboard. Old prints, tapestries, and rich paintings of landscapes and famous battles hung on the paneled walls. The room smelled strongly of tobacco, while warm saltwater breezes slipped through the open windows facing the sea. An old, roly-poly man sat low in a cracked leather chair near the blackboard, puffing on a meerschaum pipe, and nodding as they entered. As they took their seats, he grumbled in a low baritone.

"No familiar faces here. Good. I think I must be in the right place. Welcome to Humanities for First Year Apprentices. I'm Byron Morrow. I'll be your instructor."

Lucia coughed and raised her hand.

"Mr. Morrow? Will you be smoking a pipe every day?"

"Yes, I will, young lady," he grumbled, raising an eyebrow. "Is that all right with you?"

"I am allergic to smoke."

"Heaven help you in Mystics!" he exclaimed. He chuckled and waved his hand, causing the pipe smoke to abruptly stream down and snake a wispy path along the floor until it disappeared up and out the window. "Better?" he grunted.

Lucia nodded with wide eyes.

Throughout the period, Mr. Morrow enchanted Max and his classmates with an overview of the course delivered in his rolling baritone. At times, Mr. Morrow would waddle around his desk in sudden fits of passion; during others he would lean back in his chair to answer students' questions between long puffs on his pipe. They would be learning a combination of history, literature, writing, and myth. It would be a challenging course, he promised, but those needing extra help could always find him at his small white cottage beyond the Sanctuary dunes.

Mathematics and Science were straightforward and more familiar, if daunting. Math was spent taking a diagnostic test to gauge their proficiency. Max turned it in after only ten minutes; many problems had symbols he had never even seen before.

Science was hardly an improvement, as they were assigned a lengthy chapter in their text and strongly encouraged to know the earth's major ecosystems by the next class.

Taking a breather before Languages, Max leaned on Maggie's railing and watched the white-capped swells out on the ocean. In daylight, the *Kestrel* looked antique and charming—hardly the seesawing terror from which they had fled early Sunday morning. Someone tapped him on the shoulder. He turned to see Julie Teller, grinning and holding a flimsy photo between her fingers.

"Hey, you," she said with a laugh, "want to see your photo? I should win a Pulitzer!"

"Oh. Hi," said Max, standing up very straight, aspiring to her height. "Sure."

She handed him an eight-by-ten black-and-white photograph that showed a shirtless Max leaping high off the ground away from the selkies. His expression was one of sheer terror, his limbs shooting in four different directions. In the photo, Helga had turned her head to look at him; Frigga was still oblivious as she basked in the sun.

"Oh my God," Max moaned, handing it back to her. "It's worse than I thought. Are you sure you need to use it?"

"It's not so bad," tittered Julie, giving the photo another look. "It's cute!"

"It is *not* cute," muttered Max, blushing. "I won't live it down all year. . . ."

"Oh, stop it," she said, smiling. "How're your classes?"

"They're okay—I don't know how I'm going to do all the homework. . . . I like Mr. Morrow, though."

"He's the best," she gushed. "Some of us still go visit him out at his house. I think he gets lonely sometimes."

Max nodded, racking his brain for something—anything—to prolong the conversation.

"Well, anyway," said Julie, hoisting up her bag, "I've got Devices—first time, and I heard Vincenti's a killer. Gotta run!"

With a wave, Julie jogged down a path toward the woods, her shiny auburn hair swishing back and forth. Max watched her go, until Connor stuck his head out Maggie's double doors.

"Who was she? She's a stunner," Connor said as Max followed him inside and up the stairs.

"She's a Third Year," Max replied, wary of Connor's tone. "I met her in the Sanctuary. . . . She took my picture for the newspaper."

"Think she likes you?" asked Connor, sounding impressed.

"No." Max flushed. "She liked the photo opportunity."

The rest of their Languages class was already seated when Max and Connor entered. The room looked like a concert hall in miniature, its polished walls and roof designed for optimum acoustics. At the front of the room was a very large woman with curly black hair who wore a cheery sundress and an unusual coppery necklace. Once Max and Connor took their seats, she handed out printed sheets and delicate chrome headsets that blinked with bright green lights. Returning to the blackboard, she wrote:

Welcome to Languages.
My name is Celia Babel.

She turned and beamed at them, then motioned for Connor to introduce himself. He did so, followed by the others. Next she motioned for them to read their handouts. Puzzled that the woman had not yet spoken a word, Max read a passage that was printed in several different languages.

Please pick up the headset on your desk. It is a translator and it is already turned on. On the screen labeled AUDIBLE, use the arrows and scroll to Greek. On the screen labeled SUB, please scroll to your native language and put on the headset. Further instructions will follow.

Mrs. Babel waited patiently for the class to follow the instructions before she spoke for the first time. Her voice was high-pitched and a bit nasal, and the words were completely foreign—unfamiliar and spoken with a strange rhythm. Yet, to his utter shock, Max found he could understand them.

"Hello, students," the instructor said. "I'm pleased to have you in my Languages class. At the moment, you are hearing the Greek language—a language with which all of you are unfamiliar. You are *simultaneously* hearing, in your subconscious brain, these words and phrases translated into your native tongue. How many of you have difficulty understanding English?"

Max saw over a dozen hands rise high into the air. Mrs. Babel smiled at them.

"You may keep these devices for use in your other classes. Your English will improve very quickly as your brain begins to correlate it with your native language."

Everyone laughed as a Portuguese girl cheered gratefully.

"Regardless of what language we are speaking," Mrs. Babel continued, "it's a good idea to have these devices handy when speaking with me. Please shut them off and I'll demonstrate why."

Mrs. Babel removed her coppery necklace as Max flicked off his device's switch. He was suddenly assailed by a bewildering cacophony of voices. Mrs. Babel was evidently speaking—her mouth was moving—but the sound that issued forth was an unintelligible mixture of words, shrieks, grunts, and clicks. She shrugged her shoulders with a helpless smile and replaced her necklace, inviting them to don their devices once more.

"Years ago, I was stationed at a field office in Ghana. One of our informants accused me of double talk and cursed me to speak all languages simultaneously. Mr. Vincenti had this necklace developed for me as a project for the Sixth Years—it filters all the languages I'm speaking down to Greek. A bit limiting for a language teacher, but a minor inconvenience in the big scheme of things."

Sarah Amankwe raised her hand.

"I don't want to be rude," she said, "but if this device can help us to learn any language, why do we need a language class?"

"That would certainly help you to understand the spoken language and eventually speak it yourself," replied the instructor. "You'll see many older students around campus doing just that. It would not, however, help you read or write that language, to say nothing of absorbing the culture's traditions or way of life. Understanding a person's words and understanding the person is not always the same thing. In this class, we strive for cultural immersion. . . ."

The rest of the class was spent on the Greek alphabet. As Mrs. Babel spoke, labeled pictures of the Greek landscape, mythic figures, leaders, and philosophers appeared on the walls and ceiling. Max worked hard to keep up, scribbling the strange symbols in his notebook as quickly as he could.

After Languages, Max's section of First Years grabbed sandwiches and fruit from the dining hall and sat outside near their Class Tree. Hannah and her brood waddled by.

Max collapsed onto the grass, his exhaustion washing over him. He listened to the others' conversations as the sun warmed his face. But it wasn't long before a familiar voice broke in.

"Hey! It's the tadpoles!"

Max cracked an eye as Alex, Sasha, and Anna wandered over with some other Second Years.

"Hmmm," said Alex, coming to a sudden halt and sniffing the air. "Why would tadpoles smell like horse manure?"

"I dunno. But it sure does stink!" said Sasha, waving a hand under his nose.

Connor held his nose and squinted up at the older students. "We stink because we cleaned the stables. What's *your* excuse, Muñoz?" replied Connor. Almost everyone laughed, including some of the Second Years. Alex simply smiled grimly and nodded his head, moving closer to Connor.

"You know," said Sarah, rising angrily and stabbing a finger at Alex, "that wasn't funny the other night. I can't swim. Someone could have hit their head and drowned. Whatever was in the water could have hurt us!"

Alex clapped his hands to his cheeks and turned to the others, imitating Sarah. Anna laughed, but some of the Second Years fidgeted uncomfortably and looked away.

"Ignore them, Sarah," muttered Jesse, stacking paper plates and brushing crumbs off his legs. Suddenly, his soda toppled over. Jesse leapt to his feet, a large wet stain spreading across his navy pants.

Alex doubled up with laughter.

"Hey, check it out—he wet his pants!" the older boy shouted.

Jesse reddened. "You *made* that cup fall over."

"Sure. You wet your pants and try and blame someone else. Nice!" exclaimed Alex sarcastically, turning to the others.

Jesse suddenly stepped forward to push Alex. Alex laughed incredulously and stepped to the side, locking one of Jesse's arms straight and tossing him hard to the ground.

Max sat up completely as there were several shouts of protest. Jesse lay curled up on the grass, holding his elbow. Connor jumped to his feet.

"You're a bloody jerk, Muñoz!"

Connor launched himself at Alex to grab hold of his shirt. Again, Alex stepped to the side. He punched Connor hard below the sternum. Connor dropped to one knee and doubled over.

"C'mon, Lynch," said Alex with a laugh, rocking on the balls of his feet. "Don't you have a witty comeback? Let's hear it, or can't you talk?"

Anna started to giggle. Lucia reached out to touch Connor's shoulder, but he brushed her hand away and stared at the grass. Rolf stood up and stepped over to Alex, who was relaxed and grinning.

"Why don't you leave us alone?" Rolf said. "What do you think you're proving?"

"He's right, Alex," said one of the Second Year girls. "What *do* you think you're proving?"

"Me? I'm just welcoming the tadpoles to Rowan! You tadpoles are taking it all wrong. C'mon and shake my hand." Alex grinned maliciously and stepped forward to extend his hand to Rolf, who looked suddenly uneasy.

Max stepped in front of Rolf and swatted Alex's hand aside.

"Leave us alone," Max said.

For a moment, Alex looked shocked; he glanced at Sasha, who merely laughed and shook his head.

"Are you kidding me?" scoffed Alex.

Max ignored Alex's words as the older boy ridiculed him. He watched his hands instead. Max had learned that bullies always had a great deal to say before they ever did anything, and he suspected that Alex was no different.

Max was right. When the boy's hands moved up to push him, Max threw a hard, straight jab that smacked square into Alex's cheek. The punch landed so fast and hard that Alex merely blinked in shock and took a tottering step backward.

"Whoa," cried Connor, sitting up, as other students ran over at the commotion.

Someone yelled behind Max.

Max realized he'd made a mistake even before he had turned. He felt a flash of pain in his eye as Alex punched him hard from the side. The two fell onto the ground in a rolling tangle of curses and punches and groans.

Just as Max gained the upper hand, something immensely strong took hold of him, and he was pulled firmly up and away. Several Second Years hurried in to restrain Alex. As Alex screamed to be let go, Max whirled around to see who had hold of him.

It was Bob.

There was a stern, sad expression on the ogre's sunken features as he towered over Max. Setting Max's feet back on the ground, he stepped in between the two combatants. "No fighting," rumbled Bob, wagging a giant finger. "Only first day of school!"

Alex pressed his torn shirt to his bleeding mouth. With a furious scowl, he brushed off Sasha.

"We can handle it ourselves," hissed Alex. "Get back in the kitchen, you oaf!"

"Alex!" one of the Second Years warned. "Watch it!"

"Whatever." Alex seethed, fixing Max with a furious stare before composing his features into a crooked, bloody smile. "I can't even tell you how sorry you're going to be."

Still grinning, Alex spat, turned, and walked back into the Manse with Sasha and Anna trailing behind. Max put his hand over his throbbing eye. Bob sighed and motioned for Max to follow, leading him into the kitchen, where he scooped a handful of ice into a large yellow dishtowel.

"Come in, come in," intoned Mr. Watanabe as the class arrived on the second floor of Old Tom for Strategy. The instructor was a trim Japanese man in his fifties. He strolled around the room's large tables as the students took their seats. When he reached Max, he stopped.

"What happened to you?"

"Oh," said Max hastily. "Nothing. I fell and hurt my eye."

Mr. Watanabe raised a skeptical eyebrow and continued, glancing at Max's knuckles and those of his classmates.

"Welcome to your first year of Strategy and Tactics." He bowed to the class. "My name is Omi Watanabe, and I will be your instructor. So who can define strategy for me? Let's discuss what it means to think 'strategically.'"

Max tried to listen to Sarah's response, but it was hard. His eye hurt and he was still angry from the fight. Several times, Mr. Watanabe singled him out to make sure he was paying attention. By the end of class, all he could remember was that the course would be divided into Strategy and Tactics. Max thought Strategy sounded boring—lots of principles and dry theories. Tactics assignments would be taken from the *Rowan Compendium of Known Enemies, Volume One* and sounded much more interesting.

As anxious as he was for the end of class, Max knew he wasn't the only one to feel that way. Their section had Mystics next, and everyone seemed eager to see what it was all about. When the chimes finally sounded, the students hurried out in a chorus of excited chatter.

"I think Mystics will be my favorite," commented Lucia. "I put out my fire in under a minute. The Recruiter said it was very good."

Max nodded, impressed, while David gazed out a window on the stairwell, his backpack slung loosely over his shoulder. He began coughing as everyone clambered up to the second floor. Max put a hand on his shoulder.

"You okay?"

"Yeah," wheezed David, wiping his nose with a tissue. "Just taking it all in. Lots of stuff, you know."

"No kidding," muttered Max, floored by the accumulating homework. "I guess we'll watch Lucia extinguish fires all period. She did it twice as fast as I did. How long did it take you?"

"I'm not sure," said David. "I don't remember."

"What do you mean, you don't remember? How can you forget something like that?"

"My memory's pretty bad sometimes. It's got holes in it, I guess," said David, walking on ahead. Max was following when he heard someone call his name. He turned to see Jason Barrett bounding up the stairs.

"Hey, bud," he called. "I heard about your—whoa! That's a serious shiner!"

The Sixth Year boy stopped dead in his tracks to examine Max's eye.

"Yeah, I shouldn't have turned my back on him," said Max, feeling his ears burn. "I was stupid."

Jason dismissed the comment with a wave of his hand.

"Whatever," he said. "That shiner's a badge of honor! Heard you gave Muñoz a whupping that he had coming! Everyone's heard, I think!"

Max was mortified; the same thing had happened at his last school after several bullies began teasing him after his mother's disappearance. Max had beaten them badly and had nearly been expelled. He studied the white scars that dotted his small, hard knuckles.

"Can you please not talk about it?" he asked quietly.

"What?" said Jason, his smile disappearing. "Really?"

"Yeah."

"All right, but do you want me to say something to Muñoz? It's not fair for him to be picking on First Years. He's had a whole year of training, and you guys just got here."

"No—it's okay," said Max. "I can handle it."

Jason took a step back and looked hard at Max.

"My kind of guy." He grinned again, continuing up the stairs. "Keep ice on it!"

Max waved good-bye and poked his head into a classroom that made him forget all about his fight and Alex Muñoz.

Hazel Boon stood in the middle of what appeared to be a large forest. She spoke to a silver-haired woman wearing a gray shawl while Max's classmates wandered wide-eyed among the towering trees, exchanging whispers.

Looking closer, Max discovered that the room was not in fact a forest; its floor was of gray-green hardwood polished to a gleaming finish. With the exception of the doorway, each of the room's eight walls was set with a carved stone fireplace. A number of large live trees were embedded in the floor at random intervals, their branches rising high toward a pitched ceiling supported by many beams. The walls were of the same gray-green wood as the floor and inlaid with a variety of silver markings and symbols.

Miss Boon caught Max lingering near the doorway and beckoned him farther in with an impatient gesture. Max joined his classmates as they took seats in wooden chairs on an enormous Persian rug at the room's center.

"All right, students," said Miss Boon, "before we begin, I want to introduce a very special guest. This is Annika Kraken, Chair of the Mystics Department."

The old woman smiled kindly at the students and gave a polite bow as the children murmured hello.

"Instructor Kraken teaches only the Fifth and Sixth Years," continued Miss Boon. "She will be joining us from time to time, however, and will receive your utmost respect and attention when she is here."

"You're in good hands, children," uttered Instructor Kraken, nodding at the younger woman. "Miss Boon is one of the very best we've had in all my time."

She said farewell and moved slowly to the door, closing it quietly behind her. Miss Boon cleared her throat and began pacing around the room.

"When each of you completed the Standard Series of Tests for Potentials, you demonstrated a capacity for Mystics. Mystics can take many forms, but at its heart, it is the ability to channel and manipulate energy.

"Understand that Mystics is a highly individual discipline. No two among us are the same when it comes to our raw talents and our ability to access them. There are some Mystics who are able to draw upon tremendous stores of energy but inevitably waste much as they strive to harness and shape it. Conversely, there are some with considerably less 'horsepower' but who are able to utilize every last little bit. You will find that some branches of Mystics come naturally, while others are inaccessible to you. As your instructor, my goal is to help you understand your natural abilities and maximize your individual talents. Are there any questions?"

Lucia raised her hand.

"How do we know how much 'horsepower' we have?" she asked.

Miss Boon pinched her chin and nodded at the question.

"The Potentials test is one measure, but my research suggests it's an imperfect one. Some who score well on that test turn out to be hopeless Mystics."

Lucia looked hurt.

Connor raised his hand.

"Do we use wands or staves and stuff?" he asked.

Miss Boon smiled and shook her head.

"No, such tools are not necessary and can actually be dangerous," she explained. "What's more, they can only be made with Old Magic, and the greater ones are very, very rare. The temptations they offer are not healthy—most have been accounted for and destroyed."

With a sudden flick of her wrist, Miss Boon ignited a lone torch on a far wall. Smoke from the torch streamed rapidly across the room and swirled about her hands as she spoke.

"No, Connor, the Mystic's tools are their hands and the power of language. These are all that you will need to summon and shape the energies around you. This year, you will be learning the basic commands so that they become second nature."

"Would you look at that?" breathed Connor, staring at a dark, churning copy of himself that the instructor had fashioned.

Max was speechless as the smoky figure waved good-bye to the class and walked into the nearest fireplace, disappearing up the chimney. With a dismissive flick of her wrist, Miss Boon extinguished the lit torch.

"To get you started on that path," she said, eyeing them as they sat riveted, "I'd like you to form two single-file lines."

Max quickly took a place in line.

"All right," Miss Boon said with a clap, stepping around to the front. "Each of you has extinguished a fire before—it's one of the reasons you are here. Today, you're going to do just the opposite: you're going to kindle a fire in one of these hearths. This will demonstrate that as a living conduit you can both absorb and channel energy. While we do this, I will be the only person talking. If anybody speaks, laughs, or causes any kind of distraction, he or she will be asked to leave. Understood?"

They nodded. The room became silent.

"Okay," Miss Boon continued, "I'd like the first person in each line to step forward and face the fireplace in front of them."

Two girls stepped forward.

"Spread your feet slightly apart and breathe deeply. Try to relax. I want you to take a moment and listen to the beating of your heart, feel its energy. Now I want you to feel the energy in this room, the atoms and molecules buzzing in the air. Close your eyes and picture the logs in the hearth beginning to smoke; imagine the smoke coming faster and faster until suddenly the wood ignites. Now, keep your right hand at your side and spread your fingers with the palm facing forward. Good. When I give the word, I want you to raise your arm and make a tight fist. Do you understand?"

The girls nodded, their eyes tightly closed.

"Now," said Miss Boon, in an even tone of voice.

Both girls raised their hands and closed their fingers. Almost at once, both fireplaces began to smoke.

"Keep concentrating," intoned Miss Boon. "Drop your arms and repeat the motion."

The second time, one hearth showed a low flicker of bright purple flames, triggering a few exclamations from the class that Miss Boon silenced with a glance. A few wispy trickles of smoke appeared in the other hearth, but no flame.

"That's enough, you two," she said. "Well done. Please step to the back of the line."

With a quick wave of her hand, both hearths looked dark and cold. Her next command was brisk.

"Next pair."

Despite three long attempts, Rolf and Sarah failed to ignite anything. Rolf looked furious, but as other pairs went, Max saw that the task was not so easy. Only two students had been able to conjure small, sputtering flames by the time it was David and Lucia's turn.

David patiently closed his eyes as Miss Boon guided them through the process. She signaled for them to begin.

There was a flash of light, followed by an explosion.

Max found himself thrown backward, lying on the ground, shielding his eyes from the torrents of green and gold fire that roared from David's fireplace. Burning logs and embers smoldered on the floor, blasted clear from the hearth. The nearest edge of the Persian rug began to smoke.

David was the only student standing; the rest shrieked and scurried away as more sheets of green flame spilled out of the fireplace and swept above the mantel to singe the paneled wall above. Miss Boon's voice rose above the fire's roar.

"Stay down."

Miss Boon strode forward and muttered a sharp word of command coupled with a decisive sweep of her arm.

The fire did not subside.

Narrowing her eyes, the instructor repeated her command.

Max exhaled as the fire began to dim. It gathered reluctantly into small pools of green flames before winking out entirely. The stern expression on Miss Boon's face softened.

"Is anyone hurt?"

Max and the others murmured "No" as they pushed up from the floor. The floor and walls surrounding David's fireplace were badly charred and smoking.

"If no one is hurt, please re-form your lines."

David coughed and opened his eyes, looking curiously behind him where the students were slowly reassembling. Ignoring Max's stare, David merely walked to the end of the line. Miss Boon stepped back to her position, as though nothing unusual had happened. In a terse voice, she muttered, "Next, McDaniels and Boudreaux."

Max found it difficult to concentrate as Miss Boon led them through the steps. Although he tried to focus on his hearth, his mind kept returning to David's disturbing display. After several minutes, exhausted from the effort, he opened his eyes. His

hearth was smoking mightily, but no flame flickered within it. It was no different for the girl next to him or anyone else that followed.

When the last pair had finished, Miss Boon bade them take their seats. Lucia spoke first.

"Miss Boon?" she asked, uncharacteristically tentative. "What happened? What happened on David's turn?"

"He kindled a flame as instructed," was the flat reply.

"Yes, but, um, why did it *explode*?"

"Apparently he has lots of 'horsepower,' Miss Cavallo."

After class, Max waited in the stairwell while David remained behind with Miss Boon. The windows in the hallway hummed as Old Tom chimed four o'clock and Max saw Ms. Richter climbing the stairs. She turned to him as she approached the Mystics classroom.

"Why aren't you in Etiquette, Mr. McDaniels?" asked the Director.

"Oh. I'm waiting for David Menlo. He should be out any second."

"He will not be," Ms. Richter replied, opening the door. "Go on to class, Max. Tell Sir Wesley that David will be arriving late. Oh, and be sure to get more ice for that eye."

Max stammered a good-bye; he had almost forgotten that his eye was swollen and bruised. He clambered up the stairs to the room for Etiquette. As soon as he entered, he heard a voice exclaim, "No, no, not at all. Did everybody see that?"

Max stopped and saw a tall, tanned man with a shock of white hair and a cleft chin in a cream-colored suit. The man was

flanked by Max's classmates, and his bright blue eyes were studying him intently.

"Is this David or Max?" asked Sir Alistair Wesley, suddenly
plucking a silk pocket square from his breast pocket and polish-
ing his glasses.

"Uh, Max, sir," he said. "Uh, David will be late—Ms. Richter
told me to tell you."

"Uh, I see," said Sir Wesley, conspicuously emphasizing the
"uh" and refolding the pocket square. "As you are late and as your
entrance is an example of everything *not to do,* we shall use you as
an example. Please step back into the hallway."

Max hesitated before retreating several steps.

"Please reenter the room."

Max took several halting steps. Connor looked ready to
burst.

"There!" exclaimed Sir Wesley. "Slumped shoulders, shifty
gaze, shuffling feet. Hardly a projection of confidence, good
breeding, or manners."

The rest of the class giggled; Max was incredulous.

"We'll try it again," said Sir Wesley. "This time, Mr. Mc-
Daniels, I would like you to stand straight, lift up your chin, and
stride confidently into the room. As you enter, I'd like you to give
Sarah here a warm smile and walk over to make her acquaintance."

"But I *already* know Sarah," Max muttered, his face burning.

"Yes, I know you do. I want you to pretend that you do not.
Sarah, I want you to pretend that you do not notice the rather
prominent black eye exhibited by Mr. McDaniels."

Max bit his tongue and backtracked into the hall. When

called, he stood up straight and walked back into the room. He saw Sarah and tried to concentrate on her, but it was difficult with Sir Wesley's running commentary.

"Good! No! No! Shoulders back—there, that's it. Chin up! Don't look so serious; you're making a lovely young lady's acquaintance, not battling gas!"

The class burst into laughter and Max abandoned his effort.

"All right, Mr. McDaniels, we'll consider you a work in progress," Sir Wesley said wearily, turning from Max to address the others. "Now, I know that today young people fancy themselves perpetually moody and angst-ridden, but let's *pretend* we're not, shall we? Any more volunteers for *Scenario One: Winning Entry into an Occupied Room?*"

Connor's hand shot in the air.

"All right, Mr. Lynch. Have a go."

Connor disappeared out into the hall. When called, he sauntered in, pausing to lean against the doorway and raise an eyebrow as he surveyed the group with a rakish smirk. Pretending to catch an initial glimpse of Sarah, he strode toward her with slow majesty. Sarah burst into giggles; Omar buried his face in his hands. Stopping several feet away, Connor gave a low bow and raised his head to flash two rows of gleaming teeth.

"Connor Lynch at your service."

"Bravo!" roared Sir Wesley, clapping with sincere enthusiasm.

Everyone else groaned in disgust.

Max could not wait to escape from Etiquette; it had leapfrogged Mathematics as his least favorite class. He was first out the door and jogging down the stairs toward the athletic fields for Games as Old Tom chimed. M. Renard was waiting, impatient as ever as he directed them to separate facilities where they could change. When they emerged from the lockers, their instructor was bouncing a soccer ball on his foot. He motioned them over.

"First day of classes. The piggies are tired, I know. We end the day as we begin: a little hop, skip, and jump, eh? All of you know football? 'Soccer'?" He scanned the faces as the children nodded; Max noticed David was still absent.

"Good game for the legs. Builds speed, stamina, and body control. Apprentices play lots of football at Rowan, but here you will find the conditions slightly different. Here at Rowan, we play Euclidean soccer."

"What's different?" asked Rolf.

"You will see as you play," M. Renard said, allowing a little smile. "You and Sarah will pick teams. Quick, quick."

Max was chosen first by Sarah despite warning her that he had never played organized soccer. As the game started, Sarah whizzed past Jesse with the ball, passing it deftly to another girl, who ran alongside her. Rolf crashed in and stole the ball, eluding Max and kicking a long pass downfield to Connor, who fired a hard shot toward the goal. Playing goalkeeper, Cynthia tipped the ball straight up into the air and caught it short of the net.

"Nice save!" cheered Omar from midfield.

Suddenly, the ground began to shift and bubble. Small hills and depressions started to form on the field; entire sections rose or lowered several feet to form ridges and plateaus. The children stopped and shot M. Renard a frightened look.

"It is all right," he assured them from the sideline. "Keep playing!"

The game ended in a 0–0 tie. Rolf's team would have scored

if a sizable mound, rising like a sudden blister, had not deflected the ball to the side just as Rolf split two defenders and aimed a shot. M. Renard blew a whistle, and the field promptly settled to a flat plane.

"That game is impossible," complained Rolf, dribbling the ball to the sideline. "We should have won."

"You will have to struggle, adjust, and adapt," M. Renard said, shrugging. "That is the entire point. You played the game today on its lowest setting. Come see the older students play on a weekend; you will not think you have it so hard."

Back in the locker room, cupping cold water over his eye, Max's spirits fell at the thought of all he had to do that evening. He had to feed Nick, study the Greek alphabet, draw a land map of Europe, and practice kindling small blazes in his hearth. His eye throbbed. Trudging toward the Manse, all he wanted was to crawl into bed, gaze at the constellations, and sleep for a week.

~ 9 ~

A GOLDEN APPLE
IN THE ORCHARD

Ten letters lay in a little pile on Max's bed. They were from his father, and Max had read them several times. It was a late weekend morning in early October, and Max had been at Rowan over five weeks.

Things at home sounded busy. Mr. McDaniels was traveling frequently on business, determined that his efforts would convince Mr. Lukens to assign him more accounts. Max was preparing to write a letter back when David came into the room, closing the door quietly behind him.

"Hey," he muttered, flopping onto his bed across the way and kicking his shoes off.

"How was it?" asked Max without looking up.

"Stunk. Miss Kraken yelled at me for not paying enough attention. Ms. Richter came in and watched for the last half. She never says anything, she just watches. It's annoying."

After the first day, David had been removed from their Mystics class and was taking private lessons every day from Miss Kraken. The damage he had inflicted on the classroom had been repaired immediately.

"Are you excited to go into town?" Max asked, beginning his letter. What he really wanted to know were further details of David's lessons in Mystics, but David never shared them.

"Yeah, I guess," came David's reply, muffled by the pillow he had pulled over his face.

Max frowned as he wrote to his father; there were so many fascinating things about the new school and so little he could actually share. Practical considerations limited his letters to chronicling his academic struggles and assuring his father he was making new friends. Max made no mention of vegetarian ogres or talking geese.

Mr. Vincenti, Miss Boon, and the other advisors were already waiting for the First Years by the fountain when Max and David walked out the Manse's front door. Most students had abandoned their school uniforms in favor of blue jeans. Mr. Vincenti spoke up as they set out for the campus gate and the world outside.

"Ha! Exciting stuff—first trip to town and a beautiful fall day to enjoy it! Did everyone bring some spending money and an appetite?"

"Yes!" screamed the group, causing him to cover his ears and chuckle.

"Good. Now listen up—we have reservations for dinner at the Grove at seven, and the food is excellent so don't fill up on sweets! Make a point to introduce yourselves to the residents and shopkeepers. They're well aware of what Rowan's all about—in fact, many are former students or family of the faculty. Be on your best behavior and make Sir Wesley proud, eh?"

The students cheered and Max hurried along with them as they crossed the lawns and entered the forest, which was ablaze with the brilliant colors of autumn. The breeze off the ocean was crisp, and Max rejoiced in the unprecedented sum of money in his pocket—his hoarded allowances for the past two months. He chatted with Rolf and Lucia as they walked the scenic, meandering mile to the gate.

As the great gate closed behind them, Max and Connor dashed away with the others, arriving a few hundred yards later at the long stretch of quaint shops and businesses radiating from the village green. Older students milled about, ducking in and out of the nearby pizza parlor, café, and bookstore.

"Where to?" asked Connor, hopping up and down and looking in all directions.

"Let's wait for David," said Max, peering back down the road, where his roommate looked to be getting an earful from Miss Boon. Finally, David nodded and hurried toward them up the road, arriving in an annoyed fit of coughing.

"What was that all about?" asked Connor.

"Oh, nothing special. She wants me to 'be careful'—she's been on my case ever since Miss Kraken started teaching me Mystics. I don't think she likes it."

"Why would she care?" asked Max.

"She's really young," said David. "She's only, like, twenty-five. I think she's worried Miss Kraken doesn't have confidence in her."

"Kraken thinks you're going to blow up Boonie!" said Connor with a laugh.

David started walking toward a patisserie, coughing hard into his jacket sleeve. As they got closer, they heard a chorus of excited voices. A few steps later, Max understood why.

In the window, Max saw a marvelous seascape crafted entirely of sweets. There were sand castles of white chocolate, thick beds of licorice anemones, and brilliantly colored fish and sea creatures made of taffy, hard candies, and peppermints.

"Come in! Come in!" said a friendly voice from inside.

A stout man with a black beard and rosy cheeks was methodically braiding strands of bread dough. He stopped to greet them at the counter, wiping his hands on his apron.

"You must be First Years. I'm Charlie Babel—I believe my wife is your Languages teacher."

Ten minutes later, having settled on some wedges of toffee and a handful of chocolate sand dollars, the three peered into the windows of a café and saw a number of older students having coffee and pastries inside. Jason Barrett was in a corner, flirting with a very pretty Fifth Year whom Max had once seen him kissing behind Old Tom. Jason saw them staring and waved them inside.

In one swift motion, Connor mooned them.

"Hope you brought your runners!" he yelled, pressing his bare bottom against the window a second time before dashing after Max and David.

They ran for two blocks, finally coming to a sudden stop, where they gasped for breath and plundered Max's sweets. David looked reborn; his cheeks flushed pink, and Max thought it was the first time he had ever seen David so happy.

Glancing at the store window behind them, Max spied a small set of paints on display. It occurred to him that it had been some time since he'd had the chance to really draw or paint like he used to with his mother. He squinted at the price. They were expensive, but they were very nice; they looked like something a real artist would use.

"We better go hide somewhere," laughed David, rubbing his hands and glancing back up the street.

"Yeah," said Connor, looking about. "I don't want my bum picked out of a lineup. They could do it, too—they got two good looks at it!"

Connor and David dissolved into giggles again while Max tapped his finger thoughtfully against the store window, studying the set's clean little tubes of color.

"Hey, I'm going in here," said Max. "I'll catch up."

When the shopkeeper set the paints before him, Max began counting out his money almost immediately. The set had more colors than he'd ever used, and even its box was fancy with its delicate brass hinge. He sorted his bills and change on the counter but was two dollars short. The woman smiled and took his money, sliding the set into a small bag.

"I can spare two dollars for a young man who wants them that badly. You go enjoy them—maybe bring me something that you paint!"

"I will," said Max, beaming as she pushed the bag into his hands.

The trees were casting long shadows as Max, carrying his bags of sweets and paints, strolled toward the theater. Just as he passed Luigi's, the pizza parlor, he heard a voice call out behind him. Alex had emerged from Luigi's, trailed by Sasha and Anna.

"Hey, Max," Alex called out in a friendly voice. "How you doing?"

Max said nothing and watched them.

"What's the matter?" said Alex, walking toward him. "What do you have to worry about after you ran and cried to Jason Barrett?"

"I didn't tell Jason anything," Max said, glowering, switching the bags from his right to his left hand.

"Sure you didn't," Alex said sarcastically. "Just remember, Max. Jason graduates this year and I won't forget."

Alex walked past him and swatted Max's bags onto the street. The chocolates and toffees spilled out onto the pavement, but those weren't what concerned him. The case for his paints had broken and the little tubes of paint littered the sidewalk.

"Hey, I *wanted* that candy!" moaned Sasha, trotting after Alex.

Max bent to gather his things when Anna walked slowly toward him, a thin smile on her face.

"You know, that was a nice picture in the paper. You should have heard us laughing. I thought Julie Teller was going to pass out!"

Her pretty features twisted into a tight little smirk as she walked methodically over the candy and paints, grinding them with her heel. Max's heart sank as he looked at the resulting smears. Anna gave a satisfied smile and rejoined Alex and Sasha, who howled with laughter as the three continued down the sidewalk.

Max watched them go and began to shake with rage. It took all his control to smother a predatory urge that rose up within him. He could not go after them; Mr. Vincenti had threatened grave consequences for Max if he got into another fight.

He tried to clean up the mess, using the broken case to scoop up the crushed candies and splattered tubes of paint and throwing it all into a nearby wastebasket. Storming off to the theater, he had walked several blocks when he heard voices call out from above.

"Hey, Max! Up here."

He stopped near a bench at the entrance to the green. Connor and David were grinning at him from up in the branches of a gnarled tree. Connor's mouth was smeared with chocolate.

"There're lots of names and initials carved up here," said David excitedly. "I think I found one by Mr. Morrow. It says 'Byron loves Elaine '46.'"

"I can't picture old Byron as a kid," mused Connor. "Imagine a wrinkly kid with a pipe snogging in this tree a hundred years ago."

Max laughed, happy to resume the good time he had been having. With a quick step, he caught a branch and hoisted himself up to join them.

"Hey, can I try one of those sand dollars you bought?" asked David, tracing the carved lines of a limerick with his finger.

"Oh, I dropped mine on the street and they got smooshed," Max said quickly. "I threw them out."

"You should have kept them!" moaned Connor. "We could

have used them for an Etiquette scenario!" His imitation of Sir Wesley's voice was perfect. *"Scenario Number Twenty: Salvaging the Mangled Sweets of the World."*

"They're in the garbage can at the corner if you want them," sighed Max. Connor seemed to think it over a moment before letting the matter drop.

They spent the next two hours exploring the village green, climbing a bronze statue of a man on horseback and perusing the names on the granite headstones in a small cemetery. It was getting dark when they finally ran back along the cobblestones, weaving their way through old-fashioned streetlamps and converging with other First Years at the foot of the high hill.

The Grove was a sprawling, well-appointed house whose lower floor had been converted to several large dining rooms. Max followed Mr. Vincenti and a hostess down a hallway lined with maps of early New England and frayed etchings of whaling scenes. Max's section of First Years was seated in a candlelit dining room whose table was decorated with Indian corn and short sheaves of wheat bound with copper wire. Mr. Vincenti rearranged the seating to alternate the boys and girls. Max found himself sitting between Sarah and Miss Boon.

Mr. Vincenti took his seat at the head and rang his wineglass.

"I'd like to propose a little toast."

The students reached for their wineglasses filled with apple cider.

"To a month under the belts and young minds on the move!"

The glasses clinked, and even Miss Boon managed a smile as Mr. Vincenti began quizzing the group about the more memorable experiences to date.

"Any mathematicians in this bunch?"

They all tossed out David's name, except for Jesse, who offered his own.

"Who's a whiz at science?"

Sarah blushed as her name was called.

"Any budding ambassadors or diplomats among us?"

Everyone screamed, "Connor!" who received the accolade with typical bravura, wiping away fake tears.

As Mr. Vincenti continued rattling off the subjects, waiters brought steaming plates and baskets of food. Warm squares of thick cornbread, sizzling crab cakes, and plates of cod and perch drizzled with lemon were set on the table. Max nearly spit out a mouthful of sweet potatoes when Lucia and Cynthia reenacted one of Connor's many efforts to impress the older girls on campus. Even Mr. Vincenti put down his fork to laugh as Lucia swaggered about the room, sucking in her tummy and lowering her voice.

An hour into the meal, the group laughter gave way to smaller conversations; Max watched as their hostess entered the room and bent down to whisper into Mr. Vincenti's ear. Mr. Vincenti excused himself and continued their conversation in the hallway.

As soon as Mr. Vincenti left, Miss Boon turned to Max.

"You know," she said quietly, "I happened to overhear Nigel mention to Ms. Richter that the tapestry you discovered involved the Cattle Raid of Cooley?"

"Yeah," said Max, distracted. His eyes wandered back to where he could see Mr. Vincenti's very still shadow in the hallway. Something was wrong.

"Max," she said tersely. "Say 'yes.' Has Sir Wesley told you that 'yeah' is not proper English and that it's rude not to look at someone when he or she is speaking to you?"

Max flicked his eyes back toward her face.

"I'm sorry," he said.

"That's all right," she said, her voice softening. "Have you taken the time to read up on the Cattle Raid or its hero, Cúchulain?"

Max shook his head. "No, Miss Boon, I haven't had time." He reached for a piece of cornbread.

"Listen to me, Max," said Miss Boon, placing an icy hand on Max's arm. He looked directly at her, her young features so serious and strange with their mismatched eyes. "That vision was tailored to *you*. It's very important that you understand everything you can about its history and symbols. Cúchulain was a great hero and champion—people called him the Hound of Ulster for the way he guarded their kingdom, but he had to make some awful choices along the way. It would be best if you knew them, Max."

Max stared at her; his mind flashed with thoughts of his recurring dream of the monstrous wolfhound. He decided against sharing this with Miss Boon; her gaze and grip were too intense for his comfort.

Just then, Mr. Vincenti rejoined them from the hallway. His voice rose well above the many conversations.

"We have a change of plans. I need everyone to place their utensils on their plates and follow me. Quickly."

"But, Mr. Vincenti," said Connor, "you have to come see what Omar can do with his—"

"Right now, Mr. Lynch!" thundered Mr. Vincenti, who circled around the table physically hoisting the confused children from

their seats. Without a word, Miss Boon rose swiftly and started pulling the children's chairs away from the table, herding them out the door and down the hallway.

Their hostess was standing by the doorway looking frightened. "Be careful, Joseph. Be careful, Hazel," she whispered, dimming the house's lights. Other First Years hurried out from the other dining rooms, accompanied by their advisors. A dozen limousines were parked in the street, their doors open and engines running as the hostess locked the door behind them.

Max crowded into the second limousine. Mr. Vincenti slammed the back door shut, and the car raced down the street toward Rowan's gates. The street looked abandoned; all the shops and stores were dark. As they passed the church, Max thought he saw a pair of dark figures melt off its lawn to disappear behind a hedge. A few seconds later, he was thrown to the side as the limousine made a sharp turn and screeched through the gate. They wound through the trees and along the sea before coming to a jarring halt near the fountain. Max's heart froze as he heard the familiar awful wailing coming from the direction of the *Kestrel*.

Mr. Vincenti opened the door and ushered the children out as Nolan galloped from around the Manse seated astride YaYa. There was nothing old or broken about her now, Max noted. Steam billowed from the ki-rin's nostrils, her massive head craning from side to side to scan the grounds with eyes that glowed white in the darkness. And Max had never seen the normally cheery Nolan so grim. The groundskeeper shouted over the distant keening sound.

"Joseph, get the children inside. You and Hazel are to take up your assigned positions along the perimeter—Director's orders."

The Manse was a frenzy of shouts and slamming doors. Max, David, and Connor sprinted past a pair of Sixth Years who stood guard at the entrance to their hallway. The older students ordered them to lock themselves in their rooms and to be quiet. When Max and David turned to close their door, they saw Connor blocking their doorway.

"I'm coming in with you two!" he hissed. "My roommates are wankers!"

Connor hurried inside and Max shut the door, making double sure it was locked tight.

The minutes and hours ticked by at a crawl. Unable to concentrate, Max tossed his sketchbook aside as David and Connor played cards downstairs. Hearing muffled sounds from the hallway, Max got up from his bed to investigate. Connor and David stood on the stairs to the lower level, wrapped in blankets and looking frightened, as Max listened at the door. Hearing footsteps and whispers outside, Max turned to them and put his finger to his lips. Holding his breath, he silently turned the knob and peeked out into the hallway.

A small group of First and Second Years were pressed against the window at the end of the hall. Max beckoned to David and Connor, and the three of them joined the group. Rolf stepped aside to let Max peer out the window; he leaned forward to press his forehead against the cold glass.

Lanterns bobbed about the dark grounds in pairs as the faculty combed the orchard, lawns, and gardens. Away in the woods, Max saw more lanterns peeking from among the trees. He whispered to a Second Year standing next to him.

"Have you guys seen anything?"

The Second Year shook his head and motioned for quiet. Suddenly, someone at the end gasped, *"Something's happening!"*

Max was smooshed against the window as the crowd surged forward. Below, the lanterns bobbed wildly, rapidly converging at a point near the orchard's edge. A huge plume of flame erupted at the spot. Max and the other boys gave out a yell.

Something monstrous and wolf-shaped was illuminated by the sudden burst of light. It took several hunched, uneven steps on its hind legs before dropping to all fours and racing across the lawn toward the forest and the road.

"Get back in your rooms!"

Max whirled to see the two Sixth Years hurrying angrily down the hall. The boys scattered to their rooms in a sudden flurry of shuffling feet and slamming doors. Max and David ran down the steps to their bedroom's lower level. Connor flew in a moment later, locking the door behind him, his eyes wide.

"Did you guys see it? I saw it!"

"I'm not ever leaving this room," whispered David.

The three sat in silence for several minutes. Max shivered, replaying the image of the terrifying shape lowering itself to the grass and galloping across the grounds. He looked up at the sky dome, watching Scorpio twinkle into view.

"What do you think that was?" he asked softly.

"I don't know," said David, rubbing his temples. "I don't want to know."

"Maybe it was a werewolf," volunteered Connor. "Like in the movies."

"That didn't look like any werewolf I ever saw in the movies," quavered Max. "It was a lot worse. And it looked bigger. . . ."

A loud knock on the door woke Max from his sleep. Blinking, he looked around the room. Connor was asleep on one of the couches. David was huddled near the fireplace, a shapeless lump underneath his blanket. There were three more knocks, quick and decisive. Max lurched to his feet and climbed the stairs, halting at the door.

"Who is it?" he ventured, his voice slow and wary.

"It's Joseph Vincenti, Max. The danger has passed. Ms. Richter would like everyone to come to the orchard. It's chilly, so bring a jacket or a robe."

Mr. Vincenti moved down the hall, rapping on the next door. Within a few minutes, Max had woken Connor and David. The three boys shuffled sleepily with the other Apprentices out the back doors to the orchard, where the sky was a pale wash of blue in anticipation of the sunrise.

Ms. Richter stood near the first row of trees, flanked by the faculty and a dozen other adults. The hushed conversations ceased immediately as Ms. Richter's voice filled the morning air.

"Students, we have had a loss. Another golden apple graces this orchard—all too prematurely, I'm afraid."

Max watched as several older students began whispering and scanning over the faculty with worried expressions. The Director shook her head.

"No," she said. "Our loss did not occur on this campus. We lost a member of our Recruiting staff: Miss Isabelle May, whom many of you undoubtedly met during your tests for admittance here."

There was stunned silence among the students. With a solemn face, Ms. Richter continued.

"We do not, as of yet, know what happened to Miss May. Our last communication with her was one week ago, despite our best efforts to contact her since. We have been monitoring her Class Tree anxiously throughout. Mr. Morrow made the unfortunate discovery before dinner last night. Miss May's apple has turned to gold."

Several older students hugged one another. Max saw Lucia wipe tears from her eyes; he guessed that it had been Miss May who had recruited her.

Ms. Richter raised her arms for quiet.

"Shortly after we lost Isabelle, something triggered the defenses of this campus. While I apologize for actions that might have confused or frightened you, they were necessary precautions. For the first time in Rowan's history, this campus has been penetrated by agents of the Enemy."

The student body erupted in sideways looks and whispers.

"They are gone now," Ms. Richter assured them, her voice silencing the students, "and you may rest assured that all our resources will be mustered to determine exactly what has happened and what steps are necessary to ensure your safety. Until that time, no student is to leave this campus for any reason whatsoever. Failure to mind this rule will result in expulsion. Is this clear?"

Max found himself nodding and saying "Yes, Director" along with everyone else. Rubbing his arms, he realized he had forgotten to bring a jacket, and the early-morning air was unseasonably cool.

An older girl raised her hand.

"How could they be here?" she asked, her voice trembling. "Rowan is supposed to be *hidden* from the Enemy! What does this mean?"

Ms. Richter's glance was stern, her voice sharp.

"It means we have entered a time of danger."

~ 10 ~

THE COURSE

In the weeks that followed, all students had to travel in pairs, and
Rowan Township was off-limits. Faculty and older students volunteered for evening patrols and as security escorts for the
younger students. Most notable were the strange adults that had
arrived on campus. They flitted through the woods, appeared
suddenly in corridors, and stood watch throughout the campus.
The students were assured that these individuals were present for
their safety but that they were not to be approached or bothered.
Among them was one particularly alarming man with a badly
burned face. It soon became something of a dare to cross his path

at night as he walked quietly across the grounds in his black knit cap and peacoat, swinging a shuttered lantern. His name was Cooper, and Max was afraid of him.

After two tense weeks, Max was working alongside his study group in a small room off the Bacon Library. Despite recent events, the faculty had decided to keep the midterm schedule, and Max needed to score well on several of the exams. He took a handful of popcorn from Cynthia, then grumbled at his math notebook; only half of his responses matched those in the answer key.

Max yawned. It was getting late and he still had to feed Nick. As he gathered his things and zipped up his fleece, David peeked up from reading a book on the couch.

"Are you going to the Sanctuary?" he asked.

"Yeah," said Max, stretching. "Want to come?"

"Nope. I'm going to bed. You should get an escort to go with you, though."

David returned to his book. Sarah looked up suddenly.

"I'll go with you, if you want. Just let me get my coat," she said, snapping her book shut.

Lucia grinned and tossed a popcorn kernel at Cynthia, who glanced sideways from her book. Max looked at Connor, who merely raised his eyebrows.

"Uh, sure," said Max. "Thanks, Sarah."

Sarah smiled and left the room. Max turned to the others.

"What are all of you smiling about?" he asked, glancing from face to face.

"C'mon, Max," scoffed Connor. "She likes you."

"No, she doesn't," Max protested.

"Sure," giggled Cynthia. "That's why she *always* picks you in Games and sits next to you in every class. Believe me—she's not trying to copy *your* homework!"

Max glared at her.

"Sorry," pleaded Cynthia, laughing again and feigning interest in her reading.

Lucia put down her pen and snorted. Her English had improved tremendously, but now she spoke so rapidly that Max had trouble understanding her. He heard something about him being a baby and Sarah being beautiful and smart, but it was the word "festival" that caught his attention.

"What did you say about the festival?"

Lucia narrowed her eyes.

"I said she is too good for you and that you are very lucky to go to the Halloween festival with her!"

Max shot a terrified glance over his shoulder at the door.

"What are you talking about?" he hissed. "Sarah's going to *ask me to be her date for Halloween?*"

"Don't be ridiculous," Cynthia chimed in. "Sarah's far too old-fashioned for that."

Max exhaled.

"She'll simply let you know that she wants *you* to ask *her*," Cynthia added, her eyes twinkling mischievously.

"But—" Max halted in mid-sentence as Sarah reentered the room, wearing a hooded windbreaker.

"Are you ready?" she asked, walking past and waiting by the door. David rested his book on his face as Connor chuckled. Max followed her down the hall, wiping his palms hard against his fleece.

* * *

Except for a brief stretch of Indian summer, the days had been getting steadily cooler. Sarah walked the path next to Max, fiddling with a series of beaded bracelets.

"So," she said, "I've never really seen Nick up close before. What's he like?"

"Oh, he's okay," replied Max quickly. "He eats a ton, though, and he likes to attack me."

"Really?" She laughed.

"He also gets pretty angry if I show up late," added Max. "He's already shredded a couple sweaters."

"Are you late tonight?" asked Sarah, with a playful note in her voice.

Max gave a sheepish nod as they hurried up the main path through the wood.

Just then, a dark figure rose up from the nearby underbrush, shining a lantern on their faces.

Max took a step backward. It was Cooper, dressed all in black with a stocking cap pulled low. Max stood frozen, his eyes fixed on the taut, shiny scars that disfigured half the man's face.

Sarah was furious.

"How dare you come popping out of the dark like that?" she said, her voice sharp.

Cooper said nothing; he merely gazed impassively at them.

"Well?" she demanded. "Are you going to be a gentleman and apologize for frightening us?"

"Sarah," Max whispered, "don't make him angry!"

Slowly, Cooper's ruined features contorted into a sort of smirk. He doffed his stocking cap politely, revealing a head that had also been badly burnt. The scalp was left with only a few straw-colored patches of hair like ragged shoots of pale wheat. He shuttered the lantern and made his way quietly through the underbrush toward one of the shaded side paths.

Max and Sarah continued toward the Sanctuary. Max did not speak until they had shut its heavy door behind them.

"That guy seriously creeps me out."

"Well, of course he does!" shot Sarah. "Sneaking up on students at night! I should say something to Miss Boon."

"Yeah, but his *face*—"

"—gives him no right to frighten people! I'm sorry he was burned, but life goes on."

Sarah regained her composure and lingered near the opening. Her long neck and profile made a very regal silhouette against the intertwining branches. She turned to him, her eyes as dark and glittering as a doe's.

"You know, Max, I never thanked you for getting me out of the water that night when we were on the *Kestrel*."

"Oh," said Max. "It was no big thing. Anyway, you just saved me from the bogeyman, so we're even!"

He tried a weak laugh while Sarah adjusted her bracelet.

"Well," she said. "Thank you."

Leaning forward, she gave him a soft little kiss on the cheek. Max simply stood there, registering briefly that she smelled like perfumed soap. Stepping back, Sarah smiled at him before stepping out into the clearing. He lagged behind, conscious of his reddening cheeks and thankful for the darkness.

Nick was already pacing about his stall, gnawing at the base of its small tree. Sarah helped deflect his anger; the prospect of having someone new to chase seemed sufficient to appease him. Sarah laughed as she tried to outdistance Nick, who would crouch low, flicking his tail from side to side, before suddenly bolting after her. She shrieked as he quickly closed the gap, his pelt glinting red as he streaked across the clearing. Meanwhile, Max cleaned out Nick's stall and loaded up the wheelbarrow with his dinner.

Setting the crates near the lagoon, Max called Nick, who abandoned an opportunity to ambush Sarah and came hurtling out of the darkness. Sarah came trotting back, holding her side and panting.

"Oh, I love Nick!" she exclaimed. "He's adorable!"

"Hmmm. See if you find *this* adorable," Max said, opening a crate teeming with foot-long rats. The rats scattered in every direction and Nick was after them. His tail fluttered and his claws were a blur as he chased them down and eviscerated each with a swipe of his paws or a violent shake of his head. Sarah groaned as half a rat landed near her shoe. Nick trotted over and nuzzled it closer to her with his bloody snout.

"He likes you!" offered Max from where he crouched, sorting metal bars into small stacks. "He didn't offer me anything the first couple of times."

"Wonderful," Sarah said before gagging.

After wolfing down the rats, Nick waddled over and spent the next half hour alternating between the miniature ingots and the gallons of wriggling night crawlers. The lymrill then took a flying leap into the lagoon, frightening away several herons that had been sleeping among the reeds. A few minutes later, Nick emerged from the water, looking very sleek and sleepy. Climbing up on the wheelbarrow, he collapsed on the jumble of crates, claws extended and snoring, as Max labored to push it all uphill.

Sarah peeked in on her charge, the beautifully plumed

peacock, before strolling over to where Max slung the comatose lymrill over a low branch in his stall.

"Hey," said Sarah, grabbing his hand, "let's try something!"

Sarah pulled Max over to the feeding bin and cleared her throat.

"Food for Max McDaniels: twelve-year-old boy with a sweet tooth."

The bin shook, its lid rattling against the latch as golden light streamed out.

"Sarah, I don't want to eat anything that comes out of that thing!"

"Oh, hush!" said Sarah, smiling as she watched the bin. "Let's see what it offers!"

The bin stopped rattling and the golden light subsided. Sarah flipped the latch and lifted the lid. Suddenly, three heads emerged from the bin, belonging to three very angry little imps in spattered chef's uniforms. They shook their fists at Sarah and Max.

"Not for students! Not for students!" they chimed as they flung small handfuls of garbage and rotten vegetables. Sarah burst into laughter and shouted apologies over her shoulder as they ran down the hall and out the door.

They closed the Sanctuary gate and continued toward the Manse. Max was conscious of the fact that her hand had a way of brushing his occasionally as they walked along. Old Tom chimed eleven o'clock, the notes rolling across the campus while they walked through autumn leaves that drifted down in shaky little spirals.

"I like this season," said Sarah suddenly, stooping to inspect a golden maple leaf. "We don't have anything so dramatic where

I'm from. It's like the earth is climbing into bed and getting ready to sleep."

"Just wait until winter," said Max.

"I can't wait for winter! I've never seen snow before."

"Really?" asked Max, incredulous. He was well acquainted with Chicago's long, cold winter months.

"No, Max," said Sarah sarcastically. "Nigeria gets *lots* of snow."

Max said nothing and walked along, kicking aside little piles of leaves as he went. As they passed the last row of Class Trees, Sarah stopped.

"Are you planning to take anyone to the All Hallows' Eve festival?" she asked hastily.

Max stopped, too. He cast a longing glance at the Manse.

"Er, not really," he said. "I mean, don't we all have to be there anyway?"

"Well, yes, I suppose. . . . But it might be nice to go *with* someone, don't you think? I heard Rolf is taking someone . . . and Lucia was asked by a Second Year."

"You're kidding," said Max, horrified.

"Not at all," said Sarah. "Miss Boon said that most of the students take a date."

"Even First Years?"

"Even First Years," Sarah laughed, before glancing at her shoes. "I heard John Buckley might ask me."

Max heaved a sigh of relief. John Buckley was a Second Year whom Max heard was their best Euclidean soccer player.

"That's great, Sarah," said Max in an upbeat tone. "He seems nice."

"Yes, well, I'm hoping someone else will ask me first," she

said, adjusting her bracelets and looking away. Her smooth black skin looked almost blue in the moonlight filtering through the thin clouds.

"Oh, well, I hope he does," said Max lamely. "Um, it's getting pretty late and I need to get to bed. Thanks a lot for helping me with Nick."

"Sure," she said quietly. "Good night."

Sarah hugged her windbreaker closer and jogged into the Manse, disappearing up the girls' stairway with quick, quiet steps.

Saturday morning arrived, windy and wet. Max pulled on a woolly sweater and went downstairs to the dining hall. Several of his classmates were already there, finishing breakfast and talking excitedly about the upcoming trip to the Course. Located below the Smithy, the Course was normally reserved for older students, but Ms. Richter had decreed that circumstances required all students to begin immediately. Max had been unable to pry any information out of the older students; Jason Barrett had simply laughed and said, "It's made grown men weep. You'll learn a lot about yourself." Since hearing of Ms. Richter's decision, Bob had been heaping extra food on the First Years' plates and ignoring their full-bellied protests.

This morning, however, Max managed to ignore the ogre's pleas and emerged from the kitchen with a small bowl of cereal. He took a seat in the dining room next to Lucia, who made a face.

"What's your problem?" Max sighed.

Lucia gave him a frank look before pointedly resuming her conversation with Jesse. Since he had failed to ask Sarah to the dance, many First Year girls breezed by him without so much as a word. Sarah herself was still friendly, but less talkative and outgoing than before.

Max rolled his eyes, put down his spoon, and pushed up from the table. Sarah was sitting at the other end, nibbling a piece of toast and talking with Cynthia. She put her half-eaten toast on her plate as he walked toward her.

"Sarah?" said Max, coming to a stop.

She nodded, a small smile on her face. Everyone at the table had stopped talking and watched the two intently.

"Would you go to the All Hallows' Eve dance with me?" asked Max simply.

The table burst into a chorus of whistles and cheers. Sarah kept her cool and lifted her chin.

"Thank you for the invitation, Max. I will consider it."

"Okay," he mumbled, and walked back to his seat, mortified to see Julie Teller sitting several tables over, giving him the thumbs-up and giggling with her girlfriends. When Connor launched into a Sir Wesley–inspired play-by-play titled *Scenario Thirty-Nine: Awkward Request for Fall Dance Companion*, Max laughed along with the others before catching Connor hard in the forehead with a bit of muffin. Still snickering, Connor retreated to the kitchen to clean the butter and blueberry splotches off of his face.

"So," said Max, turning to Lucia, "am I out of everyone's doghouse now?"

"Maybe theirs," she sniffed, "but not mine. If anything, that is even worse—asking a girl just to prove a point. In front of everyone, too!" She shook her head and got up from the table.

There was a sudden commotion from the kitchens, and Connor came running out through one of the swinging doors.

"Not a chance!" he cried over his shoulder, leaping back into his seat.

Mum came hurtling through the door, flinging off her hairnet.

"But you're thumbing your nose at tradition!" she cried.

Mum burst into tears and Cynthia rose to console her. The hag buried her face in Cynthia's fleece, waving her hands wildly to shoo away the students who were calling out to her.

"What did you do?" scolded Cynthia, glaring down at Connor.

"I didn't do anything!" pleaded Connor. "She cornered me and told me I was the 'lucky' Apprentice who'd been chosen to escort her to the dance!"

Max spit out his cereal. Even Cynthia stifled a chuckle as Mum wobbled her head from side to side, her shoulders shaking violently with sobs. Suddenly, Mum looked up at Cynthia, searching her face while she rubbed red, teary eyes.

"I'm hideous, aren't I?" croaked Mum. "I trust *you*, Cynthia— you're no looker yourself. Am I truly hideous?"

"No, of course not, Mum," said Cynthia, overlooking Mum's insult and patting her arm. "You're unique!"

"Uniquely *hideous*?" croaked Mum, fixing Cynthia with a wide-eyed look of horror.

"No," said the entire table in unison.

"Then why won't *he* take me?" she whimpered, shooting a tragic glance at Connor, who hid his face in his hands.

"For one thing," he mumbled, "you're, like, a hundred years older than I am."

"Connor!" exclaimed Lucia.

"What?" he asked incredulously. "Oh, and another thing—she's a *man-eating hag*! Or did you all forget?"

Mum shrieked and buried her head once more into Cynthia's fleece. Cynthia tried to comfort her by patting her hair, but stopped abruptly and examined her fingertips.

"Connor, you should ask Mum to the dance," Cynthia said, a note of warning in her voice.

Connor gave Max a helpless look of panic; Max widened his eyes and shrugged.

"It's the least you can do for Mum, Connor," said Sarah. "She cooks for us every day."

"It's just one night," added Cynthia.

"And it *is* a tradition," added a passing Third Year with a knowing smile.

Mum peeked out from Cynthia's fleece and peered at Connor, who was now practically slumped under the table. She screamed and started stamping her feet, her voice escalating to a painful pitch.

"Oh, it's a fate worse than *death* to take Mum! She should go alone! Or better yet, don't go at all! Just stay at home in your cupboard and keep your hideousness to yourself!"

"Fine, I'll take you," muttered Connor, his voice barely audible amidst Mum's shrieks. *"I said I'll take you to the dance!"*

The shrieks stopped immediately. Mum whipped around, almost knocking Cynthia off her feet.

"Why, I'd be delighted," she said magnanimously, issuing a low curtsy. "I'll expect you at my cupboard at seven."

Mum strode leisurely toward the kitchen, a girlish bounce to her step.

"Don't forget about our date, my dear," she called over her shoulder. "I have witnesses, you know."

Connor moaned as Mum disappeared into the kitchen with a cackle. Soon pots and pans could be heard crashing about, Mum's shrill singing rising above the din.

"I just got a new camera for my birthday!" said Cynthia brightly. "I'll be sure to take lots of photos!"

"Yeah," said Max, roughing up Connor's hair. "Sir Wesley will be so proud that his Etiquette lessons have paid off! C'mon, Mr. Mum, we need to get to the Smithy."

Smoke poured from several chimneys jutting from the Smithy's slate roof. It was drizzling outside; rain turned the yellow leaves to mush underfoot. Miss Boon and Mr. Vincenti were waiting for them as the class hurried down the path. The advisors each held a stack of sleek navy binders. Miss Boon sipped coffee from a stainless-steel cup and offered a prim smile as Max caught a close glimpse of the binder: THE COURSE: OPERATIONS MANUAL was stamped in silver foil on the cover.

"All right," muttered Mr. Vincenti, scanning the group. "Good, good, everyone's here. Welcome to my neck of the woods—our beloved Smithy. Let's get you out of the rain—it goes without saying that you will not touch *anything* once inside. Your key cards and PIN numbers are enclosed in your binders— ah, there we go. . . ."

Mr. Vincenti opened the door, and Miss Boon ushered them inside a small entryway with a metal door on their left and a large elevator straight ahead. There was another keypad next to the door.

"Now," said Mr. Vincenti as he and Miss Boon distributed

the binders, "that door leads to the workshops. No reason for you to be in there until you take Devices. This elevator's what you want—it'll take you down to the Course's main level. In you go."

Max crowded into the elevator with the others; it was beautifully paneled and surprisingly spacious.

"Hold on tight," muttered Mr. Vincenti as the doors closed gently.

Max gripped a side railing as the elevator accelerated rapidly downward. He closed his eyes against the queasiness, focusing on the whirring sound of motors and the faint smell of machine oil. When they stopped, he was sure they must be hundreds of feet below the ground.

One by one the students stepped out into a large octagonal room with a high ceiling and gleaming walls of polished red granite. On the wall opposite was another elevator bearing the Rowan seal on its brass door. Max wandered over to look at a beautiful samurai helmet brightly lit within a glass case. He turned to the large gleaming plaque above it.

" 'The Helm of Tokugawa,' " he read, " 'awarded for outstanding leadership.' " The names of past winners were inscribed below, shining with a soft golden glow. Max turned as he felt a hand on his shoulder. Miss Boon smiled down at him.

"Come," said Miss Boon. "I'll show you my favorite."

They passed by a case displaying a huge, battered gauntlet and stopped at another in which a charred stone was suspended in the air.

"This is the Founders' Stone. It was salvaged at great cost by the refugees who fled from Solas. It's a piece of our last school— a fragment of its cornerstone. While the other awards are given to a student who exhibits one particular quality, the Founders' Stone is awarded to that rare student who personifies many."

"Wow," said Max, perusing the much shorter list and widening his eyes as he came to the last name. He turned to Miss Boon.

"Ms. Richter was the last person to win it?"

"Yes," said Miss Boon with a solemn nod. "Ms. Richter was an outstanding student and Agent before she became Director."

Max and Miss Boon wandered over to David, who was standing alone, gazing at a golden apple floating in another case.

"'Bram's Apple—awarded for sacrifice,'" David murmured. "Elias Bram. He's the one who sacrificed himself against Astaroth so the others could flee; he was the last Ascendant."

"That's right, David," said Miss Boon quietly.

"Miss Boon?" asked Max. "What *is* an Ascendant?"

She looked down at him but sounded distracted.

"An Ascendant is very rare, Max—especially in the last millennium. Our long-departed Bram was the last we know of for certain. Ascendants had great stores of the Old Magic in them; they were very powerful."

Max thought of his conversation with Miss Awolowo that night on the temple's dome; she had mentioned Old Magic might be within *him*. He shook off the thought as Miss Boon wandered away to another case, which contained a beautiful African belt layered with cowry shells. Max and David turned as Mr. Vincenti called them over to where he was standing in the middle of the room.

"All right, now you know why our older students work so hard. They want to win some of those awards! Never won one myself—you win one of those and you've done something, eh, Miss Boon? Kids, don't let Miss Boon's modesty fool you; she won *two* awards during her student days at Rowan! Which ones did you win, Hazel?"

Miss Boon flushed.

"Macon's Quill—twice," she said.

"Yes, well, as your advisor I selfishly hope there will be some awards in store for this group," said Mr. Vincenti. "But we didn't bring you here to appreciate museum pieces and awards. We're here because the Director believes your safety requires the Course."

The fidgeting and whispers ceased.

"The Course is a training tool," said Mr. Vincenti. "It's designed to let you apply and build upon the skills you've been acquiring in the classroom."

Mr. Vincenti walked over to the other elevator door.

"You are granted access only to those levels and settings commensurate with your skills," he said. "As you improve, you may pass on to new scenarios and stiffer challenges."

Rolf's hand shot up in the air as Mr. Vincenti pressed the elevator's button.

"What kind of scenarios do we have?"

"The scenarios you encounter are dependent on various inputs. The most important input is the floor you choose here in the elevator. The floor indicates the difficulty level, and at Rowan, we have nine. Very few students progress beyond Level Six. Once on the appropriate floor, you can program any number of scenario variables: environment, objectives, opponents, et cetera. The possibilities are endless."

"Cool," muttered Connor, elbowing Max.

"After each scenario you complete, the Course will assign you a score based on your performance," Mr. Vincenti continued. "That score is calculated from various factors: strategic approach, objectives achieved, time elapsed, and such. Scores range from zero to one hundred. Score above a seventy, and the analysts might store your performance in the archives and use you as an example in the screening rooms—"

Mr. Vincenti paused as the elevator doors abruptly opened. Several sweaty students emerged. To Max's dismay, Cooper stepped out of the elevator after them, dressed all in black and breathing heavily.

"Ah!" said Mr. Vincenti. "As you can see, the Course is a busy place. Students, faculty, and alumni may use it at any time. How'd it go, ladies and gentlemen?"

"We all got creamed," bemoaned a boy among a group of Third Years. "Level Three's a *killer*—they got us right before we solved the Mayan puzzle. We couldn't even use Mystics!"

"How about you, Cooper? Haven't seen you down here in years! Good to have you back."

Cooper nodded in greeting, quietly crossing to the other elevator that would take him back to ground level.

"He went down to Level Eight!" gasped a wide-eyed Second Year. "I asked one of the analysts—she said he got, like, a seventy-five!"

"Well, what do you expect from one of our finest Field Agents?" beamed Mr. Vincenti.

Max watched Cooper step inside the other elevator; the Agent towered over the students filling in around him. The elevator doors shut, and Mr. Vincenti cleared his throat.

"Well, that gives you a little taste!" he said. "Let's go down to Level One."

Mr. Vincenti held the door of the other elevator as the students filed in.

The doors closed and the elevator eased down, far more slowly and smoothly than their trip from the ground level. Sarah stood close to Max, smiling. Moments later, the doors opened onto another octagonal room, paneled in pale yellow wood. Into each wall was set a numbered green door.

"So," said Mr. Vincenti, hopping out, "let's say you've got an extra half hour on your hands and want to squeeze in a bit of practice. Once you arrive at the appropriate level, you've got basically two choices: to practice a scenario or review and analyze past scenarios in the screening room. Let's start with a scenario."

Mr. Vincenti led them to a smooth silver control panel set into the wall next to door one.

"Okay," he said. "To register for a scenario just tap the touch screen here to get started—there we go. Now, you'll register your identity with a retinal scan and select your variables from the options menus—or else leave them for the Course to define. The details are in your binders."

A mischievous twinkle entered Mr. Vincenti's eyes.

"Any brave soul care to try a scenario as an example we can use in the screening room?"

Sarah stepped forward.

"Excellent," said Mr. Vincenti, smiling. "I hate it when I have to draft my volunteers."

Mr. Vincenti tapped the screen again and quickly selected the variables.

"All right, Sarah," he said. "You have only one objective on this scenario: to try and touch the opposite wall any way you can. Got it?"

Sarah nodded and swallowed nervously.

"Whenever you're ready," said Mr. Vincenti. "Just head on through the door."

Max and the rest started cheering for Sarah as she opened the door and disappeared inside. The door closed solidly behind her.

"She's brave!" breathed Cynthia. "You'd have needed a gun to get me in there!"

"I wanted to go," whined Jesse, who was immediately beset by several doubters.

Max read the readout on the bright white screen:

Sarah Amankwe: Level One, Scenario 0A02
Time Elapsed: 00:00:14:57

When the time elapsed reached two minutes, the monitor started flashing. A moment later, Sarah emerged from the door, breathing heavily and leaning forward with her hands on her knees.

"It's awesome!" she crowed as the others greeted her with cheers and anxious questions.

"Now," said Mr. Vincenti, smiling, "you'll want to study up on your performances now and again and get some feedback. For that, you use the screening room. Let's take a peek at how Miss Amankwe fared. . . ."

Miss Boon opened a walnut-paneled door, revealing a large room with many computer monitors stationed at dark wood cubicles. Several older students, including Alex Muñoz, sat at the monitors, studying the screens intently. Alex merely glanced over at them without interest. Mr. Vincenti said a polite hello to a middle-aged woman before taking a seat at a large display. He beckoned for Sarah to take the seat next to him and activated the screen with a touch of his finger.

"Well, let's take a look at how you did," said Mr. Vincenti. "Everyone gather around and try to get a peek."

Max looked over Omar's shoulder and got a glimpse of the display. It showed a very nervous-looking Sarah at one end of a large rectangular room. The opposite wall was blinking bright green. Sarah had started crossing the room when the floor changed suddenly to a number of conveyor belts whizzing away from the blinking wall at various speeds. She was hurtled backward against the starting wall with a loud bang. She took a moment to gather herself and seemed to be gauging which conveyor belt was slowest. She started running up one positioned near a side wall. As she did so, enormous rubber balls started bouncing around the room from every direction. Time and again Sarah would approach the wall, only to be knocked off her feet and conveyed rapidly backward. Max was impressed by her perseverance, although the scenario ended without her touching the wall.

Sarah smiled as several girls cheered and hugged her.

"It does not surprise me that a girl volunteered first," said Lucia, glancing at Jesse.

"Doesn't surprise me that a girl failed it," he shot back.

"Now, now," said Mr. Vincenti. "The Course is all about *personal* development—it's not a competition. Sarah did very well for a first attempt. You can see here that the Course awarded her an eleven, which may sound low but is very good for a first try. The recommendations listed below are pretty generic—they'll be more meaningful once the Course has more of your performances to analyze."

Several students giggled as they read the recommendations listed: AVOID BALLS, MOVE FASTER, SHARPEN TIME AWARENESS. Each recommendation was coupled with two or three activities that Sarah could follow to hone the necessary skills.

"For complex scenarios, the feedback can be pages long," said Mr. Vincenti, standing again. "Each quarter you'll receive a booklet profiling your performance on the Course along with some commentary and feedback from a team of analysts. Any questions?"

"When can we start doing scenarios?" asked Connor.

"Today," said Mr. Vincenti, chuckling. "I'm a big believer of jumping in with both feet. Anyway, the system won't let you screw things up too badly."

David came over to Max once the students had left the room and begun gathering near the elevator.

"Pretty cool, huh?" said David. "I've got to go feed Maya. Want to come?"

Max shook his head immediately, eyeing one of the silver control panels.

"No," said Max with a smile. "I think I'm going to stick around here a bit."

"I thought you'd say that," said David, grinning as he stepped inside the elevator.

~ 11 ~

ALL HALLOWS' EVE

By the weekend of All Hallows' Eve, Rowan was bustling with alumni who had returned for the celebration. They had arrived from all over the world: ancient crones in wheelchairs, well-dressed men and women, and handfuls of college students wearing the sweatshirts of their respective universities. Max was surprised to see some familiar faces: several politicians, a world-famous scientist, even a movie actress who was a favorite of Mr. McDaniels's.

Max slipped past several alumni in the great hall and ducked down a back stairway. Tomorrow, the First and Second Years would play one another in a Euclidean soccer match, with the rest of the school and alumni as spectators. The First Years were convening on one of the Manse's sublevels to choose their team.

The scene was a nightmare, and Max soon had a headache. The First Years were permitted to have twenty players on the team, but each of the five sections seemed to think they had ten worthy candidates. Max and David sat off to the side while the arguments persisted, leaving the negotiations for their section to Rolf, Sarah, and Connor. Rolf and another boy were in the midst of arguing when David quietly got up and walked to the front of the room.

"Excuse me—" said David.

The arguments persisted and David began coughing.

"Excuse me—" he repeated.

Max breathed a sigh of relief when Cynthia stepped in to rescue him.

"*Everybody shut up!*" Cynthia bellowed, clamping a hand over Connor's mouth to interrupt an unintelligible stream of Dublin slang. "David's got something to say," she concluded.

David turned bright red as all eyes focused on him.

"Well," he said, his voice barely audible in the large room, "we'll never get anywhere this way. . . . We have twenty spots and five sections. Each section should choose their best four players and that will be the team."

"But that might not be the *best* twenty players," scoffed a boy from Brazil.

"Well, you can argue for as long as you want," said David. "The game starts tomorrow at nine and I want to have a team to cheer."

David sat back down next to Max while the debate continued.

"Remind me *never* to do that again," David groaned.

* * *

That night, Max could hardly sleep. He paced the room in anticipation of the match against the Second Years. Rolf, who had
been chosen captain for the First Years, decided on a lineup that
would emphasize the First Years' strengths, one of which was
Max's rapidly blossoming speed.

"Get to bed early, Max," Rolf had urged at dinner. "I'm
counting on your legs. You may be playing most of the game."

Max had promised and hurried through his visit with Nick,
who was visibly annoyed. Getting to bed early made no difference, however, and Max tossed and turned for an hour before finally creeping downstairs to fetch one of his Mystics texts. He
spent the next few hours conjuring small orbs of dark blue flame
and concentrating on making a pencil roll back and forth on his
book. Near dawn, he caught his image reflected in a dark glass
pane of the observatory dome. A small sphere of blue flame still
flickered about his hand before disappearing altogether.

"You're changing," he whispered, and collapsed into bed.

David was already dressed in his navy Rowan uniform when he
shook Max awake. Max bolted upright, knocking the Mystics
text off his bed onto the floor.

"You have to be at the field in ten minutes for warm-up!" said
David, running to get Max's soccer shoes.

Max leapt out of bed and threw on his navy jersey. A minute
later, he raced to the athletic fields, passing by the Second Years'
team as they ran through drills in their white uniforms. The
First Year players were all stretching at the far end of the field—
except for Rolf, who stood with his arms crossed. Max tried to
ignore his captain's purple face, focusing instead on his stretches

and a pair of scarecrows that had been placed as spectators in the stands.

David brought him some toast.

"Here you go. Better to be late this morning than tonight . . . ," he said with a smile.

Max narrowed his eyes as David started giggling and ran off to the stands. His roommate had enjoyed teasing him ever since Sarah had finally accepted Max's invitation to the festival.

It was a crisp autumn day with a pleasant breeze scattering fallen leaves into golden drifts. Students and alumni were already filling the stands, settling down with thermoses and spreading cotton throws on their laps. After the stretches, Sarah tapped Max on the arm, pointing over his shoulder with a giggle: Nolan was leading the players' charges across the grounds from the Sanctuary. The enormous shedu, Orion, clopped out in front; a white sheet painted with victory slogans had been thrown over his back. Max wondered how Rolf had managed to cajole the proud shedu into serving as a billboard.

Max sighed as he saw Nolan abruptly scoop up Nick to prevent the lymrill from running out on the field. Nick was entrusted to a somewhat nervous-looking pair of alums, and Nolan assembled the other charges to watch from the grass.

M. Renard strode out on the field and raised his arms to quiet the crowd. Max's stomach felt queasy. Several thousand spectators clapped and chattered with one another as they perused little programs and matched names and numbers to faces. Max's attention shifted as M. Renard's voice boomed out, magically amplified.

"Ladies and gentlemen, welcome to this year's All Hallows' Eve match between Rowan's young Apprentices!"

The crowd erupted in enthusiastic cheers. Max saw that Nick was shaking so wildly that Nolan had to retrieve him from the alumni couple. The man scowled and removed his camel's-hair coat, holding it up to examine its shredded sleeves. Wincing, Max turned back to M. Renard, who seemed to enjoy the crowd's attention as he gestured at the First Years with a dramatic flourish.

"It was only two months ago that these little globules arrived here, fat and squishy like little pats of butter!" said the Games instructor.

The crowd chuckled as Max blushed with his teammates.

"You should not laugh!" scolded M. Renard. "I see several pats of butter in the crowd. Remedial training may be in order for some of you," he deadpanned, wagging a finger in the direction of several plump women sharing a tartan blanket. One of them stood and shook her fist, shouting, "Never again!" to the delight of the alumni.

The instructor continued. "Yes, only two months ago did they arrive, but as you shall see, they have learned a thing or two. Please give them a warm Rowan welcome."

Max squinted in the morning sun, trying to make out more faces as the crowd issued a friendly round of applause.

"And our Second Years," said M. Renard, trotting over to the other team. "Who can forget them? Ah, the 'middle children' of Rowan. I sympathize with them in this match—always cast as the scoundrels, the villains, the bullies, as they compete against our poor, innocent First Years. . . . It's not fair, is it?"

The Second Years laughed and shook their heads.

"Yes, well, while it is not fair, it is life, is it not?" M. Renard sniffed. "Good luck to both teams. Play hard and be good sportsmen. And, eh, Happy Halloween!"

The crowd cheered as trumpets sounded, blown by a quartet of satyrs stationed at the far end of the stands. Max took a deep breath and trotted onto the field, adding his hand to the huddle as Rolf rallied the troops. Rolf mentioned something about "pride" and "they're only a year older," but Max's main focus was on trying to overcome his nerves. He saw Alex Muñoz take the field with the Second Years, chatting with his teammates as he leaned to the side and stretched. Alex caught Max looking and shook his head, as if with pity.

The field buckled as soon as M. Renard blew the whistle. Max was jostled off balance as a Second Year raced by with the ball, passing it quickly to a wing. The wing knocked the ball down and began to pass it around, probing for a seam in the defense. Alex Muñoz ran up from midfield in time to catch a sharp pass and line up a shot on goal before Rolf came hurtling in to knock the ball away.

Once the game had begun, Max forgot his jitters and watched the action. He was playing midfield, but Rolf asked him to focus on the defensive side of things, anticipating that the Second Years would seek to demoralize them early.

Rolf was right. The Second Years struck twice in quick succession on a visibly frustrated Cynthia, who was an excellent goalie but unaccustomed to such sudden, speedy shots. The First Years, however, rallied when one of their forwards scored an improbable goal due to a sudden shock wave in the field that knocked the opposing goalie off his feet. The crowd roared its support when the First Years threatened again, but Alex stole the ball away from Sarah and launched a long pass downfield that quickly resulted in another score. Before play resumed, Alex jogged over to whisper something to Sarah with a nasty look on his face. Max thought she might lose her composure and go after him, but Rolf quickly substituted another player for her.

Despite their lead, the Second Years began squabbling with one another as the half progressed. Max got the impression that a margin of 3–1 was embarrassing. They sniped at one another or cursed whenever the First Years managed a steal or controlled the ball for any length of time, drawing cheers from the crowd. Max noticed a definite change when he converged on the ball with two Second Years and was elbowed hard to the side by one as the other dribbled away, hurdling a series of uphill bumps that tilted to the right. Max chased after the girl with the ball when M. Renard's whistle sounded and the half came to an end.

"You can't get pushed out of the way like that," panted Rolf, running up to Max as they herded with the rest toward one goal. "You have to be more aggressive or I'm going to pull you."

"It's *soccer*!" snapped Max. "It's not even a contact sport!"

"Tell *them* that," retorted Rolf.

As the second half started, Max was sure M. Renard had changed the field settings. Its movements became more extreme and the patterns less predictable. Entire sections rose and fell in seamed ridges. Tracking a ball that arced over his head, Max turned and suddenly found himself face to face with a six-foot wall. He hoisted himself over only to see a Second Year defender reach the ball before him. The ball was passed back over his head, where it was caught on the chest by John Buckley, the Second Years' captain, who made a nice move around the sweeper and launched the ball past Cynthia into the net. The crowd cheered as John was mobbed by his teammates.

Five minutes later, Max found himself dribbling the ball and looking for Sarah upfield when he was suddenly slide-tackled hard from behind by Alex, who stole the ball and raced toward Cynthia. Alex feinted convincingly to the right before shifting his weight and sending the ball into the opposite corner, completely bewildering Cynthia. Max watched miserably as it trickled past her; the goal had been his fault. M. Renard's voice rose to announce the new score to the cheering crowd as Alex pumped his fist and shouted something to Cynthia.

Despite Rolf's frantic shouts of encouragement, Max thought the First Years were beginning to droop. These thoughts vanished from his mind as a Second Year suddenly launched a long pass in the direction of John. Max sprang into action. He overtook the older boy and was about to chip the ball to Rolf when his legs were taken out hard from under him and he crashed to the turf. Pain shot through his knee. He saw Alex run laughing after John, who was now dribbling the ball toward Cynthia.

Max watched them for a moment.

Then, the simmering presence within him snapped and roared to life with terrible force. Jumping up from the turf, he set his jaw and raced after them.

Faster and faster his legs churned, the wind strong and fierce in his face as the jerseys he chased grew larger. The gap closed with startling swiftness; Max had never run so fast. The blood pounded in his head.

Alex looked shocked as Max elbowed past him and snaked around John to steal the ball and reverse field. The crowd jumped to their feet in a colorful jumble of clapping hands and waving caps, but the shouts and cheers sounded far away. Max focused on the ball and the turf in front of him, taking instantaneous note of his teammates, his opponents, and their relative positions.

The other players now appeared sluggish; he easily outpaced a Second Year boy who badly misjudged his angle of pursuit and was left gaping as Max flew past him, leaping like a deer high over a mound that had risen before him. Seconds later, he changed directions so abruptly that the opposing sweeper fell to the ground, clutching his own ankle. His legs a blur, Max rifled a shot past the goalkeeper that exploded into the upper reaches of the net.

Immediately after the ball left his foot, Max turned and sprinted back down the field. He ran past his teammates, who tried to congratulate him, making directly for Alex, sullen and scowling as Max approached. Sticking a finger hard in Alex's chest, Max panted, "All day long, Alex. I'm going to do this to you all day long."

Alex pushed him and was restrained by his captain as M. Renard blew his whistle in rapid chirps. Max ignored the cheers of the crowd and his teammates, running back to his position so play could resume.

For the remainder of the game, he was unstoppable.

He hounded the Second Years on both sides of the field; his heart beat furiously as he scrambled up ridges, leapt over sizable gaps in the turf, and nimbly changed directions at astonishing speeds. He had scored another goal almost immediately after his first, forcing the Second Years to assign multiple players to guard him. This allowed Max to deliver consecutive beautiful passes to Sarah and the other forward, each of whom victimized the isolated goalkeeper and scored easy goals.

The game was tied 5–5 in the waning minutes when Max ran down a terrified-looking Second Year boy and stole the ball. He ignored the fire in his lungs and reversed field, dodging past a Second Year who crashed in from his left. Dribbling upfield, he lofted the ball over the head of Alex and onto a ridge, some ten feet above. A distant roar from the crowd sounded in his head as he dashed past Alex and leapt up onto the ridge without breaking stride.

His teammates simply stopped playing and watched.

Bounding over the ridge, Max beat a nearby defender to the ball and sped down the sideline. He managed to launch a shot just as he was slide-tackled by John Buckley. Collapsing onto the turf, Max followed the ball as it screamed past the goalkeeper into the net.

John was panting hard on the grass next to him. "You're a one-man army, Max! Oh my God," he breathed, coughing as he rolled onto his back.

Max pulled him to his feet just as M. Renard blew a long whistle. The game was over. Max was mobbed by his teammates, Rolf driving him to the ground as the others piled on top. M. Renard ran forward to rescue Max from the heap, hoisting him out and appraising him with a small smile.

"That was . . . *something*," he said quietly with a short nod.

"Ladies and gentlemen," said M. Renard. "I think we can all agree that this was an unexpected show. For the first time in Rowan's history, the First Years have emerged victorious. Who knew these little monsters could play a match like that, eh? Our Player of the Game is Max McDaniels!"

Max was still panting as the crowd roared and rose to its feet.

Sarah and Cynthia hugged him tightly while the rest of the class patted his back and messed up his hair.

As Max walked toward the stands, he was nearly upended by Nick, who came barreling into him. Scooping the lymrill into his arms, Max grimaced, imploring his charge to pull in his claws. Nick did so while vibrating his tail like a maraca.

Julie Teller grinned as she stood by the end of the stands holding her camera.

"That was awesome, Max! Really awesome," she gushed. "Got lots of pictures, too! Hurry back and watch the alumni game!"

Max nodded and waved, trotting off back toward the Manse to shower. He stooped to let Nick spill out onto the grass and clamber after him.

The alumni game was about to begin when Max returned to the stands, wearing his school uniform and shaking the water out of his hair. He brought a thick blanket so he could be at ease around Nick's claws while they watched the game. He settled into the second row of the bleachers with Rolf and Connor just as a persistent chant of "Coop, Coop, Coop" worked its way through the crowd. Max craned his neck and saw Cooper sitting up and over in the bleachers, bundled in his peacoat and hat. Several of the alumni players and surrounding spectators were trying to entice him out of the stands to play. Cooper gave a thin smile and shook his head.

"I heard he was an awesome player," said Rolf, munching on a hot dog. "Made the All-Rowan Team as a Third Year. Scored two goals against the alumni."

"I said hey to him one day outside Maggie," muttered Connor. "He just sort of looked at me like I was touched."

"It's not his job to be friendly," said Rolf. "In fact, I heard he's so tough he's not even assigned to a particular field office. Just goes where he's needed."

"What's a field office?" asked Max, feeling uninformed.

"We've got them all over," explained Rolf, "in most of the major cities in the world. Keep an eye on the Enemy—"

"Here he is!" sang a loud voice to his left.

Max looked down to see Hannah at the edge of the bleachers, helping the goslings up onto Max's row.

"Max! How are you, darling?" crowed Hannah. "Word around town is that you're a star! *A star!* Well, the goslings absolutely insisted on seeing you. Do you mind if they join you? Oh, you're such a dear."

The goslings hopped up and down at his feet, pecking everything in sight until Max gently lifted them up. He carefully shifted Nick over and nestled the goslings in a little row along Nick's warm back. Meanwhile, Hannah had waddled over to the fence near where M. Renard was set to begin the game.

"Hey, Renard!" the goose bellowed. *"Gonna call a clean game this year? Huh? Or are you on the alumni payroll again?"*

Max and the others giggled as M. Renard fixed Hannah with an acid glare and cleared his throat. Throughout his introduction, Hannah's taunts and obscenities could be heard during his pauses. The crowd cheered her on, and M. Renard hurried through the pregame ceremonies.

The game itself was stunning. The All-Rowan Team fought valiantly, particularly Jason Barrett. The alumni team, however, was simply unstoppable: their casual speed, strength, and agility far outstripped the students'.

As the outcome was never in doubt, Max found himself hoping for spectacular plays, and he was not disappointed. Two alumni clasped hands and hurtled a sprinting teammate up and over a thirty-foot ridge that rose suddenly at midfield. Another play had the alumni scoring a goal after the ball had traveled the entire field, player to player, without ever touching the ground.

"How can they *do* that?" whispered Max in awe as one alumnus hurdled a forty-foot chasm without breaking stride.

"Body Amplification," said Julie Teller matter-of-factly from off to his left. She snapped a photo of Max with Nick and the goslings, and smiled as she peered out from behind the camera.

"What?" said Max. Connor glanced at her and almost choked on his hot dog, scooting over quickly to make room.

"Body Amplification," she repeated. "Using your Mystic energy to Amplify your body's capabilities." She took a seat next to Max and let one of the goslings waddle onto her. "They start teaching it Third Year. It's pretty hard. You're obviously a natural, though."

"Why do you say that?" he asked.

She laughed and squeezed his arm. He felt light-headed.

"Because, whether you realize it or not, it's pretty clear you were Amplifying during your match!" Julie explained. "Most Apprentices can't outrun Olympic sprinters. You should talk to Miss Boon about it."

They spent the rest of the match chatting. Julie told Max a funny story about her little brother learning to surf back in Melbourne; Max shared with her a bit about Chicago and his dad. When she asked about his mom, Max simply murmured, "She's gone," and turned back to the field as M. Renard blew the closing whistle. The alumni had won 11–3, although Max suspected it could have been by whatever margin they chose. The two teams shook hands as spectators began to gather their things and exit the stands.

Max waved at Sarah and the rest of the girls in his section as they approached. Sarah waved back absentmindedly; her attention was on Julie.

"Hi, guys," said Sarah. "We're going to rest up and then get ready for tonight. Max, will you meet me by the girls' staircase at seven?"

"Sure," said Max, letting two of the goslings nibble at his fingertips.

"Great. See you then," said Sarah. She shot Julie a quick glance before leaving with the others.

"Hmmm," said Julie. "I don't think she likes me sitting with you."

"Oh. Sarah's really nice," said Max quickly.

"I didn't say she wasn't," said Julie, lifting the gosling off her lap and placing it back with Max. "See you tonight." Julie trotted back up toward the Manse, just as Hannah walloped the fence angrily to conclude her discussion with M. Renard.

"*Well, same to you!*" she screeched as the instructor stalked away muttering. The goslings jumped down off Max's lap and waddled to the end of the row to greet their mother.

Sarah really did look pretty, Max thought as she came down the staircase with the other girls, giggling and whispering in their formal uniforms. Sarah had adorned hers with some colorful accessories from home: a copper coil around her wrist, a cowry-shell necklace, and a small colorful pin of a lion on her lapel.

"Hi, Max," she said, smiling, arriving at the last stair.

"Hi, Sarah. Er, you look really nice," Max said quietly, certain that Sir Wesley would be mortified by his delivery.

"You do, too," she said.

"I really like your pin," he said, acting upon his father's stern directive to compliment his date on something specific.

Max blushed as she thanked him and took his arm, suddenly aware of the many adults in the foyer who had taken notice and were smiling at them.

Outside, the grounds of the Manse had been transformed. Two enormous pavilions had been erected: white canvas swooped down in graceful arcs from tall, sturdy tent poles. Underneath one pavilion were row upon row of covered serving trays. Max looked longingly at a set of life-size gravestones fashioned of white and dark chocolate that must have come from Mr. Babel's patisserie. Barrels and enormous woven baskets were stuffed with breads, apples, and sheaves of wheat or tall stalks of corn. Hundreds of jack-o'-lanterns dotted the grounds, crowded together in bunches or hovering above to illuminate the paths and gardens. Out on the lawn, several older students and alumni created eerie phantasms of ghosts and goblins, headless horsemen, and wailing banshees that galloped and loomed against the night sky before dissipating to wispy shreds of smoke.

On the parquet floor beneath the second pavilion, alumni danced to music played by an orchestra whose members were drawn from both the student body and the Sanctuary. A particularly delicate faun strummed a lute while a small man with green skin puffed his cheeks to astounding dimensions while playing

the bagpipes. Kettlemouth was there, too, wearing a little pump-
kin hat and sitting sleepily on an embroidered pillow, ignoring
Lucia's exasperated pleas to sing.

"Why is Lucia doing that?" asked Max. "He's a frog."

Sarah laughed.

"Lucia's booklet said that his kind have been known to sing,"
she explained. "And that his songs can inspire passionate love. . . ."

Max cleared his throat and quickly spied out Connor, who
was munching on a turkey leg and giggling whenever a student
hit a wrong note or an alumnus attempted a particularly ambi-
tious dance move. Max and Sarah strolled over.

"Hey, Connor," said Max. "Where's, er, Mum?"

Connor shrugged.

"I knocked on her cupboard and she started screaming that she
wasn't ready. Apparently her *girdle* was giving her some trouble."

Max and Connor snickered; Sarah frowned.

David walked up, conspicuously *not* wearing the tie that he
been wrestling with when Max had left to meet Sarah. The students chatted and waved hello to Bob, who ambled by in an enormous tuxedo, his few hairs combed carefully back.

Ms. Richter swept up, wearing a beautiful shawl of warm colors woven with Celtic borders.

"Don't let Sir Wesley see you standing in the corner like this,"
she said with a smile. "You'll be practicing 'mingling' scenarios for
weeks!"

She glanced at Max before addressing them all.

"Congratulations on the First Years' victory today. I only
caught the first half, but heard it had *quite* a finish. The alumni
won't stop talking about it!"

She stood upright and tapped her head a moment.

"Oh! As long as you're standing here, would one of you mind running down to the kitchens and getting some more cornbread? It's disappearing fast and I know Mum had a last batch baking."

Ms. Richter was off again, confiscating a bottle of champagne from some scowling Fourth Years.

"Connor, why don't you go?" said Sarah. "Maybe Mum's ready."

"Oh no!" pleaded Connor. "She said *she'd* find *me*! I don't want to catch a glimpse of her in her girdle!"

"You're impossible," scolded Sarah, turning her back to watch the faun begin an intricate number on his lute.

"I'll go," volunteered David.

"*See?*" said Connor pointedly to Sarah. "David will go. Thanks, Davie—you've saved me from an awful sight!"

David smiled as Connor gave him an exaggerated pat on the arm, then he coughed suddenly and slipped through the crowd. The others went to examine the buffet. Just then, the grounds filled with light. A great bonfire had been lit on the ridge overlooking the beach; logs were piled thirty feet high and flames roared up into the night sky. The party cheered and glasses clinked as the orchestra began an upbeat melody.

Twenty minutes later, Max was savoring the lamb and talking to Sarah about the morning's match when he stopped suddenly.

"Where's David?" asked Max.

He turned to Omar, who shrugged, looking bored as he nibbled at a baby carrot while his date, Cynthia, trailed Nolan around the party.

"I'll be right back," Max said to Sarah. "I'm going to see where he is."

Sarah nodded but said nothing as the orchestra began another song.

The foyer was empty. Max made his way down to the dining hall. He rounded the pillar and stopped dead in his tracks.

David was lying unconscious on the floor near several battered trays. Squares of cornbread were scattered around him like yellow sponges. His cheek was scratched and bleeding. One of the enormous oak tables was overturned on its side; the dishes and glassware that had been stacked upon it were shattered into thousands of little pieces.

Max looked up and gasped.

There was Mum. She was bound tightly to a stone pillar, pinned some ten feet off the ground, by writhing coils of green and gold fire. Her head hung limply to the side. One of her broad little dancing shoes had fallen off and lay at the base of the pillar.

Max turned and ran up the steps, taking them two at a time and sprinting out the front door to practically tackle Ms. Richter, who was posing for a photograph with some alumni.

"Ms. Richter!" Max panted. "Ms. Richter—come quick!"

"What is it?" she asked, turning to Max just before the flash went off.

"In the dining hall. Hurry!" Max wheezed, before racing back inside.

The Director took in the scene at a glance. Max knelt next to David, who was breathing slowly, the familiar funny whistling sound coming from his nose.

"Get away from him," commanded Ms. Richter in a calm but stern voice. Max leapt to his feet and backed away against a wall.

As she walked briskly toward the unconscious boy, Ms.

Richter raised her left hand, and the green and gold cords binding Mum dissipated to fading motes of light. Mum was lowered to the ground, where she slumped in a little limp heap next to her shoe.

Ms. Richter leaned over David, cradling his head in her hands and whispering softly. David moaned slightly and began to stir. She whispered again and David opened his eyes to blink at Ms. Richter.

"Mum attacked me!" he whispered, wide-eyed. "I just wanted to keep her away from me. I didn't *kill* her, did I?"

Ms. Richter shook her head and put a finger to her lips.

With another small wave of her hand, Ms. Richter brought the heavy table upright and collected the broken plates and scattered corn muffins into a neat pile by the kitchen doorway. A chair slid across the floor toward her.

At the Director's bidding, Max helped her lift David off the ground and sit him down. David was blinking distractedly, glancing at Mum, who was still unconscious.

Ms. Richter crouched over Mum and lifted up the hag's chin. Mum's leg kicked, and she awoke with a shriek. She spied David and shrieked again, scrambling to her feet to sob behind the pillar.

"That thing is dangerous!" she cried.

"Really?" said Ms. Richter. "He says that *you* attacked *him*, and I am totally inclined to believe it."

There was a long silence. Finally, Mum's voice could be heard, heavy and desperate.

"I thought you were playing a game with Mum—sending down a tasty little boy on All Hallows' Eve. I thought he was a party favor!"

"Why on earth would you think that?" snapped Ms. Richter. "Everyone here is off-limits, Mum. You've been told a thousand times."

"Not *that* one!" Mum cried. "That one is all right for Mum to eat!"

Max suddenly remembered back to the day the First Years had met Mum. David had fled at the sight of Bob and disappeared into a pantry. Max had not seen him come out.

"Ms. Richter! I don't think David ever went through the sniffing ceremony—I think maybe he was hiding!"

"Dear heavens!" exclaimed Ms. Richter. "David, is that true?"

David just sat there blinking sleepily.

"Mum, come out here and sniff this boy at once," commanded the Director.

Mum peeked from behind the pillar before shambling out. She paused several feet away from David. Trembling, she lifted David's arm to her nose, keeping one cautious eye on David as he sniffled. Finally, she croaked, "Done," and shuffled off dejectedly toward the kitchen. Max heard her cupboard door slam shut.

"Perhaps we just can't keep her," muttered Ms. Richter to herself, frowning. She suddenly turned to Max and put a warm hand on his cheek.

"You did the right thing to come and get me, Max," she said. "David will be fine. I'll take him to his room; you go back to the celebration. Tell the others he's taken ill."

Max nodded and walked back up the stairs.

The celebration was in full force, with people dancing and singing while the quarter moon shone high above them. Max found Sarah and Omar chatting near the dance pavilion. Sarah looked at him curiously.

"Where's David?" she asked. "Where have *you* been all this time?"

"David's really sick," Max explained. "He's gone to bed."

Omar glanced at Sarah's expression and sidestepped away just as Connor sauntered over.

"Anyone seen Mum?" he asked. "I'm terrified of what she'll do if she thinks I stood her up!"

"She's not coming," Max sighed. "I heard her in her cupboard. She won't come."

"Seriously?" said Connor, his face lighting up.

"Yeah," confirmed Max, giving Connor a look to drop the subject.

"Great! Maybe now I can get that Second Year cutie to dance with me," Connor said, scanning the crowd.

"You boys are *ridiculous*," hissed Sarah, walking quickly away. Max gave Connor a helpless look and trotted after her.

"Sarah," he called, "wait up. What's the matter?"

"I'll tell you what's the matter." She whirled around, her eyes glistening. "I've been standing over there for half an hour feeling like a fool at my very first dance. If you didn't want to take me, you shouldn't have asked!"

"What?" asked Max. "I was just taking care of David—he was sick."

"Please," Sarah sniffed. "I know you only asked me because the other girls made you. I know you'd rather have taken *Julie Teller*." She mocked Julie's wide smile and occasional hair-flip.

"Sarah—"

"Leave me alone! I should have gone with John Buckley. *He* has manners!"

Max's face reddened.

"Maybe you should have!" snapped Max.

He stormed away, circling around the Manse and heading toward the orchard and the paths that would take him to the Sanctuary. Nick could use an early feeding, he reasoned. He unknotted his tie and thought about booting aside a jack-o'-lantern.

The light and laughter from the party faded steadily. He turned back to see if Sarah was following; there was no one except for hundreds of grinning jack-o'-lanterns. Crunching leaves beneath his feet, Max paused as he saw a strange light glowing from the side path where David had buried the coin on their very first day. The light ebbed to a soft twinkle before flaring up again in a quick flash of white.

Max heard faint sounds of laughter, like children singing far away. He whipped his head back toward the Manse. The music was not coming from the party.

Brushing aside a low-hanging branch, Max stepped onto the side path. He began to follow the light that now danced deeper into the woods.

"I would not do that if I were you," hissed a nearby voice.

Max stifled a cry as a figure stepped out of the shadows, its dead white eye gleaming bright in a shaft of moonlight.

By all appearances, the man's body might have been a shadow, shifting and blending into the background. But his face was clearly visible now, appearing even more worn and haggard than when Max had last seen him at the airport. It looked like he had not slept in days; his face bore heavy stubble. His expression was grim and menacing. He stood taller and stepped forward, slipping a small pack off his shoulder.

"Hello, Max," he whispered in the same strange accent Max had heard at the museum. "I have something for you."

Max turned and bolted down the path toward the Manse, but was lifted off the ground before he had taken three steps. A hand was clamped tightly over his mouth, and the man's voice whispered urgently in his ear.

"Shhh! I am *not* the Enemy! I am here to *help*. Will you listen to me? Will you listen to me and not cry out?"

Max nodded and ceased struggling. As soon as he was lowered to the ground and felt the man's grip loosen, Max elbowed hard into his stomach and went berserk trying to wriggle free. The man wheezed, but his hold was iron. Max was hoisted off the ground again and held by a grip now so numbingly strong that any resistance was utterly futile.

"I understand you're frightened," the man hissed. "But if I really wanted to harm you, it would already be over and done with. Agreed?"

Max nodded at the white eye inches away and let his arms go slack. The man paused and then lowered him to the ground.

"You're a fighter," the man grunted. "But then again, I guess we knew that."

Max said nothing but eyed the man warily. The light and laughter from the woods were gone.

"What was in there?" demanded Max, pointing at the woods.

"I don't know," said the man simply, motioning for Max to lower his voice. "I *do* know that Rowan is strange and that it's best for foolish Apprentices not to follow mysterious laughter on All Hallows' Eve."

Max shivered, peering into the woods, which were now dark and quiet.

"How do *you* know about Rowan?" asked Max suspiciously. "How did you get on the campus?"

"The answers are one and the same. I was a student here. Like most curious students, I know a few of its secrets."

Max shot a look back at the Manse.

"I am *not* going to harm you," hissed the man impatiently.

"No," said Max, "I know. It's just . . . I was warned about you. No one told me you were a student."

"I'm not welcome here anymore," said the man with finality, slipping something out of his pack. "But I wish to return something to you."

The man handed him the small black sketchbook Max had left behind at the Art Institute. Max ran his hands over the cover, flipping it open to see the sketch he had abandoned when this man had entered the gallery. Max tucked the book under his arm.

"Why did you follow me that day?" asked Max.

The man looked around quickly and motioned again for Max to be quieter.

"I am a half-prescient," said the man, gesturing casually at the white eye that Max found so unsettling. "I *knew* to be in Chicago and to board that train, but I did not know why. Then I saw you."

Max remembered the awful way the man's eye had locked onto him.

"You have a very powerful aura about you, Max. I followed you because you were clearly one of our young ones, and our young ones have been disappearing."

Max whipped his head around as he heard a distant burst of cheers from the party.

"You and your father were in greater peril that day than you know. The Enemy has been active at art museums. They are looking for special paintings and special children, and they might have found both that day."

Max was stunned.

"Were you in my house?" Max stammered. "Was that you upstairs?"

The shadowy man shook his head.

"When I arrived, I saw the Enemy fleeing through the alleys. I thought they might have abducted you and gave chase," said the man. "But they eluded me. By the time I could return, your home was closely watched. I'm sorry I could not get there sooner—I can seldom take the fastest way."

"What about the airport?" Max hissed impatiently, a strange mix of emotions starting to well up within him.

"The Enemy was waiting for you outside those doors. I knew if you saw me, you would find another way."

"So what are you saying? That you saved me that day?" Max whispered.

The man smiled for the first time, his sharp features softening momentarily into a kindly expression.

"You'll do the same for me one day, eh?"

The man suddenly frowned and crouched low.

"I have to go," he hissed. "They're coming."

The man withdrew silently into the shadows; camouflaging hues spread over his body until only his face was visible.

"Will I see you again?" whispered Max. "What's your name?"

The man nodded and gave a wry smirk. "Call me Ronin."

The face disappeared.

A moment later, Max yelped with fright as Cooper appeared

next to him. The Agent held a long, cruel-looking knife of dull gray metal. Max started to speak, but Cooper raised his hand quickly to silence him. He never took his eyes off the woods. They waited in silence for several moments before Cooper slipped the knife back into his sleeve. He towered over Max. Cooper's voice was low and calm with a touch of a cockney accent.

"You were talking just now. Who were you talking to?"

"N-nobody," stammered Max; he had not even been sure if Cooper *could* speak.

Cooper's response was flat and immediate. "You're lying."

"What? I got in an argument and I came out here to blow off some steam!"

Cooper stared at Max for several moments. He slowly drew his knife from his sleeve and stepped off the path to the very spot where Ronin had been only minutes earlier.

"Get inside."

The Agent issued the command in a soft, even voice just before he disappeared entirely.

~ 12 ~

SECRET PRISONS

Max tensed his calves for a moment and scanned the room. A bright green circle appeared on the floor some six feet away. He leapt and landed on it, careful to keep his feet within its boundaries. A heavy ball the size of a cantaloupe whizzed toward his head; he glimpsed it in his peripheral vision and ducked just in time. A smaller green circle appeared off to his right; Max jumped sideways and landed on his tiptoes, deflecting another ball out of the air with a slap of his hand. Instantly, another circle appeared ahead; this one was moving and smaller than a Frisbee. Max sprang forward, landed lightly within the circle on one foot, and promptly pivoted to boot aside the small, hard ball that came rocketing at him from behind.

Once Max had finished the scenario, he wiped the sweat from his brow and went to the door. Mr. Vincenti stood just outside, studying the display.

"Hmmm," he mused, running a hand over his trim white beard. "I see you've scored over a forty on your last six scenarios."

Max grinned and grabbed the towel that he had left on the doorknob.

"I also see you're avoiding the strategy-based scenarios," murmured Mr. Vincenti, scrolling through several screens. "That will have to change."

"They're not as fun," panted Max.

"They're not as fun? Or you're not as good at them?" said Mr. Vincenti, raising an eyebrow and clearing the screen. "Come along, Max. I'd like a word."

Several older students waved good-bye and wished them a happy holiday as Max and Mr. Vincenti walked up the forest path back toward the Manse, making pleasant chitchat. The cold air made Max's nose tingle. Once they were in the clearing, he thought how different Rowan looked in winter: Old Tom and Maggie under blankets of snow, the dark leafless forest, and the ocean rolling cold and gray. Max glanced at the gunmetal sky that promised more snow and the small white holiday lights twined about the Manse's hedges and windows.

"How'd your finals go?" asked Mr. Vincenti as they climbed the outer steps.

"Okay, I think," said Max, waving good-bye to the departing students. Except for David, all of Max's friends had already gone.

"Mystics and math were tough. Strategy was all right, but I think I got the logic sections wrong. . . ."

"How was Etiquette?" asked Mr. Vincenti, leading Max into a little sitting room off the great hall.

"Who knows? That stuff seems kind of stupid."

"It's not," said Mr. Vincenti, shaking his head and gesturing for Max to take a seat. "Oh, I know Sir Wesley can be over the top, but knowing how to act in a given situation is a very valuable skill. You'll need it if you ever decide to become an Agent—and I'm sure they'll be clamoring for you to become one someday. Anyway, I asked all the instructors to inform me if one of my advisees was in danger of failing a course. You're safe for now."

Mr. Vincenti eased himself into a deep armchair and tapped his fingers against his knee. He seemed uncharacteristically somber and hesitant. Max listened to the small clock on the mantel tick until his advisor finally spoke.

"Max, I don't entirely know how to say this. . . ."

An icy calm came over Max. He glanced down at his wet shoes. The conversation that informed him of his mother's disappearance had begun in much the same way.

"What is it?" he murmured. "Please, just say what it is. I already know it's bad."

"We don't believe you should travel home for the holidays," said Mr. Vincenti with a sigh. "We think it's best if you stay here at Rowan."

Max did not speak for several seconds, but simply stared at Mr. Vincenti.

"Why?" he finally asked, trying to control his temper.

"You know why," said Mr. Vincenti. "We think it could be dangerous. It's for your own good."

"What about the others?" snapped Max, standing up. "*They* get to go home!"

"They are not *you*," said Mr. Vincenti gently. "They have not been targeted by the Enemy. The Enemy does not know where they live. . . ."

"Did you make this decision?" asked Max evenly.

"No, Max. This comes straight from the Director—"

Max scowled and bolted from the room. In the foyer, he glared at the luggage piling up near the doors, then thudded down the hallway toward Ms. Richter's office. His face burning, Max flung the door open.

"How can you keep me here?" he yelled.

Ms. Richter sat at her desk, gazing at him with her hands folded under her chin.

"Please lower your voice and sit down," she said quietly.

Max stood in the doorway several moments, breathing hard and watching the steam curl from a cup of tea on Ms. Richter's desk. Snow was falling again outside.

"You can't keep me here," Max said at last, managing to smother most of the rage out of his voice.

Ms. Richter's face looked very tired and downcast. "Please sit down, Max," she said. "I would like to discuss this with you."

"Why'd you send Mr. Vincenti, then?" asked Max, his anger rising once again.

"Because I had a very important meeting that could not be moved. Please sit."

Max glanced at a bit of melting snow on the room's cream-colored rug; there were shallow footprints in the snow outside the Director's office.

"Why couldn't they come by the front door?" he demanded.

"What's so secret?" He nearly yielded to the temptation to tell her that he knew all about the missing Potentials, that she was not nearly as clever as she liked to appear.

"I understand that you are angry," she said wearily. "If you wish to continue standing and yelling at me, you may do so. Or you may sit and receive answers to your questions."

Max heard footsteps behind him; Mr. Vincenti stepped into the room, his hands in his pockets.

"I'm sorry, Gabrielle," he said.

"Oh, it's all right, Joseph—I understand completely. Please have a seat and perhaps together we can convince Max to hear us."

Max glowered at the two of them, sitting so calm and composed. Taking a deep breath, he sat on the edge of a chair.

"I have to go see my dad," he pleaded. "He needs me."

"I wish you *could* go home," said Ms. Richter softly. "That is the truth, Max. It breaks my heart to keep a child from their parent—holidays or otherwise. I regret that we could not tell you sooner, but the fact is that we were exploring options that might have made such a visit possible. I'm sorry to say those options do not exist."

"I'll be just fine," said Max. "You can have an Agent watch my house...."

Ms. Richter shook her head.

"I will speak plainly, Max, so you understand and we can put this matter behind us," said the Director. Her face was grim and the softness in her voice had evaporated. "We have analyzed and discussed this situation thoroughly. You would *not be fine*. The Enemy would come for you, and not just 'Mrs. Millen' and whoever else was in your house that day. A tremendous allocation of resources would be required to ensure your safety, and I simply cannot spare them at this time. You would endanger yourself, your father, and potentially many others. It is an unpleasant decision I have to make, but I have made it."

Max listened carefully, weighing every word before he spoke.

"My father would be in danger?" he asked.

"Yes, Max. I am afraid he would be," said Ms. Richter, her voice gentle once again.

Max bowed his head; when he spoke, his voice was quiet and thick with tears.

"So, I'm a prisoner," he said. "I can't even go *home*!"

"Oh, Max," said Mr. Vincenti, patting his shoulder. "It won't be so bad! You're not the only student spending the break here, and we all celebrate the Yuletide together in the Sanctuary."

Max ignored Mr. Vincenti and stared instead at a diploma over Ms. Richter's shoulder. He kept his voice calm and even as he spoke.

"What lie should I tell my father?"

Ms. Richter sighed and placed her palms flat on her desk.

"That you failed your final exam in Mathematics and need to redo several units if you wish to avoid spending the summer here," she answered.

Max bit the inside of his cheek and nodded. He wanted to shatter the arms of the slender chair as he got up to leave. He paused in the doorway.

"But I'll be spending the summer here anyway, won't I?" he asked, staring down the long hallway toward the foyer.

"I hope that will be your decision, Max. Not mine."

Mum and Bob were in the kitchens dicing vegetables for soup when Max came in to make his phone call. Mum hummed merrily to herself as she worked, but Bob's somber frown suggested he knew why Max was there. Wiping his hands on his apron, the ogre whispered something to Mum and led her quietly out of the kitchen.

Max's father answered on the second ring.

"Are you busy right now, Dad? I'm sorry to bug you at the office."

"No, no, no—I'm glad you called! In fact, your ears must be burning, because Mr. Lukens and I were just talking about you. I mentioned you were coming home from Rowan and he just about dropped his coffee mug!"

"You're kidding," said Max, sliding down the wall to slump against a large sack of potatoes.

"Nope," his father said excitedly. "He was very impressed—said Rowan's as *exclusive* as it gets and that he's got a niece that might be interested in going. Isn't that great?"

"Super."

"Oh, and another thing," said his father, lowering his voice. "He wants to talk to you about it at their Christmas party—only the *bigwigs* ever get invited to that shindig!"

Max began thumping his head dully against the hard wall behind him; he wished the line would go dead. "Dad, I've got some bad news. . . ."

"What is it?" his father asked, the enthusiasm in his voice cooling. "Is everything okay?"

"No," said Max, dropping his head between his knees. "I bombed my math final—I'm failing Mathematics."

A relieved laugh burst through the receiver.

"Oh my gosh! You about gave me a heart attack! Is that it? Max, I think I failed algebra *twice* before it made any sense. . . ."

"No, Dad—you don't understand. I have to stay *here* over the break—otherwise I fail the class and have to stay here for summer school."

There was a long pause at the other end; Max braced himself.

"*What?*" Scott McDaniels exclaimed. "Are you saying you're *not* coming home for Christmas?"

"Yes. I'm so sorry—"

"Put someone from that school on the phone."

Max flinched as the words spat rapid-fire out of the receiver. Reflexively, he craned his neck to see if any adults were present. He held his breath a moment, telling himself over and over again that he was keeping his father safe.

"There's nobody here right now, Dad," he said quietly. "I can have somebody call you."

"I've never even *heard* of something like this! What kind of nerve does that place have? Keeping a kid away from his family because he can't do a few word problems!"

There was a long pause before his father's voice became very calm.

"Max, I want you to pack your things. I'll be picking you up at the airport as arranged—"

"No, Dad—" Max pleaded.

"I'll park the car and meet you—"

"Dad, I'm *not* coming home!" snapped Max, his frustration and guilt boiling over.

"Don't you *want* to come home? Max, I'm your father. . . . I don't care if you failed every stinking class they've got! I'm spending Christmas with my son! The Lukenses have invited us to their holiday party—"

"Oh, well as long as it's good for business!" Max snapped.

"What are you talking about?" said his father, sounding hurt. "I've already put up the stockings and—"

"Did you put up Mom's stocking?" Max interrupted.

"What?"

"Did you put up Mom's stocking again?"

"Yes! I put up your mother's stocking," snapped his father defensively. "What's that got to do with—"

"She's dead, Dad!" Max screamed. *"Stop putting up her stocking! Stop putting lipsticks and chocolates and jewelry in that stupid stocking! Mom is DEAD!"*

Max heard his own words echo in the cavernous kitchen. Closing his eyes, he curled into a ball as shame consumed him. He braced himself for a torrent of angry words, but instead his father's voice sounded chillingly calm.

"You are my son, and I love you very much. Pack all your things. I'll be there to get you by noon tomorrow. You tell that teacher or *whoever* is keeping you there that I'll call the police if they try to interfere."

He heard his father's phone rattle in its cradle before the line went dead. His mind and feelings numb, Max slowly got to his feet and hung up the phone.

"Whew! Now *those* were some fireworks!" exclaimed Mum with an excited gleam in her eye. The hag peered from around the corner, where she had nibbled an unpeeled carrot down to a nub. "I thought me and my sis knocked heads, but that takes the cake."

Max said nothing but walked toward her like a zombie. Her crooked, panting grin wavered as he came closer. Stooping over Mum, Max hugged her tight, ignoring her lumpy back and sweaty blouse and hair that smelled of mop water. The hag stiffened while Max shook and pressed his cheek against her shoulder. Several moments later, Max felt her short, thick arms embrace him.

"Shhh . . . it'll be all right, love," said Mum.

Max lifted his head and looked at the watery red eyes blinking back tears at him.

"You haven't lost a father, love," she croaked. "You've gained a Mum!"

The hag immediately began pinching Max's arm and looking urgently around the kitchen.

"We've got to *feed* you—that's what we've got to do! That's the trick—a full belly to chase the icky blahs away! Three hams and a cabbage and call Mum in the morning!"

The hag squeezed Max's hand and suddenly darted off to a meat locker, humming contentedly as she began launching hams out the door.

Mr. Vincenti was waiting out in the dining hall when Max emerged.

"My dad says he's coming to get me tomorrow morning," said Max, walking past the older man and trudging up the stairs. "He says he'll call the police if there's any problem. I'll let you and Ms. Richter figure that one out. . . . I'm going to my room and I want to be left alone."

David was staring up at the stars beyond the glass, scribbling into a notebook, when Max came in and flopped into bed.

"What's the matter?" asked David. He walked around the balcony, weaving through books and astronomical models on the floor, and took a seat on a small rug next to Max's bed.

"Everything. Ms. Richter isn't letting me go home for the break."

"Why not?" asked David. "Isn't your dad expecting you?"

Max hesitated. He had promised both Nigel and Ms. Richter that he wouldn't tell anyone about his encounters with Mrs. Millen. But the image of his father standing before a fireplace with three empty stockings flashed through his head. Max sat up, his eyes flashing with anger.

Over the next hour, he told David everything.

The wonders and horrors spilled out of him like water from a broken faucet; he told of the tapestry and Ronin and Mrs. Millen and the conversation he overheard about missing Potentials and stolen paintings. David said very little while Max talked; he simply hugged his knees and listened intently until Max had finished.

"Well, things make a lot more sense now," said David finally. "Really big things are happening," he said simply. "Or about to happen. It's been written up there for a while." He pointed up at the small constellations winking in and out of sight. "I'm sorry you're not going home, but at least I get to have some company over the break."

Max stared at him.

"Why aren't *you* going home?"

David's face lost its little smile, and he walked downstairs to retrieve a small bundle of letters. Max recognized David's handwriting on the envelopes. Each was stamped RETURN TO SENDER.

David's voice was quiet and calm. "My mom moved away."

"Well, where did she move?" asked Max.

"I don't know—she didn't leave a forwarding address."

Max sat up as David began coughing.

"I knew she would," continued David when the coughing stopped. "I knew she'd leave once she was sure I'd found another home. It was just the two of us, and she really couldn't take care of me. . . . She wasn't well."

David wrapped the rubber band back around the letters, and Max stared at the little bundle of envelopes. His own sense of injustice and outrage began to diminish.

"David, I'm sorry."

"It's okay," said David. "Ms. Richter told me to consider Rowan my home, but she didn't need to. I already did. I'm sorry you can't spend Christmas with your dad, but Ms. Richter's actually right—you're both probably safer if you stay here until they figure everything out." He glanced back up at the glass dome. "There's still some stuff I haven't figured out, either."

"Like what?" asked Max, swinging his legs over the bed.

"Everything you told me makes sense based on what I can see. But didn't Ms. Richter say Astaroth was defeated?"

"Yeah," said Max uneasily. He stood and glanced up at the glass dome. He saw a moon, white dots, and pretty constellations. But David seemed to read them like a book—a very important book.

"His symbol is all over the place," David said quietly. "Astaroth might have been defeated, but I don't think he was destroyed."

Mr. McDaniels did not arrive at Rowan the next day; no police came to restore Max to his father. Instead, Max received a phone call during which his cheerful father expressed sincere but supportive regret that Max needed to stay at Rowan over the holidays. Max was assured that his presents had been shipped express and that Mr. McDaniels would be thinking of him every minute.

Late that morning, Max ran into Mr. Vincenti in the dining hall; his advisor was finishing a roll and perusing the newspaper. On the front page, Max saw that yet another painting had been stolen.

"Did you speak to your father?" asked Mr. Vincenti.

"Yeah," said Max, still puzzling over the conversation. "Everything's fine. What did you do?"

Mr. Vincenti folded the newspaper and sighed.

"We had to influence his memory and feelings a bit." Seeing Max's face, he added quickly, "Not his feelings about you—just his perspective about you staying here over the holidays. They were very strong. He loves you very much."

The strange conversation left Max feeling mixed. On the one hand he was relieved that his father did not seem to remember the awful things Max had said; on the other, it was disturbing that a seemingly minor intervention could alter his father's memories and attitude. He tried to shake it off, running his hand up the banister wound with mistletoe and holly.

David was upstairs in the foyer, tying his scarf.

"Going to feed Maya," he said. "Want to come?"

Minutes later, the two were crunching through the snow on their way to the Sanctuary. It had snowed throughout the night, and everything was encased in a glistening white blanket.

The Warming Lodge was very snug in the winter. Sunlight streamed in from windows high along the walls, and the building smelled of fresh hay and sanded wood. Nick was sound asleep, but Maya was not. Like a silver gazelle, she walked in graceful circles around her stall while David ordered a small box of food from the feeding bin. When David opened the door, Maya glided past him and came directly to Max. She rested her smooth silver head against his hip and craned her neck to look up at him with eyes like almonds cast of gold. Max felt his spirits lift; the weariness and sorrow drained away, and he was filled with a sense of peace and well-being.

"What exactly is Maya again?" asked Max, quietly stroking her ears.

"She's an ulu," said David, leading Max and Maya toward the door. "Her kind brings quiet and understanding. She might be the last one left, though—they almost went extinct in the nineteenth century all because their skins and horns are beautiful and their blood's rumored to hold the secret to any language. Collectors and scholars and scientists wanted them."

Max was incredulous; he could not imagine anyone wanting to hunt or hurt or kill anything so graceful and giving. Maya shivered once as she stepped gingerly out onto the snow, before dipping her head into the little box of fruits and grasses.

When Maya was finished, David and Max took her for a long walk in the Sanctuary, choosing paths that Max had never taken before. They climbed high in the woods, listening to drips of water and the strange calls of many birds. Suddenly, a large drift of snow came spilling down a slope.

Max looked up and caught his breath.

YaYa was sprawled above them, on a bluff overlooking their path. Her black lioness face was matted with blood and steam rose off her body; the hoof of a very large animal was visible beneath her in a trampled bed of pinkish snow. YaYa peered at

them, sniffing the crisp air. Max saw his own reflection in her huge pearly eyes as she spoke in her strange voice that sounded of several women.

"Solstice greetings to you, Maya. Greetings, children."

She dipped the broken horn atop her head in salute.

"Hello, YaYa," said David. "I was hoping to find you."

Max glanced at his roommate; David had mentioned nothing to him.

"Were you, child? Let me come down." The huge ki-rin stood and nuzzled her face clean in the snow before descending the slope. Max stood silent; encountering YaYa in the wild was a far different experience from passing by her as she snored beneath blankets in the Warming Lodge.

"YaYa, was Astaroth destroyed?" asked David.

YaYa stepped forward; her whiskered chin came to a stop right above Max's head.

"Why do you ask YaYa this?" chimed YaYa's voices.

"Because you are the Great Matriarch of Rowan. Only you remember Solas in its glory; only you remember the light that rose up against the darkness when Astaroth came."

The words flowed from David in a lilting cant that made Max feel sleepy. He stood quietly and stroked Maya's silvery withers.

YaYa crouched and settled her great bulk onto the path. "Did you know you are just like him?" she asked after a long silence. "The words and spirit of my master echo in your young voice."

"Who was your master?" asked David. "I did not know the Great Matriarch could have one."

"My master *was* the light that rose against Astaroth. I was with him when he threw the Enemy down. Elias Bram was my master. I tried to aid him, but the Enemy was too great. My horn broke against the Demon's side, and I was cast far away before they brought down the high halls and the land was ruined beneath them."

"But was Astaroth *destroyed*?" David asked again.

"It is beyond my understanding how to destroy something so aged and evil," said YaYa quietly. "That is Old Magic and is woven into the heart and roots of this world. I have heard the Demon's body was found, but I do not know what came of it. When her master fell, YaYa sailed west with the others and left those dark days behind. . . ."

The sounds of bells and laughter came up from the winding path behind them. YaYa turned and padded away farther up the path, disappearing around the bend. David led Maya to the side of the path, just as a bright red sleigh pulled by two great chestnut horses rounded the corner. Nolan was holding the reins, laughing with Mr. Morrow, Miss Boon, and two Sixth Years.

"Hey there, you two!" crowed Nolan. "Been talking to YaYa?"

"How'd you know?" asked David.

Miss Boon leaned forward, studying them very closely as Nolan gestured at the limp hoof and red snow on the bluff above them.

"Been caring for YaYa for almost thirty-five years," he said. "I can spot her work a mile off."

Mr. Morrow took a long draw off his pipe and snuggled deeper into the folds of his woolen throw. The tobacco smelled fine and warm among the pine needles and patches of sun.

"We're a bit cramped for two young First Years and an ulu, but take this, eh?" he said.

Max stepped forward and took a metal thermos from his

Humanities instructor. Unscrewing the lid, he smelled hot chocolate.

"Thanks, Mr. Morrow," said Max, taking a quick sip.

"Not at all, McDaniels," he growled with a wink. "Happy Solstice to you two, my boys. Songs and treats in the first-floor hall tonight—eight sharp!"

"We'll be there," said Max as the sleigh continued on around the bend.

Once it disappeared, David shook his head at Max and coughed.

"No we won't," said David. "Tonight we're figuring out what happened to Astaroth."

Max heard fiddle music and singing from the great hall even before he opened the Manse's heavy doors and crept inside. Nick was fed and David would be waiting. Max stole up an old flight of servant stairs while the baritones of Bob and Mr. Morrow rose above the chorus of remaining students and faculty.

> *The rising of the sun*
> *And the running of the deer,*
> *The playing of the merry organ,*
> *Sweet singing in the choir.*

Max met David in the Bacon Library, where he had left the lights off and was working by candlelight, poring through a stack of newspapers and computer printouts.

"Take this list," he whispered before Max could sit down.

Max glanced down at a piece of notebook paper; there were dozens of book titles listed.

"We need *all* these?"

David nodded, handing Max a second candle and continuing to jot down notes in his thin, slanting script. Over an hour later, Max grunted as he stacked the last of the heavy books on the table. David was still writing furiously, seemingly unaware that Max was even there. His candle had almost burnt out.

Max sat down to take a breather, perusing some of the spines before him: *Great Works of the Nineteenth Century, Art of the Baroque, Secret Techniques of the Old Masters, Dada and Surrealism, The Genius of Rembrandt, Hidden Symbols of Bernini, A Renaissance of Art and Man, Dutch Masters of the Seventeenth Century, The Postmodern Dilemma* . . .

"David," Max hissed, overwhelmed by the thick books and unfamiliar names. "What are we going to do with all of these?"

David appeared much older by candlelight; he stopped writing a moment to look at Max.

"Astaroth isn't destroyed," said David. "I'm sure of it. The Enemy's looking for him, and it has something to do with the stolen paintings. I think some paintings may have secret clues that lead to Astaroth. But first I'll need two more books."

Max rose in anticipation, but David shook his head and said, "They're not in here. They're locked up in the Promethean Archives—a secret room below Maggie and Old Tom. I can get them, but I have to go alone. Just take these back to the room and I'll meet you there."

Max ignored David's cryptic comment and watched as David opened his backpack and started putting the books inside. Just as with Nigel's calfskin case, the books dropped inside without making a sound or dent in the sides.

"Where'd you get that?" asked Max.

"Made it," said David simply. "I'll go ahead—meet you back in the room."

David blew out his remaining candle and left as a chorus of shouts and cheers erupted from the gathering in the great hall two floors below them. Max bagged the remaining books and was about to creep out the library door when his curiosity overwhelmed him. He wondered exactly why David had insisted on visiting the Archives alone.

Max hurried down a long hallway and pressed his face against a window that commanded a fine view of the grounds between the Manse and Old Tom. Sure enough, down to his left and far below, Max saw David waddling like a penguin across the snow, trying hard to stay within the long shadows cast by the bright moon.

Then something moved in Max's peripheral vision and he caught his breath.

He was not the only one watching David.

A dark figure stalked out from the edge of the woods that bordered the front gate. It stopped and seemed to be watching David, who crouched low and crossed from the shelter of the Manse's shadows to the snow-topped hedges that lined the walk to Old Tom. Max groaned; David had chosen a terrible route that eliminated the hedge as a source of cover.

The dark figure broke into a loping trot before suddenly accelerating into a blurry streak across the fresh snow. Max smacked the window in panic.

"Run, David," he whispered. "Run, run, *run!*"

David did run. He had turned his head in time to see the

dark figure closing rapidly on him from several hundred yards away. Max could hardly bear to watch; David was *painfully slow!*

Suddenly, there was a brief pulse of dim light and David was gone.

The dark figure came to a sudden halt ten feet from where David had been. It crouched and examined the ground, whirling in all directions before it stopped.

"Cooper," Max breathed, seeing the Agent's pale features staring up at him from the lawn. The Agent walked several steps toward the Manse, keeping his eyes locked on Max, who stood frozen in the third-floor window.

"McDaniels?" said a sharp voice behind him.

Max yelped and dropped David's backpack. Scrambling to pick it up, he whirled to find Miss Boon staring at him.

"Oh," Max croaked. "Hi, Miss Boon."

"Hello," said Miss Boon, glancing at David's backpack. "What are you doing up here in the dark?" She stepped past Max and peered out the window. Max looked out, too. Cooper was gone.

"I just left the library."

"Hmmm," she said, turning away from the window to glance again at the backpack. "Well, I've got work to do and you'd better get to bed. Good night."

Miss Boon disappeared down the hallway toward the Bacon Library. Max dashed to his room, where he found David already hard at work at their table, wheezing and rubbing his chest. Many candles were lit around the room.

"I ran into Miss Boon," panted Max. "She was going to the library."

David looked up from the two large books spread out before

him; he looked anxious. He said nothing but beckoned for Max to put his backpack on a chair.

"What are those?" Max asked, peering at the enormous books. They were easily three feet tall and filled with many pages of thin, cracked paper. There was something very strange about these books; they had an unwholesome aura, and Max did not wish to remain close to them.

"Grimoires," said David quietly. "They're kind of dangerous. One is on Old Magic; the other has to do with binding spells and prisons. These aren't originals—they were copied during the Middle Ages."

Max stepped away. "Can you *read* that?" he asked, scanning the strange letters and symbols.

David nodded. "Sumerian," he said casually as he pulled the art-history books from his backpack. "You can go to bed, Max. . . . I'm okay."

Max lay awake in his bed for a long time while David's scratchy pen and small voice could be heard faintly on the lower level. He watched Andromeda, staring at the grouping of stars and trying to count how long it would be until her outline twinkled with slender golden threads.

When he awoke, he peered over the balcony to see David sprawled across the table below amid a sea of parchment and flickering candle stumps. Hurrying downstairs, Max shook his roommate awake. David yawned and glanced down at a small puddle of drool that had stained one of the grimoires' pages.

"That's a shame," he murmured sleepily.

"David," said Max, snapping his fingers under David's nose. "Are you okay?"

David blinked several times. Suddenly, he clutched Max's arm; his small grip was fierce.

"Max! The stolen paintings *aren't* clues to finding Astaroth. They're Astaroth *himself*—or at least one of them is!"

David's face trembled with exhilaration and fear at his discovery.

"Astaroth is imprisoned *inside* a painting!"

~ 13 ~

FIBS AND A FIDDLE

The ogre walked ahead, carrying a lantern in the twilight and stopping periodically to wait as Max, David, and Connor hurried to match his long strides. Snow was falling, and the sky was darkening to slate.

The door to the Sanctuary was open. A number of students and charges had crowded near the porch of the Warming Lodge, where a bonfire blazed in a large circle cleared of snow. Nolan sat on an upturned crate on the porch, cradling a fiddle and surrounded by students sipping from mugs and thermoses. Max saw a cloud of steam billow from the Lodge's doorway and caught a glimpse of YaYa's eyes glowing white from the shadows.

"Bob!" exclaimed Nolan. "We don't get to see you too often out here. What's the occasion?"

"Afternoon," said Bob with a nod. "Bob takes young ones across the dunes to see Mr. Morrow. The house is far and little ones know not the way."

"Ah," said Nolan. "Well, Byron sure will appreciate that. I hope he's on the mend—he's been sick for weeks now! Give him my best and get on back to have some hot chocolate when you're through. I'll be taking requests a bit longer."

Bob nodded and skirted the bonfire, leaving the Warming Lodge behind. Max picked his way among the seated students, waving at Cynthia and Lucia, who huddled together. On Lucia's lap, swaddled in a shaggy blanket, was Kettlemouth, who blinked his bulbous eyes and wriggled his red skin in a full-body shiver.

To Max's surprise, Julie Teller turned around to beam at him, the firelight dancing upon her pretty blue eyes and faded freckles.

"Hi," she said with a smile. "Haven't seen much of you since the break, and here we are in February!"

"Oh, I've been trying to study more this semester," Max said, fiddling with a zipper on his coat. He was thankful that Sarah was not there. It had taken two weeks for Sarah to speak to him after Halloween, and while they had resumed their friendship, she became sullen whenever she saw Julie speak to Max.

"Well, let me know if you need any help," she said. "Anything but Languages. I'm hopeless at them!"

Max merely reddened and nodded mutely, ignoring Connor's exasperated face. A quick, cheery tune got a number of students clapping, and Julie turned to watch Nolan, whose fingers and bow danced on the fiddle strings. Connor and Max hurried after Bob and David just as Tweedy began to correct Omar's mistimed attempts to clap along.

"Hey, wait up!" a voice called from behind them.

Max turned to see Cynthia stepping carefully through the snow. She was pulling on her mittens with her teeth by the time she reached them.

"I want to go see Mr. Morrow, too," she said. "Been meaning to before, but, you know."

They ran to catch up with Bob's lantern as it bobbed up ahead. When they reached the edge of the sand mounds, Bob and David were waiting for them. The ogre's coat shielded David from sudden blasts of gritty snow. Cupping his hands over his ears, Max struggled to hear Bob over the wind's howl as they resumed walking.

"Stay close to me, little ones," he cautioned.

What appeared to be little ripples in the distance were in fact towering dunes some fifteen or twenty feet high. Max and the others panted as they clambered up one face and slid down the other side. Thirty minutes seemed like hours; even Bob had to stop and catch his breath from time to time.

"Why does Morrow live all the way out here?" moaned Connor, shielding his face from another gust. "No wonder he doesn't come to class in this weather!"

"He doesn't walk this way," said David. "I think he takes another way—a secret way. This campus is full of them. You can catch them if you know how to look."

Connor whistled through his teeth and pressed David for details that were not forthcoming. Max glanced at his roommate, thinking of the night David had vanished to fetch the grimoires, just barely evading Cooper. David never mentioned the incident, and Max had let it be, embarrassed that he had been spying.

As they reached the crest of yet another dune, Bob suddenly put up his hand and motioned for them to be still. A heavy sniffing sound could be heard.

To his horror, Max saw several pairs of luminous green eyes looking up at them from below.

"Bob—" Max hissed as Cynthia clung to him and they backed away.

"Shhh!" commanded Bob, swinging the lantern around and peering down at the eyes below.

The children huddled in terrified silence for several moments while Bob stood as still as a stone, staring down at the base of the dune. Suddenly, there was a low whine that rose above the wind.

Whatever they were had gone.

"We get going," rumbled Bob. "Not far now."

"Bob," said Connor, shivering and clinging to the ogre's side, "what were those?"

"Bob knows not," he muttered. "Many wild charges live outside the clearing."

"What do you mean 'wild charges'?" asked David, his voice almost lost to the wind.

Bob stooped low to answer.

"Charges whose keepers have gone away—charges that live off on their own. Some may have forgotten that people ever cared for them."

"Are they *dangerous*?" asked Cynthia, shuddering and looking around.

Bob shrugged. "They are wild," he said, hefting the heavy thermos like a weapon and leading them toward the next dune.

Max caught the comforting smell of a fireplace even before he scrambled up the final dune and saw the cottage. Situated near the edge of a dark wood thick with fir trees, its walls were made of mortared stone crossed with timbers and surrounded by a low picket fence. Bright yellow lights peeked from behind its curtained windows. Eager to leave the wild charges and wintry conditions behind, Max and the others ran downhill toward the cottage.

"*Stop!*" Bob's voice echoed on the wind, bringing them to a stumbling halt. "Wait for Bob," he wheezed, stepping sideways down the dune and using the lantern to light the easiest way. "Little children anxious for walls and warmth. Makes little children foolish—think they are now safe and become blind to dangers."

"Why do you say that?" asked Connor, rubbing his arms and casting a longing look at the warm cottage.

A slight frown crept across Bob's craggy features. "Before Bob became cook, Bob was ogre. . . ."

The ogre knocked on the cottage's red door; a thick sheet of snow slid off the roof and crashed into the garden. The children huddled together for warmth, their backs to Bob as their eyes scanned the forest and dunes. Bob knocked again.

"Instructor Morrow?" Bob inquired delicately. "It is Bob and some students."

No sound came from the cottage.

"We brought soup for you," Bob purred. "Soooouuuuup!"

Bob looked at the children and shrugged, bending down to leave the thermos of soup by the door. Cynthia shook her head

and squeezed past Bob, turning the doorknob and poking her
head inside.

"Cynthia!" wheezed Bob. "He might be in the bathroom
or . . . *unclothed*!"

"Oh, shush!" Cynthia replied with authority. "He's sick and
he needs people to look after him. I haven't hiked this far in the
cold to leave him a frozen thermos of soup! C'mon."

Max, David, Connor, and Bob followed Cynthia through the
doorway and into a warm room with a low ceiling. Bob's back
creaked as he ducked to avoid hitting his head on a low beam.
Books were everywhere: great piles of leather tomes stuffed onto
shelves, stacked in precarious towers, or scattered in seemingly
random arrangements on the floor.

A low fire burned in a small fireplace while candles flickered
here and there amidst winding trails of wax. Mr. Morrow was
sound asleep, slumped in a cracked leather chair and buried in
blankets. He did not look well; his lips were dry and there were
purple circles under his eyes. His gray hair was matted to his
shiny forehead.

Max turned to warm his hands at the fire when, suddenly, a
familiar voice rumbled in the room.

"I'm far too fat for such tiny pallbearers."

Max and the children jumped, but Bob's face widened into a
relieved grin.

"Ah!" exclaimed the ogre. "You are awake, Instructor. Good,
good, we brought you some soup!"

Mr. Morrow fixed them with a bright eye as he drew his
blanket closer.

"Most kind of you—it'll help me take my medicine."

"Ooh," said Connor, stooping to examine a cup of bright

green liquid sitting on an end table. "Is this some sort of magic potion?"

"Yes, my boy," said Mr. Morrow in a hushed voice suggesting awe and mystery. "This very potion offers its brave imbiber a bevy of benefits both strange and wonderful. I give you . . . cough syrup!"

Cynthia, Max, and David burst into laughter as Connor set the cup down with a disappointed expression. Mr. Morrow chuckled, too, but was quickly overcome by a spasm of hacking coughs.

"How are you feeling, Mr. Morrow?" asked Cynthia. She brought over a bowl of soup poured from the thermos while the instructor pushed aside a number of spent and wadded tissues until he arrived upon his pipe. With a distracted shrug at Cynthia's question, he lit his pipe and took a long draw.

"So, Bob," inquired Mr. Morrow without turning his head, "how'd you persuade these four young rascals to visit this sick old bird?"

"Bob didn't, Instructor. They let Bob come with them."

Mr. Morrow let out a surprised grunt as Max wandered over to examine a framed photograph on the wall. The image was a younger likeness of Mr. Morrow in a fedora posing in front of the Eiffel Tower with an elegant young woman. Max thought suddenly of the carving he had seen on a tree in town: "Byron loves Elaine '46."

"Ahhh, Mr. McDaniels. Are you admiring my pretty lady?" asked Mr. Morrow.

"Yes, sir."

"That's my wife, Elaine. Cancer got her."

"I'm sorry," said Max awkwardly.

Mr. Morrow shook his head impatiently and cleared his throat.

"Don't be. It was her time. Everyone should be so lucky as to find his matched pair in this world. I'm grateful for the years we had."

Cynthia stepped over to the photograph.

"Mr. Morrow!" she said. "You were a handsome devil! Look at you in that suit!"

"Very handsome," intoned Bob in agreement, stooping lower to examine the photo over their shoulders.

"Oh, stop it!" Mr. Morrow chuckled. "You'll make this fat old thing too vain for his own good. That photograph should be in the Smithsonian!" He looked into the fire, but Max saw that he was pleased.

"Who's this?" asked David, picking up a frame perched on a pile of books. In it was a yellowed photograph of a young man in a military uniform.

"Oh, that's my son. Arthur," said Mr. Morrow quietly. "That's him right after he joined the Marines. Lost him, too—his entire platoon, as a matter of fact."

Cynthia made a furious gesture at David to put the photograph down.

"It's all right, Cynthia," said Mr. Morrow with an understanding smile. "I'm flattered that you children take an interest in my family." He motioned for David to hand him the photograph.

"The politicians chose war and he chose it, too," said Mr. Morrow, studying the photo. "I didn't understand. It's strange, really. My whole life has been consumed with the study of war—of kingdoms that rise and fall with fire and sword. It all seems very glorious until it swallows up someone you love. Life is too precious a thing to throw away on orders and absurd chains of command."

He put aside the picture and turned back to his soup, spilling a bit onto his robe. David looked depressed. Bob made a steadying gesture with his hand, cleaning up the used tissues that lay in little piles around the chair. Mr. Morrow looked up once more.

"Come now—if I'm to suffer visitors, then the least they can do is offer news! What are the happenings on campus? How's Hazel managing with my classes? Have they found those stolen children yet? Missing Potentials is serious business—"

"Instructor," warned Bob, dropping a porcelain cup he'd been washing. "They are not supposed to—"

"Not supposed to know?" exclaimed Mr. Morrow. "You mean Gabrielle *still* hasn't told them the dangers despite all her promises? That's outrageous! It's—it's *unconscionable!*"

"What are you talking about?" Cynthia asked quietly. "What 'stolen children'?"

"We should be going," said Bob, reaching for his coat and motioning to the others. "We will visit again soon."

"No, Bob," said Cynthia. "I want to hear this."

"You *must* hear this," growled Mr. Morrow, sitting up in his chair with a fierce look. The ogre sighed and peered out the window. "It's your right and responsibility to know the dangers you face. Do *any* of you know anything about this?"

Max and David glanced at each other. The wind raged outside the cottage; drafts scurried through cracks, causing the candles to flicker. Ignoring David's little shake of the head, Max spoke up.

"I do."

"What do you know, my boy?" grumbled Mr. Morrow, giving Max his full attention.

"I know that some children—Potentials—have been taken by the Enemy all over the world," said Max, speaking carefully. "I know another kid, someone named Mickey Lees, was supposed to be in our class. I guess he was last seen with Miss May, who . . . who died."

The room was very still; Mr. Morrow looked tired and sad.

"And how do you know this, Max?" asked Mr. Morrow.

"I overheard Ms. Richter talking about it in the Sanctuary. And because the Enemy tried to take me, too."

Cynthia and Connor gasped; David looked irritated and stared into the fire. Leaning back in his chair, Mr. Morrow jabbed an authoritative finger at Max.

"You tell me *everything*, McDaniels."

For the next ten minutes, he related his encounter with Mrs. Millen. Mr. Morrow puffed thoughtfully on his pipe, shushing the others when they tried to ask questions. Max glanced at Bob, but the ogre appeared lost in his own thoughts. When Max had finished, Mr. Morrow fixed him with a frank look.

"You're lucky to be alive. Your 'Mrs. Millen' was almost certainly a vye."

Max's stomach contracted into an icy clump.

"What's a vye?" he asked.

"A shape-shifter," explained Mr. Morrow. "Very crafty. Tough to detect and, according to our Agents in the field, appearing in greater numbers. Their real form is terrifying."

"Does a vye look like a werewolf?" Connor piped from near the fire. His face looked drawn and frightened.

Mr. Morrow fixed him with a peculiar, penetrating glance.

"Yes, Mr. Lynch, it might look like a werewolf to you," he said, his voice gravelly and low. "Bear in mind, however, that a vye is *not* a werewolf. The vye is larger, with a more distorted and hideous face—part wolf, part jackal, part human, with squinty eyes and a twisted snout. In human form, however, they can be most convincing. You must *never* speak to a vye, children! They are clever in their deceits, and their voices are wound with spells to ensnare you."

"How would you even know if you're speaking to one?" whispered Cynthia, shivering and scooting closer to the fire.

"There are all kinds of tricks to uncover one, but I'm a strong believer in the gut. If a vye approaches you, Miss Gilley, something will feel very, very wrong in your belly or down the spine. As they prefer to attack when your guard is down, a vye will often seek to gain your confidence first. This may give you an opportunity to identify it before . . . before it has you."

A sudden cry pierced the room.

"I remember now!" exclaimed David. "I've *seen* vyes before!"

"We all did, David," said Connor reassuringly, "from the hallway window last semester. That must have been a vye. . . ."

"No," said David, shaking his head. "Back in Colorado, before I came to Rowan. I was walking home through the woods when I saw someone off the path watching me. Something about him scared me and I walked faster. He started to follow and I ran as fast as I could. He started laughing; he was making fun of me for running slow." David began coughing, and it was several seconds before he could continue. "I turned around and he was coming after me on all fours. Changing shape, catching up, and laughing the whole time."

Max had never seen David like this before. His voice was so faint and small; he looked and sounded traumatized.

"I tripped," he continued. "I saw another one coming at me through the woods. . . . I think I screamed and fainted. When I woke up, they were gone. So were the trees around me. . . . Everything was burned. I know it sounds crazy, but I think that it all happened."

"I believe you," rumbled Mr. Morrow, patting David's shoulder. The instructor convulsed with a sudden fit of wheezing laughter. "Imagine those poor vyes' shock when they realized— pardon the expression—that they'd bitten off more than they could chew! Thinking they're toying with a poor helpless boy only to encounter *him* instead!" His laughter sputtered into hacking coughs.

"What are you talking about, Mr. Morrow?" huffed Cynthia. "David could have been killed!"

"No, Miss Gilley," said Mr. Morrow, rubbing his hand over his white stubble. "I do not think two vyes are likely to be the downfall of our Mr. Menlo. And in any case, I do not believe the Enemy is merely out to take the lives of our unsuspecting young ones. I fear a darker purpose is at work."

"Like what? What would the Enemy want with Potentials?" asked Connor.

Max and David glanced at each other again. Although David had deciphered the reasons behind the stolen paintings, the stolen Potentials remained a mystery.

"Our Potentials are our lifeblood," rumbled Mr. Morrow. "If the Enemy saps our youth, our future withers. It would be devastating to kill off our Potentials, but it would be much worse should they become corrupted to the Enemy's will. Our ranks would dwindle while theirs grew stronger. The key question is *how?* How are they managing to reach our Potentials before we do? For that I have no answer, but I fear the worst. . . ."

"And what's that?" ventured Cynthia weakly.

"Treachery!" boomed Mr. Morrow, pounding his fist into his hand. "Betrayal! Treason against humanity by one of our own! Some here scoff at the notion, but these same people can't tell me how our Potentials are being snatched away. And they have no answers for the breach we suffered last autumn."

"But why would Ms. Richter want to keep all of this a secret?" asked Max.

Mr. Morrow was silent; his rheumy eyes shot quickly from face to face. Suddenly, his features darkened and his jaw quivered.

"Because Richter's nothing but a *bureaucrat*! A *war* is beginning, children! The Enemy is on the move. Only a fool wouldn't see this rash of vyes for what they are—scouts to test our strength and will. Nothing less."

The words came quickly; he clawed at his chair with his fingers.

"War is coming, and our Director clings to process and procedure like every lousy bureaucrat before her. . . . And it's because of fear, I tell you! She's paralyzed by the thought of a mistake— that her competency will be questioned and someone will challenge her for—"

"That is enough!"

Bob's voice shook the cottage; the windows hummed. Max had never seen Bob raise his voice in anger. It was terrifying.

Mr. Morrow did not appear terrified, however. He appeared capable of violence. Slowly, however, the old man's silent fury subsided to anger and then to a weary, defeated look. He nodded at Bob, coughing hard into a fistful of blanket. He gave the children an apologetic wave of his hand.

"You're right, you're right. You bring me soup, and I go ahead and frighten you! It's this horrible flu talking—making me cranky—eh, Bob?"

Bob said nothing. He pulled on his coat and opened the door a crack. A gust of wind upset some papers on a nearby shelf. He watched them settle to the ground in slow spirals.

"We must go. Children, come along with Bob."

"Yes, yes," agreed Mr. Morrow. "You're all very kind for looking after me. Ah! But before you leave, we should have a quick lesson."

Mr. Morrow put down his pipe and leaned forward in his chair.

"I can't frighten you all about vyes without giving you a bit of defense, can I? Vyes hate bright light—causes them to lose their senses for a moment. It's a simple enough trick, but I know they don't get to it until later. You should be able to do it with the energy already in you—no need to tap other sources or gather any."

Mr. Morrow balled his hand and then spread his fingers, hissing, "Solas." The room was filled with a bright burst of light, like a massive flashbulb. Little shapes swam before Max's eyes. A moment later, the room was dim again, lit only by the fire and candles.

"You all try it. It's a simple thing, really."

Connor stepped forward, his hand in a tight fist.

"Solas!"

The room flickered with a bright golden light.

Mr. Morrow nodded and turned next to Cynthia, who looked doubtfully at her hand.

"Solas!"

The room filled momentarily with warm light. Connor and Cynthia seemed delighted with their new skill.

"And you, Mr. McDaniels," murmured Mr. Morrow, dabbing at his nose.

As soon as the word left Max's lips, the room erupted in brilliant light that subsided just as quickly.

"Last but not least, Mr. Menlo."

David shook his head and stepped to the door.

"I can do it," said David simply. "I hope you feel better, Mr. Morrow. I'll visit again soon."

Mr. Morrow nodded and offered a small, sad smile.

"I hope so, Mr. Menlo," he said softly. "And many thanks to all of you for looking in on a poor sick thing! Forgive me if I lost my head."

The children waved good-bye. Mr. Morrow waved back, looking very small and old. He reached for a nearby photo album.

Outside, Bob took long strides to the top of the first dune. He motioned for them to come quickly before disappearing over the crest. Max started to trot ahead but hung back when he heard Connor chiding David.

"Oh, come on, David. *We* all did it."

"I already know I can," muttered David, zipping his jacket and pulling on his gloves with his teeth.

"I know you can, too," said Connor, laughing, "but I want to see for myself, Mr. Magic Man!"

"Me too!" added Cynthia.

"Yeah," said Max, feeling a swell of envy. After all, Mr. Morrow said Max was lucky to have survived Mrs. Millen while

David had had nothing to fear from the vyes that chased him in the woods. "It's not fair for you to just watch all the time."

At Max's words, David stopped pulling on his glove. The smile melted from Max's face. David looked at him impassively for several seconds. With a sudden nod of his head, David flexed his hand.

"Solas," he whispered.

Max gave a yelp and fell backward in the snow as the entire sky erupted in light, illuminating the countryside for miles as though a hundred bolts of lightning had flashed at once. Max's eyes stung from the sudden exposure. Connor and Cynthia were doubled over, shielding their faces, while Bob fumbled blindly for the lantern he had dropped. When Max regained focus, he saw David standing over him, extending his hand.

"Don't ask me to do that again," he whispered, helping Max to his feet. Max nodded, his cheeks flushing in shame. Ascending the dune, David carefully placed the lantern in Bob's groping hand. With a moan, Bob lurched to his feet and placed a hand to his knotty forehead.

"Bob will be fired. . . ."

The trek back was quiet, broken only occasionally by Bob's faint and angry muttering in Russian. Max's spirits were finally lifted by the happy sounds of Nolan's fiddle, which turned his thoughts away from wild charges, lurking vyes, and missing children.

Bob turned to face them.

"Bob goes ahead. Dinner soon. Say nothing of the light," he warned, wagging a finger at them, lingering a moment on Connor's ruddy face. "If you do, Bob gets false teeth. Then Bob *finds* you!" The ogre's features twisted into a hideous, sunken smile, and he pulled the lantern close to cast an eerie glow across his face. Connor whimpered and took a backward step. With a satisfied chuckle, Bob smiled and walked on ahead, taking six feet at a stride.

"He's kidding, right?" Connor said with a weak laugh.

"Of course he is," said Cynthia, sneezing into her sleeve.

As Max and the others approached the Warming Lodge, they saw that the bonfire was still burning brightly, and a dozen students lounged on bales of hay. Nolan was putting his fiddle in its case. Julie was busy aiming her camera at Lucia, who had fallen asleep with Kettlemouth held tightly in her arms. Other students began to stir, standing up and stamping their feet to get the feeling back in their toes.

"Hey there!" drawled Nolan. "Y'all missed the music, but you're in time for dinner. Good timing either way you look at it!"

"Oh, stop it, Nolan," Cynthia blushed. "The music sounded *wonderful*!"

Max and Connor shot each other a look. Even David smiled.

"Thank you, Cynthia," said Nolan. "Did you catch a glimpse of that light?"

Max shut his eyes as he and Connor blurted, "No," while Cynthia and David simultaneously exclaimed, "Yes." Nolan raised an eyebrow.

"Never seen anything like it before," he continued. "Lit up the whole Sanctuary—"

"Oh, Nolan," Cynthia interrupted, "couldn't we hear just one more song—a quick one? Old Tom hasn't chimed the dinner bell just yet."

Nolan hesitated.

"Pleeeaaaaase?" begged Cynthia, tugging on his arm. Connor rolled his eyes and coughed loudly.

"Okay," said Nolan, looking flattered. "A quick one, then. 'Daisy Bell,' to get us thinking of spring around the corner."

Max stopped politely as Nolan began to play. He was anxious to get back to the Manse for dinner. His stomach, his bladder, and the fact that Julie made him queasy led him to look longingly toward the hedge tunnel.

Suddenly, an impossibly magnetic voice, rich and deep, began to sing.

> Daisy, Daisy,
> Give me your answer, do,
> I'm half crazy,
> All for the love of you.
> It won't be a stylish marriage,
> I can't afford a carriage,
> But you'll look sweet,
> Upon the seat
> Of a bicycle built for two.

Max stood rooted to the spot as the words washed over him. Kettlemouth had hopped away from Lucia and now sat alone on a bale of hay. His blood-red throat was puffed out like a balloon; his head pumped up and down in rhythm to the music.

Kettlemouth was singing.

Nolan got a funny look on his face and picked up the tempo. He struck up the tune again, and Kettlemouth's voice filled the clearing. Cynthia started jumping up and down, clapping her hands in wild applause.

"Oh, Nolan," she gushed, "it's beautiful! You're so very talented, Nolan! Really, I mean it. And you have such a *rugged* way about you!"

Max's whole body began to tingle with warmth. He watched as David, with a wry smile, plucked Julie's camera from a nearby chair.

Hoarse barking suddenly filled the air. Frigga and Helga, the Scandinavian selkies, were lumbering toward them from the lagoon in ground-shaking ripples as steam rose off their thick blubber. Coming to a skidding stop, the selkies began to bump each other aside in an effort to gain position next to a handsome Fourth Year boy, who was now in a passionate embrace with a redheaded classmate.

Like a shot, Tweedy bounded off his bale of hay and began to weave mad zigzags through the snow, chasing a spotted rabbit that had been chewing a stray bit of hay. Tweedy's bifocals fell to the ground, where Connor promptly smashed them as he stumbled past to plop down on Lucia's lap. She was now awake and smiled coyly at him, batting her thick eyelashes.

The song began once more; Nolan grimaced as his fingers danced mechanically over the strings. Cynthia began clapping and singing along with an enthusiasm that far exceeded her musical talents. A furious bark erupted from Frigga, who was angrily eyeing the amorous Fourth Years.

"What *she* got that Frigga no have?"

"No winter coat of blubber, that what!" barked Helga.

"*Quiet, you!*" roared Frigga, thumping her sister with an angry head-butt.

Max's heart started beating faster, fluttering like a moth in his rib cage. Julie had risen to her feet and was staring at him with a puzzled expression. As Kettlemouth's voice rose to a fevered pitch, Max took several steps toward Julie and took hold of her hand. She gave his hand a little squeeze in return; her nose was pink, and her breath smelled like peppermint. Max cleared his throat.

"Julie—"

Suddenly, she kissed him, throwing her arms around him and almost knocking him over. Her nose was cold against his cheek, and Max felt weightless. . . .

Old Tom's chimes sounded clear and cold in the winter air. Max opened his eyes in alarm; Julie backed several feet away, her face a deep scarlet. Kettlemouth had abruptly stopped his singing and hopped off the bale of hay. As though they burned him, Mr. Nolan flung his fiddle and bow into the snow and began shaking his cramped hands. A sheepish Connor apologized profusely while Lucia screamed at him in Italian. The Fourth Year boy stood by with a confused and frightened expression on his face as Frigga briskly informed him that "It not have worked out for us, anyway. You are human and Frigga is selkie."

"*Not* a word, you!" Tweedy snapped at Omar, who was giggling in fits as he tried to piece together Tweedy's mangled spectacles. Tweedy whirled to face Nolan, thrusting a paw in the direction of Kettlemouth.

"I demand that such a creature be removed from this Sanctuary! This is an outrage! That amphibian's power is disgusting and irresponsible! It's—it's not *dignified*!"

Nolan shook his head and retrieved his fiddle from the snow, wiping it clean with his sleeve. Cynthia handed him his bow while staring at her boots.

"Now, now, Tweedy," cautioned Nolan, "I grant you I didn't realize Kettlemouth's songs were so . . . *compelling* . . . but it's not his fault. Anyway, his songs just eliminate inhibitions; they don't make you do anything you didn't already want to do."

Max glanced at Julie, who avoided his eyes and gathered up her things.

Tweedy hopped over to Nolan, his whiskers twitching with incredulous rage.

"Are you insane or simply ignorant, man? Are you suggesting that I *wanted* to court some unwashed, uneducated floozy from the wrong side of the meadow? That this is some secret desire I harbor?"

"Well," quipped Nolan, giving a casual wave of his hand to slowly extinguish the bonfire, "it's no secret anymore, is it, Tweedy? But I'll be sure to speak to the Director to see if there are some precautions we should take with Kettlemouth."

A few students snickered while Tweedy stood on his hind legs, bristling and uncharacteristically speechless. Finally, Tweedy hopped after Nolan, who was now walking with several students toward the Sanctuary tunnel. Omar ran after them, erupting in periodic snickers. Lucia had taken Kettlemouth back into the Lodge, slamming the door in Connor's face. Max shivered, watching it all unfold before running after Julie, who was hurrying up the path with a girlfriend.

"Julie, Julie, wait up," huffed Max, slowing to a walk next to her. "I thought maybe you could help me with some homework I have for Strategy—"

"Sorry," Julie muttered, avoiding his eyes. "I have a practical in Devices. Gotta run."

Max watched the two girls disappear into the tunnel. He

sighed and started for the tunnel when he heard Cynthia screech behind him.

"Whatever, Connor!"

As David looked on, Connor was doing a funny, albeit cruel, impersonation of Cynthia applauding Nolan's efforts on the fiddle. He jumped up and down, clapping wildly before clasping his hands in a sudden swoon.

Cynthia looked furious and near tears. "You shouldn't talk, Connor! You were just as big an idiot as any of us!"

"Please," dismissed Connor. "Boys, are we going to let Cynthia off the hook so easily?"

Without a word, David took Julie's digital camera out from his pocket. Scrolling through several photos, he stopped at one and thrust the camera before Connor's eyes.

Connor's smirk vanished. He swallowed and blinked.

"Right, then," he said. "Well—we're late for dinner, and I'm starving."

Connor crunched through the snow for the tunnel. David slipped the camera back into his pocket and sauntered after, whistling "Daisy Bell." Squealing with delight, Cynthia rushed past Max.

"David Menlo! Let me see that photograph!"

The foyer was wet with small puddles of melted snow and boots that had been cast aside. Sounds of laughter and the smell of meat loaf issued from the stairwell to the dining hall. Just as the four children tossed their boots into a corner, Ms. Richter appeared from the hallway leading to her office. With a small frown, she looked at the mess. Suddenly, the icy puddles evaporated from the tiles while the boots arranged themselves in neat pairs against the wall. Then Ms. Richter's attention abruptly shifted to them.

"You four come with me. Now."

It was not a long walk to her office. Max shuffled along in his socks, ignoring Connor's attempts to get his attention and keeping his eyes locked on the floor ahead of him. Pushing open the door, the Director motioned them inside.

Max looked up. He intended to scream but found instead that his mouth merely opened and closed as if he were a goldfish scooped from the water.

Inside the office was Cooper. Tethered to Cooper was a vye.

~ 14 ~

MEETING THE VYES

Towering over Cooper, the vye fixed each of the children with a dark, feral stare. Its snout was wet, and its thick tongue rolled in its mouth as it shifted its weight from one hind leg to the other. Max, Connor, and Cynthia huddled together in the doorway, while David took one look at the vye and fainted, slumping to his knees and toppling over almost casually. Sighing, Ms. Richter reached down to lift David and settle him into her desk chair, stroking his hair and cupping his chin.

"Cooper," she said, "please lead that thing away from the children."

Cooper nodded and tugged gently on a silver tether that was fastened around the vye's neck. Responding with a display of jagged yellow teeth, the vye followed him slowly to a yellow settee near the French doors. Max noticed four dark streaks of dried blood on Cooper's cheek.

"Why isn't it attacking?" breathed Cynthia.

"Because Cooper's caught it in a Passive Fetter; you'll learn to make them by your Sixth Year. Very effective on vyes, but tough to get on them. Shorts out their aggression and makes them susceptible to your command. That's why the Enemy's never wholly relied on them, despite their uses."

"Where did Cooper catch it?" whispered Connor, letting go of Max's shoulder.

"Prowling near the highway into town, disguised as a salesman," replied the Director. "We think this one may have infiltrated our campus several months ago."

David stirred and sat up, and Max saw the vye shift its attention from him to David. Ms. Richter stepped away from her desk to the middle of the room.

"While Cooper's capture is relevant, it's not the sole reason I've asked you here," the Director continued. "It's my understanding that the four of you have had a very confusing ordeal—that you've been frightened by stories of vyes, missing Potentials, and the incompetent Director who's endangering you all."

Max said nothing; he didn't want to get Mr. Morrow into trouble. Furthermore, he found the monstrous vye that sat watching him quietly from the yellow settee to be a considerable distraction. As if sensing his discomfort, the Director raised her hand and addressed the vye in a commanding voice.

"Assume your false form and do not speak."

The creature's eyes glistened darkly as Cooper draped a blanket over its still form. It looked at Max, its twisted wolf-face smiling in a chillingly human manner. Max shuddered as the creature's form began to tremble, shrink, and contort; its features melted away to reveal a balding, middle-aged man with watery eyes now sitting naked beneath the blanket.

"Revolting, counterfeit things," muttered the Director. "Now we can focus on the topic at hand. Mr. Morrow is a wonderful man, but he is very ill. He said some things I am sure he now regrets, and well he should. And he is not the only one. I am a bit disappointed that some of you would discuss topics you have been specifically instructed not to."

Max shrunk before Ms. Richter's gaze. Her expression was grave, but not angry.

"Now that you've been given certain information, I'd like to set the record straight. The first and foremost question is 'Are children missing?' Specifically, Potentials. The answer, as Max apparently overheard, is *yes*. There are currently forty-two children whom we believe have been intercepted and captured by the Enemy shortly after becoming known to us. Mickey Lees is unique—the only child taken by the Enemy *after* passing the tests.

"Despite what you may have heard, however," Ms. Richter said, walking over to a large antique map of the world, "we have not been idle."

Ms. Richter placed her palm on a scanner, and the antique map slid soundlessly into the adjoining wall. A digital map of the world was revealed with numbered codes in different colors scattered across its surface. The majority, Max noticed, were clustered in New England, North Africa, and Eastern Europe.

"Each of these numbers represents a different mission involving our operatives. As Director of Rowan, I am privy to all of these missions. There are currently three hundred and twelve nonclassified missions in various stages of completion. Forty-two of these initiatives involve our missing Potentials—one mission for each child. Master Agents have been called out of retirement, the Prescients Council has been convened, and we have initiated a number of DarkMatter—er, *classified*—operations concerning this situation. Mr. Morrow—and he represents only one among many—is aggravated because he does not have access to all the facts. Incomplete data leads to incomplete conclusions. I am willing to suffer their frustrations because I must keep certain information and initiatives secret. That is the grim necessity of these times."

There was a knock on the door. Mum scurried into the room carrying an elaborate silver coffee service. The hag recoiled when she saw David, averting her eyes as she gave him a wide berth.

"Another late night, eh, Director?" inquired Mum in an anxious voice.

"Yes, Mum," Ms. Richter said, smiling. "Thank you for bringing this to me."

"It's my pleasure, love," Mum gushed. "I'm sorry I'm a bit late, but Bob abandoned me in the kitchens. I was able to manage as I always do," she sighed, "but I think we *may* have to let him go. . . ."

"Yes, Mum," Ms. Richter said patiently. "I'll be sure to speak to Bob. Now, if you'll please close the door on your way out."

Mum bowed, then suddenly stopped and sniffed the air with a quizzical expression on her face. She shot a panicked glance at the vye on the settee and gave Ms. Richter a horrified stare.

Cupping her hands to her mouth, Mum spoke in a whisper heard by everyone in the room.

"Director," she hissed, "there's a *V-Y-E* in the corner!"

With a spastic jerk of her head in the vye's direction, Mum fixed the Director with a knowing look.

"Yes, Mum, we are quite aware of the vye," said Ms. Richter, pouring herself a cup of coffee.

"Would you like me to eat it? It's no trouble at all!" offered Mum, a hopeful note in her voice.

"That's very sweet of you, but no—not just at this moment. Now, if you please, Mum."

With an indignant flip of her lank hair, Mum turned on her heel and marched to the door. Stopping in the doorway, she whirled and grinned at the vye, peeling back her lips to reveal rows of smooth crocodile teeth. With a sudden giggle, she slammed the door and was gone.

The vye looked ill.

"Ms. Richter," asked Cynthia, "would you really *feed* that vye to Mum?"

"Absolutely not," she replied, shaking her head. "Mum's been putting on too much weight and vyes are enormous. Now, back to business."

Sipping her coffee, Ms. Richter walked over to the digital map. With a brisk tap of the screen, she zoomed in on a satellite image of a large city.

"I am happy to report that progress has been made. Nine separate operations have independently converged on the city of Istanbul in Turkey. We have long suspected that there exists a honeycomb of chambers deep beneath Topkapi Palace that may have been tunneled long ago by the Enemy. A number of our

Agents believe the Potentials may be there; other teams suspect a site in northern Hungary."

"So why don't they just go in and get them?" asked Connor.

"I wish it were that simple," replied the Director. "Can any of you see why that might not be the wisest course of action?"

"Well," said Cynthia, "if it's a palace, there are probably lots of people around—tourists and such. They could get hurt, or at the very least, there would be a lot of explaining to do if they saw a bunch of vyes and Agents running around."

The Director smiled and nodded, glancing from face to face for more answers.

"You said the underground chambers are secret—or supposed to be," Max added suddenly. "If that's the case, I would want to spy them out. Even if the Potentials aren't there, the Enemy might be using the place for something else important. If so, I wouldn't want them to know that I'd found them. I'd wait to pick my moment."

Ms. Richter raised her eyebrows and turned to Max.

"I'll have to inform Mr. Watanabe that you're holding back in Strategy," she said. "Any other suggestions?"

"It could all be a trap," murmured David, his eyes wandering over the map before locking on to Ms. Richter's.

"Indeed," replied Ms. Richter, searching David's face for several moments. "Well done—all of you."

Max flushed with pride; Ms. Richter was notoriously spare with her compliments. Looking at her watch, she frowned.

"I need to have a word in private with David and Max. Cynthia, you and Connor may go. I hope this little chat has reassured you that many forces are at work to resolve this situation. And lest you think that you children will be the only ones privy to such terrible secrets, we will be sharing this information with the rest of the school. Now, I suggest you hurry off to the kitchens and see if there's anything left to eat."

Connor gave Max and David a curious look as he and Cynthia made their exit.

"Cooper, you may go as well," said the Director. "Please be sure to get treated for that scratch immediately. We don't need any complications."

Cooper nodded and opened the French doors that looked out onto the orchard. Closing the doors quietly behind him, Cooper led the vye out into the night. Ms. Richter turned her attention back to Max and David.

"I have asked the two of you to stay because I would like to hear precisely why over four dozen books on art history and a pair of forbidden grimoires are missing from the libraries."

David's eyes widened and he shot a glance at Max, but Max only dropped his head, certain of imminent expulsion.

"Cooper was quite impressed with your disappearing act," the Director said with a small smile. "Rowan has had rumors of a back door to the Archives for some time."

"I'm sorry, Ms. Richter," said David. "I got curious—I'll return the books tonight."

Ms. Richter shook her head.

"I'd prefer it if you did not, David," said the Director. "As far as I am aware, you are the only person on this campus capable of using those grimoires without peril. As such, I am more interested in hearing what you have learned than devising some sort of punishment. Would you care to share your thoughts?"

David stood. "Astaroth was never destroyed," he said abruptly. "I knew from the stars in our room."

Max was amazed at the change that had come over his roommate. David's downcast eyes kindled with energy and assumed a darting intensity that seemed to gather and process information continuously. Ms. Richter said nothing but gestured for David to continue.

"I knew Astaroth was alive," continued David. "Everything suggested he was imprisoned somehow. My first guess was that the paintings might be clues to *where* he was imprisoned . . . but the grimoires told me something else."

Ms. Richter sipped at her coffee and listened intently.

"Because Astaroth was so strong, I was curious what kind of prison could hold him," said David, pacing about the room. "I kept imagining a mountain or something huge. The answer was actually the opposite. Interwoven spells of Old Magic were used to bind him within something small and precious— a painting."

"Why a painting?" asked the Director.

David nodded. "That was my question, too, but it's not random. Paintings are perfect prisons for things like this; secret symbols and guardians can be infused into the materials, images, composition, *everything*. . . ."

"Do you know in *which* painting Astaroth is hidden?" asked Ms. Richter pointedly.

"No," said David, shaking his head.

"Really?" said Ms. Richter, raising an eyebrow and leaning forward.

David tried to meet the Director's gaze but looked away and

began coughing. Max was surprised that his roommate, normally so timid, was not more cooperative.

"I don't know if I should say," said David quietly when his coughing had stopped. "I mean, you're the Director. . . . Why don't *you* know? Maybe *nobody's* supposed to know. Maybe they just wanted Astaroth to fade away in a prison no one even knew existed, much less where to find or break it?"

"A fair point," conceded Ms. Richter. "Indeed, it has long been rumored among our faculty that Astaroth was imprisoned in a painting, but I am not aware that any Director has ever had the specifics. Based on what you've said, however, I think that time is past. We must know where Astaroth is and if the Enemy has already taken possession of him."

David cleared his throat.

"I don't know exactly which painting, but I have hunches . . . ," he said.

Ms. Richter glanced at the French doors and closed the curtains with a wave of her hand. David began pacing around the chair once again.

"First of all, the painting will have been completed sometime close to when Astaroth was defeated. That's when he was weak and we had the Tuatha de Danaan as allies—they had the Old Magic needed for the binding spells. I know the Enemy has taken modern paintings, too, but that's all just a cover-up to disguise who's stealing the art and why."

"You're sure?" asked Ms. Richter.

"Yes. Astaroth's too powerful to hold in something temporary or move from one prison to another—all of that's too risky."

Ms. Richter nodded, stirring her coffee and watching David carefully as he continued.

"I also think it would be by a famous painter. The idea is that the Enemy would assume any prison would be hidden away. Famous paintings might be in plain sight, but they don't change ownership often and can be guarded really well."

"Leading candidates?" asked Ms. Richter, nodding.

"Rembrandt and Vermeer," said David.

"Why these artists, specifically?"

David shrugged.

"Time period fits best and others had access to their paintings while they were being made," said David. "I don't think either artist would have even known their work was involved; one of our people—a student of theirs or someone who had access—would have played the pivotal role. Nothing in the Archives' records says that Rembrandt or Vermeer was one of us. Personally, I think the painting is a Rembrandt, but it's most likely any one of these four paintings."

David got up to take a pen from the Director's desk and scribble on a slim pad of paper nearby. Ms. Richter snatched up the paper and glanced at it.

"The good news is they haven't been stolen," said David.

Max tried to glimpse the names through the paper as the Director held it up but was unable to make them out in the soft light. Ms. Richter glanced at him, as though she suddenly realized that he was still there.

"Thank you, David," she said, placing the sheet facedown on her desk. She motioned for David to be seated once again. Opening her drawer, she produced a folder Max had seen before. His pulse began to quicken.

"Now for you, Mr. McDaniels," she said, removing the glossy photograph and flipping it around to face him. Max blinked at the picture of Ronin staring furiously back at him. "Can you explain why you *still* have not shared the fact that you had a conversation with this man on this very campus?"

Max had not heard from Ronin since Halloween; he had assumed enough time had elapsed that Cooper's suspicions had been unreported or dismissed.

"I'm sorry," said Max quietly. "I just thought—"

Her interjection was calm and even.

"You chose not to report this despite the fact that I told you this man was dangerous. You chose not to report this despite the fact that vyes infiltrated this campus several weeks prior."

"Is he a *vye*?" asked Max, horrified.

Ms. Richter stood and walked to the window to open the drapes and watch snowflakes float about the outside lights like tiny moths. "No, Max, he is *not* a vye. Your original instincts about him were on target, nonetheless—he is dangerous. I'm sorry to say he is a graduate of Rowan—a supremely gifted one who is quite misguided. He was cast out several years ago. His name is Peter Varga."

"But he tried to *save* me in Chicago and at the airport," said Max, confused. "He *did* save me. Why was he cast out? What did he do that was so bad?"

The Director's reply snapped through the air with finality.

"He made contact with the wrong people." Her figure remained framed against a backdrop of swirling snow and frosted glass. "You had best go get some supper, Max. You are not to speak to Mr. Varga again or say *anything* about David's research to *anyone*. I will emphasize to you that these are not polite requests I am simply making of a student; these are field orders issued by the Director of Rowan. Do you need me to explain the difference?"

"No, Director," said Max, his face reddening.

"Good," said Ms. Richter in a gentler voice. "Please get some dinner and some rest. David, I would appreciate it if you would remain a bit longer. Good night, Max."

Max left the room as quickly as he could, skirting several students and hurrying down to the dining hall, where Bob had put aside a special plate for him.

The next few weeks were a whirlwind for the students at Rowan. Everyone had been brought up to date by their respective advisors. The news of missing Potentials caused quite a shock as did the distribution of security watches to every student. These watches were thin and silver with a digital screen that was to be pressed hard if danger threatened. While these developments had triggered a buzz among the students, the real shock and gossip began one evening when Cooper brought his hunched and shambling vye to the dining hall.

"We're seeing more of these," Cooper announced to his petrified audience. "We caught this one sniffing round the gates, so the Director thinks it best you see one now—in captivity. Some of you may think you know all about vyes from your books; I thought the same until I met one in Oslo. . . ."

Cooper then gave a very practical and targeted explanation of how to spot and handle vyes. According to the Agent, a fair fight was not what they wanted. The vye's objective was to catch you unaware, even trusting. The key was early detection: a vye was much less likely to attack if it thought it had been identified. In human form, their eyes were often watery, and they had a meandering, indirect way of speaking.

"They like to think they're clever." Cooper smirked. "Catch yourself in conversation with a vye, and it'll be using ominous words and violent metaphors—toying with its prey. Turn the tables; introduce a riddle into the conversation. Vyes love riddles—it will almost always get distracted and try to solve it. Catch-22s are gold: say that you're applying for a job that requires experience, but that you can't get experience without the job. Drives them crazy—a record skipping in their heads.

"*Don't* just rely on your gut to spot a vye," Cooper cautioned. "I know that's the going tip, but it's wrong and risky. Some people can sense a vye in a heartbeat; something about it triggers a response in their genetic memory and they know a predator is near. Some people aren't so lucky. Be alert and remember to check the eyes and speech patterns. Also, remember that vyes almost always work in pairs; *always* be wary of a second vye if one is spotted. Always! The one you see might just be distracting you. If their teeth or claws ever puncture your skin, you've got seventy-two hours to get the antidote or you risk contamination."

Jason Barrett, looking very serious, asked Cooper how best to combat one.

"That depends on you and your strengths," he mused. "I think of vyes as knife-work, but that'd be risky for students. They don't burn easy, but they sure don't like bright light or bitter cold. They're quick, but not quick enough to keep pace with you if you're much of an Amplifier. There are many ways to tangle with a vye. You'll just have to figure out what works best for you."

"And how are we supposed to do that?" a nervous-looking Third Year asked.

"On the Course," Cooper hissed. "On my recommendation, vyes will be randomly inserted into your training scenarios. Effective immediately."

~ 15 ~

UNEXPECTED GUESTS

Following Cooper's dinner demonstration, there was a sharp decline in Course usage. Max had reluctantly continued his scenarios but had yet to encounter any vyes. What he *did* encounter was incessant teasing at the hands of other students as tales of Kettlemouth's song flooded the campus.

Julie now avoided him whenever she could. When their paths did cross, she muttered "Hello" and hurried off, usually flanked by a protective phalanx of girlfriends. The Valentine's Day dinner and dance had come and gone without Max in attendance. The only consolation was that Mum had reportedly hounded Connor throughout the evening, claiming he still owed her a date from Halloween.

Max put Julie out of his mind, however, as he jogged with Rolf and Sarah on the muddy path to the Smithy. It was mid-March, and there was a brisk, wet wind in the air as Rowan shook off the vestiges of winter. Small buds sprinkled the branches, shoots of grass peeked from the soil, and the sky teemed with convoys of pink-tinged clouds rolling in from the sea. The trio quickened their pace as Old Tom chimed five o'clock.

Their class had been attempting more complex scenarios as teams, and the three hoped to complete one before dinner. Three other First Years had just set the best mark, a thirty-one, on a Level Three scenario requiring them to track and capture a golden fawn. To complicate things, the scenario also offered opponents: a pack of mischievous hampersprites who attacked in swarms, clinging to one's legs until the victim was toppled and bound with tree roots.

Sarah punched in the security code, and they entered the building. Moments later, Max felt his usual queasiness of anticipation as the elevator opened to the familiar granite walls of the Course's trophy room. Sarah's speech came rapid-fire.

"Don't forget—communication is the key," she said. "Our goal is to use sunbursts and frighten the fawn to the central clearing, where we can converge on it. Rolf, you'll camp in the clearing so at least one of us is already there; plus, you're the best at Hypnotics. Max, can you Amplify whenever you want?"

"No," said Max. "But I'm getting better—Miss Boon's been giving me lessons."

"Will you try during the scenario? I think it's probably our best chance to catch it."

Max nodded but felt uneasy. There were times he feared that his body simply couldn't contain the energy that Amplification generated. Others feared it, too; Miss Boon often kept her distance during their lessons, instructing Max from across the room.

While they waited for the elevator, Max wandered over to a heavy mail gauntlet suspended in one of the cases. The gauntlet was enormous, forged for a hand twice Max's size. Its rings and plates were twisted and battered. It was the Gauntlet of Beowulf, and next to it were inscribed the names of those students who had demonstrated exceptional courage. Max's eyes wandered over the list, wondering what deeds the students had performed to merit the award. Craning his head, he did a double take. Etched above in fiery script was the name Peter Varga.

Max blinked. According to Ms. Richter, that was Ronin's real name.

Sarah's voice hissed, "Max—come on! The elevator's here!"

Level Three was paneled in tortoiseshell, the swirls creating illusions of depth in contrast to its flat silver doors. Sarah went to door three and punched codes into its console.

"Everybody ready?" asked Sarah, clapping her hands with excitement. With a twist of the knob, they stepped into another world.

Max instantly noticed the different aromas; polished wood and metal had been replaced by moss, earth, and pine. His eyes adjusted quickly to the light as he scanned the deepening sky and gauged the distance across a meadow of tall grass and low bushes bordered by an encircling hedge of forest. The sun's last rays shone orange through gaps in the western trees. Some movement caught his eye; deer were grazing in the meadow, but there was no telltale glint of gold to signal their quarry.

"Rolf, take a position near those bushes in the center," said Sarah urgently. "Keep low and choose a path downwind from those deer. Max and I will split up and head in opposite directions around the forest. Remember what Mr. Watanabe said: slow and steady. Our chances are best on the first try, so make it count!"

Max nodded and slipped into the forest, hugging the trail and avoiding the twigs and branches. He moved quickly; the sun was setting, and its light would be valuable in spotting their target's golden coat. The air was cool, but perspiration formed on Max's brow as he scanned the forest for the reflective eyes of hampersprites. Periodically, he would stop to listen but heard only the beating of his heart and the buzzing of mosquitoes.

Suddenly, a fountain of red sparks erupted like firecrackers above the forest canopy across the meadow—Sarah was in trouble! Max burst out of the forest and raced across the clearing. The deer scattered; Rolf stood up from his hiding spot. "Stay hidden!" Max hissed as he raced past him, his body beginning to Amplify. Seconds later, Max had reached the other side, leaping over a low hedge and into the dark forest.

Three hideous lime-green creatures with mossy hair and yellow cat's eyes clung to Sarah's legs like stubborn toddlers while a fourth wrestled with her hands. Hampersprites. To Max's alarm, another gang of five had taken hold of a tree root and were lugging it like a fire hose to bind her.

"Solas!" he yelled, flexing his hand and filling the forest with a brilliant flash of light. The hampersprites shrieked and shielded their eyes, permitting Sarah to fling one aside and begin peeling the others off her legs.

Max leapt away as a howling hampersprite came charging at

him. He took hold of its little arm and tossed it at those carrying the tree root. The little creatures were dashed to the side, losing hold of the root, which promptly resumed its rigid state.

Sarah had by now raised a low ring of red flames around herself. A half-dozen scowling hampersprites prowled around it, cursing in their high-pitched, jabbering voices. With a yelp, one tried to hurdle the flames, but succeeded only in catching its loincloth on fire. The creature fell to the ground while several others rushed in to smother the flames.

From the corner of his eye, Max caught a golden gleam. Watching the action, with an inquisitive tilt of its delicate head, stood the golden fawn.

"Sarah—on the path!" he hissed. "There it is!"

Sarah risked a quick turn of her head, just as she raised a burst of flame to singe a hampersprite that had slunk behind her.

"Go get it, Max!" she panted. "I've got this under control. Run!"

As if sensing the upcoming chase, the fawn swished its tail and bolted down the path. With a predatory leap, Max was after it, his feet kicking up bits of bark and soil. Max quickened his pace and ignored the sting of branches that whipped at his face, but the golden fawn always managed to bound ahead just out of reach, holding to the gentle curve of the trail.

I'll never catch it this way, thought Max. *This must be part of the scenario—speed alone can't catch it. It's sticking to the path— I have to head it off!*

Veering to the left, he sprinted out into the meadow, estimating the best angle at which to cross the clearing and intercept the fawn. He ran fast and low, trying to make use of whatever cover was available. Slowing almost to a stop, he crawled on his belly through a thicket and reentered the forest. He grinned as he heard the soft thud of trotting footsteps coming down the path. Scanning about for cover, Max leapt twelve feet straight up, onto a thick branch overhanging the trail. A moment later, he was perched above the path like a great cat lying in ambush.

The approaching footsteps slowed; something was now moving very deliberately. Max hushed his breathing and wiped the sweat out of his eyes. Squinting, he saw a shape emerge from the shadows, walking slowly and clearly too big to be the fawn. Max flickered with annoyance as he thought it was Rolf abandoning his post. Annoyance, however, withered to sickening dread as the figure stole closer on the forest floor below him.

It was the ears that triggered Max's initial rush of terror.

The vye had ears like a wolf, only longer, and they twitched with alertness as it suddenly shifted its gait and rose onto its hind legs. It took a quick step to the right, crouching to investigate the depths of the dark thicket. Then it stopped. It sniffed the air and swept its great head in Max's direction. Max held his breath, fighting the urge to scream as the vye abandoned the thicket and crept toward Max's tree.

The vye was huge: over eight feet of rangy muscle, matted hair, and sinew. It edged closer. The top of the vye's gray-black head was only a few feet away when it stopped at the base of the tree. Its head was bowed; its panting breath was hoarse and quick. Suddenly, it spoke in the voice of a woman, its tone calm and with a hint of playfulness.

"Do you have him, my love?"

"Yes, my love."

The reply was whispered from behind Max. He whipped his

head around to see the leering face and bared fangs of a second vye inches from his own.

Max screamed and let go of the branch. He flailed and kicked in anticipation of rending claws and ripping teeth.

Nothing happened. With a croak, he opened his eyes and saw that he was sprawled on the blank white floor of the spacious scenario room. Rolf and Sarah were looking at him with a mixture of shock and concern.

"What happened?" asked Rolf. "Was there a malfunction?"

"I don't know," breathed Sarah. "Max, did you get the fawn?"

Max shook his head; his chest rose in rapid beats while sweat poured off his body. He took a long, quivering breath.

"There were vyes in the scenario—" he said.

Before Max could finish his sentence, the door to the chamber opened. Nigel Bristow stood in the doorway, out of breath and agitated.

"We have unexpected guests, Max," he stated flatly. "Your father is at the front gate with another man, a Mr. Lukens. Get your things and come quickly."

On the elevator ride up, Nigel gave Max a frank look.

"Max, did you know that your father was planning to visit?" asked Nigel.

"No," Max breathed, simultaneously thrilled and terrified at the news of his father's arrival. Seeing Nigel's expression, Max blurted, "I swear I didn't, Nigel! He mentioned in his last letter that he had a surprise for my birthday next week, but I thought it was just a present."

"Who is this Mr. Lukens?"

"He's my dad's boss," replied Max. "He owns the agency

where my dad works. Oh my God, Nigel, what are we going to do? I know my dad—he's going to want to see my room, meet my friends . . . *everything!*"

Nigel placed a steadying hand on his shoulder.

"Relax, my boy. A bit of a surprise, granted, but it's not as though this is the first unexpected visitor we've received. We know how to keep up appearances," explained Nigel, guiding Max on a brisk walk out of the Smithy. "At the gate, your father and Mr. Lukens received special visitor badges that will *filter* their experience. Instead of the Rowan you know, they'll be witness to nothing more than a posh little prep school. Have faith— the badges are really quite marvelous."

"If you say so," Max said. A sudden wave of realization washed over him: his dad was here. His father whom he had not seen in over six months was here, and Max would get to see him any moment.

A sly smile crept across Nigel's face. Stopping abruptly, he scratched his chin, as though pondering a difficult question. "By the way, how do you think you would have scored on that scenario?"

Max rolled his eyes and started trotting ahead, calling back over his shoulder.

"I dunno—a six, maybe seven. . . ."

"Hmmm. And how do you think the vyes scored?" inquired Nigel with a chuckle. "An eighty? Ninety, even? Always look for the second vye, Max! *Always!*"

"Yeah, yeah," groaned Max, "like I'll ever forget now. See you there!" Max ran ahead of Nigel, making for the Manse, whose windows now shone bright and cheery.

When Max opened the door, he saw his father's mountainous figure in the foyer, wearing his olive trench coat and gesturing wildly to Mr. Lukens, who was dressed neatly in a topcoat and fedora. A large, gift-wrapped box sat on the floor, and both men wore white badges on slender cords around their necks. As Max walked inside, Mr. McDaniels stopped in mid-sentence and turned around.

"There he is!" his father exclaimed, his blue eyes brightening. "There's my guy! *Surprise!*"

"Dad!" Max exclaimed as he was abruptly hoisted six inches off the ground.

"Ugh, you're getting too big and tough for your old dad to lift! Bob, is it me or has Max grown half a foot since August?"

"A foot at least," said Mr. Lukens, tipping his hat. "Good to see you, Max. Happy birthday. I hope I'm not intruding—your father was kind enough to let me tag along after our pitch in Boston. Funniest thing, though, trying to find this place. I could have sworn it wasn't on the map until your dad finally spied it! I must be getting old." He chuckled and retrieved a slim black box from his coat.

"Hi, Mr. Lukens," said Max, stepping over to shake Mr. Lukens's hand and accept the present. "It's very nice to see you. Thank you for the gift."

"Oh, it's nothing," said Mr. Lukens with a dismissive wave. "I hope you like it. It's a tad personal so you might open it in private."

Max nodded and slipped the package into his pocket.

"Actually, we've got Mr. Lukens to thank for letting *me* tag along," gushed Mr. McDaniels. "Told me a few weeks ago I'd be going to the meeting—this was his idea! It was everything I could do not to spill the beans that I'd be popping in for your birthday!"

Nigel quietly slipped into the foyer and gave a little wave.

"Dad," said Max, tugging at his father's elbow, "this is Mr. Bristow. He's—"

"In admissions," Nigel interjected, engaging Mr. McDaniels in a friendly handshake. "I had the pleasure of meeting you at the airport."

"Of course, of course," Mr. McDaniels said, pumping Nigel's hand. "How could I forget? Nigel, please meet Bob Lukens— head honcho of my agency. Actually, if you're in admissions, you're probably just the guy Bob wants to see. He has a niece in-terested in—"

"Scott," Mr. Lukens interjected, "let's not torture Mr. Bristow just yet. It sounds as though dinner is being served. Maybe Max can give us a tour and we can corner Mr. Bristow before we have to catch our flight . . . ?"

"I've got an idea," said Nigel. "Allow me to take you to dinner to celebrate Max's birthday. I'd be happy to answer your questions there. Max, why don't you show your dad your room while I offer Mr. Lukens the express tour? Meet back here in twenty min-utes?"

"Perfect," said Mr. McDaniels, looping an arm around Max.

Max hoisted the gift-wrapped box and started up the stair-case, turning back to see Nigel leading Mr. Lukens into a sitting room. Mr. Lukens smiled politely, his eyes following Max and his father's progress up the stairs.

"So," said Mr. McDaniels, his face shiny from the climb,

"surprised to see me? Think I'd miss your initiation into the terrible teens?"

"I'm really glad you're here," Max said, relieved to see his third-floor hallway empty. "I missed you!"

He gave his father's badge a hopeful glance and opened the door.

"Well," he said, wincing, "here it is. . . ."

His father took a step inside the doorway and stood silent for a moment. Max froze. The light from David's reading lamp was reflected in the glass dome where Andromeda was fading in the night sky. David was curled up in bed, an open grimoire on his lap, while he closely examined a large Vermeer print. He spoke without so much as a glance at the door.

"Hey. How was the scenario?"

Max shut his eyes tight and gulped.

"Uh, fine," said Max. "Dad, this is my roommate, David Menlo. . . ."

David's head snapped up to gape at Mr. McDaniels, who stepped past Max, laughing and extending his hand. David started coughing profusely as he slid the grimoire under his pillow, alternating panicked looks between Max and his father.

"Nice to meet you, Mr. McDaniels," David peeped.

"Call me Scott, David. Mr. McDaniels is my father," he said amiably while looking around the room. "Well, they sure don't give you much space, but I guess this is cozy enough!"

Humming to himself, Mr. McDaniels ambled down the stairs to examine a framed photograph of their family taken before Bryn McDaniels had disappeared. David poked Max in the shoulder.

"What's going on?" David hissed. "Does your dad know about Rowan?"

"It's okay," whispered Max. "He's wearing a visitor badge that hides anything funny. Why aren't you at dinner?"

David shrugged. "Got wrapped up in my book—wasn't hungry."

"Did I hear you say you haven't eaten?" said Mr. McDaniels, his head popping up from the stairwell. Both Max and David jumped.

"Uh, yeah," said David. "But I can get something later—they usually keep leftovers in the kitchen."

"Nonsense! You're coming to celebrate Max's birthday with us!"

"Oh, that's okay," muttered David. "Thanks, though."

"Nonsense again!" cried Mr. McDaniels.

"Give in, David. He'll drag you if he has to," Max said with finality.

"It's true!" Mr. McDaniels conceded, planting a kiss on top of his son's head. "Oh, it's good to see my birthday boy! Let's unwrap your present and get going—my fuel tank's near empty."

"If you insist." Max grinned, sliding the large box across the floor. He peeled off handfuls of wrapping paper while Mr. McDaniels chuckled in anticipation and winked at David.

"Wow, it's, uh, great!" said Max, trying to sound enthusiastic as he studied the box. "Thanks, Dad!"

"What is it?" asked David, leaning forward.

"It's a Beefmeister 2000!" crowed Mr. McDaniels. "You boys will be able to grill your favorite meats and veggies *right here at school*!" Max's father seemed to swell with pride.

"Oh, it looks really neat," offered David. Max shut his eyes and waited.

"'Neat?'" exclaimed Mr. McDaniels. "Is the Great Wall of China *neat*? The Grand Canyon? Then don't make the mistake of underestimating the Beefmeister 2000! David, what would you say if I told you this product could handle anything desired by the summer sportsman? *Anything*—from steaks to rotisserie chicken to a delicate salmon fillet! And with its EZ-Clean patented surface, cleanup's not just easy, it's *fun*!"

David's eyes widened. He shot an incredulous glance at Max, who merely shrugged.

"And that's not all," said Mr. McDaniels with a sly wink. He slipped an envelope out of his pocket and handed it to Max.

Max tore it open and read the enclosed certificate.

"It says twice a month, I'll be receiving a shipment of assorted meats. . . . Thanks again, Dad."

"That's a great present, Mr. McDaniels," said David, his hand positioned oddly in front of his face. "Awesome."

The McDanielses left David to change and walked back to the foyer, but Mr. Lukens and Nigel had not yet returned. The sounds of supper could be heard from the back stairs off the great hall.

"Let's go take a peek down there, Max," said Mr. McDaniels, veering toward the stairwell. "It'd be fun to meet some more of your classmates!"

"Uh, we'd better not. David will be here in a minute, and so will Mr. Lukens."

"Aw, c'mon," chided Mr. McDaniels, already disappearing down the stairs.

In desperation, Max looked once more for Nigel before

scurrying after his father. He froze at the bottom of the stairs as he heard his father's voice call out.

"Miss Aloha! How are you?"

Max hurried around the corner to see Mr. McDaniels standing by the head table, shaking the hand of a very surprised Miss Awolowo. His broad face was beaming as he surveyed the large hall full of students, who had stopped eating to gape at the unexpected intrusion.

"Hi, everyone," Mr. McDaniels boomed, giving a friendly wave. "I'm Scott McDaniels—Max McDaniels's dad!"

The room was silent; a few students gave awkward waves. Max saw Alex Muñoz doubled up with laughter at one of the tables. Catching Max's eye, he puffed out his cheeks to mock Mr. McDaniels's girth. Anna and Sasha were red and shaking with laughter.

Undaunted by the silence, Mr. McDaniels rocked back and forth.

"Visiting from Chicago," he explained with his usual good cheer. "Max's birthday's coming up—*the big thirteen!*"

Max felt hundreds of eyes shift from his father to him. Ears burning, he nodded and tugged at his father's sleeve. Suddenly, Nigel descended the stairs accompanied by Mr. Lukens and David.

"I thought you might have stolen down here," Nigel chided, looking at his watch. "I told the Grove we'd try to be there by seven, so we'd better be on the move."

As Nigel finished his sentence, the dining hall was illuminated by a flash of light. Mr. Lukens smiled and placed a small camera back in his pocket.

"Wonderful shot," he explained, upon seeing Nigel's frown. "My niece will love getting a sense of daily life—"

"I'll be happy to send you some brochures, Mr. Lukens," Nigel replied tersely. "Please do not take any more photographs of the students; it is illegal to do so without their parents' permission."

"Of course," said Mr. Lukens. "Please accept my sincere apologies."

"Apology accepted," said Nigel, taking Mr. Lukens by the arm and lightly steering him toward the stairs.

Four unfamiliar adults were waiting in the foyer. As Max reached the top of the stairs, Ms. Richter's voice called to the new arrivals from the hallway that led to her office. They nodded at Nigel and filed past Mr. Lukens to disappear down the hallway.

"Well, now," Mr. Lukens quipped, as though speaking to himself. "Someone *quite* important must be down that hall. . . ."

As Nigel held the door for Max and David, another flash illuminated the foyer.

"Mr. Lukens," Nigel snapped. "I thought we'd agreed that photographs are not permitted."

Mr. Lukens held up his hands in a defensive gesture.

"I thought the prohibition was against having students in the photographs. Surely you don't object to a photo of this magnificent chateau?"

Nigel said nothing, but Max saw a vein throb in his forehead. Mr. Lukens breezed past him and down the steps to the fountain.

Dinner was a tale of two conversations, with Mr. McDaniels entertaining Max and David at one end of the table while Nigel and Mr. Lukens were engaged at the other. Mr. McDaniels was describing the many merits of Bedford Bros. Crispy Soup Wafers to an attentive David when Mr. Lukens called over.

"Scott, Mr. Bristow just asked what it takes to be successful in advertising. What do you think?"

"That's easy," chortled Mr. McDaniels, wiping his mouth before continuing to speak. "You've got to love your client and love their products! Without that, it's just a job, and if it's just a job, you won't be successful."

"Cheers to that," said Nigel, raising his glass. "Here's to doing what you love—what's that they say? 'If you love what you do, you'll never work a day in your life?' Anything to add, Mr. Lukens?"

Mr. Lukens paused a moment, shooting Nigel a mischievous grin. Max thought he looked like a little boy who had been caught cheating at something trivial.

"Oh, I think Scott said it well enough," he said. "A bit idealistic, perhaps. My bias is that successful advertising requires you to shock your audience—catch them unaware and, eh, go for that jugular."

Mr. Lukens beamed and shrugged his shoulders.

"Most of the time, you've only got that one shot to get them, so it'd better count," he added, before glancing at his watch. "My God—is that the time? Scott, I hate to say it, but we've got a plane to catch."

Mr. McDaniels looked at his watch and frowned, looping an arm around Max in the process. "I guess we do," he said softly, forking a last bite of potato.

Nigel had Mr. Lukens drop them at the gate, insisting that it would save valuable minutes for their trip to the airport. They all piled out of the car and said their good-byes. After Nigel had collected the visitor badges, Mr. McDaniels gave Max a long, fierce hug and whispered that it would not be long until Max would be coming home.

Max watched as the car's taillights shrank to small red dots before finally disappearing. David waited patiently near the gate as Nigel put a hand on Max's shoulder.

"Happy birthday, Max," said Nigel. "I'm very glad you could see your father, if just for a few hours. Now, if you don't mind, I'd like you to tell me anything you know about the irrepressible Mr. Lukens."

"I don't know," said Max, fighting the heaviness in his heart. "He seems nice—he brought me a present."

Nigel's smile wavered.

"What was it, if I might pry?" asked the Recruiter.

"I don't know yet," said Max, retrieving the slim case from his pocket. "He told me to open it in private."

"Max," said Nigel, "that is a decidedly odd request. Do you mind if I have a look?"

Max shook his head. Nigel plucked the box from his hand and removed its silver ribbon. A moment later, Max saw a glint of gold as Nigel flipped open the black velvet lid. Inside was a jeweled dagger with a green handle. Nigel studied it a moment before his eyes widened in apparent recognition. The blood drained from his face.

"Dear God," he muttered, fumbling in his pocket.

"What?" said Max as Nigel retrieved a slim phone and began frantically punching numbers. Nigel held up a finger for quiet.

"Gabrielle? Nigel. Abort the mission. Dear Lord—abort, abort, *abort*! I'll explain everything—have to go!"

"Nigel!" Max yelled, feeling a queasy sense of panic. "What's going on?"

Nigel ignored him and pressed another button on his phone.

"This is Nigel Bristow, Senior Recruiter. Emergency intercept requested of two subjects in black rental sedan bound for Logan Airport. First four characters of license plate are DL42. . . . *Top priority!* Apprehend both subjects—use caution and do not harm them!"

"Nigel!" Max screamed, trying to snatch the phone from the man's hand.

Nigel hugged Max close to him.

"It's going to be okay," he said, herding Max over to where David stood looking petrified. "But we need to get inside immediately."

Clutching the dagger, Nigel led them toward the Manse, their footsteps spraying wet gravel as they ran.

~ 16 ~

ROWAN'S NEW RESIDENT

Max paced back and forth by the fountain, ignoring Miss Awolowo's pleas that he sit. For the past two hours, David had sat quietly, trailing his fingers through the mist that rose like little wraiths from the fountain. A murder of crows took flight from the dark woods near the gate just before Max saw headlights emerge into the clearing. A limousine was making its way slowly along the road that bordered the ocean. Max kept his eyes on the approaching car even as he noticed Nigel descending the Manse's front steps.

"Max, please listen to me," the Recruiter said. "Your father is in that car, but—"

Max bolted up the drive, meeting the car halfway as it turned and made its way toward them. He smacked his hand against the black windows, but the car did not slow until it finally came to a stop near the fountain. Nigel looked helpless as he stepped between Max and the car.

"Max, *please*—let them do their jobs," he pleaded.

The back doors to the limousine opened, and an unfamiliar man and woman emerged, followed by Cooper. Max looked through the open door and saw his father lying limp and still inside. Max's hands shook uncontrollably.

"*You!*" he screamed at Cooper, trying to step past Nigel at the Agent. "What did you do to him?"

Cooper ignored Max and gestured to his companions to lift Mr. McDaniels out of the car. Max felt Nigel's hands holding his shoulders.

"Max," Nigel pleaded. "It's going to be fine—"

Max shoved Nigel off to the side and rushed at Cooper.

The other man saw Max coming and moved to intercept him. Max reacted, ducking as the man's arms reached out, then punching hard up and into the man's ribs. Cooper stepped quickly around the car, putting it between Max and himself as the woman went to grab Max's wrists. He was too quick, slipping out of her grasp and springing up onto the roof of the limousine. Cooper was calmly backing away toward the fountain, his face composed and unafraid; Max was determined to change that.

Max leapt.

Cooper stood unmoving as Max hurtled through the air.

Suddenly, the Agent disappeared behind a wall of water as the fountain suddenly emptied itself to form a protective dome around him. Max shrieked as he landed on top of it. He clawed furiously at the improbably tough, shimmering surface to get at the shadowy, rippling figure behind it. The water began to hiss and steam, giving way before him. Max pried apart an opening and forced his head and arm through.

Cooper held a sheathed knife to Max's throat.

"Poor choice," the Agent whispered.

Suddenly, Cooper gritted his teeth, and the knife fell from his hand. Gasping, he dropped to his knees, crumpling to the ground like an aluminum can being crushed by invisible hands. Max was set gently on his feet by some unseen force as the barrier dissolved, its waters streaming over his shoes to fill the fountain once again.

Max saw David standing on the fountain's rim, his face deadly serious as he focused on Cooper's motionless body. A crowd had gathered on the front steps of the Manse, and Miss Awolowo was doing her best to get them back inside.

Max ran to his father.

Nigel and the woman held Mr. McDaniels between them; the man Max had punched sat propped against the limousine, holding his side and taking uneven breaths.

"Your father is fine, Max," grunted Nigel, straining under Mr. McDaniels's weight. "Unconscious, but fine. Lend us a hand and let's take him to a guest room."

Ignoring the stares and whispers, Max helped carry his father inside.

* * *

The next day, Scott McDaniels lay sleeping on top of a four-poster bed, wearing one of Bob's enormous flannel shirts; it draped over his not insubstantial body like a nightgown. Max placed a fresh washcloth to his father's forehead.

"Feeling better, Dad?"

His father smiled and squeezed Max's hand.

"A little," he said. "Just give me a minute."

Max sat at a small desk and gazed out a white-curtained window at the orchard below. A number of Fourth Years were walking down the path, laughing.

"Want me to close the window?" Max asked.

"Nah," he said. "Breeze feels nice."

Max tapped his knee and watched his father's mammoth torso expanding in slow, ponderous breaths. He turned away and studied the room's woven mats of dried grasses and furniture of dark woods, wicker, and smooth green cushions. Max left his seat to explore the private bath of cool stone tile and silver faucets. Finally, his dad's voice rumbled from the other room.

"What?" said Max, poking his head around the corner. Mr. McDaniels was now sitting up; the damp washcloth had fallen onto the floor.

"The museum," he mumbled. "The Art Institute—on Mom's birthday. You weren't lying to me, were you?"

"No," said Max, sitting on the bed next to his dad and retrieving the washcloth. "That's the day this all started, I guess. That's the day I found that room and saw it."

" 'It' what?"

"The tapestry. It was my vision—it let the people here know about me."

"I had no idea," croaked Mr. McDaniels, shaking his head

and looking around the room. "No idea that anything like this existed, much less that my son was a part of it. . . ."

There was a soft knock on the door, and Max went to open it.

Mum came hurtling through the door, holding a tray of toast and tea.

"I came as soon as they'd let me," she panted. "Oh, you poor things! Let Mum take care of the nice, big man."

Setting the tray on the bed, Mum tittered and danced an excited little jig at Mr. McDaniels, who stood speechless against the wall. Max quickly inserted himself between his father and the hag. Mum began petting Max's hand and humming contentedly, but her crocodile eye remained fixed on Scott McDaniels.

"Mum," said Max firmly, "I'd like you to meet my dad, Scott McDaniels."

"Oh, how delightful!" exclaimed the hag, using the introduction as an excuse to try and tunnel past Max.

"And," said Max, blocking her path, "seeing as he's a *guest* and not a meal, I'd like you to sniff him. Now."

Max ignored his father's groan and focused on Mum, who recoiled in apparent shock and embarrassment. She glanced in panic at Mr. McDaniels and then at Max before laughing indulgently.

"Your son, Max, is quite the teaser," she said, wagging her finger. "He forgets that Mum is a *reformed* hag. Surely some primitive sniffing ritual is unnecessary and unseemly, don't you think?"

"It *is* necessary, Mum, and you'll do it or I'll go get an instructor."

Mum laughed off Max's demand with polite indifference.

"Would you like a tour of the kitchens, sir?" she inquired sweetly. "There's quite a feast in store for dinner this evening."

"Mum!" snapped Max. "You sniff him right now or I'll go get David."

Mum shrieked and shot a glance at Max.

"You *wouldn't.*"

"I would," insisted Max. "I can have him here in two minutes."

"Oh, these silly games we play." She rolled her half-lidded eyes at Mr. McDaniels. "If your son and I weren't dating, I'd never put up with it—"

"Mum!"

"Fine!" she roared, reaching past Max to seize Mr. McDaniels's wrist in her meaty hand. His father gave a startled yelp and practically climbed the wall behind him.

"He's moving too much!" she snarled over her shoulder. "I can't work like this!"

"It's okay, Dad," Max assured him. "It'll be over in a second."

Shutting his eyes, Scott McDaniels stopped struggling and let the plump, ferocious-looking creature squeeze and pinch at his arm before running her quivering nostrils along its length.

"Done!" she bawled, flinging his arm aside. *"And it's a crying shame, too!"* The hag looked Mr. McDaniels over from head to toe and shook her head sadly, before stalking out and slamming the door behind her.

"Oh my God," muttered Mr. McDaniels, thick beads of sweat running down his forehead.

"That's the hardest part," Max promised. "Now that she's sniffed you, you're okay."

Mr. McDaniels did not answer but merely glanced down at

the enormous flannel shirt he was wearing, its sleeves cut in half
so their length would accommodate him.

"*Who* does this belong to?" asked Mr. McDaniels slowly.

"Bob. He's our other chef. . . . We should go meet him, too."

"I need to lie back down," Mr. McDaniels muttered, peeling back the covers and crawling beneath them. "I'll meet Bob
later."

There was another quiet knock. Annoyed, Max walked over
and wrenched the door open.

"Mum—" snapped Max.

Cooper stood outside.

"The Director would like to see you," he said softly.

Max stared at the man's scars and the scattered patches of
light blond hair visible now that Cooper had removed his cap.
Glancing back at his father, Max saw he was lying still with the
washcloth flung once more over his eyes.

"I don't know if I should leave him here alone . . . ," said Max.

Cooper nodded, in apparent understanding.

"I'll watch over him," the Agent volunteered, clearing his
throat and glancing down at Max. "Or I can get another . . ."

"No," said Max, looking hard at Cooper. "No, I'd rather it be
you."

Cooper's granite features softened. He bowed his head and
quietly shut the door, standing outside as Max left the guest wing
and made for Ms. Richter's office.

David was already waiting when he got there, along with Nigel.
The dagger Mr. Lukens had given Max lay on the Director's desk.

"How is your father?" asked Ms. Richter, motioning for Max
to take a seat.

"He's doing okay," said Max quietly. His face began to turn red. "How is that man? The man I hit . . ."

"Three broken ribs," said Nigel. "Fortunately, he was wearing Nanomail. . . . I should consider myself lucky that it was *him* on the receiving end and not me."

"I'm sorry," said Max, looking away.

"You need to control that temper of yours, Max," said Ms. Richter, examining the dagger. "But by all accounts, we were very fortunate last evening, broken ribs aside. Max, do you know anything about this dagger?"

Max shook his head.

"It's a replica of a famous dagger—the Topkapi Dagger, given as a gift to the shah of Persia. It was lucky for us that Nigel recognized it," explained Ms. Richter.

Max listened carefully, positive that he had heard the word "Topkapi" before. He turned in his seat and looked at the Director's digital map, which was activated and glowing on the opposite wall. The map showed the city of Istanbul; number codes indicating individual missions formed a wide perimeter around a particular section of the city.

"Topkapi Palace," he breathed. "That's where you said the missing Potentials might be."

"That's right," said Ms. Richter, glancing at David. "It was a trap. Mr. Lukens is in the service of the Enemy. Apparently he couldn't resist a little gibe that he believed would go unnoticed until it was too late."

"Where is he?" asked Max.

"He escaped," she said. "Others came to his aid and we might have endangered your father had we pressed the issue."

"Is Mr. Lukens a *vye*?" asked Max.

"No, Max," said Ms. Richter. "He is not a vye; he is merely a man in the service of the Enemy. Just one of many, I am sorry to say. The Enemy's promises are very tempting. . . ."

Ms. Richter placed the dagger back within its case and snapped it shut.

"Mr. Lukens's arrogance saved many lives," she said softly. "But our little victory has disturbing implications. The Enemy knew precisely when and where our people would strike."

Her eyes locked onto Max's.

"I have already informed David. Neither of you is to spend any time alone with a member of this school's faculty or senior staff—with the exception of myself, Nigel, or Miss Awolowo. If anything suspicious occurs, you are to activate your security watch immediately. You are to keep this watch on your person at all times. Is that understood?"

Max frowned.

"What about my Amplification lessons with Miss Boon?" he asked.

Ms. Richter nodded.

"They are to continue—Cooper or I will also be in attendance. Now, I know you have midterms this week. I suggest the two of you get some studying accomplished while Mr. McDaniels is resting."

David got up and went to the door, but Max lingered to ask a question.

"Ms. Richter, what's going to happen to my dad?" he asked quietly.

The Director was gazing out the window, massaging her hands. She turned and smiled at Max.

"He is most welcome to stay here, of course. Rowan will be his home."

Max almost knocked the portraits off the wall as he ran back to his father's room, bursting with the best news he'd had in months.

A week later, however, his joy was forgotten as Max rubbed his temples and stared at the last question in his exam booklet. It stared back in small black letters:

> 50. Prioritize the following strategic components according to their importance in the scenario described above.
> __ Position
> __ Resources
> __ Initiative
> __ Flexibility
> __ Information

Max sighed and glanced out the window; a number of older students were throwing Frisbees that bucked in the lingering gusts from the previous day's storm. The early-afternoon sun coaxed radiant hues from the grounds, as Rowan's campus had blossomed quickly with spring. Max looked longingly at clean stretches of emerald lawn and walkways bustling with daffodils and tulips, Peruvian lilies and Spanish bluebells. The *Kestrel* bobbed on a brilliant cobalt sea.

Cynthia was the only other student left in the classroom. Mr. Watanabe had already begun to grade the midterms; his pen shot across the pages like a typewriter carriage.

"One minute left," muttered Mr. Watanabe.

The instructor smiled at Max and turned back to the completed exams. Cynthia rifled through the pages of her test with a revolted expression on her face. With a few despondent slashes of his pencil, Max randomly assigned numbers to the blank spaces before surrendering his exam.

Connor and David were waiting on Old Tom's steps, chatting in the bright sunlight.

"So?" asked Connor with an expectant grin.

"Failed," said Max, hoisting his backpack higher on his shoulder. "How was it for you guys?"

"I squeaked by," admitted Connor. "I peeked at David's, though. Sickening, really—chock-full of correct answers with little side notes questioning Watanabe's assumptions."

David shrugged, looking sleepy.

"Whatever." Max grinned. "Forget that test. Midterms are over and we're going off campus!"

"Yahoo!" whooped Connor, flinging his bag aside and sprinting to intercept a Frisbee that skimmed over the grass nearby. Catching it neatly in one hand, he whirled to toss it to an expectant Fourth Year girl but accidentally flung it far out over the rocky bluff and down onto the beach below. "Sorry!" he yelled, wincing under a verbal barrage as he loped back sheepishly to retrieve his bag.

The three made their way toward the fountain to join their classmates.

Once Cynthia finally arrived, the First Years headed out to Rowan Township. Mr. Vincenti, Miss Boon, and several other faculty members and adults went with them. Max focused on one in particular—his father, who had been slowly acclimating to life at Rowan and had come to join them. They walked along to-gether, smiling as Connor provided running commentary regarding people and places as they went. Connor took special pains to point out one student, who was pestering Miss Boon about her Mystics exam.

"And that—*that's* Lucia over there. Italian. Fiery. She practically attacked me with her lips when Kettlemouth—that's her charge—started singing back in February. She claims it was the frog, but I say *chemistry. . . .*"

"You can judge for yourself, Mr. McDaniels," said David with a grin. "I've got a photo of them on my computer. Actually, I use it as my screensaver."

"You said you'd delete that!" protested Connor, shooting Mr. McDaniels a glance and turning scarlet.

Max was anxious to show his father Rowan Township and thrilled that Ms. Richter had decided to resume chaperoned visits—if only over the protests of many teachers, including a recovered and unapologetic Mr. Morrow. While Rowan offered endless opportunities to explore, the students had been confined to its grounds for months and were becoming a bit stir-crazy.

Max and his friends left their bags with a heap of others at the base of the tree where Mr. Morrow had carved his name decades before. Then they dragged Mr. McDaniels to Mr. Babel's patisserie, where the display window had changed with the seasons. It now featured white-chocolate saplings whose branches cradled spun-sugar birds' nests laden with marbled chocolate eggs. Behind the counter, Mr. Babel worked on a magnificent cathedral made of brownie slabs and chocolate tiles.

Max eyed the display case as Mr. Babel walked around the

corner to introduce himself to Scott McDaniels. Once he heard his father slip into "salesman voice," Max knew he would have some time to choose carefully from among the hundreds of sweets lining the glass cases.

"Oh, no you don't!" huffed Sarah, clamping a hand over his eyes. "Not until *after* you break the records next week."

Max glowered at her playfully. His marks in Training and Games had been approaching several Rowan records, and Sarah had assumed the role of his unofficial trainer. She blinked at Max's evil look, before abruptly wiping her mouth clean of crumbs.

"Let's go sit outside," she suggested sympathetically, while Connor and David bought large wedges of broken chocolate bunnies that were being sold at a discount.

"Be out there in a minute," Mr. McDaniels said, before lowering his voice. "Can you *believe* he hasn't even heard of Bedford Bros. Crispy Soup Wafers?"

"Dad, they're not your client anymore."

"I know, I know," said Mr. McDaniels, shrugging with a rueful smile. "That doesn't mean it's not a quality product. . . ."

Max gave a relieved sigh as his father resumed his conversation with Mr. Babel; it was the first real sign that Mr. McDaniels was recovering from the many surprises of the previous week.

The students walked outside, where Miss Boon was sitting on a park bench and writing feverishly in her journal. She glanced at them and nodded as they filed past to gather at the tree where they had left their bags. Several First Years began climbing the tree, swinging their legs over its thick branches. Rolf called down to Max from a branch some fifteen feet above.

"Think you can jump up here?"

"I think so," said Max, glancing over at Miss Boon, whose face was buried in her book.

"No adults are looking," said Rolf, peering around the green. "C'mon, it'll be good training for Renard."

Rolf began to count; Max tensed his legs and braced himself for a leap. Before Rolf reached three, however, Max's concentration was broken. Alex Muñoz and a half-dozen Second Years had wandered over.

"Showing off, Max?" inquired Alex innocently.

"Nobody asked *you* over here," said Sarah.

"You *still* have a crush on this kid?" Alex snickered incredulously. "Better get it out of your system before he packs it on like Daddy."

Alex smiled as Max turned red; he looked Max dead in the eye.

"Anna thinks Daddy's due for a heart attack within the year, but I'm giving him two," said Alex. He puffed out his cheeks and patted his belly, mimicking Mr. McDaniels while Anna and Sasha giggled. Max's hands started to shake.

"Don't," whispered David.

"Where is Daddy, anyway?" asked Alex, just as Mr. Mc-Daniels's booming laugh could be heard from the patisserie. "Oh my God!" he laughed. "He's in *there*? He's eating *chocolate*? That's too perfect—guess Anna was right!"

Anna and Alex snickered; Max felt David's small hand holding his school sweater. Connor hopped off a branch and stepped between Max and Alex.

"Just curious, Muñoz—what *do* you have against Max?" inquired Connor. "Is it that he bloodied you up last fall? Or maybe it was the way he ran circles around you in front of the alumni on Halloween? Is that it?"

"Shut up, Lynch!" spat Alex.

"Or *maybe*," Connor continued, his finger wagging under Alex's nose while his voice sank to a whisper, "it's the fact that Max is going to break all the records next week while you're not known for anything around here other than being a bloody jerk."

Alex stood silent for a moment, a murderous look on his face. His lip twitched; he seemed to be expending all of his energy in his effort not to reach out and throttle Connor. But then a chilling calm came over the Second Year's features. He flashed a wicked smile over Connor's shoulder, directly at Max.

"Connor sure is a witty guy," said Alex. "A guy like that should have his tongue cut out. Who knows? Maybe someday he will. Still, he has a point. Maybe I *am* jealous. Think you can get to that branch faster than I can?"

Max glowered at him before glancing again at the branch.

"It's not even a question and you know it," he said.

"So, prove it to me," chided Alex. "Put me in my place."

"You don't have to prove anything, Max," David breathed. "He's planning something."

"Come on, Max," Alex goaded. "You just said it's not even a question. Prove it to me!"

"Fine," said Max. "When Sarah counts to three."

"Can she count that high?" Alex sneered, pushing past Connor and positioning himself next to Max at the tree's base.

Sarah ignored the insult, choosing instead to clear everyone a few feet away from the tree. Max's adrenaline surged as Sarah began to count. When she reached "three," Max crouched low to spring when Alex stepped suddenly on top of his foot, pinning it to the ground. Grabbing the back of Max's head, Alex slammed Max's face into the tree trunk and scrambled up his back to make a mad leap off of his shoulders.

Max staggered backward, holding his hand against his forehead, which burned like fire. Alex was hanging from the branch by his fingertips, cackling maniacally and ignoring the furious shouts from the other children.

"See?" he crowed. "I reached the branch first! Muñoz wins! Muñoz wins!"

With a sudden convulsion, Max sprang up onto the branch. Before Alex could move, Max had seized him by the shirt and dangled him with one arm out over the ground. Alex strained and wriggled helplessly in his grip.

"Boys!"

The voice seemed distant and unimportant. Max focused his attention on the bully whom he held like a rag doll. Alex had stopped struggling and simply looked at Max with a mixture of shock and fear.

"Boys!"

It was Miss Boon screeching with hoarse rage from across the square. Their Mystics instructor was walking very quickly toward them, her face white with anger. The other children parted. Arriving at the base of the tree, the teacher folded her arms and glared up at them.

"Max McDaniels! Pull Mr. Muñoz up to that branch. Then both of you climb down here this instant! *This instant!*"

Reluctantly, Max pulled Alex back toward the tree, allowing the Second Year to grab hold of the trunk. Breathing heavily, Alex muttered "Freak" under his breath before scooting to a lower branch and hopping down. Max clambered down a moment later.

Miss Boon stabbed a finger at the two boys. "Fighting? Flaunting your abilities off-campus? What on *earth* would possess you to act so stupidly? Do you know what could happen if you'd been seen? Did you even stop to think that you *might* be seen?"

Miss Boon looked from face to face, her rage slowly subsiding to an icy calm.

"He tried to kill me," Alex accused. "You saw him, Miss Boon!"

"Be still, Mr. Muñoz. I don't require a crystal ball to see that your predicament had something to do with the bloody lump on Mr. McDaniels's forehead. Do either of you have anything sensible to say in your defense?"

"I'm sorry," Max said quietly. He had never seen Miss Boon so angry.

"'Sorry' isn't good enough!" she snapped. "This is going to result in some serious punish—"

Just then they heard a man's frantic call for help. Miss Boon kept her eyes locked on the boys a moment longer before turning her head in the direction of the patisserie. Max's father and Mr. Babel came barreling outside. A second later, a waist-high surge of melted chocolate oozed from the doorway and spilled out onto the sidewalk.

"Help!" cried Mr. Babel again. Miss Boon and the children ran over just as the near-finished cathedral slid out the door and was swallowed up in a chocolate gurgle.

"What happened?" exclaimed Miss Boon, checking the street

for tourists. A number of older students and faculty hurried over from the coffee shop and pizza parlor, including Mr. Vincenti.

"I don't know!" panted Mr. Babel, slogging to the doorway and trying unsuccessfully to staunch the flow of chocolate with his body. He groaned as the white-chocolate saplings slid past his reach and also began to sink. "I don't even know where all this chocolate came from!"

"Is the coast clear, Joseph?" asked Miss Boon.

"I think so, Hazel," Mr. Vincenti panted, confiscating a coffee cup from a Third Year who was intently filling it with chocolate. He handed the cup to Mr. McDaniels, who looked carefully at its contents.

Miss Boon took one last glance up the street before raising her hand and muttering a few words. The chocolate stopped pooling on the street; it hardened instantaneously. Great cracks, like fault lines, zigzagged across its surface as the mass solidified into a block. Mr. Vincenti leaned forward to help Mr. Babel free himself from the chocolate, knocking off a large chunk to reveal the submerged cathedral. Mr. Babel moaned at the sight of his ruined masterpiece.

"Any idea what happened?" the advisor asked.

"None," wheezed Mr. Babel. "One minute I was cleaning the soda lines, the next I was waist-deep in chocolate. Could one of the students be behind this? You know—a spring prank?"

"It's possible one of the older students could have done this," Mr. Vincenti mused.

"Let's not overlook the younger ones," Miss Boon interjected, casting a smoldering glance at David. "After all, many of them were in the patisserie shortly before this happened."

"They couldn't have done this, Hazel," laughed Mr. Vincenti, helping himself to a small shaving of chocolate he had scraped off with his car keys.

"You're quite mistaken, Joseph," Miss Boon growled. "In any event, it's time Mr. Muñoz and Mr. McDaniels got their things and accompanied me back to campus."

Max's cheeks burned as his father's eyes fell on his bleeding forehead.

Mr. McDaniels frowned and put the cup of chocolate down on the sidewalk. He examined Max's forehead.

"What happened, son?" he asked.

"He's fine, Mr. McDaniels," called Alex, smiling. "You just go ahead and enjoy that chocolate, sir."

"Alex!" hissed Miss Boon. She turned to Max's father. "Scott, my apologies, but Max must return to campus immediately. His behavior today has been unacceptable. I won't get into the details, but—"

"You can call me 'Mr. McDaniels,' young lady," said Max's father.

Miss Boon paused, momentarily speechless.

"It's *okay*, Dad," Max pleaded. "I'll see you back on campus. Please stay here with Connor and David."

"Yeah," said Connor quickly. "David and I got loads to show you, Mr. McDaniels."

Mr. McDaniels looked at Max once more before turning to Connor and nodding.

Max and Alex slunk away from the crowd and walked over to the tree. As Max retrieved his bag, he noticed a folded slip of paper sticking out of a zippered pouch. He trailed a step behind Alex, who was dragging his feet toward Miss Boon, and unfolded the note.

Nice jump. Get back to campus!
Go to Rattlerafters ASAP.
Be alone. Check your RCOKE.
—Ronin

Max whipped his head around, half expecting to see Ronin's white eye locked on him from behind a tree or among the crowd. Crumpling the note, Max took one more look around before hurrying to where Miss Boon and Alex were waiting.

~ 17 ~

THE HOUND OF ULSTER

It was well after dinner by the time Max was able to slip away from his classmates and make his way alone to Rattlerafters Library. His father had expressed his disappointment that Max was unable to avoid fights at yet another school. But for Max, the experience had more disturbing implications. He had not *decided* to leap after Alex and seize him, it had just *happened*—as swift and involuntary as a blink or a sneeze.

Passing a trio of older students, Max climbed Old Tom's stairs two at a time. He had never been up to Rattlerafters before, but he knew the library was shunned by most of Rowan's students and faculty. Occupying the attic of Old Tom, the Rosetta Library owed its unpopularity and nickname to its location directly beneath Rowan's chimes. Beams, books, and furniture were shaken up every hour on the hour.

The long, low attic smelled of dust and book leather; to Max it resembled a book graveyard more than a working library. Near the entrance, a slender spiral staircase disappeared up into a dark room housing the building's clockworks and chimes. Max moved quickly past it; Old Tom had always seemed to him a living thing, and something about the dark space above made him uneasy.

Max settled himself into a rickety wooden chair at a long table. Flicking on a table lamp, he sneezed and brushed a layer of dust off the table. There was little doubt in Max's mind that Ronin had caused the distraction at the patisserie to slip him the message. Ronin's note had been brief but was relatively clear; "RCOKE" clearly stood for Max's *Rowan Compendium of Known Enemies.* He opened his bag with uneasy anticipation, pulling out the heavy book and spying another folded letter between its pages. Max opened the letter and scanned its jittery script.

Dear Max,

i write in greatest urgency. The Enemy has begun a great work of which the missing Potentials are but a part. The Enemy believes Old Magic exists once again among our Order, and this signals an opportunity to recover Astaroth.

Max, the Demon is not dead, but imprisoned in a painting! Furthermore, the

Enemy believes it is already in possession of the accursed thing. Many works now hanging in museums are clever forgeries—the stolen paintings in the newspapers are merely to divert Rowan's attention from other thefts that have gone undetected. . . .

There are whispers of a matchless child—a child whose arrival they have foreseen and whose help they require to free the Demon. Verifying the existence and identity of this child is of great interest to them.

Max—your name is known and has been mentioned many times in their councils. Be on your guard! There is at least one traitor among you. Rowan is not safe. i am close and watching—look for me at Brigit's Vigil. incinerate this!

Ronin

Max scanned the letter several times, committing its details to memory. "Brigit's Vigil" was a mystery, but much of the letter made grim and disturbing sense. He had to speak to David immediately. David was operating under the assumption that the four paintings he had identified still hung safely in their respective museums, now under careful watch. And David might well be the matchless child the Enemy was seeking.

He crumpled the letter in his fist and reduced it to ashes with a blue flame.

As Max's eyes followed a drifting flake of ash, the room suddenly shook with the deafening sound of Old Tom's chimes.

Max clamped his hands over his ears and pitched forward in his chair, eyes screwed shut. His eardrums rattled and vibrated for what seemed an eternity until the bells finished striking eight o'clock.

Opening his eyes, Max yelped as he realized he wasn't alone in the old library. Miss Boon was standing some ten feet away.

"I'm sorry to surprise you," she said. "I gather this is your first visit to Rattlerafters?" She took a deep breath and looked around. "I used to come here, too, when I wanted to be alone."

Max nodded as the ringing subsided in his head.

"Some students said they'd seen you come this way," she explained, gesturing toward the stairwell. "I hope I'm not disturbing you."

Flustered, Max zipped his backpack and started to get up from the table.

"No, but I already said I'm sorry," he said quietly.

The corners of her mouth stiffened a moment before relaxing into an amused smile.

"I'm not here to discuss your behavior this afternoon. Please have a seat—I'd like to talk to you."

Max casually swept the letter's ashes off the table while Miss Boon took the chair opposite him. She reached into her bag and produced a thick book bound in worn green leather. Interlacing Celtic designs in faded gold ran along its borders. IRISH HEROES AND FOLKLORE was stamped on the front cover.

"What's this?" asked Max.

"Interesting question," mused Miss Boon. "I happen to think it may be *you*."

Max looked across the table. Miss Boon leaned forward, her

mismatched eyes locking on his as she raised her hands and murmured a word of command. Instantly the book sprang open, its pages flipping past until they stopped at an illustration of a fierce-looking warrior standing in a chariot. His black hair was plaited and he clutched a barbed spear in his hands. Max read the chapter title aloud: "Cúchulain—The Hound of Ulster." The name sent a tingle up his spine.

"Not '*koo*-choo-lane,'" Miss Boon corrected, "koo-*hull*-in. Yes, Max, this is the very person I'd been hoping you'd research in an effort to better understand your vision. You have thus far refused to look for him, so he has come looking for you."

Max balked at her tone and eyed his watch.

"Is everyone else doing research on their visions?" Max asked, trying to stall. "Because I'm having a hard enough time with classes as it is. I don't think I should be taking on any more work."

Miss Boon glanced quickly at the stairwell and gave Max a guilty smile.

"Fair enough. You see, Max, I'm really asking you for a favor. I want to understand more about your vision. I know it had something to do with the Cattle Raid of Cooley. But I need to know more—I need to know *precisely* what you saw."

Max's stomach tightened up. There was something in her eagerness that reminded him of Mrs. Millen.

"I'm not sure," Max lied. "It's kind of hard to remember. Why's it so important?"

"Most of the time, a vision is something pretty and without much meaning behind it," she said. Max fidgeted uncomfortably; Mrs. Millen had wanted to know if his tapestry had been pretty. "But yours is a bit different. Your tapestry was of a very definite person. From what little Nigel told me, your vision illustrated a very particular scene. If it's true, that's very rare. Almost unique, in fact. I've been doing a lot of independent research on visions, and I don't know of one like that in over four hundred years. Since before Rowan was founded."

Max took a quivering breath; he already knew the answer to his next question.

"Who had the last one?"

"Elias Bram," she said.

Max thought of the last Ascendant's apple floating in the Course's trophy room.

"You think he had the same vision I did?" Max asked.

"No. His was very different. But, unlike all the others—and similar to yours—his was tied to history and myth. According to Bram's letters, it was of the Norse god Tyr placing his hand in the mouth of the Fenris Wolf. Do you know the tale?"

Miss Boon smiled at him; she always seemed pleased when she knew something that someone else did not.

"The Fenris Wolf was a monstrosity," she explained. "It was capable of wreaking unimaginable havoc unless it could be controlled. No chain could bind it, and so the gods, in secret, procured a cord wound with spells so as to be unbreakable. When they challenged the monster to test his strength against the cord, the wolf laughed but was suspicious of such a feeble-looking fetter. It agreed to be bound only if one of the gods would place a hand in its mouth as a gesture of good faith. Only Tyr stepped forward."

Max winced. "What happened?" he asked.

"The Fenris Wolf could not break the magic binding," she continued. "When it realized it had been caught, it bit off Tyr's hand and swallowed it. Tyr had made a mighty sacrifice, but the monster was rendered harmless until Ragnarok—the End of Days—when it would burst its bonds."

"Didn't Elias Bram sacrifice himself at Solas?" Max asked. "So others could flee?"

"He did," said Miss Boon, looking closely at Max. "I take it you can now imagine why I want to help you understand your vision."

Max was not so certain.

"It's like I told you," he said. "It's hard for me to remember. Maybe we should talk about it with the Director."

Her eyes widened momentarily and she shook her head.

"No, no! This is just between us." For a moment, she looked sheepish. "Ms. Richter doesn't know I'm doing this research. She might think it's taking time away from my . . . teaching duties. You understand, don't you?"

Max glanced from her face to the book several times before finally nodding.

"Good. I thought you would." She smiled and pushed up from the table. "I'll leave this with you in the hope that you'll read it. Perhaps it will jog something in your memory. I'll see you tomorrow."

Max hesitated, before blurting out a final question.

"What's Brigit's Vigil?"

Miss Boon turned around.

"Where did you hear *that* term?" she asked, her nose wrinkled up in curiosity.

Max panicked; he had obviously made a terrible mistake.

"I heard Mr. Morrow say it," he lied. "It just made me curious. I'd never heard it before."

Miss Boon smiled and walked back over.

"Byron *would* like that term—he's a romantic," she said. "Come here and I'll show you. This is one of the few spots on campus where you can get a good view of it. I think there's enough moonlight tonight."

She guided Max toward several small windows at the far end of the library. It was dark outside, and the sea was a calm sheet of black glass. Miss Boon pointed at a large rock jutting out from the water some fifty yards from shore.

"*That* is Brigit's Vigil," she sighed. "It's an old legend here at Rowan, but fading fast, I'm afraid. It dates back to the founding of this school. It's a bit sad or romantic, I suppose, based upon how you look at it. You see, among the survivors that fled here aboard the *Kestrel* was Elias Bram's wife. Her name was Brigit. It's said that before Elias ran to meet Astaroth during the great siege, he begged his wife to flee with the others. She refused to leave his side until he swore an oath to come for her, to follow over the sea and rejoin her in this new land.

"As you know, Bram was never seen again after Solas fell. After the survivors reached these shores and this school was built, Brigit spent her days wading in the surf, looking east in hope of her husband's return. He never came. The legend says that one day Brigit disappeared and that rock emerged offshore in her stead. Some people—like Mr. Morrow, I'd imagine—insist the rock resembles a woman, dressed in a nightgown and staring out to sea."

Max pressed his nose against the window and squinted. It was too dark to see the rock in any detail.

"Try as I might, I don't see it—not even by daylight." Miss Boon sighed. "Tell me later if you can. I think you'll get very

familiar with Brigit's Vigil while you and Alex are scrubbing the
Kestrel. Good night, Max."

Max watched her go in a series of brisk, efficient steps across
the room and down the stairs. He checked his security watch. He
still had forty-five minutes before the chimes would sound again.

As Max smoothed down the book's pages, his fingers seemed
to crackle with electricity. The Hound of Ulster stared back at
him from the book, his handsome face brimming with youth and
purpose. Max leaned back to read, setting his watch to beep several minutes before the chimes.

> Cúchulain's tale takes place in Ireland at a time when
> that country was not united but divided into four great
> kingdoms. Like many heroes, Cúchulain was the son of
> a god: the sun deity, Lugh, who took the form of a
> mayfly and flew into the wine cup of a noblewoman on
> her wedding day. After drinking the wine, she was spir-
> ited away with her maidens to the Sidh—the Land of
> Faerie—as a flock of swans.
>
> This noblewoman was sister to the king of Ulster,
> northernmost of Ireland's four kingdoms, and thus
> many warriors searched for her throughout the land. A
> year later, the king himself came upon a house where his
> sister was found with a small child. The baby's name was
> Setanta. It was decided that he should come to live with
> the king when he had reached boyhood.
>
> Some years later, as the noble children of Ulster
> played on the field, a youth appeared and stole away their
> hurling ball to score a goal. As the boy was unknown

and uninvited, the other children turned on him. Instead of fleeing, the youth ran wild among them, making each give way before his fierceness. The boy announced that he was Setanta, bidden by his mother to seek the king.

At the king's court, Setanta was prized above all other youth. Thus one day he was invited to join the king's company for a feast at the home of the blacksmith, Culann. In these days, smiths were vital to a kingdom, and Culann's stature rivaled even that of the king. The king's company had departed for the smith's home before Setanta had left the playing fields, and the boy was left to travel alone across the countryside.

It was dark when Setanta approached the smith's house, which was filled with light and the sounds of laughter. It was then that Setanta heard the growl of the smith's hound, which had been loosed to protect his lands at nightfall. As the great wolfhound crouched to spring, Setanta hurled his ball with all his strength down the beast's gullet, nearly splitting the creature in two. While the animal howled, the boy took hold and dashed its body against a stone until it was torn to pieces.

Max stopped breathing and read the paragraph again. It was horribly familiar. This was the very dream that had haunted him ever since he had seen the tapestry. He thought of the monstrous hound with its shifting face. *"What are you about?"* it always demanded of him. *"Answer quick or I'll gobble you up!"* Max covered his mouth and glanced at his watch. He knew he needed to speak

to David and that Nick would be getting hungry, but both would
have to wait.

When Setanta looked up from the hound's body,
he saw that the king's men had assembled around him.
Culann the blacksmith was angry.

"I welcome thou, little lad," said Culann, "because
of thy mother and father, but not for thine own sake. I
am sorry for this feast."

"What hast thou against the lad?" asked the king.

The smith replied, "It is my misfortune that you
have come to drink my ale and eat my food, for my
livelihood is lost now after my dog. That dog tended my
herd and flocks. Now all I have is at risk."

"Be not angered, Culann my master," said the boy.
"I will pass a just judgment upon this matter."

"What judgment would thou pass, lad?" asked the
king.

"If there is a pup of that dog in Ireland, I shall rear
him till he is fit to do his sire's business. Until that day,
I will be the hound to protect his flocks, his lands—
and even the smith himself!"

The men laughed at the fierce boy's pledge, but the
king weighed the words and marked them a fair offer.
On that day, the boy left behind his childhood name and
became known as Cúchulain—the Hound of Culann.

Cúchulain was fierce and proud and anxious to become a warrior. So it was that one day he overheard the
king's druid and advisor remark that the child who took

up arms that day would have the greatest name in Ireland but his life would be a short one. Upon hearing this, Cúchulain raced to the king, demanding his right to take arms that very hour.

"Who put that idea into your head?" inquired the king.

"The druid," responded the boy.

Having great respect for the druid's councils, but ignorant of the latest prophecy, the king relented, and Cúchulain ran off to the smithy. No weapon could be found to match the boy's strength. Spears and swords were shattered until at last, the king allowed the boy to try his own. Only these proved true. When the druid saw this, he cried out, "Who has told this child to take arms this day?" to which the king replied that it was the druid himself. When the druid denied this and told the king of the prophecy, the king was furious and confronted his nephew.

"You have lied to me!"

"I have not," replied the boy. "You asked only who put the idea in my head and I answered truthfully. It was the druid!"

Although the king was saddened, he acknowledged the boy spoke the truth. And so it was that Cúchulain took up the king's arms and became Ulster's champion.

Cúchulain's legend spread rapidly. Fighting on foot or from his chariot, he conquered Ulster's enemies. It was said that in battle he shook like a tree in the flood and his brow shone so bright he was near impossible to look upon. Chief among his weapons was the "gae bolg"—a great spear whose wound was always fatal.

Cúchulain's greatest feats occurred during the Cattle Raid of Cooley, a war sparked by a squabble between husband and wife. The queen of Connacht, another of Ireland's four great kingdoms, argued with her husband over whose heritage and possessions were greater. The two matched each other until it was revealed that her husband owned a magical white-horned bull named Finnenbach. The queen could find no equal among her herds and, consumed by jealousy, sent her emissaries to Ulster, where she sought Finnenbach's rival, the Brown Bull of Cooley. Her offer refused, the queen resolved to take the bull by force.

The queen chose an auspicious time for her raid into Ulster. The men of that kingdom suffered from an ancient curse that weakened them for a time each year. As the queen's armies raided north, the men of Ulster were bedridden and powerless to stop her. Not being born in Ulster, Cúchulain was spared the curse and stood alone against the queen's armies. Cúchulain came upon them at night, killing the outriders and leaving only heads behind as a warning to turn back. So devastating was his onslaught that the queen's soldiers quaked at the mention of his name and the armies were brought to a standstill.

The queen sought desperately to negotiate with him, promising riches and reward if he should give way. Cúchulain refused these temptations until, finally exhausted by his efforts, he agreed to a bargain. In exchange for halting his nightly attacks, he would meet a single champion of the queen's each day. While the two fought, her armies could continue on their march. If and when the queen's champion was defeated, her armies were obligated to stop and camp.

Each day, Cúchulain met a different champion at the river and fought while the queen's armies raced deep into Ulster. So impressive were his feats that Morrigan, the death goddess, watched from above in the form of three ravens. Finally, the queen sent forward a kinsman of Cúchulain's who now served Connacht. Preying upon Cúchulain's loyalty, the kinsman pleaded with the youth to give way—as a favor to one who had raised him. Reluctantly, Cúchulain stood aside and relinquished the field. Galloping ahead, the queen's riders seized the bull and rushed back to Connacht with their prize.

Once reunited, the magic bulls went mad in an attempt to destroy each other. In their rage, the bulls devastated the surrounding countryside and were never seen again.

Max put the book down. He tried to envision the tapestry he had seen at the museum. His mind wandered over its threads of green and gold, the brilliant glow that erupted from the scene within it. He understood that scene now. The sleeping soldiers were the weakened men of Ulster, unable to protect the Brown Bull of Cooley. The approaching warriors were undoubtedly the soldiers of the queen of Connacht. Cúchulain stood tall in the distance.

While the images were clear to Max, the interpretation of the story was not. After all, Cúchulain had *failed*—the queen was able to get the bull despite his acts of heroism. Was Max somehow destined to fight the good fight but fail? Was *his* life to be short? Max turned the page and poked gingerly at the bump on his head. His eyes fell upon a discolored illustration of a wounded warrior tied to a stone pillar. The heading read "The Death of Cúchulain."

Max quietly closed the book.

His head ached and his mind raced with too many questions to count. With a sigh, he slipped the book into his bag and walked once more to the windows. The campus was quiet; just a few lanterns bobbed along the paths. Max turned to go when a small flash of green light danced on the window. It disappeared suddenly. Squinting, Max hooded his eyes against the window's glare and peered deep into the night. Another pinpoint of green light shot from the black mass of Brigit's Vigil. It bobbed and hovered in front of Max's eyes before disappearing a moment later. He stayed at the window another ten minutes, but the light did not return.

~ 18 ~

SMUGGLERS ON THE NORTH ATLANTIC

The morning sky beyond the observatory dome was a pale blue. Max frowned with concentration beneath it, flipping through a thick booklet full of glossy charts as David came downstairs to join him at the table.

"What did Ms. Richter say?" asked Max, turning the booklet sideways to read a particularly detailed chart.

"Bad news," said David. "Two of the four paintings are actually forgeries—the Enemy has already stolen them."

Max looked up. "Which ones?"

David retrieved two posters from his desk: one was a Vermeer of a girl reading a letter; the other was a Rembrandt depicting Abraham's sacrifice of his son, Isaac. Max stared at them, abandoning his booklet on the table.

"I don't get it," said Max, glancing up. "If they wanted to hide the fact that some paintings were stolen, why wouldn't they just replace all of them with forgeries? Then we wouldn't even know they were after paintings."

David nodded.

"It's a good point, but the forgeries needed to be real—made by hand, that is. Any traces of enchantment would have aroused suspicion. Not too many people can forge a Rembrandt or a Vermeer, so they would only be able to leave behind forgeries for a few," said David. He leaned down to read the spine of the booklet Max had been reading earlier. "What does your Course Analysis say?" he asked.

Max shook his head slowly from side to side.

"I'm never sure with these things. I wish they'd write them in English." Max pushed the slim white booklet full of crisp blue graphs and analyst commentary toward his roommate.

"They say some good things," David allowed, skimming through it. He selected a paragraph from the summary page. "'McDaniels continues to demonstrate capabilities well beyond the normal Apprentice spectrum. As illustrated in scenarios MMCD048, MMCD071, and MMCD093, his Amplification abilities are at Agent levels and will continue to be monitored very closely. Relative to peers, McDaniels is among the top four in scenarios involving live adversaries, including four scenarios with random vye generation. Ratings on Strategy Execution continue to be high, and McDaniels's aggressiveness should prove to be an asset if it can be applied more selectively. Due to exceptional physical abilities, McDaniels currently has the highest Course rating among both First and Second Year Apprentices.'"

"That *does* sound pretty good!" said Max, perking up considerably. David started giggling.

"What?" said Max, his smile frozen at the sound of David's sudden laughter.

"Well, you can read the rest," his roommate said, failing to suppress a smile as he handed the booklet back to Max. "Second paragraph, summary section."

Max scanned the page, murmuring aloud as David picked up a discarded sock and sniffed it before dropping it in a hamper.

"'McDaniels's slide from the top spot is as imminent as it is inevitable. His combination of gutter ratings on Strategy Selection coupled with high marks on Strategy Execution are a disaster waiting to happen; the operational equivalent of running very fast in the wrong direction.

"'Running very fast in the wrong direction seems to come naturally to McDaniels and has been a common theme in his more amusing scenarios. We can recommend MMCD006, MMCD-052, and MMCD076 as personal favorites, although other colleagues swear by MMCD037 as a candidate for this year's highlight reel. Unfortunately, these tendencies are a fatal flaw, and we recommend McDaniels's scenario options be restricted to those emphasizing Issue Identification and Strategy Selection. In his long-term interests, McDaniels should be prohibited from accessing those scenarios that allow raw physical execution to overcome glaring strategic flaws. One can only hope that a steady diet of Strategy scenarios will help him overcome lazy mental tendencies and build a strong foundation for longer-term success.'"

Max blinked twice and flung the booklet on the table. He whirled at David.

"Can they write that?"

"Don't take it all so personally," said David, slipping on his running shoes. "What happened with your Strategy midterm?"

"Failed it," Max replied, casting a final angry glance at his booklet. "But at least Boon passed me on my Mystics midterm—then again, I think that's just so I'll talk to her about my vision. Does she ask you about yours?"

David turned toward his wardrobe to change shirts.

"Not really. I told her I forgot mine," he said.

"I said the same thing, but I don't think she believes me. . . ."

Max trailed off as he caught a glimpse of David's chest in the wardrobe's mirrored door. A long, ugly scar trailed down its center from chest to navel. The small, pale boy pulled on his athletics shirt.

There was a knock at the door.

David shuffled up the steps. A moment later, Max heard a bloodcurdling shriek.

"Get it away from me! *Get it away from me!*" Mum's voice screeched.

"Max, I think it's for you," called David evenly.

Bounding up the stairs, Max saw Mum backed into the hallway, slumped against the wall with her hands over her eyes. A small basket was overturned on the floor; a variety of nutrition bars were scattered around.

Mum stabbed an accusatory finger at Bob, who chuckled softly.

"You *knew* that Max lived with that thing!" she sobbed. "That's why you insisted Mum do the knocking! You could have given me a heart attack tricking me into standing face to face with that hideous, wretched thing! *A heart attack!* Oh, it was so gruesome!"

David rolled his eyes.

"Sorry, Mum," interjected Max. "Er, what are you guys doing all the way up here?"

Bob started to speak until Mum shushed him with a furious waving of her hands.

"You keep quiet!" she hissed. "Just you wait and see what I can hide in a grilled-cheese sandwich! Ooh! The soup will be even better!"

Mum started giggling and seemed to forget the original purpose of her visit. Bob cleared his throat, causing her to blink several times. Suddenly, the hag launched into a dramatic curtsy.

"Max McDaniels, we have come to nourish your body and provide an honor guard on this blessed day of greatest promise."

"Excuse me?" asked Max, raising his eyebrows.

"Bob and Mum are here to walk you to your tests," Bob translated.

Mum glared at Bob for the intrusion.

This was the morning that the First Years would be undergoing their monthly fitness measures—a series of events similar to a modified decathlon. The periodic tests were not normally a matter of great interest except that Max was now very close to breaking several records. He looked down the hallway to see several sleepy Second Years who had poked their heads out their doors, apparently roused from sleep by Mum's shrill voice. Alex Muñoz's brooding face was among them.

"Thanks for the . . . escort!" said Max, ushering David out the door and shutting it behind them. "We'd better get going."

Mum took a slimy, possessive hold of his arm as the four walked down the hall. She insisted that David stay well ahead, so she could keep an eye on him. Several Second Years wished Max good luck as they passed; Alex merely closed his door. For the past week, the two of them had endured their daily punishment in relative peace, scraping and scrubbing the *Kestrel*'s hull in tense silence.

As they reached the stairs, Mum fished a nutrition bar from her basket.

"Eat this," she whispered. There was a sly hint of conspiracy in her voice. "I got them special just for you. It wasn't easy, I can tell you! They're very *modern!*"

Max *was* hungry and glanced down at the granola bar in its silver wrapper. He unwrapped it and took a bite, causing Mum to swoon with pleasure and flash her fierce crocodile smile.

"Don't tell anyone I gave you that," she breathed quickly. "I'm not sure it's legal."

"I won't," Max promised, ignoring David's giggle and giving her a nod of reassurance.

Despite the early promise of a clear day, wisps of cool, damp fog blew in off the ocean. David ran back to their room to grab sweatshirts, returning just as Old Tom rang eight o'clock. The four had to hurry toward the athletic fields, which shattered Mum's hopes for a stately procession. She cursed the entire way.

Seeing YaYa alerted Max that something was unusual. The ki-rin's great head was visible near the bleachers. Max called ahead to David.

"Is that YaYa? What's she doing here?"

David just turned and gave a little smile.

They rounded the Field House to see the bleachers filled with several hundred students and faculty, who burst into a cheer as Max arrived. Nick raced toward Max, running tight little circles around him and shaking his tail with a metallic whir. Max bent down and scooped him into his arms. The lymrill promptly hooked his claws into Max's sweatshirt and relaxed, becoming a considerable dead weight.

Max turned and scanned the chattering crowd. Jason Barrett was there, hollering and clapping with most of the Sixth Years. Sitting on one of the lower seats was Julie, holding her camera and laughing at something said nearby. She snapped a quick photo of Max. Mr. McDaniels was there, too, waving wildly and sitting with Mr. Morrow, who puffed steadily on his pipe.

Hearing a whistle, he turned to see M. Renard impatiently shooing away Hannah, who did not appear at all pleased about it. She waddled toward Max, the goslings in tow.

"Hello, dear," her honey voice cooed. "Good luck today. We're all rooting for you. And I had a few words with *that man* to keep it fair."

"Thanks, Hannah," Max said, taking another glance at the crowd, not at all sure he wanted an audience. The whistle blew again, and Max trotted to where M. Renard had gathered the class. The instructor had a cold and blew his nose into a handkerchief with a loud honk.

"All right, my little sausages. Today you make me proud, yes?"

The children nodded.

"We will do the tests in alphabetical order, as always, except for the races, which will be paired by your most recent times. Ignore all these people—focus on each task and do your best. Does anyone have anything to say?"

Connor raised his hand.

"Yes, sir." He leaned across the circle of classmates and jabbed a finger in Max's chest. "We went through a lot of trouble to drum up this crowd, so don't you screw it up!"

Everyone burst into laughter; even M. Renard cracked a smile as he brought the whistle to his lips to signal the first task. Max shook his hands loose and took a long look at the stretch of track before him.

An hour later, Max was consumed by assorted cheers, roars, honks, and shouts. Hoisted onto the shoulders of Jason and another Sixth Year, he caught his breath and looked far across the fields to where his javelin's flag fluttered in victory. YaYa stood to her full height and bowed; David held Nick tightly to keep the lymrill from hurting himself. Mr. McDaniels almost trampled a row of students in his hurry to reach the field, while Mr. Morrow merely doffed his cap and waved from the stands, his expression strangely sad. The Humanities instructor raised a bottle of champagne to Max and took a sip before passing it back to Mr. Watanabe and Miss Boon, who followed suit. Max waved back, trying to ignore Mum's nearby shrieks that he owed his triumph to her "miracle treats."

"That's something, Max," said Jason, raising Max higher. "Only thirteen and the best in Rowan's *history!*"

Jason hosted a celebration party in his room, a timbered Viking hall. Some forty students lounged about, playing cards and darts or simply content to sprawl about in small groups, listening to music or tiptoeing through a minefield of pizza boxes to scavenge for leftovers.

Max was having the time of his life. After weeks of adhering to a strict diet, he now stuffed himself with pizza and sweets. Even better, he sat and talked with Julie, who seemed to have forgotten all about their awkward kiss during Kettlemouth's song.

In mid-afternoon, the party was interrupted by a series of loud knocks on the door. Max's spirits sank as Jason opened the door and Miss Boon peered in at him, her face pinched and angry.

"Max," she called, "please get your things and come with me."

Max wiped his hands on a paper towel and stood.

"Do I have to go *today*?" he pleaded. "I thought maybe—"

"You thought what?" she interrupted. "That you'd attained some sort of carefree 'celebrity' status this morning? No, no, no. Need I remind you that *both* your party and punishment were well earned? Alex Muñoz has been down at the dock scrubbing that ship for the last hour. Now get your things."

Max's face turned crimson; he bit his tongue. He murmured "Good-bye" and "Thank you" to everyone, avoiding Julie's eyes in the process. Tugging on his sweatshirt, he followed Miss Boon down the hallway.

Max swung his lantern in wide circles, periodically overcome with great surges of anger and embarrassment. The fog had become so thick that he found himself stumbling into hedges. Old Tom was a hulking block of flat gray; the gas lamps dotting the grounds sprang to life, their lights appearing as will-o'-the-wisps in the gloom.

Storming past Maggie, Max heard the ponderous slap of heavy waves and the shrill cry of seagulls. As he descended the winding stairs to the beach, he began to make out the *Kestrel* hovering in the air above the dock, tethered by a dozen slender ropes. Miss Kraken had provided the enchanted ropes that had raised the heavy ship as if it were a helium balloon.

Alex stood under the boat, scrubbing up at it halfheartedly with a stiff bristle brush. Clinging to the area of the hull that normally rested beneath the waterline were millions of barnacles whose hard shells made the task an arm-numbing chore. Alex and the miserable weather promised to make it particularly unbearable.

"Surprised you bothered to show up," huffed Alex, scrubbing vigorously now that Max had arrived. "Must be nice to get away with whatever you want."

Setting his lantern down, Max said nothing and merely went to select one of the long-handled brushes lying next to a mop bucket. Alex snorted with contempt and turned his attention to the hull.

Max took a long look at Brigit's Vigil before setting to work. Its shape could hardly be seen through the fog, and Max wondered if Ronin was indeed there, as he suspected—nestled deep among the rocks and crabs and swirling brine. Despite Max's now daily visits to Rattlerafters, Ronin had sent no word or signal since the day Max received his letter. And Max had not ventured out to Brigit's Vigil, wary of the water since the campout on the *Kestrel*. Picking a spot away from Alex, he began scrubbing in a sudden fit of energy.

They had worked in silence for almost an hour—Alex in disdainful stabs, Max in busy arcs—when Old Tom's chimes sounded from over the ridge. Alex turned and tossed his brush past Max, where it clattered against the metal bucket.

The Second Year hissed, "Keep scrubbing, Maxine— keep scrubbing or I'll tell Miss Boon that Rowan's little hero is neglecting his duties!"

"Whatever, Muñoz," Max snapped. "I probably got twice as much done in the last hour as you have all week."

Alex just smiled and shook his head incredulously.

"You really are an idiot. Did you know that? An idiot," he said again, stretching each syllable. "Our punishment isn't about scrubbing the *Kestrel* clean! Hell, Miss Boon could do that in five minutes with a bit of Mystics. It's about standing out here as punishment. Scrub till you break your back, Maxine. No one cares, you moron. Man, wait till Daddy's blubber catches up with your brain—they probably won't even admit you ever went here!"

Max stopped scrubbing. His words were soft.

"Don't you say a thing about my father."

"I don't have to." Alex shrugged with a laugh. "You should hear what everyone says about him! You think it's a coincidence he 'helps out' in the kitchens? I don't. Personally, I think Daddy's just trying to snag some extra meals. . . . No wonder I hear Mommy took a hike, huh?"

The words slapped Max across the face. Alex suddenly became vividly clear despite the tatters of fog blowing across the dock. Max dropped his brush off to the side. Alex's smile faltered a moment—a flicker of doubt—before he resumed.

"What?" he asked. "You want to fight me? Aren't you scared without Bob or Miss Boon? They're not here to save you this time. . . ."

Max shook his head and took a step forward, grinding his toe into the dock to test his footing. A hoarse quake rose in his voice.

"I'd worry about myself if I were you."

Alex frowned and took a small step backward. Suddenly, his face contorted with shame and disgust.

"Fine!" he muttered as if to himself. "Fine. Let's do this. One condition, though."

"Name ten," whispered Max. "They won't help you."

Alex's eyes glittered as he smiled.

"No watches," he said. "I don't want you crying for help in the middle of this!"

Max glanced down at his security watch, its small screen fogged by mist. He had been explicitly warned never to remove it. But Alex slipped his own watch off and snickered at Max's hesitation.

Unclasping his watch, Max placed it on the dock.

As he expected, Alex's foot shot out just as Max stood back up. Stepping to the side, Max caught it and swept under the boy's other leg, spilling him hard.

Alex scowled and scrambled quickly to his feet; Max stood completely still, trying very hard to control the rage that flooded every inch of his being. Alex advanced at him, breathing heavily and circling around to try to position Max against a heavy wooden post. Feigning a rush, he suddenly stopped and raised his hands.

The wet dock turned slick with ice beneath Max's feet.

Max tried to jump, but the lack of friction caused his feet to shoot out from under him. He fell heavily, hitting his head against the post. In a moment, Alex was on him, pinning an elbow against his throat and throwing wild punches.

Anger erupted within Max. He seized Alex's wrists, causing the older boy to gasp in pain. With a violent heave, Max flung Alex off of him.

Max sprang up in a heartbeat. Alex was sprawled on the dock, and before he could even move, Max was upon him.

"Let's hear it, Muñoz," Max panted. "Let's hear *everything* you want to say. Let's hear all about my family!"

With a sharp crack, Max's fist tore through the wooden plank immediately to the right of Alex's head. Smoke rose from the deck. The Second Year shrieked and writhed in terror but could do nothing to break Max's grip.

Emotions flooded Max's heart; he shook and tears streamed down his face.

"I don't hear anything. Is that even *possible* with you?"

Crack!

"All out of insults for my dad? Why don't you tell me how stupid I am?"

Crack!

"No? Then tell me something about my mom! Why don't you tell me where she went? Sounds like *you* might know! *Go ahead and tell me!*"

Crack! Crack! Crack!

Three more holes were punched in the surrounding dock, which was now smoking heavily and hot to the touch. Max raised his bleeding hand again, and then froze. Alex had stopped struggling and lay very still, a cool drizzle falling on his blank face.

For a moment, Max thought he had killed him, that he had throttled the boy to death in his rage. But then Alex suddenly focused his eyes and gave Max a look of mute horror. Max blinked.

His anger dissipated into the fog. He released Alex and rose slowly to his feet.

"You're not worth it," he sighed.

Alex lay there for several moments, breathing heavily. He groped at his face, apparently feeling for any damage that might have been done. Blindly, he sought out the holes in the dock, tracing their splintered edges with his fingers. Climbing sluggishly to his feet, he coughed and stumbled past Max, who watched in confused silence. Alex became sick, throwing up over the side of the dock. Wiping his mouth and coughing again, Alex reached out with a trembling hand and flung Max's watch far out into the gray swells. The Second Year watched it sink and stared at the water for several moments. When Alex at last turned around, he held a long, thin knife—the same ugly weapon Cooper often carried. He was crying.

"Alex," Max said with measured calm. "You're not supposed to have those things outside the Training Rooms."

Alex said nothing; his face contorted in a silent scream of rage, fear, and humiliation. His shoulders shook as he switched the knife to his left hand.

"Alex!" Max hissed. "What do you think you're doing?"

The answer was a murderous sweep with the knife, its tip swooshing past Max's chest as the younger boy jumped backward, gaping in disbelief. Sobbing, Alex shifted the knife to his right hand and stabbed upward. Max leapt backward out of range, almost slipping off the pier and into the water.

"Alex—stop it!" Max said. "The fight is *over!*"

Then, over Alex's shoulder and through the fog, Max caught sight of a figure approaching quickly from the beach.

"Help!" Max shouted. "Miss Boon? Over here—help!"

Alex stopped and turned, squinting into the fog. He bent down and let the knife slip through one of the jagged holes Max had made in the dock. He rose and stumbled toward the figure.

"Miss Boon?" Alex called. "Thank God you're here! Mc-Daniels tried to kill me!"

Max was about to raise his voice in protest when he froze; the approaching figure did not move like Miss Boon, and it was far too tall. Bile rose in Max's mouth as he recognized what it was.

"Alex!" Max cried. "Get away from it! That's *not* Miss Boon!"

A vye was loping up the dock.

Alex's hands fell limply to his sides, and in a flash, the vye swept the boy up and crushed him to its hip.

"Let him go!" Max shrieked, running down the dock toward the creature.

A deep-throated growl rumbled from the vye, ending in a high-pitched whine. It clutched Alex closer and stooped to seize Max. But Max was too fast, launching himself at the vye like a missile. The top of his head smashed into its snout. The vye gave a startled yelp and dropped Alex, giving Max time to land an off-balance kick that caused the bony leg to buckle.

Alex was unconscious. The vye was between them and the beach. While the older boy's watch was only some twenty feet away, Max could not get it without momentarily abandoning him. Seizing Alex's limp hand, Max dragged him backward away from the vye, which now scrambled after them on all fours.

The shock and horror of his sudden realization almost made Max laugh: Nigel's voice practically screamed inside his head.

"Always look for the second vye, Max. Always!"

The blow to the back of his skull was so hard that Max was unconscious before he could feel the taloned hands take hold of him.

Max groaned and forced open his eyes. It was dark. His neck was clammy, and his joints ached as a fever coursed through his body. Some sort of fur was piled on him, and it stank—a nauseating reek of animal fat and musky hair. He gagged and retched only to find that his limbs were bound tightly to a hard surface. Tossing his head from side to side, he tried to nuzzle the revolting fur away from his face, knocking over several glass objects in the process. His body rose and fell in a smooth roll that made his stomach queasy. Timbers creaked and strained nearby.

I'm on a ship, he realized.

He heard footsteps above; a doorway clattered open, and a shaft of moonlight streamed into the room at an angle.

"I think one is awake," said a man's voice. Tentative. Older.

"Which one?" came the familiar voice of a woman. Max squirmed and felt the sweat roll off him in smooth little beads.

"The feisty one," said the man. "It is time for his shot."

Something blocked the moonlight; a terrifying silhouette was projected on the wall.

Max heard stairs strain under slow footsteps. He struggled with all his might against his bonds, but they held fast. A face peered into the cabin. Max felt a wave of primal horror as he met its eyes: cold, animal eyes—*appraising* eyes—with a distinct gleam of human intelligence. The moonlit cabin only hinted at its features: the sharp glint of a tooth, the wetness of its snout, a glittering eye, its wolfish ears. Max held his breath as they gazed at each other for several moments. The vye carried an unlit lamp that began to glow as the monster's contours and features danced and shifted. By the time the cabin had filled with a dim yellow light, Max looked upon an older, gaunt man with small black eyes and wearing a loose, dirty overcoat. The man hooked the lamp to a small chain that hung from the cabin roof.

"Good evening," he said, inclining his head in greeting and making his way to a cooler wedged within a large coil of rope. Max watched in silence. After rummaging through the cooler's contents, the man wheeled around and displayed an enormous syringe, far larger than any needle Max had ever seen. He steadied himself as the ship rolled before shuffling over to Max.

"Time for your shot," the man explained, squeezing a bit of clear liquid out of the syringe.

"Keep away from me!" Max pleaded, straining against his bonds. His head was burning.

"Tut, tut," cautioned the man, rolling back the filthy fur cover. "You need this medicine—unless you want *these*." The man opened his mouth wide to reveal jagged fangs poking through his gums. "You see, Peg scratched you—didn't mean to, but it couldn't be helped with you struggling and all."

"It was you on the dock," Max murmured, searching the man's face. "I kicked you."

The man smiled and dismissed it with a wave of his hand.

"You were frightened," he said. "It was a natural thing to do."

"I'm hungry. I don't know what day it is."

"Your fever was very bad," the man said sympathetically. "You've been asleep for three days now. I can get you something to eat in just a minute, after your medicine. You see, we don't

want another mean old ugly vye. No, sir, got enough of us running around as it is. We want you just the way you are. Now hold
still. This might pinch a bit."

The man pulled up Max's sweatshirt to expose his stomach. Max clamped his eyes shut, trying desperately to ignore
every instinct that screamed at him to buck, flail, and protect
the vulnerable spot. The needle stabbed like a flame as it entered; tears streamed down Max's face while his hands flopped
and clawed against the wooden plank. Then suddenly, the pain
was gone.

"There, there," soothed the man, slipping the needle out of
sight. "All done. You may call me Cyrus."

The cabin seemed suddenly very small; Max broke out in a
sweat.

"I need air, Cyrus," he croaked.

The man frowned at that request. He stepped over to the
cooler and stowed the syringe before starting up the stairs.

"I'll check with Peg," he muttered, disappearing out the
hatch.

Max heard a series of whispers from up on deck. A moment
later, Cyrus crept back down and hovered over Max, deftly loos-
ening the complex knots and cords that bound him. Shaking in
fits, Max rose to his feet.

"It's cold up there," Cyrus said. "Keep this over your shoulders. It'll keep you warm."

Max fought his gag reflex as the man wrapped the strange fur
over his shoulders; bits of dry skin and fat still clung to it as
though some great animal had been skinned in haste.

"Where's Alex?" he mumbled as the events from the dock
started to seep back into his memory.

Cyrus grunted and pointed to the bunk above, where Alex lay similarly bound and fast asleep. His face had an unhealthy pallor.

"He's fine," Cyrus whispered, ushering Max toward the steps. "Just sleeping. Here—eat this."

A biscuit was pressed into Max's hand; it was coarse and damp and smelled of mold. Despite his hunger, Max balked.

"There's nothing better till we land unless you want to share our rations," said Cyrus. "We've got plenty of meat. Fresh meat. Say the word and I'll share some—just don't tell Peg!"

Max did not want to guess what kind of meat a vye would have. He forced himself to chew the mealy biscuit, which had the consistency of carpet.

It was cold on deck but not unbearably so. The cloudless sky was sprinkled with stars that looked impossibly sharp and bright. The moon bathed the surrounding sea in shimmering waves of light, spotlighting chunks of ice that bobbed in the water. Ghostly icebergs loomed in the distance as the ship made smooth, swift progress over the gentle swells.

Cyrus led Max toward a red glow, steering him across a deck cluttered with wooden crates and ropes that lay strewn about the deck. The red glow was revealed to be an iron kettle suspended over hot coals. Near the kettle sat a woman knitting.

That woman was Mrs. Millen.

She looked up at Max, her eyes two unnatural pinpricks of cold light gleaming in the darkness. Her throaty chuckle came flooding back like a nightmare.

"Hoo-hoo-hoo! How are you, Max McDaniels? Didn't know if I'd ever get to see you again! Come have a seat next to Peg—I won't bite!"

Max tried to resist as Cyrus moved him nearer, but he had no strength. He was close enough now to see her face clearly. She wore no makeup and looked much older. Her mouth was sunken, and she gummed her lips as she rocked, knitting swift loops of black wool into a shroud.

"You've grown," she muttered.

Max collapsed heavily onto a crate next to her, helped by Cyrus, who took his own seat at the opposite end. Max's head swam with fever, and for several minutes he simply watched his breath waft away in little billows of mist. The night was silent except for the occasional click of knitting needles and the soft crashing of coals as they were consumed.

"Where are we going?" Max asked in a small, weak voice.

"A secret place," she tittered, gumming her lips.

"Where?" Max breathed.

The needles stopped and Cyrus began to fidget. Peg's hand suddenly shot out. She seized Max's wrist and jerked his arm out over the shroud.

A knife flashed.

Max gave a shrill cry of pain as the blade sliced across his palm.

Drops of his blood pattered softly onto the cloth, which began to glow with a dull green light as it absorbed them. She tossed his hand back at him with disdain. The knife disappeared into her robes, and the green glow faded from the shroud.

"Peg asks the questions," she spat, "not bad little boys who make her go a-chasing for many months and many miles."

With a sudden lurch, her face hovered inches from his. Flecks of spittle sprayed from her mouth, and long fangs extended from her lower jaw as her anger quickened. Max almost toppled backward off the crate.

"If I had my way, you'd be in my meat locker, you little maggot!" Peg spat. "You're lucky that you're worth something and Peg's got her orders." The vye panted for several moments, examining every detail of Max's terrified face as her anger receded into smug composure. Millimeter by millimeter, the teeth slid back into her gums and her mouth sank again into a soft mass.

"Yes, yes, big plans for this one," she muttered, taking up her needles once more. "Marley and the Traitor say so. . . . As long as he's the one we want. If not—*hoo-hoo-hoo!* He belongs to Peg!"

Max was taken back down to the rank cabin, where Cyrus dressed the fresh wound.

"You mustn't upset Peg," the old man cautioned, tightening the labyrinth of ropes and knots around Max, whose eyelids fluttered with pain and exhaustion. "You mustn't do that. There'd be nothing I could do to help you."

Cyrus forced another biscuit and some water into Max's mouth before taking the lantern and disappearing upstairs. The cabin went black. Max heard Alex breathing. He knew that soon his father would be waking up and helping Mum and Bob prepare breakfast in the kitchens. Charges would be fast asleep in the Warming Lodge. David would have their observatory all to himself. Max did not think David would like that and hoped that Connor would move in.

The ship shuddered as it pressed through heavier seas.

What would Ms. Richter tell his father?

How had the vyes gotten onto Rowan's campus?

Was Cooper looking for them?

Would YaYa look after Nick? Or would it be Nolan?

The thoughts passed like street signs—some profound, some vain and silly—as Max tried to contemplate a world without him. With a sigh, he wished that Nick and the goslings could be there with him, and then fell into a dreamless sleep.

~ 19 ~

THE CRYPT OF
MARLEY AUGUR

When Max opened his eyes, all he saw was darkness. He shut them again and tried to conserve his energy. He was being carried; something had been placed over his head.

It was impossible to piece together the rest of his voyage; he was not sure if he had sailed for days or weeks. There were fleeting glimpses of daylight and the soft patter of rain. Periodically they were permitted to relieve themselves in a bucket. The last Max could remember, he had awoken to see Peg hovering over him with a black shroud, muttering in a low, strange language.

And now he was bounced along, slung over the vye's shoulder as he was carried down many stairs. Each step jolted his body. A door opened and Max felt cool, musty air filter through the wrapping around his head.

"You are late, Peg," said a voice from his right. It was deep and authoritative.

"Couldn't be helped," mumbled Peg, her mouth frighteningly close to Max's ear.

Max was dumped into a chair, and the cover was removed from his head. Pretending to be unconscious, he let his head fall to the side. Then, like a stain spreading throughout the room, a *presence* approached. It was very cold. The air seemed to vibrate and tingle.

"Which is the one the Traitor spoke of?"

"This one," said Peg. She tapped the top of his head with a hard-nailed finger. "He's pretending to be asleep."

Max ignored her. He kept his eyes shut tightly and focused through his fever. An acrid vapor burned his nostrils despite the heavy, wet air. Water dripped from somewhere; the space sounded very large. Max heard something moving somewhere off to his left.

"It is all right, boy," said the voice, hollow but not unkind. "Open your eyes."

Max lifted his head as his eyes slowly adjusted to the gloom. He looked first for the source of the unfamiliar voice but could see only two small lights in the darkness. Alex saw them, too; he sat in a nearby chair, gripping it in terror and staring silently ahead.

They were in a cavernous room of cold stone; the high walls and pillars were wet with moss and shaggy growths. The only light came from oil lamps and a small fire to Max's left. Suspended over the fire was a small cauldron that released foul-smelling fumes in sputtering fits. Beyond the cauldron were long wooden tables covered with beakers and flasks encrusted with black residue. Many books, ancient and tattered like David's grimoires, lay scattered upon the tables. What really caught Max's attention, however, were the paintings. Behind the tables, dozens of paintings were hung on the dark, wet walls like some ghastly mockery of a museum gallery.

Max looked for the way out but saw Cyrus, in wolf form, sitting at the base of stone steps that climbed up into inky blackness.

A voice in Max's ear made him jump.

"Have a nice trip, dear?"

Peg's face grinned at him in the dim light. Her hair was wild, and her cheeks had sunken to cavernous hollows.

"Peg, leave him be." The voice spoke in calm, commanding tones. "This is a great day for our guest; do not spoil it needlessly."

Peg scowled and retreated to a high-backed rocking chair near the cauldron. She retrieved two needles and continued work on another shroud.

"Where are we?" said Max, his voice sounding small and young in the cavernous chamber.

"You are in Éire, my son. Ireland. You are among friends in a land of poets and kings."

"Is that you over there?" Max whispered, staring at the small bright eyes in the dark.

The icy points of light bobbed against the darkness as something came closer. A startling figure loomed into view.

He was almost seven feet tall, Max thought, and his bones creaked as he stood to full height. Steel-gray hair was wound into braids near his temples. A tarnished circlet crowned his head; an open band of thick silver encircled his neck. Frayed linen robes hemmed with intertwining designs in fading green hung loose about a great, gaunt frame. What flesh remained was drawn and decaying. His features tightened into a small smile while two pinpoints of pale green light flickered from within deep eye sockets.

Max writhed and looked away as the figure stood over him.

"I know I am not fair to look upon," said the creature sadly. "That is to change."

The creature patted Max's arm and Max almost fainted; the touch was ice and the flesh felt as damp and moist as the surrounding earth.

"That one is strong," hissed Peg from the corner. "We should bind him."

"He is a beardless boy." The creature chuckled softly. "He is our guest, not our prisoner. He will see the wisdom of our words."

The creature turned to Alex. "And what is your name, my son?"

Alex squirmed under the attention of the creature.

"Alex Muñoz."

"You are most welcome here, Alex," the creature said. "I sent Peg for *that* one. How did we have the good fortune to acquire your company, too?"

"They were both on the dock," Peg giggled. "They were fighting. We saved this one from becoming a *murderer*. Isn't that right?"

The creature cast a stern glance.

"Is this so? Why would you raise your hand against a brother?"

"I *hate* him," Alex spat suddenly, glancing at Max. "I hate everything about him!"

After weighing the words for several moments, the creature motioned for Peg. She draped a black shroud over Alex's shoulders as if he had just come in from the cold. Max leaned forward.

"What are you going to do with us?" Max demanded. "Where are the others?"

Cyrus bared his teeth from where he sat on the staircase. Ignoring Max, the man walked slowly to one of the tables in a stiff, lumbering gait. "You've done very well, Peg." He sounded distracted as he stirred something in a caked flask. "This one will most certainly have his uses."

He returned to tower over Alex.

"And what was your vision, my child?" he commanded. "Be quick. Be truthful."

"We are wasting time!" she said, her voice low and furious. "This boy is of little value—just like the others! I agree with the Traitor—it is the McDaniels boy we want!"

The creature slowly turned its attention on Peg, and for the first time, Max saw the murderous vye avert her eyes. Peg retrieved a thick book and pen from the table before hurrying back to her chair. The creature's gaze lingered on her.

"I will be sure of that," he said at last. "Perhaps *you* will explain to our Lord that his suffering was prolonged because of your stupidity. If we waste the cauldron's contents on the wrong child, it will be *your* head that rolls."

Peg gummed her lips as the creature turned back to Alex.

"Now, my child, share with me your vision," the creature continued. "How did you awaken to the greatness within you?"

"Alex, don't tell them anything!" Max hissed.

"Shut up, McDaniels." Alex turned to the creature. "If I tell you my vision, will you let me go?"

"No," said the creature. "Not yet, anyway. But I can promise other things."

"Like what?" asked Alex, stirring.

"Power" was the reply. The word saturated the air and echoed rich and heavy throughout the chamber. Alex squirmed and sat up in his seat.

"Command," the creature continued. "Recognition. Reward. All you desire deep down in your heart. Rowan is in winter; her flowers are few and fading. Why toil as a servant of mankind when you can be its master?"

Alex said nothing. The rotting creature smiled at him.

"Does Peg frighten you?" he asked, pointing at the vye, which sat watching them with narrowed eyes.

Alex nodded.

"Why fear Peg when she could be your *slave*?" asked the creature.

"Alex!" Max whispered. "Don't listen. It's a lie!"

Alex shot Max a dark look.

"No," intoned the creature, rising to its full height. "It is *not* a lie and he knows it. Don't you, Alex? *You* know I speak the truth."

Alex nodded slightly. "I'll tell you," he whispered. "I'll tell you."

The creature grunted its approval and began pouring a gurgling liquid from a crusted flask into a wooden cup.

Alex told a tale of a day when he spied a giant oyster in his father's swimming pool that had suddenly opened to reveal a black pearl the size of a billiard ball. Throughout the story, Max heard the sound of Peg scribbling the account into the thick book on her lap.

"A glorious vision," said the man, bending to offer Alex a sip from the cup. "You are *not* whom we seek, but I salute the greatness within you."

Alex looked doubtful. He sniffed at the liquid and wrinkled his nose.

"Do I have to?" he asked.

"If you truly desire all I have promised," the creature said, closing Alex's fingers around the cup. "Our Lord shall soon be free to rule and all shall be as I have said. He does not reward cowardice, however—"

"I'm *not* a coward!" insisted Alex, swallowing the concoction. He gagged and retched but managed to force it down. Black liquid dribbled at the corners of his mouth. He dropped the cup to the floor, grinning defiantly at Max. Suddenly, the older boy's eyelids closed and his head fell forward as the shroud began to shimmer and glow. To Max, it looked as though Alex had just drained a cup of tar and died on the spot.

"What did you do to him?" Max yelled, his words echoing in the large stone space.

Peg started giggling and resumed her knitting.

"He has begun his journey," said the creature thoughtfully, patting Alex's head and stooping to retrieve the cup. "And now we can turn to you. I've been very anxious to meet you, Max McDaniels."

The thing turned again and looked down at Max.

"Tell me, child. What was your vision? What did you see that day when you became known to us?" His tone was kindly and inviting.

"I don't remember," Max said evenly, looking away.

"Do not be difficult," the creature warned. "You *do* remember! I still remember mine, and it occurred centuries ago."

"You're one of us?" Max asked, incredulous.

"I am *not*," snapped the sharp reply. "I renounced that Order long ago."

"Who are you?" Max demanded. "Why are you doing this to us?"

The creature turned and placed Alex's cup back on the table, his voice heavy and sad.

"Tell me, boy. Is the name Marley Augur known to you?"

"No," replied Max, shaking his head.

"Is the name Elias Bram known to you?"

"Yes," said Max.

The air in the chamber grew colder; the massive figure was very still.

"And what do you know of Elias Bram?" asked the creature quietly.

"He was the last Ascendant. He sacrificed himself at Solas so some could flee—"

The creature's lank gray strands of hair whipped around as it turned; its face was a trembling mask of stretched and tattered skin.

"Lies!"

The word shook the chamber like an earthquake. A glass beaker fell and shattered on the floor. Max shrank and shut his eyes.

"Those are lies," the creature repeated, its voice softening to a low rumble. "Forgive my anger; the injustice of your words salts old wounds. Bram did not sacrifice himself that day. He sacrificed me. My body. My honor. My legacy."

"You were with him?" asked Max. "*You* were at Solas?"

"I was," the creature said, nodding. "It was I, Marley Augur, the blacksmith, who sounded the alarm when the Enemy was sighted. It was I who fulfilled my duty and ran to the breach while Bram ran to his wife. It was I who staunched the tide while Bram *lingered*. . . ."

Augur's voice rasped; the small green lights in his eyes danced and flickered.

"I felled many, ere I was broken." He sighed, bowing his head.

"But then, you're a hero," breathed Max.

The towering thing shook its head violently and glared at Max.

"A hero? No, boy, I most assuredly am *not*. Heroes are remembered! Heroes are secured a place in the memories of their people. They are not left to rot, unburied, *unwept*, and *forgotten on the field*!"

Max winced as the creature's voice again rose in pitch and intensity. Peg giggled softly in the corner.

"But I was spared that day," returned the hollow whisper. "Spared by an Enemy blessed with a wisdom and goodness that had been hidden from me. Before I fell, the Lord Astaroth saw my quality. He commanded his servants to bear my body away. I was given a seat of honor, and I have learned the errors of my old allegiance. I have a new Lord, and it is for him that Marley has begun his great work."

Max suddenly flushed with anger.

"What 'great work'? You're just a traitor seeking revenge!"

"You are young, boy," said Augur calmly, arranging beakers on the table. "Do not be so hasty. Revenge is a powerful force, a force that has birthed many great things. Vengeance lends purpose; it is vengeance that has kept me alive these many years to create my masterworks."

Max shrank against his chair as Augur leaned closer. Slowly, gently, the man swung Max's chair around.

Max cried out as he saw them against the far wall: dozens of children standing pale and ghostly in the shadows of a large alcove. Each was draped in a black shroud, swaying on unsure feet. Some appeared to be mere zombies, staring ahead with sightless eyes; others betrayed a hint of awareness as they gazed at Max.

"The children shall serve our cause, and they shall be rewarded. When Astaroth is victorious, they shall hold dominion and rule as noble lords upon this earth!"

One girl with tangled brown hair caught his eye. To Max's horror, she whispered, "Run."

"Oh my God," whispered Max. "*Look* at them! Look at what you're doing to them!"

"*I am sparing them betrayal! I am sparing them my pain!*" roared Augur, spinning Max's chair away from the children to face the stairs again. In a spasm of anger, he seized Max's face. Max gasped—the fingers were so cold he feared his heart would stop. Augur relaxed his grip; his other arm pried the hand away.

"I have heard Bram's apple was salvaged," Augur muttered, walking away quickly to a chest pushed against the wall. He opened the lid and reached inside. "I have heard it is prized as a trophy! That it hangs in a place of honor . . ."

Something heavy landed in Max's lap. It was a large apple, its wrinkled, moldy skin marbled with many veins of tarnished gold.

"This should hang in its stead," intoned Augur. "It *will* hang in Bram's stead, and *you* will help me place it there."

The vyes then descended on Max. Peg held her knife to Max's throat while Cyrus tied him tightly to the chair with a heavy rope.

"Wait—" said Max, straining to lift his chin away from the knife.

Augur dismissed him with a wave of his hand.

"The time for talk is past," he said. "Astaroth shall judge what to do with you."

"You'd better pray you're the one," Peg hissed in Max's ear just as Cyrus gagged Max with a filthy rag. "If not, the elixir's worthless and Marley will be in no mood to save you."

The vye tapped a sharp nail against his head and left him. Sweat poured off Max. He strained against the ropes, but Cyrus's knots were clever and only cinched tighter. All the while, he kept an eye on Peg, who had begun appraising paintings like an art critic, occasionally plucking one off the wall. Max gave a little groan as he saw Peg select the Rembrandt and Vermeer that David had identified as likely prisons.

All the while, Marley Augur chanted slow, strange words in his deep voice.

The chamber became very still—as if every living creature and even the surrounding earth and stone bore witness to the ceremony.

Max felt a sudden flash of pain as Peg's knife reopened the wound on his palm. He had not seen her approach. She pried his fingers open, pulling the skin apart and squeezing the flesh until his hand felt cold and weak.

Peg brought a shallow bowl of Max's blood to Augur. The blacksmith's solemn chanting became louder; his fingers beckoned at the blood as if seeking to draw something from it. Max looked away as Augur dripped and stirred his blood into the cauldron. Staring at the apple in his lap, Max fought to control his breathing as he watched the firelight dance on the gold that marbled its surface.

The chanting faded into silence.

"The incantation is finished," Augur croaked. "The elixir is complete."

Peg grinned and tittered as she selected a large canvas and propped it before him. It was a terrifying painting—the image of a wild-eyed giant devouring the body of a man.

Marley Augur dipped a heavy-bristled brush into the cauldron. A thick, shimmering glaze was applied to the giant's face.

"You are free, Astaroth, to walk once again as Lord upon this Earth. The Old Magic of your enemies recalls you to life and releases you from your bonds!"

Augur bowed his head while Peg and Cyrus edged away.

Nothing happened.

"Put more on!" hissed Peg, but Augur spun and glowered at her.

"I will spend nothing on more of your foolish guesses!" Augur snapped. "Bring the next!"

Augur repeated the ritual with several more paintings, becoming increasingly agitated.

"So help me, Peg," muttered Augur, a rising anger in his voice as he scraped and stirred the cauldron's remaining contents.

Max held his breath as the Vermeer was brought forward, the one with the girl reading her letter at the window. A trembling whine sounded from Cyrus's throat; the vye loped back to the staircase, almost disappearing within its shadows.

When the elixir was wasted on several more paintings, Augur's rage was hideous; he snapped their thick frames like matchsticks.

Augur stood bowed and panting while Peg propped up the Rembrandt, her face white with fear. Max's eyes swept over the familiar painting's dark and stormy surface. An angel had arrived to stop Abraham just before the old man sacrificed his son. Abraham appeared surprised; the knife fell from one hand as he covered the son's eyes with the other.

With a disdainful glance at Peg, Augur scraped the brush around the cauldron's rim and dabbed it on Abraham's face.

"Peg, you are fin—" he began.

"Wait!" shrieked Peg, backing away from Augur. "*Something's happening!*"

Max squinted at the painting, trying to make out Abraham's face beneath the shiny elixir.

His breathing came to a halt; the only sound he heard was his own heartbeat.

Abraham was looking at him.

There was an ancient, knowing wisdom to the eyes— something deeply unsettling about the way they wandered over Max's face and bindings. They might have been a million years old.

Marley Augur and Peg bowed low before the painting.

"Astaroth, you are recalled to life by your loyal servants," said the blacksmith, his voice filled with reverence. "Walk this Earth again, my Lord, and bring order with your rule."

Max's fear boiled over as the eyes ignored Augur and continued to look at him. His hands trembled, and the hairs on his neck stood on end.

With a furious surge, Max shattered the chair and bindings that held him. Spitting out the gag, he clutched Augur's apple and bolted for the stairs. Cyrus rose from his seat and blocked Max's way.

"Solas!" Max yelled, flexing the fingers of his wounded hand and filling the chamber with a flash of blinding light.

Max leapt over the vye as it howled and doubled over. He sprinted up the steps and threw his shoulder against a stout door, but it would not budge.

"*Stop him!*" roared Augur from below.

Panicked, Max saw the door was barred with a heavy cross-beam. He pushed it back just as Cyrus began to scramble up the stairs on all fours. Max shrieked and forced the door open, stumbling out into a cold, dense fog.

He exited what appeared to be a tomb, darting and weaving among gravestones that rose out of the damp mist. The vye came crashing after him.

Max grunted in pain as his knee clanged into a thick length of metal jutting from a fence. Ignoring the ache, he ran on in a desperate search for the cemetery's exit. He tried to Amplify again, but nothing happened.

Suddenly, Max saw a tall gate standing open nearby. He limped through it, stopping to swing the gate shut just as he saw the huge silhouette of the vye closing in through the fog. The gate was too heavy and slow. Max abandoned it, the sound of the vye panting behind him triggering a fear so terrible that he gave a cry and churned his legs faster. A tall tree stood at the crest of a steep bank. Max made for it, racing uphill and planting his foot for a great leap.

The vye swatted his ankle out from under him, toppling him to the grass and scrambling on top of him. It tried to pin his shoulders with its great claws, while its hind legs scrabbled wildly for better purchase. Max rolled onto his side, whipping up his arm to shield his throat from the snapping, snarling jaws. The vye's teeth sheared through his sleeve and across his forearm. Max grunted and thrust his arm forward, driving back the jaws, as Cyrus tried to tunnel under Max's arm toward his face.

Unable to Amplify, Max started to give way, and the jaws snapped closer. In desperation, he jammed his other fist down the creature's throat, forcing Marley Augur's apple deep into its gullet. The vye gave a horrible yelp of pain and surprise, bucking wildly to free itself. Max held on with all his might, forcing the apple ever deeper. They rolled on the ground, locked together, until the vye convulsed violently and gave a quivering exhale. A moment later, it was still.

Max rose shakily, using his sweatshirt to staunch the bleeding and wipe away the saliva. There were several dime-sized punctures in his forearm, and his wrist and hand were bleeding freely. Max scanned the fog to see if Peg or Marley were coming. There was no movement—only a brisk wind that chilled the sweat on Max's neck. Several black birds croaked in the branches above, looking down with small, cold eyes.

"I've got to go," Max murmured. "I've got to get help."

He squinted at the sky: no sun, no stars, nothing to gauge the direction he was facing or even the time of day. Grimacing, he peeled off his sweatshirt and tore it into strips, tying them tightly around his arm to slow the bleeding.

The vye was sprawled out in the tall grass, its tongue swollen and purple-blue. The reality of what he had just done sent a shiver down his spine.

He peered once more in the direction of the cemetery and the haunting words he had read in Rattlerafters echoed in his mind.

The child who took up arms that day would have the greatest name in Ireland, but his life would be a short one. . . .

Massaging his knee, he struck out in the direction opposite from the graveyard. *There must be a road nearby,* he reasoned. He trotted along in the gloom while arguing with himself.

You're doing the right thing, Max.

The damage is done—Astaroth is already awake.

You'll only get yourself killed. Think of what that would do to Dad!

This isn't the Course. This is real life.

You can send for help. Cooper or Ms. Richter can save those children!

They'll still be here—

Max slowed to a halt, doubling over as the pain in his arm flared. Wincing, he applied more pressure to the wounds. As the wounds began to clot, Max suddenly admitted to himself that soon there would be no one to rescue. The other children would surely be gone by the time Max could summon help. In his mind's eye, he saw the faces and eyes of the hopeless children. He recalled with awful clarity the emaciated girl who had begged him to run.

He turned and ran back toward the cemetery. The crows called out a shrill greeting as Max passed the tree where the vye lay. He retraced his path until he arrived at the fence he had stumbled into earlier. Rusted and bent well away from the rest was a black iron rail that tapered to a sharp point. Max shook it back and forth, twisting and kicking at its base until it snapped off in his hands.

The makeshift spear felt awkward as Max stole from gravestone to gravestone. The fog was lighter now; he could see the dark entrance to the crypt. Creeping to its open doorway, he heard the sounds of hurried movements—the yawn of a heavy door, the clink of metal and glass. He slipped quietly down the stone stairs. A few steps from the bottom, he stopped and hugged the wall.

There was Peg, some twenty feet away, grumbling as she gathered an armful of chains from a pile on the floor. She shambled back to where the children were kept. Max peered around the stairwell; Augur was packing beakers and jars and instruments into an assortment of chests. A great trapdoor had been opened in the floor near where Alex was slumped.

Suddenly, Peg dropped the chains. She sniffed the air.

"Hoo-hoo-hoo! Perhaps we needn't leave after all!"

Max ducked back into the stairwell, but it was too late. With a triumphant cackle, Peg bounded toward the steps on all fours, her body rippling into that of a monstrous vye. Max braced himself on the stairs as she took one last leap and hurled herself at her quarry.

Max brought up the spear.

The impact nearly jarred the weapon out of his hand, but Max held firm. Their eyes met for one horrible instant; Peg's expression was one of absolute shock. The old vye screamed and wrenched herself backward off the spear point, her limbs flailing like a spider's. Dragging her bulk, she gurgled and collapsed some fifteen feet away—a bloated vye with reddish-brown fur, clawing at its belly.

Clutching the spear in his trembling hand, Max stepped into the chamber.

Marley Augur stood by the trapdoor, staring at Peg. He shook his head sadly and turned to Max, who edged toward the children, giving the dying vye a wide berth.

"Put that down," Augur rasped, glancing at Max's bloody spear.

"I won't," Max panted, backing against a thick pillar.

Marley Augur straightened to his full height and walked toward him. Like a disapproving parent, the creature reached to take away the crude spear. Max swung the poker with all his strength, bashing the creature's hand aside.

A faint green mist gathered around the undead thing.

"Put that down or I shall become angry," said Augur, his voice rising.

"I won't," Max hissed. "Let them go!"

The temperature dropped, and Marley Augur seemed to grow larger. He extended his hand once more, but not at Max. A massive blacksmith's hammer flew to his hand from the opposite wall, its head a murderous wedge of dull black metal. Hefting the hammer, Augur glared down at Max. The green mist swirled around his legs.

"You *will* serve our Lord. Whether whole or broken . . ."

Just as Augur stepped forward, a sheet of brilliant flame

roared up before him. Max pressed against the pillar while Augur retreated a step in confusion, glancing at the painting where Astaroth lurked, watching. An unexpected voice called out.

"Leave that child alone."

Ronin stood on the bottom stair. He was dressed all in gray and breathing heavily. Peeking out from the sleeves of his coat were two long knives. In a flat, calm voice, he spoke to Max.

"Get the children and lead them out. I will deal with this traitor."

"Ronin!" Max screamed. *Astaroth is in that painting!*

Ronin glanced at the Rembrandt. He raised his hand, and sheets of flame roared up from the ground to engulf it. But the dark painting was unharmed.

A low, rumbling laugh came deep from Augur's belly. The room grew even colder; the flames between Max and the blacksmith drained away into the floor.

"*This* is Rowan's army?" the creature rumbled. Within Augur's eyes, light pulsed with quickening life as he hefted the massive hammer. "I am far greater than you, little whelp. As this child are you to me. Older magic and deeper purpose course through Marley Augur—"

Max Amplified just as the hammer came crashing down. It pulverized the stone tiles where Max had been standing while he sprang away to the alcove where the children stood cocooned in their black shrouds. Augur's hammer swung over him, sending up a shower of sparks as it collided with the pillar, which cracked and groaned from the impact.

In a flash, not one Ronin but three circled around Augur in a whirl of knives, feinting and attacking. The blacksmith swung his hammer in mad pursuit, shattering wood and stone and glass in a terrifying frenzy. The walls of the crypt shook with great flashes as though in the midst of a thunderstorm.

Max tore the black shrouds away from the children who were conscious and shoved them in the direction of the stairs, screaming at them to come to their senses and hurry. They staggered away in confused groups of two and three, hugging the walls and shuffling toward the cool daylight above.

By the time all the shrouds had been thrown aside, there were still a dozen children left in the alcove, their heads hanging in slumber. Max began trembling as his body absorbed more energy from the fight around him. Hoisting a child onto each shoulder, he dashed across the floor, over Peg, and up the steps, where he tipped them onto the wet grass. Diving back into the crypt, Max froze in horror as he saw Augur's hammer crash down onto Ronin's head. But the hammer only slammed into the floor as Ronin's decoy dissipated and promptly reformed as though made of magnetized smoke.

The real Ronin had maneuvered behind Augur. He raised a double-barreled shotgun from the folds of his overcoat. The blast echoed in the chamber with a great metallic twang.

Augur buckled and stumbled forward, but nothing more. Ronin was forced to leap back as the hammer swung around to crumple the shotgun's barrel.

By the time Max had spilled the last two children onto the grass, the chamber had begun to collapse. A flash of light erupted from the doorway, and he heard Ronin curse. Max yelled at the conscious children to pull the others back and dashed again into the crypt.

Ronin swayed near the pillar. The false images had disappeared, and he was without a weapon.

"Ronin!" Max screamed, running down to him.

"One more, Max. Get him and *go!*" Ronin gasped, hugging the pillar and staggering around it as Augur advanced toward him, stepping over a shattered table.

Max looked at Alex slumped in the chair; just beyond, Astaroth's eyes watched Max intently.

"What about the painting?" Max yelled.

"Get the boy and go!" Ronin bellowed. *"Keep them away from the stairs! Augur can't go aboveground!"*

Ronin ducked under a hammer blow that tore a jagged chunk out of the pillar. Reaching into his coat, Ronin flipped what looked to be a dull metal hockey puck into the center of the chamber before dodging another murderous hammer swing.

Max ran down to Alex, tossed him over his shoulder, and glanced at the painting.

Astaroth smiled at him.

As Max wheeled to run for the stairs, something tripped him. He dropped Alex and fell to the floor. Peg was at his feet. Gasping for breath, she pulled herself up to Max's face. Her features alternated between the slavering monster and the wild-eyed woman who had pursued him in Chicago.

"You're coming with me," she gurgled. "Down, down with Peg into the darkness."

Max stretched his neck away from the searching talons and focused on his uninjured right hand; he felt searing blue flame ignite and writhe around it. Clapping his hand on her face, he shut his eyes through a sudden gasp and horrible smell. Slowly, the vye's body stiffened and rolled away, its face a smoldering ruin of fur and flesh.

Max got to his feet, then grabbed Alex's hand and dragged him toward the stairs. Ronin limped after them, but Augur let loose a terrifying howl and swung his hammer. It caught Ronin squarely in his back with a sickening sound.

Ronin tumbled across the chamber and landed in a mangled heap by the stairs. He did not move.

"Stay where you are!" bellowed Augur, stabbing a bony finger at Max.

"They're all outside!" Max cried out, locking eyes with Augur while feeling for Ronin's hand. "You can't get them!"

"It matters not," said Augur, lowering his hammer and walking slowly across the room. "Astaroth is awakened, and we still have *you*. Your worth is far greater than those little souls."

Max tried to Amplify, but he was spent. Gritting his teeth, he struggled furiously to drag Ronin and Alex up the stairs. His arm was bleeding badly and it throbbed; Ronin was so heavy. Suddenly, three clear beeps sounded in the chamber. Ronin squeezed Max's hand very hard.

"Go," Ronin whispered.

Gripping Ronin's hand tighter, Max heaved himself backward just as the metal puck exploded.

Max had a sensation of floating. There was a high-pitched ringing in his ears, but the fog felt very cool and soothing on his face. He lay still, breathing deeply. To his surprise, he realized that there was still a hand clasped in each of his. He glanced down from where he lay against the top stair. Half-submerged in a chalky soup of stone and soil were Ronin and Alex. Alex was unconscious; Ronin's eyelids fluttered as he stared blankly up.

"I'm broken," he murmured. "My legs—"

"Shhh," whispered Max, letting go of Alex and gripping Ronin's wrist with both hands. Ignoring Ronin's sharp, sudden intakes of breath, Max pulled him from the rubble to lie on the pearly grass.

Max staggered back to Alex and took hold of his wrist. Suddenly, Max heard something deep within the earth that made him gasp and let go.

A muffled cry of rage and despair shook the ground.

With a gathering trickle of pebbles and masonry, Alex began to sink. Panicked, Max seized his hand and strained with all his might. It was no use. Something far stronger than Max McDaniels had hold of Alex and was pulling him slowly, inexorably, back into the tomb. Despite Max's gasps and pleas, Alex was wrenched from his grasp and swallowed by the earth.

The shivering children had gathered around Ronin. He was blinking and looking up at the sky, very calm and pale. Making his way through the other children, Max knelt down and took his hand.

"You're always saving me," Max whispered.

"You're worth saving." Ronin smiled. His green eye was tired but very bright as it blinked at Max. The prescient eye was going dark, its milky whites fading to dead gray.

"We have to get you to a hospital."

Ronin shook his head and smiled, squeezing Max's hand.

"Pocket . . . ," he gasped, closing his eyes.

Deep within his coat, Max found what Ronin had intended. It was a security watch. Max pressed its face as hard as he could again and again until a message suddenly flashed on its small screen.

COMING. ETA 27 MIN.

Max fought off his exhaustion and cradled Ronin's head to his chest, rocking back and forth as his mother had done with him long ago. The other children sat around them silently, gaunt little ghosts staring mutely into the fog. When the Agents arrived, he thought they must be angels.

~ 20 ~

FATHER AND SON

Max awoke to the smell of something roasting, something delicious. A breeze of lilac skimmed across his cheek from a nearby window, and he stirred in a bed of smooth sheets. His forearm ached. He touched it and found it was wrapped in thin layers of a spongy material. Max slid upright, resting his back against the headboard. It was twilight, and the room was in shadow: deep purples and blues except for a sliver of yellow light under the door.

Walking slowly out the door and into a hallway, Max heard a chorus of laughter. He steadied himself against the wall with his bandaged hand, ignoring the buzzing in his head and stumbling forward.

A number of adults were having dinner around a large table. A dark-haired woman saw him first, glimpsing him in the door-way during a sip of wine.

"Well, hello there," she cooed, as though to a lost puppy.

The other adults ceased talking and looked intently at Max.

"He must be famished," said an apple-cheeked man with a strong Irish accent. "Use a bite to eat, could you, Max?"

Max's head felt light. He nodded and let the man steer him to a seat at the table, next to a younger woman with red hair. She smiled and fixed him a plate of roast chicken and wild rice. Max grabbed a large piece of chicken and stuffed it into his mouth.

"Sir Alistair must have his hands full with this one," chuck-led a man with glasses.

"Hush!" said the dark-haired woman. She smiled at Max and pushed the plate of carved chicken closer to him. "Welcome to the Dublin safe house, Max."

Suddenly aware that he was eating in a strange house with strange people, Max put down his piece of chicken. His eyes searched from face to face.

"I'm Max," he whispered.

"We know—we know all about you, Max McDaniels." The apple-cheeked man beamed. "You're very welcome here."

Like water through a breaking levee, the memories flooded his mind.

"The Potentials!" he gasped. "Ronin! What happened to them? I tried to save Alex, but I couldn't. He was pulled away from me. Astaroth is awake!" He almost toppled backward.

The red-haired woman caught his chair and eased him

forward. She smoothed back his hair and gently quieted him. Max was still for several moments, studying the little flames on the candlewicks.

Footsteps sounded from the hallway, and in walked three men wearing dark clothes that seemed to shift and blend in with the room. To Max's surprise, Ms. Richter followed on their heels. She gave a cursory nod to the group before her gaze fell on Max, sitting small and hunched at the table. Her eyes twinkled as she studied his face.

"Well, colleagues, our guest is up and about." Her voice was soft and serious. "Hello, Max. How are you feeling?"

Max frowned at his arm, where the spongy fabric covered the deep gashes and punctures from Cyrus's teeth. The memories of their struggle on the hilltop were very vivid.

"Alex Muñoz," Max murmured. "He's gone. . . ."

"Yes, I know," said Miss Richter gravely. "It was his watch that summoned help. That crypt is being excavated and examined now. In fact, that is where I have just come from with these gentlemen."

Max looked at the men in the strange clothes who were now helping themselves to the food. He could not take his eyes off the fabric that seemed to swim with grays and blacks and greens and browns. One of the men, blond and handsome with a weathered face, smiled and stepped over to Max. He kneeled down and pinched part of the fabric off his shoulder so Max could feel it. Rolling it between his thumb and forefinger, Max was fascinated. It was slick to the touch, impossibly smooth but utterly flat, allowing no candlelight to reflect from its surface.

"Nanomail," the man grunted. "New version—in beta. I'm Carl. I was the one who got your call."

Something in the man's manner reminded Max of Cooper.

They each had the same directness: a calm, clipped way of speaking that suggested an intense, disciplined nature.

"Thank you, Agent Drake," said Ms. Richter. "That will be all. If the rest of you would please excuse us, I would like to have a word with Max."

Glasses were raised to Max as he followed Ms. Richter out of the dining room.

They went outside to sit on a porch of weathered stone and knotted wood. The moon had risen high and bright over the trees, and the air was very still. Max looked hard at the Director, who seemed lost in thought as she gazed out over the countryside. There were a thousand stories and secrets in her face, Max thought; they were etched in deep seams across the forehead and in tight little crow's feet at her eyes. Her pupils looked like drops of mercury in the moonlight.

"How long have I been gone?" Max asked.

"Thirty-seven days," said the Director.

Max drooped in stunned silence.

"Thirty-seven days lost, but forty-two children gained," she said, turning to smile at him. "Not a bad bargain. Forty-two children will be reunited with their families because of you, Max. You are a hero."

"But Alex is gone," Max said with rising anguish. "They have Astaroth, and he's awake!"

Ms. Richter patted his hand.

"Shhh. You did what you could do, and that is all a person can ask of himself. You went well above the call of duty for a thirteen-year-old boy, Max."

"Did Ronin survive?" Max asked quietly.

Ms. Richter wrinkled her nose in curiosity. "Who is Ronin?"

"Peter," Max blurted. "Peter Varga. He saved me. Is he okay?"

"Ah, I think he will be, Max. I do," said Ms. Richter, with a small smile. "It's a curious name Peter chose for himself. Do you know what a 'ronin' is?"

Max shook his head.

"A ronin is a samurai—a wandering samurai without a master. Such a notion would appeal to Peter, I suppose. Peter is going to live, but he was very badly injured. Whether or not he walks again remains to be seen. He is here—the moomenhovens are doing their very best."

Max said nothing; he was not even sure what a "moomenhoven" was. But he *was* sure that without Ronin, he would still be trapped beneath the earth with Marley Augur. His throat felt tight.

"Try to put Peter out of your mind for the moment," said Ms. Richter. "No one knows better than you that something very serious has happened and that dark times may be coming. I need to know everything that has happened starting with the day you were taken. . . ."

Max told Ms. Richter about the attack on the dock, his journey across the ocean, and the trials in Marley Augur's crypt. None of it seemed real to him; he felt as if he were telling someone else's story.

"What *was* Marley Augur?" Max asked. "He said he used to be one of us."

"What he *was* is certainly different from what he *is*," she replied. "He was, by all accounts, a very noble and valued member of our Order. However, it sounds as though his misery has transformed him into a revenant—an unquiet spirit consumed by thoughts of vengeance. Unfortunately, as a blacksmith, Augur's talents clearly lay in craftsmanship and enchantment—the making and unmaking of things. These are slow, methodical magics well suited to the task of freeing Astaroth."

Max frowned and tried to blot out the memory of Astaroth's little smile amidst the smoke and noise of Augur's crypt. He looked out over the dark countryside.

From the Director, Max learned that the ropes supporting the *Kestrel* had been cut, resulting in what appeared to be a horrific accident. The ship had crashed down and obliterated half the dock beneath it, causing the *Kestrel*'s guardian to wail and churn the waters. It was feared that Alex and Max had been crushed, their bodies swept out to sea. These fears were seemingly confirmed as their apples had turned to gold in the orchard. Three days later, it was discovered that the apples had only been coated with gold. The *Kestrel*'s crash had been nothing but a diversionary tactic to hide the fact that Max and Alex had been kidnapped. Search parties were deployed, but the trail had already gone cold.

As she finished her story, Max asked a question that was troubling him.

"What's going to happen to Ronin?"

"We shall do our best to heal him and then we shall have to see. I suppose it will depend somewhat on his condition."

"The vyes couldn't have gotten to the orchard," Max said somberly. "They had help. There *is* a traitor at Rowan, I heard the vyes and Marley Augur talk about it!"

"I know all too well about the traitor at Rowan," the Director said sadly. "Yesterday, the traitor was taken into custody. Without a struggle, thank God."

"It's Miss Boon, isn't it?" Max asked very quietly. Goose

bumps raced up his arms when he thought how dangerous it must have been to be alone with her in Rattlerafters.

"Miss Boon?" exclaimed Ms. Richter, suddenly incredulous. "Why in heaven would you suspect Hazel?"

Max's face reddened in the dark; he felt very stupid.

"She . . . she was so curious about my vision; she kept asking me about it and asking me not to tell anyone. She assigned my punishment for fighting with Alex. She made me go down to the water where the vyes were waiting."

"Ah, I see," said Ms. Richter, nodding sympathetically. "I expect Hazel wanted to keep your conversations secret because she knew I would not approve; she was pursuing a branch of analysis that I had discouraged. And the whole school knew about your punishment."

It looked as though the Director was trying very hard to control her emotions.

"It was Mr. Morrow," she said at last. "He was the traitor among us."

Max sat in stunned silence. His mind swam with thoughts of the gravel-voiced lessons, the rivulets of pipe smoke, and the little cottage beyond the dunes.

"It can't be Mr. Morrow," Max snapped. "He didn't think you were doing enough to catch the traitor! How can it be him?"

"He said those things because he realized full well that Bob would report your conversation back to me," she replied. "And in some ways, I think he was speaking the truth. Deep down, I believe he *wanted* the traitor to be identified and apprehended."

"But why would he do it?" pleaded Max. "Are you absolutely sure it's him?"

"We're sure," said Ms. Richter, reaching over and patting his hand. "He was very sick and lonely. And he was never quite the same after his wife died. Apparently, the Enemy claimed to have his son—a son Mr. Morrow thought was lost over thirty years ago. In addition, the Enemy promised him long life free from the pain and pills that had come to dominate his existence. I think the prospect of many healthy years reunited with his son gnawed at his mind until he succumbed at last."

"I don't believe it," said Max. "I don't believe that Mr. Morrow would sacrifice so many kids just to see his son again. He's not that selfish!"

"I don't think he believed he was sacrificing them, Max. The Enemy insisted that the Potentials were a bargaining chip—a brutal but necessary lever that would force his stubborn Director to consider their overtures of peace. It is no secret that Mr. Morrow never supported my appointment as Director. I think he very much wanted to believe that *I* was the one endangering lives and that he acted on behalf of the greater good."

"But how did he even do it? How did he help the Enemy find the Potentials?"

"That matter is still under inquiry. However, I believe that he found a way to exploit Isabelle May. When her apple turned to gold, interception of Potentials ceased, leading many to deduce that *she* was the traitor. I think her death gnawed at Mr. Morrow—his health deteriorated soon after."

Max shivered, and Ms. Richter placed her jacket over him.

"But the Enemy also knew about the raid at Topkapi Palace!" he exclaimed suddenly. "Why would Mr. Morrow have told them that? Why would he endanger all those Agents?"

"Because once the Enemy had ensnared him, once he had committed to this course of treachery, it was a simple matter to manipulate and twist him further. The Enemy cautioned that the Potentials were protected by powerful spells that would harm them if they were taken by force. And thus, ironically, to keep them 'safe,' Mr. Morrow had been obliged to warn the Enemy of our movements. All in all, it was a neat little plan that could have resulted in considerable losses. Fortunately, Mr. Lukens's private joke tipped us off that an ambush was planned and that a traitor was still in our midst. This would explain why Mr. Lukens has disappeared—that man probably has more to fear from the Enemy than from us."

"How is my father?" asked Max quietly.

"At first, he was inconsolable," said Ms. Richter. "And angry. He is overjoyed at the turn of events and very anxious to see you. Though that will have to wait a few days, until your arm has healed a bit more."

Max was consumed by a sudden urge to leave the porch and burrow somewhere deep in the woods. "I wish none of this had ever happened," he said. "I wish I'd never seen that tapestry."

Ms. Richter smiled sympathetically. Her eyes shone like disks of polished silver.

"Did you know that there are eleven dewdrop faeries out on the lawn right now?" she asked.

Max stood and squinted into the dark, leaning against the porch railing.

"I can't see them," he said.

"Ah," she said, standing next to him. "There's one just below us."

Ms. Richter pointed her finger directly at the ground below. She muttered a word and a small bulb of golden light grew into being. Within the enveloping light was a tiny girl with the fluttering wings of a dragonfly, dressed in a silken nightgown. She held a small basket and flitted to and from the blades of grass like a hummingbird.

"They collect the evening dew to feed their families," she said. "They're beautiful, aren't they?"

"Yes." Max was entranced by the delicate little form swooping below him. "Why couldn't I see her before?"

"You're still very young," said Ms. Richter. "You don't *expect* to see them and consequently you can't. By the time you leave Rowan, you'll see a whole world of magic that you didn't know existed. But it's not just echoes of Old Magic that makes this world such a wonderful place. There are mountains and rivers, plains and meadows, oceans and tides. Architecture and orchestras, discovery and achievement—humans striving for mastery in one thing or another for thousands of years. These are the great things.

"But there are the little things, too," she said, smiling. "For me, there are my morning walks in the gardens. My kettle telling me the water is hot. The fierce love in Mum and Bob's bickering. . . . *There's* a pair for you! Two beings that started on very dark paths yet have been won over by all that is so very good. These are the things I fight for, Max. These are the things for which I am willing to face and endure the less pleasant realities of this world."

Max sat and thought about her words. The dewdrop faerie's light dimmed as she skimmed away over the grass toward a lone tree in the dark field.

It was hard to see Cooper in the fading daylight as Max climbed out of the plane. The dark-clad Agent stood motionless on the private runway with his hands clasped in front of him. He opened the limousine's door and ushered Max inside.

"It is good to see you, Max," said the Agent quietly. "I'm glad you are well."

Max thanked him but did not otherwise speak during the ride; instead he looked out the window and waited patiently to see his father.

The sky was nearly dark when they reached Rowan. The town's shops were closing; the wall of trees bordering the campus was tall and black. At the gate, Cooper rolled down the window as the car was surrounded by grim-looking strangers. They peered inside at Max and Cooper, scanning their faces with a red light before they were permitted to pass. Max turned and watched the gate close behind them as the car continued on the winding road that would take them to the Manse.

"Who are they?" asked Max.

"Extra security," muttered Cooper. "Rowan's been a busy place. Lots of defensive measures going in. Until those are ready, we've got extra manpower."

Max looked up and saw the fountain illuminated with waves of watery light. Beyond was the Manse, its windows bright and its walls thick with ivy and flowers. He stepped out and listened to the distant surf, his eyes following the walks across the lawns and flower beds to Old Tom and Maggie. Beyond was the dock where he and Alex had been snatched away.

The door to the Manse opened suddenly. Miss Awolowo came swooping down the steps to engulf Max in a fierce hug. He was nearly crushed in a swirl of indigo robes, clicking beads, and gleaming bands of heavy gold. The woman shook with warm, joyous laughter as she held Max by the shoulders and looked him over.

"My boy, my boy," she cried, pushing the hair out of Max's face and squeezing his hand. "Welcome home."

Tears welled up in Max's eyes and he closed them tightly. It was as though Miss Awolowo had wrung out a sponge: all the emotions that Max had walled away so carefully within came seeping out. Max found himself sobbing into her shoulder, his grief and fear and triumph rushing out along with his tears.

"It is all right." She sighed. "You are home again and you are safe."

"I know," Max answered, wiping his nose on his arm. "It's just been . . . a lot."

"More than a young man should bear." She nodded, rising to her regal height and holding his hand. "But you return a hero, nevertheless. A champion of Rowan! Let's take you to your father."

Cooper nodded good-bye and strode off toward the gate as Miss Awolowo herded Max through the foyer and up the stairs. Max could hear students yelling and bustling about as dinner was concluding in the dining hall.

When the door opened, Max and his father looked at each other a long time. Mr. McDaniels examined Max from head to toe, pausing at his arm and hand, which were still enveloped in their spongy wraps.

"You're hurt," he said quietly.

"I'm okay, Dad," said Max, stepping inside and burying himself in his father's shirt.

Max did not leave his father's suite for several days. Classmates knocked and Connor slipped funny little notes under the door, but Mr. McDaniels permitted no visitors while Max cocooned, trying his best to put the horror of his experience and his black thoughts behind him. As students took their finals, the Mc-Danielses played cards and listened to ballgames on the radio, living off sandwiches brought up by Mum or Bob.

One night, however, Max decided to leave his father's room and visit his own. The rumor of his appearance spread before him, and he was forced to ignore many curious faces on the way.

David was inside their room on the lower level, pulling on his shoes.

"Hi, Max," said David softly, finishing his knot.

"Hi," said Max, gazing around the room and at the brilliant stars above.

"I was just going to feed Nick," said David.

"I'll do it," said Max. "I want to see him."

Hanging on David's wall was a poster of the Rembrandt painting from which Astaroth had smiled at him.

"That was the painting, you know," Max said quietly. "You were right."

David nodded and went to throw the poster away.

"I wish I'd been with you, Max," David said solemnly. "I wish they'd taken me, too."

"I know," said Max, glancing at the trash can. "Astaroth's awake now. He'll be getting stronger. . . ."

David looked intently at him.

"We will, too."

Nick was already pacing his stall when Max arrived at the Warming Lodge. Upon hearing Max's voice, the lymrill froze and swiveled his head toward the door. Max smiled and tightened the thick leather apron around his waist. Instead of rushing Max, however, the lymrill merely inched forward and sniffed at his ankle. Giving Max a reproachful glance, Nick climbed back into the small tree that served as his perch. He yawned and swished his tail slowly from side to side.

"Come on, Nick," Max pleaded, stroking the soft red-and-copper fur at the top of his head. "Don't be mad. I didn't mean to be away so long."

Nick twisted in the tree to expose a sinewy back full of lethal-looking quills. The branch groaned under his movements; Max guessed Nick must weigh a hundred pounds or more of muscle and metallic quills. He buoyed the straining branch with a hand.

"Come on," Max cooed. "Let's go outside. It's nice out. I may have even seen a skunk. A nice juicy skunk! Hmmm?"

The lymrill did not move. Max slid around the tree branch to glimpse his face. Their eyes met for a split second before Nick closed his and pretended to be asleep.

"Oh, this is ridiculous," Max snapped, scooping his hands under Nick's warm belly and hoisting the heavy animal onto his shoulder. The lymrill relaxed his body into a dead weight.

Max staggered to the food bin.

"Food for one sulking Black Forest lymrill," he growled, stepping back as the bin shook. Crate upon crate of metal bars and writhing, furry rodents appeared. Nick was not inclined to make the ensuing job any easier, remaining draped over Max's shoulder as he grunted and loaded the crates onto the wheelbarrow. Muttering under his breath, Max wheeled the towering mound outside.

Instead of pawing at the crates as he usually did, Nick focused his attention on Max. He tensed his muscles and lowered himself to the ground as though preparing for a charge. Taking the hint, Max sprang away through the dark clearing, cackling as the lymrill closed the gap to swipe at his feet. Nick gave an irritated yowl as Max suddenly Amplified and rocketed away. Max whooped and galloped back toward the pond, leaping across a patch of marshy grass. Finally, Max heard a patter of little snorts right behind him. He braced himself for the inevitable blow that caught him a nanosecond later.

Nick pounced on his chest, knocking the wind out of him. Even through the leather apron, the claws felt dangerously sharp. Nick looked down his snout to survey Max with shining eyes. With an anguished mewl, he suddenly nipped Max's nose hard with his small, sharp teeth. Max yelped and rolled Nick off of him. The lymrill trotted back toward the wheelbarrow in visibly better spirits.

While Nick finished washing his claws and snout in the pond, Max rolled the empty crates back to the Warming Lodge. When he returned, he found Nick waiting patiently outside, his wet fur sleek and glistening. Despite Max's pleas and threats, the lymrill refused to come inside. Old Tom chimed eleven.

"Well, I have to get back," said Max finally, striding off toward the hedge tunnel. "You can stay here or come along."

The lymrill waddled alongside him, its quills vibrating occasionally in sudden fits of satisfaction.

On the night of the farewell feast, Max held Nick in his lap and gazed out his father's window, watching students file toward the Sanctuary in chattering groups. Mr. McDaniels was rummaging through his closet while Nick tried to wriggle off of Max's lap to swat at the fireflies that hovered just outside. One group of students stopped and turned to look up at the window. Max recognized Sarah, Lucia, and Cynthia in their formal uniforms. They waved; Lucia blew a kiss. Max waved back and hoisted Nick up to see Sarah, who had helped to care for him while Max was gone. In his excitement, the lymrill tore a hole in Max's shirt and knocked a vase off the small writing desk.

"How do I look?" asked Mr. McDaniels.

Max swiveled around and saw his father wearing a navy jacket and yellow tie. The jacket was several sizes too small and strained to contain Mr. McDaniels's ample waist.

"Er, you look nice," said Max.

"No, I don't," said Mr. McDaniels, laughing. "Nolan's jacket looks ridiculous on me."

"Then why are you wearing it?" asked Max.

"Because I can't exactly wear Bob's pajamas to the farewell feast," said his father, laughing.

"You can go without me," said Max, turning back around to watch the fireflies.

His father sat beside him.

"We can't stay in this room forever," said Mr. McDaniels. "I think it's time, Max."

Max listened to the breeze rippling through the orchard and let Nick waddle off him to sprawl on a mound of laundry.

"Everyone will want to know what happened," said Max. "They probably blame me for Alex."

"They might," said his father simply. "And so you might feel bad and I might look ridiculous, but we're still going to live our lives. . . ."

Max glared at Nick, who was nibbling at his last pair of dark socks.

* * *

The Sanctuary was more crowded than Max had ever seen. By the time the McDanielses arrived, the commencement ceremony was ending. Hundreds of students, faculty, and alumni sat around long candlelit tables, sipping champagne and nibbling hors d'oeuvres as Ms. Richter awarded the last diploma to a beaming Sixth Year. Tea lights shimmered on the pond, swirling slowly in the wakes of Frigga and Helga, who turned lazy circles in the water. Dozens of giant phosphorescent seashells decorated the clearing, each illuminating the surrounding grass with a radius of soft yellow light.

"Want some champagne, Dad?" Max asked as a faun passed by with a tray of drinks.

"Dear God, yes," muttered Mr. McDaniels. He reached for a glass while the faun gave his shoes a peevish glance.

The McDanielses sat toward the back at an unoccupied table. Max bowed his head and focused on the sound of water lapping at the lagoon banks as people caught sight of him and began whispering. Glancing up, he saw Anna Lundgren and Sasha Ivanovich staring daggers at him from several tables over. Max ignored them and turned to Ms. Richter, who now stood to speak.

"We're very proud of all of our graduates," Ms. Richter said. "And while we permit our beloved Course analysts a few more minutes to put the finishing touches on their highlights reel"— here the older students groaned—"I'd like to dedicate this moment to Rowan's annual awards. That is, unless you'd prefer to simply wait for the film."

The student body began to yell and jeer in protest. Sir Alistair hid his face in a napkin.

She chuckled. "Well, I *suppose* we can squeeze them in. As you all know, these awards are very special at Rowan; each of them symbolizes qualities that are a necessary component of what we do and what we stand for."

As Ms. Richter finished her speech, six gleaming glass cases on tall stands of polished wood materialized near the head table. Inside, lit from within, floated the artifacts from the Course trophy room.

"Would you look at that?" breathed Mr. McDaniels, pinching Max's elbow. It was now very quiet in the Sanctuary.

Ms. Richter then awarded Macon's Quill to a blushing Fifth Year girl for her academic achievements, while the Giving Belt went to a student known for her diligence in the Sanctuary. Max clapped hard along with the Sixth Years when Jason Barrett's name was called for the Helm of Tokugawa. Jason strode forward from the tables of graduates, eliciting a laugh from the audience when he produced a pen and pretended to carefully write his name on the plaque.

Ms. Richter cleared her voice and continued.

"It is exceedingly rare for an Apprentice to win one of these awards." Max felt his stomach tighten as the audience turned toward him once again. "And yet I can think of no student during my tenure as Director who has been more deserving. To present this award, allow me to introduce an alumnus and former winner, Mr. Peter Varga."

Max's head shot up.

A blushing, plump little woman in a nurse's uniform emerged from behind a row of seated faculty, pushing Ronin in a wheelchair. Several of the alumni exchanged glances and whispers; the students offered a smattering of hesitant applause.

Ronin looked drained but happy. He shared a few quiet words with the Director, who amplified his voice with a wave of her hand.

"I would not be among such fine company if it was not for this young man," he croaked, shutting his eyes from the effort. The audience was utterly silent. "Nor would dozens of children who will soon return to their families. For outstanding courage before the Enemy, the Gauntlet of Beowulf is awarded to Max McDaniels."

A roar of cheers overwhelmed Max as he made his way dazedly toward the head table. Ronin's head hung heavily, but he was smiling as he offered a trembling handshake.

"When did you get here?" whispered Max, taking his hand and leaning close so Ronin could hear him over the applause.

"Few hours ago." He smiled, closing his eyes once again. "Insisted on it."

"You shouldn't have come," Max said. "You're not well yet!"

"Not yet—but he will be," interrupted Ms. Richter, placing her hand on Max's shoulder. "Mr. Varga is not present just for your award, Max; he will finish his rehabilitation here. Congratulations, my boy! Now go take your place."

Max shook her hand, glancing up at the fathomless silver eyes. He walked over to his award. The gauntlet's dented plates and rivets gleamed inside the lighted case. More cheers erupted, and he looked down to see his name written in flame.

Max found it almost impossible to concentrate for the remainder of the awards ceremony. He felt very small and exposed, doing his best to clap dutifully for the remaining winners. As Ms. Richter brought the ceremony to a close, Max looked for Ronin but he was already gone.

* * *

Two days later, most of the students had left and the Sanctuary was quiet. Under a hot afternoon sun, Max caught his father's throw and tried to herd the goslings away from the wrapped sandwich he had left lying on the grass.

"There you are!" a familiar voice called out. "Come here, my darlings! Mother's all soft and gorgeous again!"

Max looked up to see Hannah waddling toward them from the hedge tunnel. Walking behind her was Julie Teller.

The goslings abandoned Max's sandwich and went off honking toward their mother. Julie stepped gingerly around them, looking very pretty in a blue summer dress.

Max glanced at his father, relieved to see him nibbling on his sandwich and chatting amiably with Frigga and Helga as the sisters basked on the banks of the pond.

"Hi!" said Julie, coming to a stop.

"Hey." He grinned, shielding his eyes from the sun. "Are you leaving today?"

"Yeah. I wanted to come say good-bye for the summer." She looked down at her shoes. "I have something for you."

Max fumbled for words as she handed him a little unsealed envelope of pretty stationery. "Uh, thanks," he finally said, turning the envelope over in his hands.

"I read it during Humanities—in *Morrow's* favorite book, of all things! It made me think of you."

Max flipped open the envelope.

"Oh God!" she laughed, covering her mouth. "Don't read it now!"

"Sorry!" Max exclaimed, snatching his hand away from the letter.

"Well, have a good summer, Max. You can write me if you like. My address is on the back, and it would be nice to hear from you."

Blushing furiously, Julie leaned forward and kissed him on the cheek. A second later, she was gone, walking quickly back over the grass toward the Sanctuary tunnel. Max watched her go; her figure grew smaller with every step until she disappeared into the dark green foliage.

He dropped his ball and glove on the ground. Reaching inside the envelope, he retrieved a folded sheet of stationery. The words were written in careful, graceful script:

> *Give not thyself up, then, to fire, lest it invert thee, deaden thee; as for a time it did me. There is a wisdom that is woe; but there is a woe that is madness. And there is a Catskill eagle in some souls that can alike dive down into the blackest gorges, and soar out of them again and become invisible in the sunny spaces. And even if he for ever flies within the gorge, that gorge is in the mountains; so that even in his lowest swoop the mountain eagle is still higher than the other birds upon the plain, even though they soar.*
>
> *—Herman Melville,*
> *Moby-Dick*

Max read the note several times before folding the paper again, careful to keep its original crease. Placing it in his back pocket, he breathed in deep and watched a flight of black swans streak across a sky the color of marigolds. Frigga and Helga slid silently back into the water, leaving father and son alone in the Sanctuary. Mr. McDaniels was smiling now. He pounded his mitt as he took up a spot near a tall backstop of hay bales. Max reached for his glove. His first throw was high.

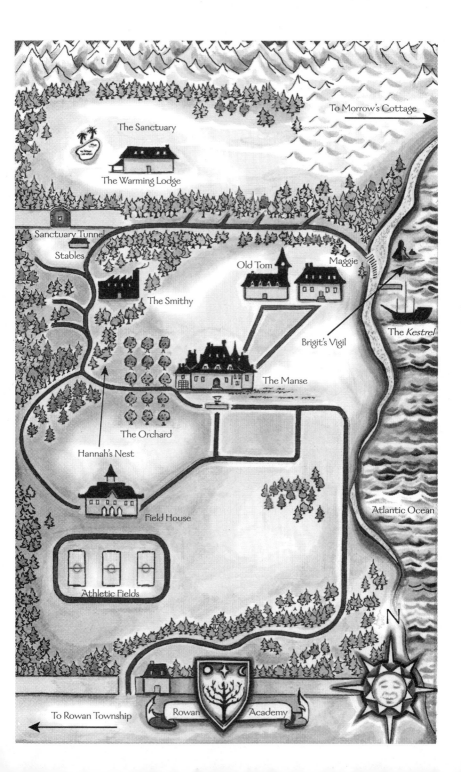

Acknowledgments

My deepest thanks to the family, friends, and students who have inspired my creative endeavors and encouraged me when things were hard. Special mention goes to those who have commented specifically on the manuscript and illustrations, including: John Neff, Victoria Neff, Matt Markovich, Chris Casgar, Jacquie Duncan, Josh Richards, and Gerald Zimmerman. For their wit and wisdom throughout, my deepest gratitude to my editors, Nick Eliopulos and Jim Thomas, and my agents, Tracey and Josh Adams. For her beautiful sense of design, I'd like to thank Joanne Yates Russell, and for his inspired cover illustration, Corey Godbey.

While there are many wonderful tales of Cúchulain and his heroic feats, I'm especially indebted to the work of Thomas Kinsella, whose translation of the Táin Bó Cuailnge captured my imagination and served as the backdrop for my synopsis of the stories of both Cúchulain and the Cattle Raid.

Finally, I'd like to thank my mother, Terry Neff Zimmerman. Without her tireless support and brilliant feedback, Max might never have made the leap from thought to page.

ABOUT THE AUTHOR

Originally from the Chicago area, Henry H. Neff teaches history and fine arts at a San Francisco high school. *The Hound of Rowan* is his first novel. You can visit the author at www.henryhneff.com.

THE TAPESTRY
BOOK 2

THE SECOND SEIGE
Coming in 2008